PRAISE FOR *HOLLYWOOD DEAD*

"[A] terrifically over-the-top
nonstop action and dark hum
including those new to the se

"The surliest hero in literature,
enough grotesque entertaining description to satisfy thriller
fans and gore fans alike."

—*San Francisco Book Review*

"Kadrey is writing a new Sandman Slim novel every year,
and it's not like he's short of material: his winning formula
of mixing deadpan, hilarious hard-boiled swearing and zero-
fucks-given attitude with painstakingly researched apocrypha,
daemonology and magic could yield up dividends forever."

—Boing Boing

"[The] ability to mix highest violence and weirdness with ten-
derness and compassion is where Kadrey shines, and it's why
the series is not only worth reading, but rereading."

—Charles de Lint, Fantasy & Science Fiction

"Hollywood Dead reads like a grindhouse film on the page,
and delivers exactly what the movie-poster themed book
cover promises. . . . Kadrey's prose is fast, fun, and makes the
novel's pulpy concept shine."

—*Zyzzyva*

"Part fantasy, part gothic horror, part crime noir. . . . Filled with knowing winks about pop culture and told at a breathless pace that can't be bothered with actual chapters."

—*Union-Tribune* (San Diego)

"My kind of hero."

—Kim Harrison

"I hope Kadrey keeps putting out Sandman Slim books for the next 20 years. They're that much fun to read."

—*Wired*

"[Kadrey's] use of arcane lore is more in-depth and profoundly informed than any in urban fantasy. There could be a whole encyclopedia about the magic, monsters, and cosmic geography of Sandman Slim. Like one of his clearest influences, the horror master H. P. Lovecraft, Kadrey rips the skin off the real world, revealing the supernatural nerve endings and metaphysical meat underneath. And his prose couldn't be more visceral if it were carved into flesh."

—*Entertainment Weekly*

HOLLYWOOD
DEAD

Also by Richard Kadrey

Sandman Slim Novels

Sandman Slim

Kill the Dead

Aloha from Hell

Devil Said Bang

Kill City Blues

The Getaway God

Killing Pretty

The Perdition Score

The Kill Society

Another Coop Heist

The Everything Box

The Wrong Dead Guy

Metrophage

Dead Set

HOLLYWOOD DEAD

A SANDMAN SLIM NOVEL

RICHARD KADREY

HARPER Voyager

An Imprint of HarperCollinsPublishers

HarperCollins books may be purchased for educational, business, or sales promotional use. For information, please email the Special Markets Department at SPsales@harpercollins.com.

Harper Voyager and design are trademarks of HarperCollins Publishers LLC.

A hardcover edition of this book was published in 2018 by Harper Voyager, an imprint of HarperCollins Publishers.

FIRST HARPER VOYAGER PAPERBACK EDITION PUBLISHED 2019.

Designed by Paula Russell Szafranski

Library of Congress Cataloging-in-Publication Data has been applied for.

ISBN 978-0-06-247419-3

19 20 21 22 23 LSC 10 9 8 7 6 5 4 3 2 1

Sandman Slim wouldn't exist without the music that inspires me and keeps me writing. This book is for Lustmord, Klaus Schulze, Bohren and Der Club of Gore, (early) Tangerine Dream, and Nine Inch Nails.

Life being what it is, one dreams of revenge—
and has to content oneself with dreaming.

PAUL GAUGUIN

So much time and so little to do. Wait a
minute. Strike that. Reverse it. Thank you.

Willy Wonka and the Chocolate Factory

ACKNOWLEDGMENTS

THANKS TO MY agent, Ginger Clark, and everyone else at Curtis Brown. Thanks also to my editor, David Pomerico, and the whole team at HarperCollins. A special thanks goes to James Sime and Isotope, the best comic shop in San Francisco. As always, thanks to Nicola for everything else.

THERE'S DEAD AND there's Hollywood dead, and those are two very different things.

Dead is just dead. In the ground. Pennies on your eyes. A cold slab of meat with no slaw and definitely no dessert.

But Hollywood dead? That can be a lot of things. Yeah, you're still a slab of meat, but now you come with curly fries and hot apple pie.

Hollywood dead is movie dead. When the director yells "cut" you get up and have a donut, and someone makes sure your hair is perfect. When you're Hollywood dead you can die a hundred times and still come back for the sequel.

Hollywood dead is the dead everybody thinks they want because nothing is final, everything is negotiable, and you'll even get a producer credit if you keep your mouth shut and do what you're told. That last is the hard part. When you're Hollywood dead it's hard to sit still and take orders. Hollywood dead is party dead and you never want to hear last call.

Hollywood dead is the best kind of dead and the worst. Hollywood dead means you can go to the movies and have a smoke, but if you're out in the sun too long you start to rot and stink. Hollywood dead makes you very careful about cuts and scratches because you don't exactly heal anymore.

Hollywood dead gets you thinking about making everyone else regular dead. The good news is that if you're lucky and you play your cards right, you might just get the chance to do it.

DON'T LET ANYONE tell you that shooting a gun in a bowling alley isn't loud. It's very loud. Incredibly damn loud. The noise bounces off the smooth paneled walls and rattles every nerve in your skull. Of course, everything down here under the mansion is soundproof, so my target practice doesn't bother anyone else. But I should have brought some earplugs. The tissues I jammed in my ears are pretty undignified and I don't have a lot of dignity left to spare. I mean, I was dead and now I'm alive, but I'm still sort of dead. Not pork-chop-dropped-in-a-parking-lot dead, but dead enough that Tinder is out of the question. That's why I'm shooting the shit out of Eva Sandoval's bowling alley.

There's something very satisfying about seeing bowling pins explode when they're hit with a .45 slug. But I'm annoyed with myself. I left an open frame on the right lane, only killing nine out of the ten. And yet that's still better than the seven-six-ten split I left on the other lane. I need to practice. My body hasn't moved in a year and I have to get it back in shape. Whatever Wormwood has planned for me, I'm definitely going to get punched and I'd like to be able to hit back harder than a marshmallow Peep.

Sandoval and her entourage come in while I'm reloading. She frowns and her lackeys cluster in back of her like confused ducklings. I'm not exactly sure why. I mean, I'm working for them. Maybe seeing a corpse loading a Colt .45 wasn't in their day planner.

I say, "Take it up with HR."

"Take up what?" says Sandoval.

"Whatever is bothering your Mouseketeers. They look like they just saw Lemmy's ghost."

When I'm done reloading, I hit a button and an arm slides out of the back of the bowling lane on the left, sweeps away the debris, and loads another ten pins in place. I raise the Colt and cock it, sighting on the one pin. But Sandoval walks over, puts her hand on the pistol, and lowers it.

"Exactly what are you doing?" she says.

"Target practice. I need to get my eye back."

She looks around the alley.

"My grandfather built this. My father updated it, and I use it with guests."

"Sounds great." I raise the Colt and fire. The one pin explodes. Everybody except Sandoval cringes.

I say, "I'm a guest."

"You're an *employee*."

"Independent contractor, if you want to get technical."

I raise the Colt and she pushes it down again.

"If you needed weapons practice you should have told me. I would have arranged something less deranged."

"I thought deranged was why you wanted me. Otherwise you could have hired any number of local knuckle draggers." I smile at the people behind her.

"What I want is for you to have a basic modicum of self-control and sense of responsibility. If you can't do that, we should part ways and void your contract right now."

Ouch. She got me where it hurts.

"Anything else?"

"Yes," she says, leaning in close to my ear. "I don't like being fucked with."

I give her a smile and slip the Colt into my waistband at my back.

"See, now we're speaking the same language. Okay. You can have your alley back. If you give me your granddad's name, I'll write him an apology note. I've got connections in Hell, you know. They'll get it right to him."

She probes a shattered bit of bowling pin with the toe of her designer pump, clearly biting down what I'm sure is a clever retort.

"If you're through playing the idiot, let's go upstairs and talk business."

"Sure. But remember. I might be an idiot, but you're the idiot who hired me. You have to expect a certain amount of breakage."

Sandoval looks me up and down and says, "And put a glove on that grotesque hand. It makes me sick."

I flex my prosthetic left hand. I can't argue with her on the ugly part. The hand was a present from a monster. Really, my whole left arm looks like something that belongs on a mechanical insect. It's still good at giving the finger, but I restrain myself now.

While I slip on my glove, she leaves with her entourage in tow. I give them a few seconds before leaving the bowling alley. I might be an idiot, but I know they need time to cool down. Just like I know I have to keep pushing them. If they get pissed or flustered enough, they might drop some useful piece of information. But I can't go too far too fast. Sandoval could have their necromancer pull the plug on me and I'd be right back in Hell with no body and a pack of new enemies. I've got to play this right. Dance around the edges of being a complete asshole.

The problem is, I'm not the best dancer.

On my way out, I flick off the bowling alley lights. Too bad they found me. I kind of like it down here. Especially the soundproofing. It would be a good place to play the monster and slap the shit out of one of them until they told me what's really going on.

I MEET UP with them in Sandoval's office, where I woke up yesterday. It's a nice room. Nice furniture covered in pretty silks and leather. A nice pool table. A nice TV the size of Kansas. It's all so fucking nice it's like a museum. I halfway expect a stuffed grizzly bear and maybe some wax Neanderthals in the corner. No such luck. It's the same six assholes I've been staring at since I got back.

Sandoval is the boss, that much is clear. Black hair, a deep tan, and a dress cut low enough that you could autopsy her and never touch the edges. She's pretty, she knows it, and she isn't above using it. It's tedious just looking at her.

"I take it that you're feeling better today," says Sandoval.

I glance at the other idiots in the room.

"Better is a relative thing. I feel better than dead, so, yeah, I guess I'm feeling swell."

"It looks like your motor functions are coming back, too. That's good. You're going to need them," says Barron Sinclair. He's the only other one who talks much. He's heavyset. Long gray hair and perfect little beard. He's one of those guys born with an old face. He could be fifty or seventy. He's also sick. I can smell the drugs in his system. Metallic and bitter as lemons. Sinclair tries to look calm, but he's scared. Whatever he has, it must be bad if he can't find any magicians who can cure it. He's worried about what's waiting for him in Hell, especially since I wiped out Wormwood down there. Good. That's more incentive for him to want me alive.

"Eva keeps telling me that, but she won't say what I'll need them for."

"That's what this meeting is about. I think you're coherent enough to discuss your mission," she says.

I look at her.

"My mission? That sounds so noble. Am I going to rescue your kitten from a tree?"

"Not quite," she says, shooting me a feral smile. "You're going to kill someone."

"Probably a lot of people," says Sinclair.

"That's what I figured. Who's the lucky guy or gal?"

She points to one of the other cockroaches that follow her around. A young, cocky guy with a face built for punching.

"Roger here can give you the *details*. Roger?" says Sandoval.

I hold up a hand as Roger opens his mean little mouth. He closes it again.

"Is Roger going to be giving me orders? Are any of these other idiots?"

Sandoval crosses her arms.

"I suppose not."

"Can any of them help me stay in my body?"

"No."

"Then fuck 'em."

Roger and the other roaches' heartbeats spike. I smell sweat. Roger starts to open his mouth again. I raise the Colt and point it at his stupid face.

"Hush, Roger. Grown-ups are talking."

He clamps his mouth shut. I put the Colt in my waistband at my back. Okay. Enough of that stuff for now. Everyone is nice and rattled. Let's see if someone says something interesting.

Sandoval stares at me, wondering if she made a huge mistake. When she doesn't say anything, Sinclair steps forward.

"It's not exactly a hit," he says. "Though I suspect there will be a considerable number of casualties. What we need you to do is stop an event."

He coughs wetly and wipes his mouth with a monogrammed hankie. When he's done I say, "What kind of event?"

"Stupendous," says Sandoval. "Cataclysmic."

"Can you narrow that down a little?"

"No. All you need to know is that something awful will happen on Sunday unless you stop it."

"And if I do I get put back in my body for good, completely alive?"

She raises her eyebrows a fraction of an inch, even as she says, "That's the deal."

The silk slippers they gave me are absurdly comfortable. I wiggle my toes in them, telling myself that this pack of jackals *is* going to keep its end of the bargain.

"I'd still like to know what kind of event."

"I told you. No."

"You see, it would help to know what I'm walking into. Am I knocking over a *quinceañera* or stopping a nuke launch? You get my meaning? It's about preparations, appropriate tools, and my general attitude."

"Maybe we should tell him," says Sinclair.

"No," says Sandoval. "It's a trick."

I look at Sinclair, then back at Sandoval.

"I know it has to do with the Wormwood bunch that broke away and opened their own lemonade stand without you."

"No," says Sandoval. "You do what we say and you get your body back. That's all you need to know."

I don't say anything long enough for the room to get uncomfortable. Sandoval gives me the stink eye and I give it right back.

"I think we should tell him," says Sinclair.

Eva shakes her head.

"No."

I wait, wiggling my toes. Not saying a word.

Finally, Sinclair blurts, "It's a ritual. A magic ritual."

Sandoval whirls around and slaps him hard enough to leave a mark on his cheek.

I say, "What kind of ritual?"

Sandoval stares at Sinclair, breathing hard. Sinclair touches his face where she hit him. Despite things, he says, "When you joked about a nuclear launch you were closer than you realize."

"The other Wormwood has a bomb?"

"They might as well have," says Sandoval. She turns from Sinclair and looks at me. "The splinter faction are in possession of a ritual that will utterly destroy Los Angeles."

Sinclair says, "It will trigger similar destruction all over the world. Berlin. Tokyo. Sydney. Anywhere we, the true Wormwood, are concentrated."

"They hope to wipe us out in one massive action," Sandoval says.

I listen to their hearts. Check the microtremors on their faces. They're telling the truth.

Well . . . fuck.

I say, "With all due respect to Berlin, Tokyo, and wherever the fuck else, I don't care. Let's talk about L.A."

"They're out to destroy our entire infrastructure," says Sinclair.

Sandoval says, "Then they can pick off the stragglers one by one."

I look over at the roaches.

"Any of you have a cigarette?"

"There's no smoking in the house," says Sandoval.

"I wouldn't think it matters, seeing as how you're all going to die."

"What do you mean?" says Sinclair. "You won't take the job?"

"Not if you keep lying to me."

He frowns.

"What do you mean?"

"I mean you're Wormwood. Why do you need a dead man to do your dirty work? You're global and yet you can't find one single asshole who can handle this job for you?"

"I think you might overestimate us at the moment," says Sandoval quietly.

"The other faction took many of our best and brightest," says Sinclair. "Or killed them."

"Besides, you have a unique set of skills," Sandoval says.

It's making more sense now.

"That's why you gave me back the Room of Thirteen Doors. You don't just need someone who can stop the ritual. You need someone who can get to it."

"Exactly."

"That means you don't know where it will happen."

"Correct."

"But you're absolutely sure it will happen Sunday."

"On the new moon, yes," says Sinclair.

I look at them both. They're still telling the truth.

"What day is it now?"

"Wednesday evening."

"Wednesday? Why didn't you bring me back sooner?"

"You don't just snatch a soul from the afterlife willy-nilly," says Jonathan Howard, their necromancer. "It needs to happen at the right time."

He's taller than me. British, with wire-rim glasses. He carries the weird smell of death that all necromancers have. Rotting flesh. Nasty hoodoo potions. They try to cover it up with cologne, but that just makes it worse.

I walk over to him.

"What about fixing my body? Does that need to happen at some super-special time too?"

He leans back from me a little.

"No. That can happen anytime."

"You sure?"

"Completely."

I pat him on the arm.

"You better be, Johnny, 'cause I'm not going back to Hell alone."

I turn back to Sandoval.

"Let's hit the fucking road. Where do we go? Who do I kill first?"

"I have no idea," she says. "We thought we'd leave that up to you. You seem to have a knack for these things."

I look at Sinclair.

"Is she serious? You don't have a where *or* a who?"

"I'm afraid not."

"Okay. How do you contact the faction? A phone number. A name."

"They've hidden themselves well. We don't have anything."

"Fuck."

I look over at the roaches. They're no help. Not a flicker of intelligence anywhere in the bunch.

"Here I was expecting Lex Luthor and what I get is a bunch of runaways picking pockets at the bus station."

Sandoval looks at her watch.

"The clock is ticking, Stark. Your body is already starting to break down."

"A cigarette would really help me think."

"Tick-tock," she says.

I take a breath and lean back on the pool table.

"Then we have to make them come to us," I say. "Make them think you have something they want so they'll come after it. Maybe a counter-spell that can blow up their ritual.

Now, here's the hard part. Someone's got to take that fake spell and stroll out of here with it. Let themselves get kidnapped, then bring one of them back here for questioning. Any volunteers?"

I glance around the room knowing the answer but hoping Roger might be enough of a suck-up that he'll raise his hand.

No such luck.

"I think you win the coin toss, Stark," says Sandoval.

"I had a feeling I would. I wish you'd told me all this earlier in the day. I can't really get started until tomorrow, Thursday. That's cutting things close."

"I told you. We couldn't bring you back any sooner," says Howard.

"You're lucky you brought me back at all. I was one hot second from being double dead."

Howard frowns.

"Dying in Heaven?"

"Being murdered, technically."

"You do find trouble everywhere," says Sandoval.

"I was just looking for the buffet line."

"Is there anything we can do to get started now?" says Sinclair. There's the slightest edge to his voice. He doesn't like all this chitchat. Yeah, he's scared, but he knows something he's not telling me. Probably what's really going on. I believe that these creeps don't want to get blown to rags, but I wonder what they *do* want. I'll put beating information from Sinclair on my to-do list for tomorrow. For now, I just talk to him.

"Do you have a rat in your organization? Don't answer. It was a rhetorical question. For things to be this out of control, of course you do."

"They're worse than you think," says Sinclair.

"What do you mean?"

"Assassinations," says Sandoval. "Slow, but steady."

Sinclair chimes in.

"Mostly the heads of other offices. Pieter Holden in Vienna was first."

Sandoval holds up one finger, then two.

"Megan Bradbury in Chicago and Franz Landschoff in Cairo are the most recent."

I look over at the roaches, then back to them.

"You're sure it's the faction doing it?"

"There's no question," Sandoval says.

"Not just a rat then. A great big rat." I go to Sandoval and stage-whisper, "Eva, do you think it's one of these assholes?"

She looks over at her mute bugs.

"Don't worry," she says. "I trust all of these people with my life."

"Good. 'Cause if it's one of them, we're completely fucked."

"What's your idea?" says Sinclair.

"Put the word out to all of your people. A courier is taking something life-or-death important across town tomorrow afternoon. Make it to one of your other offices."

"You think the faction will try to intercept the courier?"

"They better or you can relax and eat finger sandwiches until they blow your asses up."

"And you with us," says Sandoval. "I take it that you're going to play the courier?"

"Since none of you stepped up, I guess so."

She looks at the roaches.

"All right. You know what to do. Spread the word about the courier to all of your subordinates."

"Make sure they know I'm the only thing between their ass and the next coal cart to Hell," I add.

"Go," says Sandoval. "Start making calls."

I hold up a hand.

"Not yet."

Everyone looks at me.

"If someone doesn't give me a cigarette, the deal is off."

Roger reaches into his jacket and tosses me a pack of Shermans.

"Got a lighter?" I say.

"I thought you were Mr. Magic. Light it your-fucking-self," he says.

"Thanks, Rog. You're a pip."

They all file out.

"We'll be working tonight, Stark. What will you do to occupy yourself?" says Sandoval. "And keep in mind that you're barred from the bowling alley."

"Then I'm going out."

"Where?"

"Out. I want to smoke. I want to see things. I want to have a drink with people I don't hate."

She doesn't believe me.

"Calm down, Eva. Where am I going to go? I'm in hock to you. I'll be back in a couple of hours. Just make sure your cherubs do their jobs."

She checks her watch and says, "Two hours."

"I'm going to need some money."

"Why?"

"Unless things have changed in the past year, liquor isn't free."

She stares at me.

"I don't carry cash."

"Of course you don't, your highness."

I look at Sinclair.

"How about you? You too good to touch filthy lucre?"

He pulls a wad from his pocket enclosed in a gold money clip. Peels off a twenty.

"Don't fuck with me."

He peels off another.

"Keep going. I tip big."

I stop him at a hundred dollars. He holds the bills out like I might bite his hand off. It's tempting.

I walk to a shadow and put the bills in my pocket.

"Don't wait up."

"I don't want you coming back drunk," says Sandoval.

"Don't worry. I'll look pretty for class pictures tomorrow."

One more step and the shadow swallows me.

I know those two are going to fuck me over, but I don't know how, and until I do I'm going to have to dance their dance, take my lumps, and smile the whole time. Howard is the one I need to keep an eye on. The necromancer is the Blue Fairy to my Pinocchio and I want to be a real boy again. If things go sideways, the others can fry. Howard though? I won't let anyone touch a hair on his stinking head.

I step out of the shadow onto Hollywood Boulevard a few blocks west of Las Palmas and Maximum Overdrive, the video store where I live. Or used to. Who knows now? Up ahead, Donut Universe shines like the Virgin Mary doing barrel rolls over Lourdes, so I head over.

BEFORE I GO inside there's the matter of Roger's cigarette. There's no one on the street I can bum a light from, which leaves me with one option. I put the smoke in my mouth and cup my hands around it. Whisper some Hellion hoodoo. A small flame flickers up from my palm, just big enough for me to spark the cigarette. It's a relief, and I don't mean just getting to smoke. I haven't done any hoodoo since coming back and I didn't want Sandoval and Sinclair to see me in case I blew it. Now I want to try something bigger, but what I'm best at is breaking things, so I'll wait until there's something I want to see in pieces.

The Sherman is a decent smoke in its own way, but it doesn't have the bite of a Malediction, the most popular cigarette in Hell. I had a whole box stashed upstairs at Max Overdrive. Wonder if they're still there. More important, I wonder if I should even go near the place again. What if I run into Candy? The last time she saw me, I was dying with a knife in my back. I've been gone a year. What's her life like now? A year is long enough to move past whatever grief she might have felt back then. The good news is that I saw her outside Max Overdrive the night I came back from Hell, so I know she and the store are still around.

The truth is, I want to run inside and see her right now. But what if things don't work out with Wormwood? It's almost Thursday and I could be gone again by Sunday. Is it fair to stumble back into her life when I could just as easily stumble out again? The answer is simple. Seeing her now wouldn't even be close to fair. So, for the moment I'll keep to myself and see how this insane fucking situation plays out. It's a lonely feeling, but I'm almost used to that.

What's really getting to me is that as much as I missed her in Hell, it's a hundred times worse being back. My perfect, beautiful monster. During my last look at her she was in her Jade form, tearing Audsley Ishii apart. That's how you know someone really likes you. Anyone can give you chocolate and flowers, but when they'll disembowel someone for you? That's true love.

I crush the Sherman under my heel and go inside Donut Universe.

The smell that hits me is almost overwhelming. Familiar and alien at the same time. Hellion food tastes like what a butcher shop throws in the trash and then a hobo sleeps on it for a couple of days. But what's on the shelves in this shop . . .

If I have to die again, let it be in Donut Universe. Bury me in old-fashioneds and éclairs. Burn me in the parking lot and let me drift up to Valhalla on a wave of holy sugar and grease fumes.

When it's my turn, I step up to the counter, where a pretty young woman asks me what I want. Like the rest of the Donut Universe staff, she wears little antennae with silver balls on the end. The balls bop gently as she speaks. My friend Cindil wore antennae like that when she worked here. Back before she was murdered. I can't ever come in here without thinking of her. But I brought her back from Hell and now she has a pretty decent new life. She even plays drums in Candy's terrible band. Or she did a year ago. Where is she now?

Goddammit. Memory is such a bastard when you don't know if any of it's true anymore. Candy. Cindil. Max Overdrive. L.A. That's hard to lose and maybe harder to get back when you don't know if you can keep it.

"Sir?" says the antennae girl. "Do you want a donut?"

Fuck me. How long have I been standing here? I can't even interact with actual humans without looking like a lunatic. Take two.

"I'll have an apple fritter and a cup of coffee."

She rings them up and tells me the price. I hand her one of the twenties and when she tries to give me change I say, "Keep it. I'm just happy to be back here."

She smiles and says, "Welcome back," like she means it, and it kind of breaks my heart. She's nice. I forgot what that's like. I try to smile back at her, but I'm not sure I'm getting it right. I mean, my face does *something*. Whether it's a smile or not is up to her.

The good news is that when she brings me my order she doesn't pepper-spray me. That's a beginning. I feel like a kid on his first date, proud he didn't spill whiskey on his girlfriend's dress or puke on her when he drank too much.

"Come back soon," she says as I pick up my stuff.

"If I'm still alive next week, I'll buy out the whole damn store."

She laughs and says, "It's a date then."

I nod and get out before I blow the moment.

More than I already have, I mean.

At the corner, I take a long sip of coffee. It's funny. I remember what they served at Donut Universe as being pretty good, but I can barely taste this stuff at all. I unwrap the apple fritter and take a bite. It's the same thing. I feel the dough in my mouth, but I can't taste anything. Another sip of coffee and another bite of fritter. I chew until I can't stand it anymore and spit the fritter into the gutter. It's not the food. It's me. I can't taste it. Another side effect of being only half-alive. At least the cigarette had a little kick. And I could taste bourbon the other night. This half-alive situation is getting on my nerves. I'll do whatever it takes to get right again.

If cigarettes and liquor are all I can handle until I'm fully alive again, there's only one place I can go. I head for Ivar Avenue and Bamboo House of Dolls. And it better be there. I swear if it's gone, Wormwood won't have to worry about the faction.

I'll nuke L.A. myself.

FORTUNATELY FOR EVERYONE, I don't have to drop even a single bomb. As soon as I spot the neon, my whole body relaxes. I need a drink more than ever to wash the last mealy remnants of the fritter out of my mouth. But I don't want anyone here to know I'm back, including Carlos, the bartender. I step into an alley and throw on a glamour so no one will recognize me. There are still eighty dollars of Sinclair's money in my pocket. That should be enough to get decently horizontal.

But I don't go inside right away. Instead, I stay on the street letting the moment soak in. A day or so ago, I was standing at the pearly gates. Just a few hours before that, on the road for a year with a dog pack of psycho marauders tearing up the Tenebrae, killing and burning everything in our path. Standing here now, just a day later, all that feels like a bad dream. Mouthfuls of dust, road rash, and the kind of burning fear that's indistinguishable from anger. But here and now it's just cigarette smoke, couples whispering to each other, and the sound of bird chirps and horns as Martin Denny spins on the jukebox. It's a little overwhelming, but in a good way. I take one last gulp of L.A. night smog and go inside.

At first glance, not much has changed inside. It's still the best punk tiki bar in existence. Old Cramps and Germs posters hang on the walls. Plastic hula girls and coconuts carved like monkeys are lined up behind the bar. And Carlos is there, solo as usual, doling out beer and whiskey to the rabble. What's changed is the crowd. It's still a mix of fanged and feathered Lurkers and civilians, but they're quieter than I remember. Bamboo House of Dolls used to be shoulder to shoulder any night of the week. Tonight you could fire a cannon in here and not hit anything but the wall. Over in the back corner is a minuscule stage where Carlos has installed the death knell of any good bar—a karaoke machine. It's good to be back inside, but the state of the place is depressing. Most of the stools by the bar are empty, so I take one at the far end away from the door. Yeah, it's quiet now, but I've had enough things creep up on me in here that I know I won't be able to relax with my back exposed like that.

Maybe that's what's wrong with the place. Have any flesh-eating High Plains Drifter hoedowns, skinhead assassination attempts, or hoodoo firefights happened here since I've been gone? Maybe not. And maybe people miss the danger. Maybe Bamboo House of Dolls isn't the same if you're not risking your life every time you walk inside. Carlos should have hired an evil clown to hide in the rafters and chase people around with a cleaver every now and then. It sure would have woken up these sad sacks.

Carlos comes down the bar and gives me a hello nod.

"What'll you have?"

I open my mouth and—like an idiot—almost say "Aqua Regia," my favorite Hellion brew. Instead, I clear my throat, tell myself to focus for a goddamn minute, and manage to croak, "Jack Daniel's. A double. Neat."

"You got it," he says, and heads back to the bottles and hula girls.

It's ridiculous how happy it makes me just hearing his voice. The moment I do, the bar becomes more real, the smells and sounds more solid. Who cares if I couldn't taste a fucking do-nut? This is my home away from home. Literally these days. I don't even know if I have a home here anymore. For all I know, money got so thin at Max Overdrive that they tossed some throw pillows upstairs and now rent it out on Airbnb. I won-der if they would mention that I used to keep Kasabian's head in the closet or point out all the blood that's soaked into the floor. I would if I was them. It gives the place character. Who wouldn't pay a little extra to sleep in a real-life Hollywood murder flat?

When Carlos brings me my drink I put down a twenty.

"Keep it."

He picks it up and tosses it back on the cash register.

"Thanks."

I look around the place once more.

"It's quiet in here. Quieter than I remember."

"Yeah? You been in before?"

"About a year ago. It was a lot more crowded. Loud and lively."

He looks around the place too.

"That it was. Things change though. Crowds change."

I sip the Jack. Swirl it around in my mouth and swallow. It burns just right and washes away the last of the fritter.

"Do you ever miss the noise?"

He thinks for a minute.

"Sometimes. Not always. Sometimes it was nice. Other times, it was something else entirely."

"I remember it used to be a little dangerous around here."

He lays out coasters and says, "Only if you consider dying dangerous."

"When you think of the old days, what do you miss most?"

"The people. The old regulars. Some still come in, but others . . . they're gone for good."

I take another sip of Jack.

"This is L.A. Nothing is ever gone for good."

He smiles.

"Maybe that's what we need. A reboot. Bride of Bamboo House of Dolls."

"Son of Bamboo House of Dolls."

He gives me a look.

"You a Frankenstein fan? I had a buddy who used to like old movies."

"What happened? You're not friends anymore?"

Carlos brings over the Jack and a glass. Pours himself a drink.

"He's gone with the wind."

"Left town?"

"Dead."

"I'm sorry."

He looks up as the jukebox begins to play Martin Denny's "Quiet Village."

"Me too," he says. "I mean he could be a real asshole sometimes, but you know?"

"I have friends like that. Pains in the ass, but they keep things interesting."

"Exactly. But he's gone, so what are you going to do?"

"Get yourself a necromancer?"

He rolls his eyes dramatically. "I get enough of those gloomy bastards on trivia night."

I almost spit out a mouthful of whiskey.

"You have a karaoke machine *and* you do bar trivia?"

He nods slowly.

"Pathetic, isn't it? But you do whatever it takes to keep the doors open." He gives me a hard look. "What, you never compromised anything to stay alive?"

I wipe my mouth with the back of my hand.

"I've compromised plenty. More than I like to think about. But damn, trivia and karaoke?"

Carlos downs his drink in one swallow.

"I know. I sold my soul. But when I win the lottery— boom!—they're all gone."

"You wouldn't quit the business?"

He chuckles and pours us both another round.

"I'm a bartender. Some people are cops or priests or movie stars. Me? I pour drinks and keep the jukebox cool."

As the music fades away, someone behind us blows into a microphone.

"Testing. One. Two. Can you hear me?"

The crowd murmurs.

A young guy wearing a pale blue pullover and a tech-startup haircut is hunched over the mic at the karaoke machine. He points to a young woman across the room.

"This is for you, Cherie."

I can't help but smile when I see her. This is a taste of the old Bamboo House of Dolls. A clueless tourist slumming in a weirdo bar and he picks up a pretty young thing. Only his paramour is a Jade and if he does or says the wrong thing, she's going to bite him and drink his guts like a milkshake. I'm almost tempted to tell him, only then he starts singing that Barry Manilow song "Mandy," but substituting "Cherie" in the chorus. That's when I decide to let Darwin sort out his fate.

I finish my drink and get up.

"I think that's my cue to get moving."

Carlos puts out his hand and we shake.

"Don't be a stranger. You're allowed to come back more than once a year."

"Believe me, Carlos. I will if I can."

He gives me a funny look.

"How did you know my name?"

Shit.

"I must have read it on Yelp or somewhere."

He nods, not entirely buying it.

"Okay. Well, come back on a Tuesday and play trivia with those necro bores. I'll throw in a lot of old movie questions."

I give him a nod and leave.

Carlos, you have no fucking idea how much I want to make that happen.

I WANDER ALONG the boulevard. It's a nothing night. Cars honk at jaywalkers. Knots of wandering tourists are disappointed at how boring Hollywood and Vine really is. The Egyptian Theatre is dark as a repair crew works on the electric lines out front. There's more action down by the wax museum and Ripley's Believe It or Not!, but the lights are too bright and it's too close to the Chinese Theatre. An off-duty creep in a Spider-Man costume chats up a bored Wonder Woman who's about two puffs of a Virginia Slim away from beating him to death with her shield. Really, I'm not ready to go back to Sandoval's Castle Grayskull and I'm trying to distract myself from lurking outside Max Overdrive in hopes of catching a glimpse of Candy. I've already done that once since I got back and she almost caught me. There's no percentage in taking a chance like that again, so of course, I do it anyway.

Lucky me, there's nothing happening there either. Candy is upstairs or out, so I'm basically staring at a dark storefront like a tweaker trying to work up the nerve to rob the place. But unfocused staring sometimes pays off. Through the front window, I get a glimpse of Kasabian moving around inside. He's talking to someone and smiling, and for a second I get fifth-grade giddy that I might score a look at that cute girl who sits next to me in history class. Instead, it's Alessa—Candy's girlfriend. Candy met her a few weeks before I died and they became lovers soon after that. I mean, I told her it was okay with me, and it was. Candy had always dated girls and the fact she was with me didn't make her desire to be with other women magically disappear. Now, though, things are different, and for the first time I feel jealous of the two of them. They had a year together that I'll never get back.

They're a year closer and I'm on the street like a goddamn lost dog wondering if I'll ever find my way back home.

Thinking about it, though, maybe this is a good thing and I should shut up and not get so maudlin. Candy watched me get murdered and Alessa was there to help her through it. And Alessa has obviously forgiven Candy for lying to her about who she really was. Alessa didn't know Candy was a Jade when they started dating. She also only knew Candy as Chihiro, the identity she had to adopt to stay out of a federal lockup. When someone gets hit with secrets like that all at once and they stick around, that makes them good people and someone who really cares about you. So, yeah, Alessa is a lot more all right with me now than she was before I died.

But none of that stops me from wanting to charge inside and see Candy right now. Instead, I step into a shadow before I do something truly stupid.

I come out in my room in Sandoval's mansion. I want another drink, but that means going into her office, which means I might see her or Sinclair, and in my current mood I'm not sure either one of them would leave with their head on their shoulders. Instead, I throw my clothes in a heap in the corner and get into bed. I'm suddenly a lot more tired than I was a couple of hours ago.

My dreams are about bombs exploding and L.A. being wiped off the map. It's all in slow motion, so I get a good look at the city flying apart, burning bodies tossed into the air with flaming palm trees, the fire moving up the hills, scorching everything along the way. The Hollywood sign flies apart. The Griffith Observatory explodes when the concussion wave hits it. I try to distract myself with all of this cinematic carnage, but it doesn't work. Swirling around the center of things is everyone I know and care about: Candy, Kasabian, Vidocq, Allegra, Brigitte, Carlos, even Alessa. They're whipped around in a sun-bright vortex, pulled down into a boiling mass of nothingness. A swirling singularity so incandescent it turns to ash not just their bodies, but every particle of their being, so that there's nothing left of them for Hell or Heaven, meaning they just fade from existence like they were never there. And all I can do is watch and let it happen because I don't know how to stop it.

Fuck Wormwood. Fuck the faction. If I can't stop the ritual, *no one* lives. No escape jets or yachts heading out to sea for this crowd. They get swallowed in the burning madness with the rest of us. I'll laugh and laugh as they cry and cry all the way down into nonexistence when it finally hits them that all their money and power isn't going to hold their atoms together in the coming shitstorm. The feeling isn't satisfaction. It's more like revenge. And sometimes that's as close to satisfaction as you're ever going to get.

WHEN I WAKE up in the morning, there's a black suit waiting for me in the closet. It's a Hugo Boss. Of course he'd be the go-to guy for Wormwood. In World War II, he made uniforms for the SS. There's also a dark purple shirt and a pair of Italian shoes by the bed.

When I try everything on, they're a perfect fit. That's unsettling. I'm going to assume that Sandoval or someone figured out my size by eyeballing me. It's either that or someone sneaked in here while I was asleep and measured me like they were getting me ready for a coffin.

Normally I don't like playing dress-up, but Sandoval, Sinclair, and their roaches look startled enough when they see me in James Bond drag that it's worth it.

"You look very convincing," says Sinclair.

"Except for the face," says Sandoval. "Really, Stark, you're much too ugly to be a Wormwood associate."

I whisper some hoodoo and put on the glamour I used last night. Again, Sinclair and the roaches are startled. To Sandoval's credit, she just looks me over like she's selecting which lobster in the tank to eat for dinner.

She says, "Much better. Almost human."

I adjust my tie in a mirror on the wall.

"Thanks. You're looking pretty Maleficent yourself. Curse any kids today?"

"No, but Sinclair and I punched a lovely hole in the Japanese stock market."

"It seemed a good time to bring down some Yakuza-controlled companies that have aligned themselves with the faction," he says.

Sandoval grins broadly.

"There'll be blood flowing in Tokyo tonight."

"Sounds like fun," I say. "Me, I prefer a good thriller. Ever seen *The Usual Suspects*?"

"Stop it. We don't have time for your nonsense. And neither do you."

I close in on her and Sinclair.

"I only bring it up because the whole story hinges on a huge lie. You see my point?"

Sinclair scratches his ear. A nervous tic.

"We did what we talked about. All of us."

"So, everyone knows that a courier is going out?"

Sandoval says, "Calm down. We said as much as we could without being too obvious. If there's a traitor in our organization, he or she knows that you'll be moving an important package."

There's a briefcase lying on the pool table.

"What's in it?"

"Random financial records," says Sinclair. "Nothing the faction can use against us."

I look at them both.

"You better not have fucked this up because my only other alternative is to start killing your staff and hope someone squeals."

"Why don't you just do that now?" says Sandoval. "That sounds more efficient than this courier scenario."

"Sure. I could start with you and Barron. How do I know that this whole thing isn't a setup? Maybe you two are the rats and you just want to see if anyone can get through to your faction pals."

"Don't be absurd. We're the injured party."

"Then don't tell me who to kill and when. It unsettles my tranquil disposition."

"We've done our part. Now you do yours," says Sinclair.

Sandoval glances at her watch.

"The car will be here soon."

I pick up the briefcase.

"Nice. What is this? Rattlesnake?"

"Alligator," Sinclair.

"I knew it was something cold-blooded."

Sandoval's cell phone rings. She exchanges a few words and hangs up.

"The car is here. The driver knows where to take you. It's one of our law offices in Westwood."

"Do you know the driver?"

Sandoval gives me a look.

"Philip? He's worked for me for years. I trust him."

"I mean, if I get snatched, he might not be in shape to be your driver anymore."

She looks at Sinclair. "I hadn't thought of that."

She looks back at me.

"That's why we wanted you. Your sick little mind."

"You have any spare drivers lying around? Ones you don't like as much?"

"No. Do you, Barron?"

He shakes his head. "I've known my driver for years."

"Just one big happy family," I say.

I weigh the briefcase in my hand. It's very light. That means there aren't any bombs in case they change their minds about me.

"I'll do my best to keep him alive. But if it comes down to him or me, well, you know."

Sandoval glances at her roaches.

"Just do your job and leave the rest to us."

Before I start for the door I say, "Where's Howard?"

"In the library. Why?"

"I'll try to keep the driver safe. You do the same with Howard."

"Why do you think he might not be safe?" says Sinclair.

"No reason. It's just that I'll be very cranky if anything happens to him."

Sandoval looks back at me.

"The car is waiting."

Sinclair says, "Good luck."

"Thanks."

As I reach the front door Sandoval calls after me.

"Don't get any grand ideas about betraying us or running off. The spell Howard used to bring you back is very specific and not something just any necromancer can duplicate."

I open the door but pause. "That reminds me. Does Howard like movie trivia?"

"I don't know. Who cares? What does that have to do with anything?"

"Just curious. If he brings me back right, I know the place to take him for a drink."

It's a hot day, even for L.A. The sky is clear, but the cat-piss smell of Sandoval's eucalyptus trees makes the air feel heavy. The driver is holding the limo door open for me at the head of the circular driveway. I get in and it's twenty degrees cooler. Is the driver from the Arctic or does he know about my not-quite-alive situation and think he needs to keep me on ice so I won't stink? Or maybe he knows what's going to happen next and he's trying not to sweat. There's nothing I can do to help that, so he better buckle up tight.

As he pulls away from Sandoval's house and takes us out through the gates of the estate I say, "You're Philip, right?"

He glances in the rearview mirror.

"Yes, sir."

"Well, Philip, do you know who you work for?"

"Ms. Sandoval? Of course."

"You know what she does for a living?"

"I know that's she's in international finance."

I wish I could see his eyes. It would help me know if he's lying. His heartbeat's up a little, but he's not panicked. Just curious about getting the third degree from a stranger in the backseat.

There's a small but well-stocked bar on the left wall of the limo. I find the bourbon and pour myself a few fingers. Look at Philip again in the rearview.

"You ever heard of Wormwood?"

He shakes his head. "No, sir. Should I?"

I try to think of a delicate way to ask the next question but don't come up with anything.

"Is this car bulletproof?"

"Yes. Why do you ask?"

"No reason. But if I tell you to hit the gas or bail out or get on the floor, don't ask questions."

Now his heart is racing. Even though it's Ice Station Zebra in here I can smell him start to sweat.

"Are we in danger?" he says.

"It depends on what you mean by 'we.'"

"Am *I* in danger?"

"That's the first smart thing anyone's said to me today. And, yes, you really are. So do what I tell you."

"Yes, sir. Thank you for the warning."

"Just remember to duck if I say so."

"Yes, sir."

He's quiet after that.

WE'RE ON THE part of Sunset Boulevard that winds like a drunk anaconda through Beverly Hills and Bel-Air. Most of the drive is a dull blur of walled compounds where good, up-standing American families debate whether their artisanally raised mutts deserve domestic or imported champagne with their prime rib kibble. But it's the side streets that are where the action is. These Sunset flatlanders are mere paupers with millions of dollars, while the side streets lead to gated Xana-dus where the toilets are gold and the trash doesn't end up in landfills but gets a gentle yacht journey out to the open sea, where it receives a Viking funeral, complete with human sacrifice. I can't help but wonder how many associates of Wormwood and the breakaway faction we're passing on our way west. Odds are that some of them live right next door to each other, filling Easter eggs with thermite and hiding razor blades in apples as Halloween surprises for the unen-lightened in the neighborhood. I'm trying to work up some sympathy for the big-money families that have no Worm-wood connections, but it's hard to do. Whether it's Beverly Hills, Bel-Air, or Pandemonium—Hell's capital city—odds are anyone living in this kind of luxury has a body or two buried in the greenhouse. No, this patch of land is a No Sympathy Zone. They don't give it, so they shouldn't expect it. Whether it's death by Wormwood, a bad stock market, or Daddy's drinking, they're on their own. Islands of privilege in a sea of shit and bad karma. When the tide rises, they better know how to swim, because no one is tossing these gold-plated Capones a life preserver.

Which makes me wonder what kind of deal Sandoval and Sinclair will offer me to not murder them after I'm completely back in my body. Whatever it is, it won't be enough and they probably know it, which means they're going to fuck me over at their first opportunity. I need to focus and be ready for when it happens. I let an idiot send me to Hell once. It will be embarrassing if I do it again.

It's about halfway between the Playboy Mansion and the Bel-Air Country Club that I spot the van behind us. Black with dark, tinted windows, no plates or brand insignia on the front. I tell the driver to turn left on Hilgard Avenue, then swing onto a side street.

"Oh god," he says. "Is it happening?"

"What did I say about questions?"

"Not to ask them."

"Right. Now, do you have a cigarette lighter?"

"Yes, sir."

"How about a handkerchief?"

"Yes."

"Give them to me."

As he hands them back, I take one last slug of bourbon and stuff the handkerchief into the neck of the bottle.

The moment we turn off Sunset, the van speeds up. With luck, being on a side street will get us away from traffic and minimize collateral damage, but I'm not counting on that last part.

The van floors it and slams us from behind. The limo starts to spin out, but Philip gets control and stops us before the car flips. We've done a one-eighty, though, which gives us a perfect view of the van as five men in sharp suits and balaclavas pile out, shouting and waving shiny new SIG 552 rifles—very serious weaponry that makes me wonder if taking prisoners is a priority.

"What do I do?" shouts Philip.

I roll down a side window.

"Get on the fucking floor."

I light the handkerchief in the bottle and throw it at the welcome committee. A small but satisfying fireball explodes in the street, scattering the gunmen and sending a couple of them into frantic pirouettes, beating out the flames on their suits. I don't want to see Philip get shot over my fun, so I step outside and take a couple of badly aimed swings at the closest shooters. All of my instincts make me want to crack their skulls, but I let my punches miss by a mile. I keep reminding myself that I *want* to get taken hostage, so when the five of them swarm me, I go down without a fight. Two of them haul me up while another grabs my briefcase. I can't see what the others are doing, but when I hear a single gunshot I know exactly what it means: Philip didn't make it.

Fuck. Shooting an unarmed driver cowering on the floor, that's just mean, even for Wormwood.

One more thing to remember for the Fuck Wormwood ledger.

They shove me into the van, bind my hands, blindfold me, and peel out. We drive for a long time.

No one talks, but I hear a lot of grunts and moans. Probably from the shooters I torched. It's small satisfaction, but I'll take anything right now.

Except for Philip, things are going pretty much the way I'd hoped. The faction snatched both me and the case. They could have just shot me, but they didn't, so that means they want information, which I'm more than happy to give them. I just wish this blindfold wasn't so tight and I could see something. If they're wearing their balaclavas in the van it means they still don't want me to see their faces, which means they're not necessarily planning on killing me. At least not right away. I'm going to have to improvise from here. And I can't use hoodoo because they'll know I'm a ringer and that will blow my chances of getting any useful information from them.

So I wait.

The drive takes a long time. We're not moving for a lot of it and when we are, it's at about five miles an hour. That means we're probably on a freeway. The closest one is the 405, but are we going north or south? And are we staying on that one route the whole way?

I slow my breathing and try to relax. Theoretically that's a good thing, but relaxing while blind lets my mind wander and the first thing that comes into my head is, I wonder what Candy is doing right now.

Nope. None of that shit. That will make me crazy, distract me enough that I'll miss clues, and maybe get me shot. No, anything is better than thinking about Candy right now. I move my bound hands around so I can touch my wrist and feel my pulse. Count to sixty and start again, trying to time the drive. It's well over an hour. In most towns that would mean we're halfway to Argentina, but in L.A. it means we could be circling the block looking for parking. Still, it keeps my mind off Candy.

Finally, the van makes a sharp right turn. The tires crunch over something for a few seconds. Probably gravel by the sound. Then we're back on solid pavement. When we stop, there's the sound of a motor opening a large door. As it closes, the sound echoes. We're probably in a warehouse. Now all I have to do is narrow it down from among the other ten thousand warehouses in L.A., while not getting shot. I hate multitasking.

Someone grabs my lapel and pulls me out of the van. I stumble getting out and a couple of them grab me before I can fall. Good. They're concerned about keeping me in one piece for now. I can work with that. Someone pulls my blindfold off and I feel even better. Everyone still has their balaclavas on. Good. They want me to live. Now I just need to give them a reason.

One of the shooters drags me to a metal folding chair in the middle of the room. He's limping and I look down long enough to see a burned pant leg.

"I hope there's no hard feelings," I tell him. "I was aiming for the van."

He shoves me into the chair and cuffs me on the ear before joining the others behind me. I turn and look at him.

"Ow. Fuck you."

A feminine voice from my other side says, "Don't look at him. Look at me."

I turn back around. She's tall. Long torso, legs, and arms. In her spare time she could be a fashion model or a basketball player. Smart. Tall is good for these situations. It lets the interrogator loom menacingly. She's wearing the same suit and balaclava as the guys who snatched me. That's okay.

What isn't okay is the cattle prod she's holding.

She takes her time coming over. Points at me with the business end of the prod.

"Who are you?" she says.

"I work for Eva Sandoval."

She moves the cattle prod back and forth like shaking her head no.

"That's not what I asked. Who *are* you?"

Oh, right. A name. That's the kind of thing I should have thought about instead of mooning over Candy.

"Miles," I say. "Miles Archer."

She pulls the cattle prod back and slaps it against her hand.

"Mr. Archer, answer my questions and you'll get to go home. Don't and . . ."

She shoves the prod into my stomach and gives me a good quick jolt.

"Understand?"

I look up at her.

"I'm not sure. Can you repeat the question?"

She jams the prod back into my gut and leaves it there longer this time. I'm a little out of breath when she takes it away.

"I think I got it that time," I tell her.

"Good. What's in the briefcase?"

I look down and see it sitting by her feet.

I shrug.

"It's financial papers. That's all I know. They don't tell me much."

"What do you do for Eva?"

"Lots. I move things around. I talk to people. I take care of problems."

She leans in a little closer. I could probably snap her neck from here.

"A fixer," she says. "That's my job, too. You ever kill anybody for Eva?"

"No. That's where I draw the line."

When she shocks me this time, it's on the inside of my

thigh, close enough to my balls to make them consider finding work elsewhere.

"Okay. Yes. A couple of times."

"Who were they?"

"Just some punks. One was selling company information out the back door. The other was a dog who needed to be put down."

"A liability."

I take a breath. "A big-mouth drunk and meth head. He was heading for trouble and taking the company down with him."

"What company is that?"

"Southern California International Trade Association."

Another shock, this time back in the gut.

"What company?"

"Wormwood Investments."

"Good," she says. "You might wonder why I'm asking you these particular questions."

"Actually, I was wondering when the sushi class started. I forgot my knife, but there's tuna in the briefcase."

Another shock.

I say, "Yeah. I was curious about the questions."

She gets closer, staring down at me like a buzzard sizing me up for lunch.

"I'm just trying to establish a basis for trust. If you're going to live, we have to trust each other."

"I'm all for that."

"Here's my problem though, Miles. It seems to me that you're very chatty for a man in your profession. If you are who you say you are, I'd expect a bit more discretion. And balls."

She points the cattle prod between my legs and I flinch just like she wants me to.

I say, "You mean I should encourage you to torture me? When I can tell you already know the answers to most of those questions? No thanks. I'm not getting my teeth kicked in for that."

"I should ask you harder questions?"

"You should untie me and I'll spring for drinks at Chateau Marmont. Short of that, yeah. Ask me something fucking real."

"What's the address you are going to?"

"I don't know. The driver did." I turn around and shout at the guys behind me. "He could have told you, but one of these assholes shot him."

She shocks me in the ribs and I turn back around. I'm starting not to like her.

"Focus on me, Miles."

"I don't know the address. It was in Westwood."

"Was it a bank? A person? A café?"

"A law office."

"All right. That's something. And you say it's just financial papers?" she says.

"That's what they told me."

She holds the cattle prod about an inch from my face.

"Do you know who we are?"

"I have a pretty good idea."

"Who?"

"You're the faction. The other Wormwood."

She moves the cattle prod like she's going for my eye and this time when I flinch, it's 100 percent real. Seeing that, she smiles.

"You're wrong. We're the *only* Wormwood. The Wormwood you work for is sick. A bloated tick full of diseased blood."

"And who are you, the Salvation Army? You bring down companies like the other Wormwood. You fuck people over when they're alive and you make money on their damnation when they die. I don't see much difference between you two."

She opens her hands wide.

"Because you're part of the old system. All you see is the method. You don't consider the reasons. The outcome."

"Okay. Convince me. What makes you so special?"

She taps the prod against the palm of one hand like a teacher tapping a ruler.

"If the old, diseased Wormwood gets its way, you'll barely notice a ripple in the world. They want power, money, and influence in the afterlife. We, on the other hand, will overturn existence. When we're through, this world and the next will be clean and pure. All the old, corrupt systems washed away."

I lean back.

"Is that supposed to impress me? You sound like every supervillain in every comic book ever written."

She swings down the prod and gets me in the ribs. Holds it there for a while. This time when she stops I can hear the shooters behind me laughing.

"Forgive me," she says. "It's a real problem in this line of work. Broad goals always sound a bit like hollow threats. It isn't until you get to the specifics that you find the true vision."

"But you're not going to share that with me."

"Do you want to die right here, right now?"

"Goody. I get a choice?"

"Yes, but the window is closing. Do you want to die?"

"Not particularly."

She rests the cattle prod on my shoulder while she goes on.

"If I let you live, will you deliver a message to Eva for me?"

"That depends on what it is."

"It's a warning. The last she or any of her people will receive. Will you deliver it for me?"

"Like I said, it depends. If I think it's going to get me killed, no."

"Fair enough," she says. "Here's the message: *Dies Irae*."

I look up at her.

"Day of Judgment?"

She smiles broadly and steps back.

"Look at you, Miles. An old altar boy, I bet."

I shake my head.

"Mom worshiped vodka and dad worshiped not being around either one of us, so not really."

She nods.

"Then I'll tell you: 'Dies Irae' is also 'Day of Wrath.' And that's the message I want you to give to Eva. Judgment day is coming soon. Wrath will fall like fire from Heaven," she says. "Eva and her people can join us or quit altogether. Just walk away. By this time next week, the Wormwood you know will be gone. There will be only us."

"And judgment and wrath."

"Exactly."

"I think I can remember that."

She gives me a quick zap in the gut.

"I'm positive I can remember."

"Good for you, Miles. You get to live for now. But just to make sure you don't forget, the boys are going to help you remember."

She kicks me in the chest, knocking me to the floor. The shooters rush over and put the boot in hard. I curl up in a ball, taking their kicks when what I really want to do is peel off their skin and drag them down the Hollywood Freeway behind the van they brought me in.

The things we do just to be alive again.

After a few minutes, the interrogator says, "That's enough." A couple of the laughing boys pick me up and toss me back into the van. She sticks her head in after me.

"What's the message, Miles?"

I get up and sit back down on the wheel well.

"Two parts rye, half a part sweet vermouth, a dash of bitters. Add a cherry if it's your birthday."

She nods.

"Good boy. Now get him out of here."

The six creeps get back in the van. Two sit up front. One sits on either side of me on the floor. The other two are across from me, leaning on the door. The one on the right pulls the blindfold back over my eyes. Each of them has a distinctive bulge under the arm—aside from the rifles, they have pistols in shoulder holsters.

We pull out of the warehouse, crunch across the gravel, and head who the fuck knows where. Goddammit. I need to get back in the warehouse before the interrogator gets too far away.

A moment later I hear lighters flick and matches scrape.

This is followed by the smell of cigarettes and weed. I hold my hands out and say, "Think I could have one of those? I promise I'll keep quiet. And about the fire thing earlier, that was uncool and I'm very sorry."

There's silence for a minute, then someone up front says, "If it will shut him up, give him one."

Someone takes a step toward me. From the sound of it, it's one of the two across from me. I hold out my hands and he puts a cigarette between my fingers. I hear a lighter flick on and lean into it. My hands are still bound together with plastic cuffs, so this is really going to hurt.

The moment I feel the cigarette spark, I grab his arm and pull him toward me. His head smashes into the side of the van hard enough that I hear his skull crack. I push him back against the far wall, then pull him down on top of me. I'm strong enough that I snap my hands out of the plastic cuffs. My prosthetic left arm doesn't feel a thing, but it hurts like hell as the cuffs cut into my right wrist.

Still under him, I get the pistol from his holster and fire blindly in every direction until the thing is empty. Then I drop it and yank off my blindfold. The other shooters in the back are all down on the floor. The guy in the passenger seat turns to take a shot, so I kick the guy whose skull I cracked into his face. His gun goes off into the roof.

I spin around to find the other door shooter with his pistol a few inches from my face. I move my head just as he fires. My ear goes deaf, but I get my hands around him so when he tries to fire at me, he ends up spraying the back of the van. The moment he stops shooting, I roll, pull his arm across me, and break it. His pistol falls and slides away. Out of the corner of my eye, I can see the goon who was sitting on my right try to get a shot at me. I can't reach the fallen gun, but the shooter I wrapped around myself has a knife in his belt. I pull it and use him as a battering ram, stunning him and pinning the other shooter against the wall. He tries sneaking an arm around his pal to get a shot at me. I grab the hand. Lean in and jam the knife into his throat, twisting the blade. When I pull it out, arterial spray jets onto the wall and he twitches like a dying bug. My human shield has been working on my back and sides with his one good fist and elbow. I slit his throat and push him at the other shooter on my left. But he's flat on his back with a bullet in his head. Someone got lucky. Hope it was me.

I grab the pistol that slid into the back of the van. Dive on the floor as the passenger up front fires at me. One of his shots grazes my side and I empty the pistol into the back of his seat. When he falls, he bounces off the dashboard and lands on the driver. The van swerves and slam into something. In the back it's a water park of blood. The crash sends me Jet Skiing up front. I crash into the passenger seat as the van comes to a stop.

The airbag explodes in the driver's face, knocking his head back. I hurt like I just climbed out of a cement mixer, and the shot that grazed my side burns like hell. But I don't have time to whine right now.

I slap the driver until he wakes up. When he sees me, he lurches back against the door. I let him get a good look at the bloody mess in the back before putting the knife to his throat.

"Take me to the warehouse."

The van is resting against a stop sign on a service road. He doesn't say a word but hits the ignition. The engine grinds. I press the knife harder.

"You better hope it starts or I'm going to carve off your face and make you eat it."

He tries it a couple more times before the engine catches and holds. In a few seconds, we've turned around and are running back the way we came.

While he drives I take the pistol from his shoulder holster and put it in my waistband. The rifles are tangled up in the meat market in the rear of the van and it takes a few seconds to pull one free. I check it to make sure it's loaded, then jam it into the back of the driver's head.

"How much farther?"

He points with his free hand.

"Around that corner up ahead."

"Don't go all the way to the warehouse. Stop where I tell you."

When we're about thirty yards from the warehouse driveway I tell him to pull over.

I move around the seat and put the rifle in his face.

"Did you shoot the limo driver?"

He shakes his head. Hooks a thumb at the mess in back.

"It was Bill."

"Bill a friend of yours?"

He shakes his head again. "No. He was a real asshole."

"When we run into each other in Hell, tell me how it feels to die for an asshole."

I pull the trigger once and toss him in the back with the others.

As I step out of the van, blood flows out the door in a mini-waterfall—think an elevator–in–*The Shining* level of blood. I look at myself in the van's side mirror. In my bloody suit, I look like the maître d' at a Texas Chainsaw cookout. My shoes squish with each step as I limp to the warehouse. For a second I think about going back to the van and digging around for someone's cigarettes, but they're probably as soaked through as my suit.

At the end of the driveway I hunker down, trying to stay out of sight of any security cameras. Every part of me hurts. If I could be anywhere else right now, my first choice would be in bed with Candy. My second choice would be in the closest ER that has hot tubs in the rooms. They have those, right? Hot-tub hospitals? I should Google that. I might just have a million-dollar idea. Maybe Sandoval will back me if I don't kill her. Scratch that. I'd rather shoot her and Sinclair. I'm just not gentry material and killing them sounds like more fun than a mansion.

I'm still mourning my hot-tub millions when the warehouse door slides open and a Mercedes coupe drives out. I can't see who's behind the wheel, but the car has to slow when it reaches the gravel at the end of the driveway. That's when I step in front of it and open up with the rifle.

I blast a few rounds through the windshield—but only on the passenger side. I have a feeling whoever was interrogating me isn't the chauffeur type. Closing on the Mercedes, I spray more rounds into the side windows, keeping the driver off balance until I can get there.

I'm at the driver's door when the rifle goes dry. I ditch it and smash the window with the butt of the pistol. There's a woman inside with her hand in her coat.

I put my gun to her head.

"Take out your hand slowly and put them both on the steering wheel."

She does what I say. She has short blond hair and even sitting down, I can tell she's built long, just like my interrogator. Plus my briefcase is sitting on the seat next to her.

I say, "Pop the trunk and get out of the car. Slow and easy."

I hear the trunk unlock and pull the door open for her. She gets out and looks me over.

"I don't suppose any of my men are still alive?" she says.

"We can go look. They're just down the road. Pieces of them, anyway."

"I'll pass."

When I frisk her I find a very nice Glock 17 in her jacket and a punch dagger in her pocket. I keep the pistol and knife and toss her phone into the weeds. She smiles at me.

"You had a perfect opportunity to cop a feel and you didn't do it. What a gentleman."

"If I put a couple of rounds through your knees would it change your opinion?"

"See?" she says. "You asked before doing it. You weren't an altar boy, but I bet you were a Boy Scout."

"Troop Six-Six-Six in Hell. You should have seen our jamborees."

She nods toward the trunk.

"I'm supposed to get in there?"

"That's the idea."

"I guess a bribe isn't in the cards."

"Unless you have a pair of men's shoes not full of blood, there's nothing you have that interests me."

She starts for the rear of the car. As she steps into the trunk she says, "You ruined your nice suit."

"I'm hard on clothes."

"You're a fall. A little red looks good on you."

I look up and down the road.

"Where the hell are we?"

"City of Industry."

"That's a long drive back."

"If you say so."

"What's your name?"

"Marcella."

"Is that your real name?"

"No, but it's the name I always wanted."

"Good. People should die with their true names."

I close the trunk and get behind the wheel. Marcella's balaclava is on the passenger seat next to the briefcase. I use it to wipe some of the blood off my face. Sure, I could take her back to Sandoval's through a shadow, but I really want to drive this Mercedes. And I really want her to bounce around the trunk while I do it. I start the car and jam it into gear. We take the corner on two wheels and Marcella makes a satisfying thump in the back.

IT'S NINETY MINUTES back to Sandoval's mansion. The car gets some funny looks when traffic slows, but mostly it's smiles and waves. I'm in Hollywood camouflage, hiding in plain sight. Most people think I'm a stunt driver heading home from a movie set in my prop car. The rest think the bullet holes are decorations. Gangster chic. When anyone checks me out, I give them a cool-guy nod and a thumbs-up. I'll end up on a lot of people's Instagram accounts tonight.

The Mercedes is on its last legs when I get to Sandoval's, barely creaking up the hill. I punch the intercom beside the gate and tell them who I am. Even wave at the camera so they can see my face.

A voice crackles from the speaker: "Where's the limousine?"

"In a police impound by now. Don't ask about Philip. He's not coming back."

There's a moment of silence, then the gates swing open. The last fifty yards up to the circular drive are dicey. The car finally commits seppuku halfway around the circle. Steam geysers from the radiator. Darker things leak from below. I'm not much better. Sandoval, Sinclair, and the roaches huddle at the front door, and when I walk over I leave a trail of red footprints. Eva takes a step back when she gets a good look at me.

"Oh my god," she says. "Is that blood?"

"On me? Yes."

"On my driveway."

"Yeah. Plus a little oil and gasoline probably."

She points at the Mercedes.

"You can't leave that there."

I wipe my bloody hands on my suit. It doesn't help much.

"I'm not your valet. You want it moved, get one of your roaches to do it."

I go back to the car, pop the trunk, and pull Marcella out. She's sweaty but in decent shape, all things considered. However, she's dizzy enough that I have to hold her arm like we're on a prom date as I walk her over to the welcoming committee.

"Who the hell is that?" says Sandoval.

"This is Marcella. Say hello, Marcella."

She spits on the ground.

Sinclair says, "Is she with the faction?"

"No. She's my fiancée. I thought I'd bring her home to meet the family."

When she gets her balance back, she pulls away from me.

"Give them my message," she says. "You said you would if I let you live."

"You're right. I did say that."

I look at Sandoval and Sinclair.

"Dies Irae."

Marcella laughs. "Boy Scout."

"Hush."

"Dies Irae? What is that?" says Sandoval.

"I'm told it's 'Day of Wrath.'"

Marcella takes a step toward them. I grab her arm again.

She says, "Your judgment is coming and it will be harsh if you don't repent and come to us willingly."

"You're insane. We'll kill you all," says Sinclair.

"To live, you will walk away from your operations. All of them."

"This is ridiculous," says Sandoval. She looks at me. "Why did you bring her here?"

"She asked me questions at the end of a cattle prod. Now I'm going to return the favor."

"No, he's not," Marcella says. "He talks tough, but he's adorable."

Sandoval touches Sinclair on the arm.

"That's wonderful. She has no idea who he really is. Take off that silly face, Stark, and show her."

Marcella stares at me as I let the glamour fade.

"Hi. My name is James Stark."

"Better known as Sandman Slim," says Sinclair.

Sandoval says, "Bitch."

Marcella looks from me to them.

Then she laughs, shaking her head.

"You're as adorable as him. But Sandman Slim is dead. Everyone knows it."

"*Was,*" says Sinclair. "We brought him back."

Sandoval says, "That's what we can do. So you can keep your threats and Day of Wrath nonsense to yourself."

Marcella shakes her head again, not laughing this time, but still not believing.

"You've told so many lies you don't know when you're doing it anymore."

"Make her believe, Stark."

"That's the idea."

I take the blindfold from around my neck and put it over her eyes.

"Don't mind the blood," I tell her. "None of it is mine."

"Where are you taking her?" says Sinclair.

"Where we can have a heart-to-heart in private."

Sandoval points to my shoes.

"You can't go through the house like that."

"Watch me."

I take Marcella's arm and lead her inside, grinding my bloody heels into the carpet all the way downstairs to the bowling alley.

WHEN WE'RE INSIDE I turn on the lights and take her blindfold off. Marcella looks around.

"You've got to be kidding me. This is your torture chamber?"

"Like it? It belonged to Eva's granddad. She lets me use it on the weekends."

"It's not the weekend yet."

"This is a special occasion."

I grab a folding chair from the back of the room, pull Marcella to the end of a bowling lane, and push her into it.

"Won't it be hard for me to take my turn from down here?"

"I doubt you'll live long enough for it to be an issue."

"Come on, Boy Scout. We both know you're not going to—"

I pull her gun from my pocket and fire at her head, close enough that she has to duck.

She says, "You missed."

She looks cool, but I can hear her heart going like a jackhammer.

"You sure? Maybe you're right—I haven't done much shooting in the last year. I'm still getting the hang of it."

"Because you've been dead, Mr. Sandman Slim?"

"You still don't believe? You saw me change my face upstairs."

She leans back in the chair and crosses her legs.

"Just because you're Sub Rosa doesn't make you Sandman Slim. You and the fools upstairs, you don't scare me. This is Hollywood. Any good makeup artist could give you those scars."

"Hey, I earned these scars."

Marcella sighs. "When does the torture start? Or is this it?"

I fire a few more rounds, this time at her head and her

feet. She has to curl up into a fetal position on the chair to not get hit.

I say, "Tell me about the faction."

"No. Tell me about Hell, Sandman Slim."

One of her chair legs explodes when I shoot it. She goes down on her side. It knocks the wind out of her.

I grab another folding chair and slide it down the lane to her. She opens it and sits down.

She says, "I think the woman upstairs is going to be mad if you keep shooting her furniture."

"After what I did to your men, you really don't think I'll hurt you?"

"I think you're a killer. I think you're vicious and an animal when cornered. But, no, you're not going to hurt me. It's not something you do or you would be doing it already instead of playing William Tell."

"I'm not Sandman Slim. I'm not a torturer. Damn. I don't impress you at all."

"Not much."

I put the gun in my waistband and walk quickly down the lane. She tries not to react, but her shoulders stiffen when I get close.

"If I proved to you that I was Sandman Slim, would you talk?"

"But you're not, so what does it matter?"

"But if I did?"

"Not even then, Boy Scout."

"Let's test that."

I yank her to her feet and pull her into a shadow at the end of the alley.

When we're in, I push her ahead of me into the streets of Pandemonium.

The smell hits her first. It's what gets most new arrivals. Sulfur. Burning blood and shit. The sour fear sweat of a billion losers. I don't like being here. I sure didn't plan on it and now that I've done it, I wonder if it's a huge mistake. But there's one thing I have going for me. I'm used to this misery. Marcella isn't, and so far, she's not handling it well. She's a few feet ahead of me, on her knees, puking into a ditch full of burned vehicles and charred Hellion bones. I sit down on the collapsed wall of a deserted building.

When she's done, she takes off her jacket, uses it to wipe her mouth, and throws it into the ditch. She tries to stand, but her legs are too shaky.

"How are you doing this?" she says.

"Doing what?"

"The special effects. They're good. Did you get Disney to build it?" She staggers to her feet and sweeps her arm at the ruins. "Mr. Stark's Wild Ride, right next to the Matterhorn and the spinning Sleeping Beauty's castle."

I'm actually impressed at her bullheadedness.

"You don't believe this is Hell."

"Not for a second," she says.

"How do you imagine Hell?"

"Two more minutes with you."

"What would it take to convince you this really is the bad place?"

She kicks a stone away with the toe of her shoe. "You can't. This is nothing God would make or permit."

I walk over to her.

"Maybe you're right. Maybe it's all fake."

I push her into the ditch with her puke and the Hellion dead.

"I'm going back to the bowling alley. You stay. Walk around. Explore. Enjoy yourself. I'm going to have lunch."

I go out through a shadow and leave Marcella behind. I'll give her five minutes. Now that I think about it, when I go back I should look around for some Maledictions. If I don't get a real cigarette soon, I'm going to start gnawing on the roaches' skulls.

Marcella is interesting. Altar-boy jokes. Dies Irae. God wouldn't make or permit Hell. She talks a lot churchier than I'd expect from a Wormwood creep. But I guess it makes sense that Wormwood has some pull in the religion industry. It's a good way to control the masses. A little fear and they're all yours. I wish I could see inside her head so I could figure out what her Hell really looks like. Maybe it would scare her, because my Hell sure as shit doesn't.

Should I go to Candy tonight? No. We already talked about this. Shut up.

I check the time. Four minutes. That's long enough.

I walk back through the shadow and check the ditch. She's not there. I look in the abandoned building. She's not there either.

Fuck.

I yell, "Marcella." Nothing comes back. I climb a pile of cinder blocks to get a better look around and spot a couple of bug-ugly Hellion Legionnaires at the end of the block. They're running somewhere fast. I jump off the blocks and take off after them. Sure enough, when I get around the corner, there's Marcella swinging a pipe at the two soldiers. A third one lies at her feet with something sharp sticking out of his chest. I'm still sore enough from the van that I don't feel like throwing fists with Legionnaires, so I pull my gun and shoot them both in the head. Marcella jumps at the shots. Stares as they both blip out of existence.

I head over to her and when she sees me, she sags against a toppled streetlight. Her face is smeared with dirt and a little blood. Her shirt and sleeve are torn. The Hellion at her feet isn't quite dead yet. It's leaking black blood fast, but it's tough. It keeps crawling after her.

"What the fuck are these things?" she screams.

"Hellions. Fallen angels."

She looks around, starts to say something, raises and drops her hands in a gesture of futility.

"Why did you do this to me?"

"Do you believe now?"

"Why did those others disappear when you shot them?"

"It's what angels do when they die."

She looks at the Hellion crawling for her, then at me.

"Make this one disappear."

"Did you stab him?"

"Yes."

"Then you do it."

She purses her lips and hovers over him as his hands reach out for her. The Hellion wheezes and growls low. When it drops its hands for a moment, Marcella smashes its head in with the pipe. The Hellion sags on the sidewalk and disappears. When it's gone, she leans back on the streetlight.

When I'm close enough, I take the pipe from her hand and throw it away. I don't want her getting any ideas.

"Do you believe yet?"

She looks up at me. Nods.

"I didn't until I stabbed him. I felt the metal in my hand. It was real and sharp, and when I shoved it into his chest, I knew it wasn't a trick."

"No. It wasn't."

She looks around.

"How long did you spend here?"

"Eleven years, the first time."

"And you were alive the whole time?"

"Yeah. You're one of the only other living humans to ever see the place. Congratulations."

She flexes her fist. Her knuckles are red where she must have punched the Hellion before stabbing it. Marcella is tough. I wish she was on our side.

"Get me out of here."

I take her hand and pull her into a shadow. We come out again in the bowling alley. She collapses on one of the lanes. I let her sit there for a while.

"You're a torturer after all," she says. "You sure had me fooled."

"I wouldn't have had to leave you there if you weren't so full of shit."

She looks at me from the floor.

"You can take me back there any time you want, can't you?"

"Yes. I can."

She shakes her head, picks up a piece of one of the pins I shot earlier, toys with it. Tosses it away.

"I'm sorry, but I can't tell you anything."

Now I'm getting annoyed.

"Why not?"

She gestures back at the shadow we came through.

"Because now I know what will happen to me."

"You mean damnation? If you tell me you're afraid you'll be damned?"

"I know I will."

"You faction types must have some good preachers."

She smiles, but it's exhausted and unconvincing.

"The best."

"Then you're going to want to help me, Marcella."

"Why?"

"I hate to break it to you, but you're already going to Hell for the things you've done. And when you get there, I'm the one who can get you out."

That makes her laugh.

"My my. The salvation of my eternal soul rests with Sandman Slim."

"The world is funny that way."

"And if I still won't tell you?"

"I'll put you right back in the ditch."

She looks at me.

"I think you would."

"Test me."

"Okay," she whispers. "Ask your questions."

I hold out a hand to her.

"Get off the floor. Let's pretend we're people for a minute."

I help her up and we sit on the padded seats by the scoring table.

"You ready?" I say.

"You'll really come for me if I help you?"

"I haven't lied to you so far. Well, except for my name. But you're lying to me about your name, so we're even there."

She rubs her hands together nervously.

"Ask your questions."

"Let's start with what's going to happen. The way I heard it, you're going to nuke L.A."

That makes her chuckle.

"It's a cleansing and consecration of the land. But, yes, the Los Angeles you know will be wiped away."

"And you'll do it with a ritual."

She nods wearily.

"Yes."

"Does it happen Saturday or Sunday?"

With her thumb, she draws a cross in the dust on the table. Wipes it away with her fist.

"You might want to fire whoever is getting you your information."

"It's not this weekend? Then when?"

"Tomorrow."

"Friday?"

Finally, some good news. Wormwood wants me to clean up their mess by Sunday, but I'll have it done tomorrow. Then Howard does his spook show and I'm home free. I could be talking to Candy by sometime Saturday.

"Where does it happen?"

"The Chapel of St. Alexis."

"I never heard of it."

"Most people haven't. It was condemned about twenty years ago and hasn't been used since. After it closed there was a split in the congregation, so they were never able to raise enough money to repair it."

"Then the faction stepped in and promised to foot the bill."

She draws a smiley face in the dust, then wipes it out too.

"Yes. The ritual will take place in the crypt under the church."

"When?"

"Vespers."

"Sunset."

She cocks her head.

"Are you sure you weren't an altar boy?"

This is it. I know the what. I know the where and I know the when. I even know the why, but who gives a damn about that?

"Is anyone there now, setting up, maybe?"

"No one will arrive until just before the ritual begins."

"How are they getting away? Car? Truck?"

"They're not."

I look at her.

"What does that mean?"

She draws aimless lines in the dust.

"They're not leaving," she says eventually. "The officiants are all volunteers."

"Martyrs."

She looks down the alley.

"Yes. And unlike me, they'll go straight to Heaven."

"That's what the preachers told you, but it's not going to happen. Even if they pulled it off."

She stops doodling.

"What do you mean?"

"Whoever's been running your crew is a liar or woefully uninformed. No one gets into Heaven anymore."

She narrows her eyes.

"That doesn't make sense."

"It does to the angels determined to keep human souls out."

"That's not possible."

"And you think we should fire whoever's giving *us* information? Where have you guys been? There's a new war in Heaven, Marcella. God tried to open Heaven to all souls, saved or damned. A handful of winged pricks disagreed and Heaven has been sealed shut ever since."

She crosses her arms.

"I don't believe you."

"I don't care, but think about this: Why would I lie to you now? What would it get me? You've already told me everything I want to know."

She shakes her head. Keeps shaking it.

"That can't be right. It's not true."

"Believe what you want. I have things to do, like changing out of this suit." Shifting my weight, I can feel the blood squelch in my shoes.

She looks at me.

"What happens to me now? Are you going to kill me?"

"No. I might have more questions for you later."

I leave her and go to the door.

"I'll have them bring a mattress and some food down for you. There's a bathroom through that door over there."

She looks around.

"It's a funny place for a slumber party."

"Be good and we'll play Twister later."

When I start out she says, "You know that if you don't kill me, the others will."

I stop.

"No one is going to bother you."

"You're so sure I'll make it through the night?"

"You'll be fine. But don't try to leave. I'm putting some wards on the door. The idiots upstairs will be able to bring you food and things, but if you try to go . . ."

"Then I'll die."

I carve some runes in the door frame with her punch dagger.

"No. But you'll get knocked out by a jolt like a cattle prod up your ass."

"No fair. I didn't get anywhere near your ass."

"I never play fair. That's how I got out of Hell."

"Good night, Sandman Slim."

"Good night, Marcella."

I finish carving the wards and go upstairs. I tell the roaches what to bring her. None of them will get near me in my bloody butcher suit, so I'm reasonably sure they're listening to my orders.

When I'm in my room, I lock the door and strip off every piece of clothing. Some of the blood has dried. Bits of it flake off and land in the carpet. Somehow, I don't think anyone is going to be using this room for a while after I leave.

I toss the clothes on the floor and get in the shower. I stay in there a long time, letting the steam burn the stink of Hell and that van off me.

WHEN I GET out of the shower, I check my side and right wrist. There's still a deep red slash where the bullet grazed me. My wrist aches and blood still trickles from the edges of the cuts where the plastic cuffs bit into me. My arms and back are covered in bruises. This isn't right. I should be more healed by now. This half-alive skin suit is second-rate stuff. Until Howard puts me back together again, I'm going to have to be more careful in fights. Though with any luck, tomorrow night is the last time I'll have to worry about that.

It's only a little after five, but I'm suddenly very tired. I decide to lie down for an hour and then go check on Marcella.

When I wake up, it's after dark. I've slept three hours. There are streaks of blood on the sheets where my wrist rested. Now when I check it, it's healed. It's the same with my side. The red has gone out of the bullet wound and the skin has almost closed. This is good to know. My body takes longer to pull itself together and it uses more energy, so I'll get tired faster. I need to remember that in case things get hot at the chapel tomorrow.

I get dressed and go down to the bowling alley. I can hear Marcella in the bathroom when I stick my head in. There's a rollaway bed near the wall and a tray of uneaten food on the seats by the ball return. No problems here. I leave and go back upstairs before she sees me.

When I go into Sandoval's office it's just her, Sinclair, and Howard inside. They're deep in discussion when I come in but quiet right down when they see me.

"Am I interrupting anything?"

Sandoval goes to the bar and pours herself a drink.

"Did you have a nice nap? I hope no one disturbed your beauty sleep."

"Yeah. Sorry about that. I didn't think I was going to sleep that long. It's this body. It runs down fast."

She looks at Howard.

"Is he telling the truth, Jonathan? Is there something wrong with his body?"

"There's nothing wrong," says Howard. "He's simply in a liminal state between life and death. Consequently, his system runs a bit slower than normal. But aside from occasional bouts of fatigue, there should be no other impairments."

"You're sure? Our lives and holdings are riding on this man," says Sinclair.

Howard looks at me like I'm a bug under a microscope.

"I understand that you were tortured and overpowered several people today. How did you feel while doing it? Any mental or physical problems?"

I hold up my wrist so that the others can get a good look. It's healed but scarred and bruised, covered in patches of livid reds and purples. Sandoval and Sinclair frown at the sight.

"No problems at all. It wasn't until I got back that I turned to jelly."

He waves a hand at me.

"You see? No problems. He was able to perform his job, return, and is now awake, refreshed, and completely coherent." He looks at Sandoval. "I know you're not used to dealing with creatures such as this but trust me, Eva. He is functioning perfectly normally."

Speaking of normal, I pour myself a drink at Eva's bar.

"Thanks, Howard. And if you ever call me 'creature' again, I'm going to cut off your tongue with bolt cutters."

Sandoval pats me on the arm.

"Careful, Stark. You want Howard to be your friend on your trip back to the world of the living."

"Just tell Dr. Frankenstein to watch his language."

"Of course. I'm sure he understands what a sensitive snowflake you are," she says.

"What were you and Sinclair gossiping about when I came in?"

She looks over at him.

Sinclair says, "There were two more assassinations. Jared Glanton and Tetsuya Shin."

"Here in L.A.?"

"No," says Sandoval. "Jared was in our New York office, Tetsuya in Buenos Aires."

"And they were the heads of their branches?"

"Yes."

"Good. At least the pattern is confirmed. Which one of you runs L.A.?"

"That would be me," says Sandoval.

"Then you're not going to get a bullet in the head."

"What makes you say that?" say Sinclair.

"Because they're going to blow us up, Barron," Sandoval says.

"Ah. Right."

She looks at me. "That's enough of you questioning us. What did you learn from that horrid woman in the basement?"

I glance at Howard, but he's staring at a painting on the wall and won't look at me.

"I've got good news. The ritual is tomorrow. And I know where and when."

Eva goes over to Sinclair. They whisper to each other for a minute.

"Are you sure?" he says. "We were told it was the weekend."

"She might be lying," Sandoval says.

"She wasn't. I made sure she knew it wasn't in her best interest."

Sandoval holds up a hand.

"Don't tell me what you did. I don't want to know."

"Don't worry. There were no bolt cutters involved."

"Not another word."

Sinclair says, "Where will the ritual take place?"

"At the Chapel of St. Alexis. Exactly at sunset."

He looks at Sandoval.

"That's right downtown. We could have a hundred armed associates there by then."

"That's a great idea," I say. "Scare them off so they disappear and reschedule the ritual without us knowing when or where."

"How do you want to handle it, then?" says Sandoval.

"I'll take care of it myself. I don't think there will be many faction people there because the ones who show up are committing suicide."

"How will you do it?" says Sinclair.

"I'll know when I see the setup, but I imagine I'll basically just kill them all and take their stuff. Is that okay with everyone?"

Sandoval says, "It's fine with me."

"Me too," says Sinclair.

Howard just grunts.

"Will you need anything from us?" says Sandoval.

"Body armor would be nice. Until I'm a hundred percent back, I'd like to keep bullets at a pleasant distance. I also need a couple of boxes of nine-millimeter ammo, plus three extended round clips. And bullets for the rifle I took from Marcella's boys. A hundred rounds of 5.56 × 45 millimeter."

"I don't understand," says Sandoval. "Can't you simply use magic to kill them all?"

I shake my head.

"I won't know that until I get there. There could be wards, charms, enchantments. A million little tricks that could slow down my hoodoo. I want to keep my body in one piece and that means being prepared for anything. Besides, sometimes a gun is just quicker."

Sinclair has been scribbling notes on a piece of paper. When he's done he looks over at me.

"Aside from the armor and the guns, is there anything else you need?"

I finish my drink.

"Yes. Before I have another one of these, I want a goddamn cigarette."

Sandoval goes to her desk and pulls out a box of Nat Sherman Classics. Tosses it to me along with a gold lighter.

I sniff the box.

"Thanks, Santa."

She nods at me.

"Eat something before you have more liquor. We want you in decent shape for tomorrow."

I nod and head back to my room with my presents.

"I'll get something when I'm out."

"Where are you going?" says Sandoval.

"I'm taking a walk. Personal stuff."

"What I mean is, will it be dangerous?"

"My ego might get bruised, if that's what you're asking."

Howard says, "Remember to take care of your body. The healthier it is, the easier your transition will be. Damage it too much and I might not be able to bring you back fully."

"You just be ready tomorrow night, Dr. Frankenstein. This monster wants to be able to eat donuts again."

"What the hell does *that* mean?" says Sinclair.

"Don't worry about it. Just be ready."

I STILL HAVE some of Sinclair's cash burning a hole in my pocket. Bamboo House of Dolls has good drinks and good food, so that's destination two. Before that, though, I need to make one other stop.

It's closing time at Max Overdrive and Kasabian is hustling the last customers out the door. It's Friday night so I know what happens next. I light a Sherman and wait for it. Sure enough, in a few minutes, the door opens again and more people file out. Allegra is in the lead, followed by Brigitte Bardo. Candy and Alessa are last. They're laughing, holding hands as they head out for a night of drinking, and my heart stutters for a minute. It's one thing to wish them happiness in the abstract, but it's another to see Candy laughing and in love without me. It hurts, but I'm a big boy, so I stay in the dark across the street and finish my cigarette.

Kasabian is still in the store putting money and discs away before heading out to join them. I wait until Candy and the others are out of sight before stepping into a shadow.

And step out again in the back of Max Overdrive. I watch Kasabian for a minute. He looks good. The mechanical body Manimal Mike made for him moves smoothly and naturally.

He even has a few upgrades. His hands look human, not like the metal claws I remember. He's wearing a bulky track suit zipped up to his neck to hide his stainless steel torso and legs. The suit hangs loose on him like someone deflated him. Still, he looks happy and healthy enough. Time to ruin all that.

I walk into the light.

"Evening, Kas. Long time no see."

I should have waited a little longer. He was going through the day's mail and the moment I speak it all goes up in the air and floats down like New Year's confetti. He stumbles back and slams into the wall, stays there like a butterfly pinned to a board.

I hold up my hands and say, "Before you reach for the gun under the counter, I'm just here to see how you're doing."

He points at me and doesn't say anything. Finally, he sputters, "Fuck you."

I approach him slowly because I really don't want to get shot tonight.

"Everything's fine, man. Calm down."

He relaxes a little and put his hands to his head.

"Fuck you, man. Why won't you stay dead?"

"Nice to see you too, Kas."

He leans heavily on the front counter and stares at me.

"Shit. It really is you."

"It really is."

"And you're not here to kill me?"

"When I crawled out of Hell last time I wasn't exactly thrilled to be back. This time I am."

He stares a little more.

"How did you do it?"

"Get back?"

I make it to the counter and offer him a cigarette. He takes it with trembling fingers. I light it for him and look the store over.

"I didn't do it," I tell him. "Truth is, I didn't know if I'd ever make it back. It was some other people who brought me back."

He frowns.

"I don't mean to sound harsh, but why? It's been a year, man. Things . . ."

"Things have changed. You've all moved on. I get it and I'm not going to barge back in and expect you to throw me a party. But that doesn't mean I don't care about you assholes. I need to know how things are."

He puffs his cigarette.

"You mean how Candy is."

"That's a good place to start."

"How she is is there's a big box of your shit in the closet where you used to lock me up. No one goes in there. No one looks at it. You've been cleared out and put away. Get it?"

I light my own cigarette.

"I take it that means Alessa has moved into our place upstairs."

"*Their* place," he says. "Not yours. Theirs. I told you. Things have changed."

There it is. *Things have changed.* I'm not surprised, but it's still a kick in the teeth.

"Are they happy?"

"Like a basket of kittens. And it gets a little aggravating sometimes for those of us, you know."

"Alone?"

"Yeah."

"What ever happened to Fairuza?"

Fairuza is a Lurker, a Ludere. Blue skinned and very sweet. She and Kasabian were an item last time I saw them.

He taps some ash on the counter.

"She's long gone. Remember that night Allegra killed the French chick who poisoned Vidocq?"

"I ditched the body, so yeah."

He shakes his head.

"She never got over it. Had a nervous breakdown and everything. Doesn't want to have anything to do with any of us."

"I'm sorry."

"Don't sweat it. It's the story of my life."

"Speaking of Vidocq, I didn't see him when the others left. How is he?"

He looks at me.

"You've been spying on us? There's a word for that: stalker."

"That's why I came in tonight. I don't want to be that person."

"Thanks for making me your shrink."

"So, where is Vidocq?"

He shrugs.

"Don't know. I haven't seen him for a while. Allegra dumped him after the thing with the French chick."

"He was kind of an idiot, chasing after a girl he hadn't seen in two hundred years."

"I'm not sure you're in a position to judge, window peeper."

"How's Brigitte? Working?"

He reaches back and pulls a Blu-ray box set off the wall.

"She's doing fine. She's the star of a big cable series. Plays an international spy and hit woman. But she's a good guy, you know? Anyway, she spends a lot of time kicking the shit out of everybody in six-inch heels."

I turn over the box set. *Queen Bullet*, it says in shiny red letters. The back is mostly stills of her snapping necks and shooting bad guys, dressed in miniskirts and evening gowns. She looks like she's having a ball. Good for her.

I slide the set back to him.

"And how's the store? Still in business, I see."

Kasabian sighs.

"It's doing good. Alessa had the idea to sponsor movie nights every month and Candy lets bands play here sometimes. We put the floor shelves on wheels so we can push them out of the way."

"That really is good thinking. Are you still getting those special movies?"

"All the time."

A witch friend used to use her hoodoo to find us movies in other realities that were never made in this one. Then she'd snag us a copy and we'd rent them for a fortune.

Kasabian hands me another disc.

On the front is a drawing of a burning giraffe holding a butterfly net and wearing a cowboy hat. I hold it under the light to make sure I'm seeing it right.

"What the fuck is this?"

"*Giraffes on Horseback Saddles*," he says. "Screenplay by Salvador Dalí and starring the Marx Brothers."

"This is what's keeping the lights on?"

He takes the disc back and hands me another.

"Right, I forgot you have no sense of humor. This is more the stuff that's keeping us going."

There's a horned red guy smoking a cigar on the front. The cover says, *Hellboy 3,* directed by Guillermo del Toro.

I hand it back to him.

"That makes more sense. I'm glad you didn't all lose your minds while I was gone."

He turns around and gives me a look.

"Don't worry about us," he says. "We're doing fine and making more money than ever."

"Don't stab me in the heart so quick. I'm not ready to die again."

"Okay. But sometimes you have a high fucking opinion of yourself. I mean, if you came back to save us, we don't need it."

"Understood."

I look around the store, feeling like it was a bad idea coming here. The place looks great. Clean. New posters on the wall. And unless Kasabian was lying, they're making money, which we never did when I was here. It makes me wonder if I was the thing holding the store back. Candy and Kasabian, too. Maybe it's more than them getting over me. Maybe it's that I was the problem in the first place. If that's true, I'm not really sure what I came back for. It's sure not to fuck up everybody's lives again. I'm going to have to think about it. See if there's some small place I can still fit in.

Kasabian is wiping his cigarette ash into a trash can when he says, "So, who brought you back?"

"You don't want to know."

"*Yes,* I do. First time you came back from Hell you were alive. This time, I don't know. I saw you die. We all did."

I look at him.

"Wormwood. It was Wormwood who brought me back."

He frowns.

"Those crazy Illuminati bastards? Why would they do that?"

"I'm working for them. But only for one more day."

"What the fuck are you doing for people like that?"

"Trying to save your life, for one thing. They might be complete assholes but there's a worse bunch of assholes that want to blow L.A. off the planet in less than twenty-four hours."

"Oh," he says. "Is that why you're here? To tell us to get out of town?"

"No, because I know when and where it's going to happen and I'm going to stop it."

He looks at me.

"Are you sure? I mean, I can get to LAX in an hour. Burbank airport even faster. And don't worry. I'll leave a note for Candy and Alessa."

I tap a finger on the counter.

"Stop it. I told you. I've got it handled. After I take out the bombers, I'm free. I don't owe Wormwood anything. I fact, I plan on killing a whole lot of them soon."

He puts his hands over his ears.

"I don't want to hear this shit. Don't you understand? None of us have had to hear about one of your Superman murder sprees for a year. And I think I can speak for Candy and Alessa too when I say we don't want to. Things are quiet. We do our jobs and we have fun. We have okay lives. Please don't fuck that up."

I look at him, trying to gauge his level of bullshit. Kasabian has never forgiven me for cutting off his head, and I can understand that. Part of me wants to believe that he's saying all of this because I'm in a weak position and it's his chance to finally get some revenge. But it's not that. He doesn't have a heart for me to listen to, but I can read his eyes and the frightened microtremors around his lips. He's telling the truth. Barging in here like this, I might as well have driven a tank through the front door. At least I waited for Candy to leave so she didn't have to see this disaster.

"You're right," I say. "I just had to know how things are. I'm going to go now. Do *not* tell Candy I was here."

He looks at me like he doesn't trust me. "Is that a threat?"

"No. It's me asking you politely to keep Candy out of this."

"Okay," he says grudgingly. "I just didn't like your tone there at the end."

"Sorry. I'm going to take off."

I'm starting to step into a shadow when Kasabian says, "Hey, I'm not telling you to fuck off forever. Just don't pop out of the dark like the Grim Reaper and scare the piss out of me."

"Got it."

"For what it's worth, I know Candy misses you. We had a drink on your birthday. Just the two of us. She got kind of misty-eyed and everything."

"Misty-eyed? I suppose that's better than nothing."

"Beggars can't be choosers, right?"

"That's what they say."

As I'm about to leave, a poster on the wall catches my eye. It's for a drive-in theater called the Devil's Door.

"Is that Flicker's place?"

"Yeah," says Kasabian. "She reopened about three months ago. Fixed the place up nice. You ought to go see it."

"I just might."

"See you, Stark."

"Later, Kas."

I step through a shadow but don't go out anywhere. I stay in the Room of Thirteen Doors and just breathe the cool air.

That didn't go the way I'd hoped. To tell you the truth, I'm not sure what I was looking for, but it wasn't "You being dead is the best thing that ever happened to everyone." I'm going to have to think about this more before I do anything. Maybe check in and see if Vidocq wants some company. Two assholes without a country. I wonder if he's still living in my old apartment. Maybe he wants a roommate. It doesn't sound like anyone is going to be inviting me back to Max Overdrive anytime soon. But I'll worry about that later. Got to keep my head clear and get through the next twenty-four hours. After that, whatever happens, I'll be home and alive. Hell, if it comes down to it, I can get a sleeping bag and bed down here in the Room, which, now that I say it, sounds incredibly depressing. I wonder if I can squeeze some money out of Sandoval for finishing the job early. Then maybe I could get my old room at the Beat Hotel. A bathroom, a bed, and clean towels that don't stink of Wormwood corruption would be fine with me. And I'd be back in Hollywood full-time. It's not exactly an ambitious plan, but the world is coming at me hard and fast. One step at a time is all I can handle right now.

At the moment, however, I have to figure out the rest of my

night. I'm not ready to go back to Sandoval's place and I'm sure as hell not going to Bamboo House. Kasabian is right. There's a fine line between looking in on your ex and stalking, and I'm right on top of it. What's depressing is that even Donut Universe is useless to me right now. But I have one more alternative, and it's not a bad one at all.

I STEP INTO a shadow and come out due west of Max Overdrive.

Sure enough, it's right where I remember. Because the entrance faces north, Flicker calls the place the Devil's Door. The drive-in is surrounded by a high black wall covered in flames and horned dancing girls. There are eyes over the entrance and teeth around the edges so that when you enter, it's like you're diving right down the Devil's gullet.

I go through another shadow and come out by the concession stand. It's all overpriced drinks and expensive popcorn that you're happy to pay for because all the money goes back to keeping the last old-school drive-in in L.A. open for business.

On the screen, Alan Ormsby is chewing up the scenery as he mock-marries a corpse from the local cemetery. The movie is *Children Shouldn't Play with Dead Things* and Alan's blushing bride will be snacking on his guts before the honeymoon is over. It's a beautiful print of one of the first color zombie movies ever made. I wonder where she found it.

It's wall-to-wall cars below the screen—a full house. There are even a few rented hearses in between the sports cars and SUVs. About half the crowd milling around the food stand is in makeup and filthy zombie rags. That's why it takes me a few minutes to recognize her. She's in zombie drag too, talking to an undead ballerina and a cowboy spinning a lariat made of vertebrae.

I don't know Flicker's real name and I don't know anyone who does. I know she's Chinese. I know she comes from heavy Sub Rosa money. And I know that she doesn't talk to her family anymore because they don't approve of the kind of hoodoo she practices. But she's one of the best at what she does and this drive-in is proof of that.

Out of habit, I get a hot dog and watch the movie for a few minutes. It really is a glorious, noble mess, with a spooky ending that makes you want more, but I'm glad they never made a sequel because it could never be this good.

When Flicker's zombie friends shamble back to their car, I wander over to her.

"Hi, Flicker. I love what you've done with the place."

She looks at me and does a little double take.

"Stark? I heard you were dead."

"Still am, Flicker. But just a little."

"I guess that's better than the alternative."

I give up on the tasteless hot dog and toss it in the trash.

"I'm working on getting completely undead with a necromancer in Beverly Hills."

She swivels her hips and shoulders a little when she says, "Beverly Hills? My. Isn't that a little uptown for you?"

"Tell me about it. I get a rash just saying the words."

She takes my arm and leads me around the back of the concession stand, where it's quieter. When we get there, she says, "Aside from being dead, how are things?"

"Could be worse. At least I'm at the movies."

She smiles. I point to the screen.

"I like what you've done with the place."

She leans on the wall next to me.

"Thanks. It seemed like the right thing to do with my *waipo*'s money."

"I'm sorry to hear your grandma died. You must have been close."

"She's the only one in the family I could stand to be around. We were besties the last few years of her life."

"How did your folks take you using your inheritance to reopen the theater?"

She rolls her eyes to the heavens.

"They were furious when she left me everything. Then when I blew it all on repairs, a new screen, and a new parking lot, they officially cut me off."

"That doesn't seem right."

"They still had fantasies about me marrying a nice lawyer and having Ivy League babies. The inheritance was supposed to be my dowry. Fuck that."

"Since you repaved, can you still do that trick with the parking spaces?"

Flicker is a land witch—a geomancer. All of her power is concentrated in certain patches of ground. Power spots that only she and a few other magicians know about. The Devil's Door sits right on top of her personal spot.

She waggles her eyebrows.

"It's easier than ever. The lines separating the parking spaces are held in place with spring bolts. I can pivot them into any hexagram I want. Stick around. Fulci's *Zombi* is up next. I'll show you after that."

"Thanks. But I have a pretty big day tomorrow."

"You and your necromancer?"

"Fingers crossed that he knows what he's doing."

"You'll be fine. Second-raters don't last too long in the Hills."

"I hope you're right."

She turns to me, leaning on her shoulder.

"If you ever need to do any big rituals, just call. I can shape whatever you need in twenty minutes."

"Thanks. You taking commercial clients too?"

"Hell yeah."

"Cool. I'll spread the word."

"Just wait until you're alive again."

I look over at her. "What? You've got a problem with us Revenant-Americans?"

"Hey, some of my best friends are dead. But you look like you're running a quart low."

She touches my hands and head.

"Your aura is shit."

"It feels that way, too. I like your zombie suit, by the way."

She makes a face.

"You think so? I thought that maybe I should have used more blood."

"Nah. I've seen plenty of Drifters. They weren't bloody unless they were feeding."

"That's a relief. If you like this outfit, you should have been here for our Marlene Dietrich festival. I wore a tux and white tie all week."

"I bet you were a knockout."

"You're goddamn right."

"What's your next festival?"

On-screen, the dead are clawing their way up out of the ground.

"We're doing a seventies week. Everything made in or about the seventies. From *Foxy Brown* and *The Getaway* to *Boogie Nights* and *Dazed and Confused*. You should come by. I'll be in *Roller Boogie* sequined booty shorts and skates all week."

"I'm sold."

She crosses her arms and looks me over.

"I'd tell you to dress appropriately, but I know you're incapable of not looking like a broke-ass biker. Don't worry though. I've got an ex's Nehru jacket that will fit you perfectly."

"I'm not sure I'm the Nehru type."

"Too late. You said you'd be here."

"You got me."

We walk back around to the front of the concession booth and she hands me a folded broadsheet.

"Here's a calendar with the rest of the shows this month. You got a car?"

"I can steal one easy enough."

"Awesome. Bring your girl Candy around too."

I rub a knot on the back of my neck.

"That part I'm not sure about. She's not exactly my girl anymore."

She looks around, embarrassed.

"Damn. I'm sorry I said anything."

"Don't be. She's happy and that's all that counts."

Flicker grabs a bag of popcorn through the concession

window and eats a couple of pieces. She says, "It's big of you to say that, but we both know that's not how these things work."

"No, but if I keep telling myself it is, maybe I'll start to believe it."

She taps the broadsheet.

"Definitely come back for *Taxi Driver,* then. I know you love misery."

"I'll be here."

She holds out the popcorn. I take a couple of pieces to be polite.

"And seriously," she says. "If there's anything I can do to help with your undead situation, just ask."

"Thanks. I'll see you soon."

"Take care, Stark."

She squeezes my hand and I step into a shadow to the campy screams of Alan Ormsby and his dumb friends being eaten.

ROGER AND ANOTHER of Sandoval's roaches bring me my gear in the morning, so I spend the rest of the day prepping it and myself.

I take everything out behind the mansion, deep into the eucalyptus grove. The body armor fits well, but it's cop style with a lot of padding around the neck. That's nice in terms of protection, but makes me feel like I'm being strangled. They left the clothes I died in in a storage bag in my closet, so I was able to get the black blade and na'at. With the blade, I cut off the collar padding. I'll just have to turtle my head in if things get too up close and personal. The armor over my body feels fine, except where it rubs yesterday's gun wound. The damned thing is technically healed but still tender to the touch. That's more than a little aggravating, but there's nothing I can do about it now, and anyway, it won't be an issue after tonight.

I run one box of ammo through the Glock, using the trees to practice head and torso shots at different distances. Then I run the same drill with the rifle. Both guns feel smooth and ready to go. The na'at is up next. I spin it over my head like a whip, splitting open tree trunks and ripping down limbs, then twist the grip and reconfigure it into a sword, running through a whole series of *Seven Samurai* exercises. Last, but not least, I twist the grip again so that the na'at extends to its full length. I shove the tip through one of the smaller trees, twist once more so that the far end opens into a fork whose tines are bent backward on themselves. With one good pull, I yank the fork through the tree, splitting it in half. It comes down with a pleasantly loud crash.

The black blade I test last. I haven't held it in a long time and it feels a little alien in my hand. Still, the balance and weight are good. I run through some close-quarters stabbing and slashing drills. I'm not used to fighting in armor. Before long, I'm sweating and panting like an asthmatic hog. But it feels good to be moving, and the more practice I get, the quicker I'll work out the stiffness in the armor.

From behind me, I hear, "Excuse me."

I'm in the middle of a sequence of kill moves, so when I hear the voice, I spin without thinking and throw the blade. It buries itself deep in a sapling next to Roger's head. When he doesn't move, I go over to him, not sure if he's had a stroke or just enjoys the view.

"Oops. What do you want?"

He takes a few steps back from the blade.

"Nothing," he says.

"You know, you really shouldn't sneak up on someone when they're getting ready to murder people."

"I'll remember that."

"Why are you here?"

He looks at me, a little giddy at being alive.

"No reason."

"Did Sandoval send you?"

"Yes, but don't worry about it."

"Don't be shy, Roger. It's just us here."

"Yes," he says. "Just us."

I pull the blade from the tree. He flinches like I pulled it out of his ass.

"Is it because of the noise?"

He nods.

"The neighbors have been calling. They think it's fireworks and this being the fire season, well . . ." He trails off.

"No problem. I was about done anyway." I peel off the armor and toss it to him. "You take that. I'll get the rest."

"Of course. I'm happy to help."

I start gathering my gear. I put the ammo and Glock in a duffel bag and sling the rifle across my shoulder. When I head back, Roger follows.

I say, "How long have you been with Wormwood?"

"Eight years," he says.

I look back at him.

"You look a little young for that."

"I started as an intern."

I stop and turn to him.

"Wormwood has interns?"

"Yes. We do a lot of outreach to exceptional students in a broad range of specialties."

"Do they get college credit?"

"Of course."

"For helping destroy the world?"

"Mostly it's for assisting the senior associates."

"So, a lot of typing and filing."

"Among other things," he says.

"What other things?"

"You know. Animal sacrifice. Elementary soul binding. Demon summoning."

When we're at the edge of the grove I turn around, letting Roger bump into me.

"Are you a senior associate?"

He shakes his head.

"Upper midlevel."

"Impressive."

"Thank you," he says warily.

I put an arm around his shoulders.

"Roger, just between you and me, did you ever murder anybody for Wormwood?"

He clears his throat, not sure how to answer. I can feel the gears in his brain turning as he works out the lie.

"Never."

I look at him.

"When I say murder, I don't mean did you stick a knife in someone's ribs, I mean *kill*. Magic. Poison. Maybe you just filed the paperwork for a hit."

"No," he says. "Never anything like that."

"Okay."

I look back at the mansion.

"Are any of your other friends—the other roaches—are they killers?"

"Nope."

"I find it hard to believe that Eva and Barron would surround themselves with a bunch of helpless baby birds. Are you sure *none* of you are killers?"

"Positive," he says. Then, "We're not all like you, you know."

"Like what?"

Now that we're close to home, Roger's growing an extra set of balls.

"A maniac."

"I'm not a maniac, Roger. I'm a killer. And I'm asking you all these questions because, while I was out there under the lovely trees, I started wondering if Eva and Barron planned to kill me after I do their job, and if you roaches are the ones who are supposed to do it."

He hands me back the body armor.

"You made a bargain with Wormwood. We honor our bargains. If we didn't, how would the organization have survived this long?"

I look at him for a minute. He's finally telling the truth, or what he thinks is the truth.

I say, "That actually makes sense."

"Of course it does. We're Wormwood. Not the government."

"Okay, you're dismissed. But don't sneak up on me like that again. Next time, I might not miss."

Roger goes to the back door of the house and calls, "Have a good time tonight. I hope you don't get killed or anything."

Then he gives me the finger and goes inside.

I watch him go and think about my stupid life. I'm working for Wormwood. Killing for Wormwood, in fact. I'm half-dead. I have no home. No money. No girl. No friends that I'm sure of. Food tastes like shit. Whiskey tastes just a little better than fruit punch. I have no Maledictions. No Aqua Regia. I'm afraid to let anyone important know I'm back. And I just got told off by a middle-management twerp. I'm not saying that I should have stayed in Hell, but if anyone who knew me from the old days Downtown—back when I was Sandman Slim, the monster who kills monsters—saw me now it would be downright embarrassing.

AFTER I SHOWER off some of my humiliation, I put on my old coat and go to Sandoval's office. She and Barron are both on their laptops. She's at her desk and he's at a table nearby. There are prescription bottles and a bottle of water. He catches me looking at them.

"Don't worry. It's nothing contagious," he says. "And it's not cancer."

"Then what is it?"

"A curse, as far as anyone can tell. I was poisoned by something not in any normal medical journal."

"It must be high-level stuff if none of your magicians can cure it."

"It is. Top-notch."

"Hurts?"

"Like a son of a bitch."

I want to say, *Good,* but instead I say, "Sorry."

"Forget him," says Sandoval. "Do you have everything you need for tonight?"

"Probably not. But I have everything I can think of."

"That will have to do then."

She looks at my duffel bag.

"Do you have any more room in that?"

"A little. Why?"

"You have one more task tonight. Since the faction will be performing an unknown ritual, we would like any and all mystical materials and artifacts they're using. That way, we can analyze their methods and perhaps get a step ahead of them."

I drop the bag on the floor.

"I thought I was just supposed to stop the damned ritual. You now want maid service too?"

"Yes."

"Forget it. I'm going to kill everyone, then burn the place."

"Feel free," says Sandoval. "But after you recover the artifacts."

"What if I forget?"

She gets up from her desk.

"That would void our agreement and you can spend the rest of the weekend with your friend Marcella, watching your body rot down to the bones."

I'm definitely killing all of them when this is over.

"I'll bring back what I can. But I can't guarantee it'll be everything."

"Bring back enough that we believe you put in a good effort. Enough that we can decipher their plans. If you do that, Howard will go ahead and fully restore you to life."

I pick up the bag again.

"Tell him to be ready for me."

"He will be," she says.

I leave the office with a bad feeling in my gut. Killing I'm good at. Playing retriever, I'm not. But what choice do I have? And if that's what it takes to get back to where I want to be, fuck it. I'll back up a truck to the chapel and pry every pew out of the ground and every cherub off the wall.

Before I take off, I go to the bowling alley to see if there's anything else I can get out of Marcella. When I come in she jumps up from the mattress and runs to the far wall. Crouches there like an animal. When I get closer, I can see why. Her shirt is gone. Her face and arms are bruised. Both eyes are black and swollen. There are marks on her chest like bug bites. I try to get closer, but I can tell she's about three seconds from jumping me. I set down the bag on a chair and stay where I am.

"I told you it would hurt if you tried to leave."

She laughs.

"Leave," she says. "I didn't try to leave, you idiot. A bunch of your friends came down here in the night. They asked the same stupid questions you did, only they weren't as polite."

"What are those marks on your chest?"

She runs a hand over the bug bites.

"You like these? They're cigarette burns."

"Who did it?"

"I don't know. A guy. A young guy."

I take out the Shermans and show her one.

"Were the cigarettes like this?"

"Yes."

Roger.

"First off, I didn't have anything to do with this."

"I know, Boy Scout."

"Second, I'll make sure it doesn't happen again."

"How? It looks like you're on your way out."

"Trust me. It's taken care of."

Marcella takes a few steps toward me.

"You want me to trust you? Then don't leave me alone like this. I know my gun is in that bag. Give it to me."

"I'm sympathetic, but I'm not stupid."

"Then leave me something," she says.

The bruises are bad, but they're not what get to me. It's the burns. That kind of thing is methodical. Thought out in advance. Someone's idea of a good time. And even though Marcella is an asshole, I told her she'd be all right down here.

I reach into my coat and take out the black blade.

"You see this knife? It means a lot to me. There's only one other like it in the world. If something should happen to it, I'm going to be angry. If someone tried to use it on me, I'd be even angrier. Understood?"

"Understood," she says.

I hold it out to her. She shakes her head, so I set it on one of the scoring tables. It's not until I've picked up the duffel and am over by the door that Marcella snatches up the knife. She frowns at it.

"What the hell kind of knife is this? It looks like it was made by Fred Flintstone."

"Remember those Hellions from yesterday?"

"A wee bit."

"They made it. That's bone."

She holds the blade up to the light.

"This knife is from Hell?"

"Yes. And keep your hand away from the blade. It'll cut through just about anything. Take a finger or your whole hand off before you know it."

"And you're giving it to me?"

"Don't be stupid. It's a loan. I'll want it back when I'm done."

She raises her hand and brings the knife down on one of the folding chairs. It splits into two pieces.

"Nice," she says.

"Yes it is. Like I said, don't lose it. But feel free to kill anyone who comes in here who isn't me."

"You don't have to tell me twice, Boy Scout."

"I'm going now. No one will bother you while I'm gone."

"But you're giving me the knife anyway."

"I don't think they will, but I've learned not to underestimate people's desire for self-destruction."

I close the door quietly and go back upstairs to Sandoval's office.

The roaches have joined her and Sinclair.

"Good. You're all here."

Sandoval looks surprised.

"I thought you'd left."

"There's just one thing before I leave."

Faster than he can blink, I grab Roger and hit him. The first punch breaks his nose. The second and third fracture his jaw. I let him go so he falls on the floor, bleeding all over Sandoval's nice Persian rug. While he's still down there, I pull the Colt from my waistband and point it at the closest roach. It's a woman with red hair and a white rose on her lapel.

Sandoval yells, "Stark! Have you lost your mind?"

"Shut up."

I press the Colt against the redhead's temple.

"What's your name?"

"Sandra," she says.

"Sandra, teacher has to leave the room for a while. Your job is to take the names of any bad boys or girls who try to go downstairs to the bowling alley. Can you do that for me, Sandra?"

"Yes."

"Good, because if anything else happens to Marcella, I want to know who to kill first."

"Stop it, Stark, or the deal is off," says Sandoval.

I point the Colt at her.

"That's not much of an epitaph, Eva, but oh well."

I cock the gun.

Sinclair gets between me and Eva.

"Listen to me," he says. "Nothing will happen to the woman downstairs. I'll see to it personally. Just put the gun down and finish the job. You're so close to being whole again."

I look from Sandoval to him and back to her. Roger moans on the floor. For the first time, she seems genuinely scared.

I lower the hammer on the Colt and put it away.

Sinclair says, "Let's pretend that none of this ever happened. We'll have Howard get set up as soon as you leave, so that he'll be ready for you when you get back."

"Good."

I look over at Roger.

"And get rid of him. I don't want to ever see Roger again."

"Fine," says Sinclair.

I look over at Sandra.

"Remember. You're in charge while I'm gone."

"I remember," she says.

I look at Sandoval. She's not scared anymore. She's trying to figure out the best way to fuck me over.

"See you soon, Eva."

She says, "You've proven you can hurt an unarmed boy. Now prove that you deserve your reputation. Hurt people who can hurt you back."

"That's the plan."

"And bring me back my artifacts."

"In an Easter basket with ribbons on top."

I step into a shadow and get out of there before I change my mind and snuff all of them.

THE CHAPEL OF St. Alexis is an old Spanish-style mission, the kind you see all over Southern California. There's nothing very impressive about it. It sits behind a rusty chain-link fence. The front doors are padlocked. Most of the stained glass windows are broken. Part of the roof has collapsed, leaving some of the roof beams exposed. Even the crooked cross over the front is a mildewed rotten tooth.

I don't know why anyone would want to spend a fortune putting this hovel back together again. Of course, aside from fear, the God business runs on sentimentality. That's the only explanation. Unless it's a real estate scam. I'd feel a lot better about the place if I thought that was what was really going on. But I'm probably wrong. I usually am about these kinds of things. The chapel is just the obsession of a lot of poor slobs who've been convinced that fixing it up will buy them a ticket straight to Heaven. Man, are they going to be surprised when they get there.

The sun is already starting down, so half of the chapel is in shadow. I step through it and come out in the crypt below.

No one is here yet, but someone was working on the place. The floor has been swept clean and there are halogen floods around the walls, lighting up the crypt like it's noon on the solstice.

There are small vaults all around the crypt, three high, and each holding a single coffin. Extra-holy or extra-wealthy parishioners, I guess. Maybe old priests. Really, who cares? They're dead and won't mind my using their crusty corpses as a duck blind.

I climb behind a coffin in one of the second-tier vaults directly across from the crypt entrance. It's deep and dark back here. Smells of dust and old bones. Not really comforting, but it's good cover. The way the lights are set up, they throw some nice shadows into all the vaults, except the ones directly in line with the lamps. That might be useful later.

I try to get comfortable while I wait for sunset, but after a few minutes of wrestling with the armor I'm beginning to regret asking for it. Then I catch a glimpse of my still-bruised wrist and it reminds me of why I wanted it. I check the sight on the rifle for the hundredth time. Make sure I can reach the Glock inside my coat and the Colt at my back. I wish I had a drink. I wish I had a smoke. I wish I was at Flicker's drive-in with Candy and a stolen Cadillac the size of Texas. And I wish whoever chooses the spots for these ceremonies could quit the Bela Lugosi bullshit. It's always a crypt. It's always a cemetery or a spooky old mansion where a family was murdered by a serial killer or angry Girl Scouts when they didn't buy enough cookies. The next hoodoo ceremony I crash better be at Musso and Frank so I can get a decent martini when the killing is over.

I hear scraping from far away. A murmur of voices. The scrape turns into the sound of a door opening. More voices and, now, footsteps. A lot of footsteps. More footsteps than I was hoping for.

A few seconds later, they start filing into the crypt.

Shit.

There's a lot of them. A *lot*.

Five magicians and ten heavily armed guards. Silly me hoping that, for a ceremony this important, those numbers would be reversed. Nothing I can do about it now except hunker a little farther back into the vault and wait to see how the scene plays out. I could start shooting now, but the magicians aren't set up, and with the amount of firepower they have, they could escape while I'm dealing with a shitstorm. No. I've got to let the magicians start their ceremony and hope it distracts the guards before I do anything. That means patience, and I hate patience.

As if they know I'm waiting, the magicians take their sweet goddamn time about setting up. First, a carpet goes down in the middle of the crypt. Then they unfold a portable altar and start laying out the goods from a wooden trunk. And holy shit, they pass every single fucking one around so that each magician can bless it before putting it on the table *just so* and moving on to the next item. I swear, these clowns must be getting paid by the hour. I don't know how much crap they have in that trunk, but we could be here until the Rapture starts and Elvis makes his big comeback.

Finally, one of the magicians closes the trunk. There are ten items laid out like the sephirot in a kabbalistic tree of life pattern. When they seem satisfied with the spread, they join hands and begin a low chant.

Kill me now.

The chant isn't any better or worse than a hundred other chants I've heard, but the thing about chants is that they can go on for-fucking-ever. This one feels like it's going for a record. Maybe it's just me getting antsy, but even a few of the guards start looking restless. Thank you for validating my annoyance. Now hold still while I kill all of you.

Eventually, the magician at the base of the tree frees his hands and picks up a nearby knife. He slices his left palm and dribbles blood between the items on the table, creating the paths that connect each sephira. When he's done, he picks up something from the lowest position on the tree and holds it up before him. It's a gold medallion or a large coin. Either way, I can't resist. The moment he opens his mouth to utter some hoodoo, I use the rifle to put a bullet straight through the center of the coin and into his forehead. It takes a second for everyone's brain to process what they just saw, and in that second I open up on the rest of the magicians. I get three of them with head shots, but the fourth I hit in the shoulder. By then, the guards have figured out my position and opened up on me. What seems like a hundred rounds pepper the vault where I'm hiding. Before I can slip through the shadow in the back of the vault, a couple of shots hit me in the chest. The armor stops them, but the force is like being hit by a reasonably large buffalo. It knocks me backward into the shadow.

While the guards concentrate their fire on the vault where I'm definitely not, I use another shadow to come out on their side. I blow through my first clip quickly and take down three of them. The other seven figure out where I am, but before they can open fire on me, I slip out the back of that vault . . .

. . . and come out in a vault on the opposite wall. I fire down on them while their backs are to me. I get three more of them before they zero in on my new location. Just as I'm changing clips and getting ready to bail out of there, a ricochet flashes right across the vault where I'm hiding, snapping off the rifle's trigger, so fuck my luck again.

I fall back into a shadow and come out behind them on the floor of the crypt, holding the rifle by the barrel and swinging it like a baseball bat. I knock two down on their faces and finish them with the Glock before disappearing again.

The last two guards make a break for the door with the injured magician between them. To his credit, the magician pushes away from them and screams hoodoo into the crypt. This gives me plenty of time to get behind the guards, snap the na'at out into a sword, and take off both of their heads.

The remaining magician, pale and leaking blood from his bullet wound, is smart. I recognize his hoodoo. It's going to rain mystical flaming knives down on me—or so it seems until, at the last minute, he replaces a couple of words of the spell. Instead of knives raining down, he pulls down one of the walls on me.

I barely get out of the way in time.

The sound of the crash echoes off the rock walls of the

crypt in a deafening slap. I bark Hellion hoodoo and a pillar of fire rises from the floor, shooting directly at him. He steps back and grabs an object off the tree of life, tossing it into the fire. As it hits he screams hoodoo and the fire sort of turns inside out, transforming from flames to water. He whirls to throw a curse at me, but I step into a shadow and come out behind him.

Good thing too. He pulled down another section of wall where I was standing.

When I'm right behind him I say, "Boo."

He freezes and I put the Glock to the back of his head.

"I know you want to die by hoodoo like a real warrior magician. I get it. And that's why it's going to happen like this."

I shoot him and let him fall on the floor with the dead guards. Fuck him. Fuck magic. Fuck the faction. And double fuck whoever shot me in the chest.

I open my coat—which has more than a few bullet holes in it, thanks, you fuckers—and pry the bullets out of the body armor. Toss them on the floor with the other dead dopes.

The trunk is empty, so it's not very heavy when I pull it over to the altar. Sandoval and Sinclair aren't going to be happy when they see what I'm bringing them. Most of what the magicians were using in the ritual has been shot to shit. It's all twisted metal vessels, splintered wooden idols, and shattered vials. The only thing intact is a vellum scroll. I shove everything else into the trunk but set the scroll aside. Whatever it is, it's probably worth something and I'm going to want leverage over Wormwood until I'm 100 percent alive.

When I open it, the scroll is just a jumble of geometric

shapes and runes laid out in a grid pattern. I can't read a word of it, and I don't get a chance to decipher it with hoodoo because there's an ominous *crack* above me that runs down the walls and rumbles the floor.

With two walls missing, the room is collapsing. As I grab the trunk, the halogen lights start going out. I find a shadow in the dying light of the very last one and dive in.

I come out of a shadow across the street. Car alarms are going off for blocks. Lights are coming on in the nearby houses. The street shakes as the chapel groans and snaps, crashing down onto itself until it's one big holy crater in the ground. I'm covered in dust from the vaults, asbestos, and who the hell knows what else that's raining down from the dead chapel. I stay there just long enough to make sure I'll leave a good trail of toxic shit on the rugs when I'm back at Sandoval's mansion. But as people gather to gawk at the wreckage, I drag the trunk into a shadow. Back to Beverly Hills and my brand-new, shiny, perfect life.

I'M NOT SUBTLE when I return to Sandoval's. I come in right through a wall in her office, dragging the trunk behind me.

She and Sinclair jump when they see me.

"Goddammit, Stark. That was amusing the first time or two, but not anymore. Come in through a door like a human being."

I drop the trunk and it kicks up a little cloud of dust.

Sinclair frowns.

"What are you—and it—covered with?"

"The Chapel of St. Alexis. We're pretty much all that's left of it."

"You were supposed to kill a few men. Not make a scene," says Sandoval.

"I wasn't the one that cratered the place. It was one of the faction's magicians."

"You destroyed it? The whole chapel?"

"You're not listening. *I* didn't do it. I was just going to collapse the crypt. A faction magician collapsed the building."

"And you let him," she says.

"I didn't know he was doing it—there wasn't exactly time for a zoning commission meeting. I barely got out of there with your Easter basket."

Sinclair says, "What's wrong, Eva?"

"The faction lost a valued piece of consecrated ground tonight. They won't take that lightly."

I shake some dust off my jacket and onto the floor.

"Hey, I just saved L.A. And you. Why don't you be happy about that for two minutes before you go off again?"

She looks at me.

"Yes. I suppose you did."

She looks at the trunk.

"Are those the artifacts?"

"That's them. But they got a little banged around in shipping."

"Let me see."

I use my boot to push the trunk in her direction.

"Have fun."

She shakes her head.

"No. You open it."

"You think I put a bomb in there? Maybe snakes? Maybe a snake bomb?"

"I think I know how your brain works now and I believe that it's deeply damaged by your time in Hell. Therefore, you open it."

I look at Sinclair.

"Why don't you do it?"

He just takes a pill from one of his collection of bottles.

"I have to agree with Eva. It would be better for everyone if you did it."

I look around for the roaches.

"How are Roger and Sandra doing?"

"Sandra is fine," says Sandoval. "Roger is in the hospital."

"Poor guy. You know, I got tagged tonight, too. Shot twice in the chest. It really hurts."

"I'll weep for you later. Now, the trunk."

I say, "Tough room," and kick the trunk open.

They approach it with caution.

Sandoval says, "Put everything on my desk."

"I'm not your fucking butler."

"Just do it."

I drag the trunk to her desk, sweep everything off it, and dump the remains of the ritual objects. They clatter out in a heap.

"It's garbage," says Sandoval.

I look at her.

"I told you there was some breakage."

"What happened to it?"

"Remember when I said I got shot? That should have been a clue that they didn't give this stuff up peacefully. There was a firefight, both bullets and hoodoo."

She and Sinclair go to the desk and look things over.

"These are useless," Sandoval says.

I pick up part of a broken wooden idol.

"No they're not. Given a little time, any reasonably bright magician could put them back together. You must have a hundred of them on your payroll. If you're going to complain, complain to them."

Sinclair picks up the remains of a golden pitcher.

"He's right, you know. Even in such poor shape, I recognize a few of the artifacts. Our people could put them back together."

Sandoval screws up her lips in a sour expression like she just licked the bottom of a bus station chair.

"Fine," she says. "They'll have to do."

I go over to her.

"That's it then. I've completed my part of the bargain. It's time for you to pay up."

"I know."

"When can we get started?"

She picks up pieces of the artifacts, glances at them, and drops them again.

"Howard is still setting up. He wants you to rest up for the evening. We'll call you when he's ready."

Hell.

"Fine. Do you have any painkillers lying around? And I don't mean aspirin. Vicodin or something like that? My chest is killing me."

Sandoval glances at me and goes back to sifting through the artifacts.

"In fact, we did have some Vicodin, but we had to give it to Roger before the ambulance came. Poor boy."

She looks at me.

"Poor you."

I look at her eyes.

"It's not polite to lie, Eva."

"Take the bourbon on the sideboard and go to your room. We'll call you when Howard is ready."

I'm tired and I don't feel like starting a fight when I'm this close to home. I take the bottle and a glass and get out of there.

I SHOWER OFF chapel dust and the smell of old bones. There's a full-length mirror in the bathroom, so when I'm done I check myself out. It's a pitiful sight. Like my early days in the arena, before I got my scars. I'm basically one big bruise, from my shoulders down to my ankles. The bullet wound in my stomach doesn't hurt anymore, but it's still a little pink when it should have faded to a regular scar by now. At least when I'm fully me again, the wounds will heal quickly. I should be presentable to the world in less than a day. Maybe I'll take the time to see Vidocq and ask about crashing with him for a while. When that's settled and I don't look like I went ten rounds with a stegosaurus, maybe I'll go to Max Overdrive and Candy . . .

But is that the right way to handle things? Just walk in and say, *Hi, honey. I'm back from the dead. Who wants tacos?* I'm just not sure what else to do. Should I send a note? Do it in skywriting? I sure as hell don't want Kasabian telling her for me. What's the polite way to come back to the world of the living? The last time I came back from Hell I wanted to kill everyone, which made things a lot simpler. Now I have to deal with people's *feelings* and worry about *what's good for the relationship*. It was a lot easier being a monster. Just kill kill kill all day.

I miss it sometimes. But I miss Candy more.

I get the scroll out of my coat and look it over. It's nothing but angular scribbles. I wish Father Traven was here. He was great with languages. He'd have this thing translated by the time I finished my first cigarette. I'll show it to Vidocq when I go over there tomorrow. Maybe there will be something in one of his books.

Really, I should go downstairs and check on Marcella, but after what I did to Roger, I'm reasonably sure she's all right. Besides, she has my knife. I'll get it back from her later. Right now, I'm very tired. Fuck this body. It runs down so fast. But that will be over with soon. Everything is going to be fine.

Before I know it, I'm asleep. In my dreams, I'm back in Hell. Actually, in the Tenebrae, the wasteland just outside of Hell. I'm with the Magistrate. He ran a mad horde of marauders across Hell looking for a secret weapon he was going to use to storm Heaven. Things didn't work out, but he was the smartest son of a bitch I ever met. When I met him, there were at least a hundred people and dozens of vehicles in his horde. Now it's just the two of us. I'm his chauffeur. He sits in the backseat of his Charger babbling about the war in Heaven. Switching from language to language before I can recognize any of them.

Finally, he says, "What is the shortest distance between two points?"

I look at him in the rearview mirror.

"Swordfish."

"Come again?"

"It's a joke from an old movie. What's the secret password? Swordfish."

"I see. Well, it is not swordfish this time. Would you like to know the answer?"

"Sure."

I hit the accelerator. Feel the RPMs rumble from my feet and up into my chest as the Charger tears up the cracked desert road, leaving a gray cloud behind us.

The Magistrate takes my Colt and puts one bullet in the chamber. Spins it and slams it shut. Puts the gun to his head and pulls the trigger. Nothing happens.

He says, "The answer is death. In nothingness, distance has no meaning."

"But death isn't nothingness. I'm dead and I'm here now."

He puts the Colt to my head.

"Perhaps you are not dead enough."

"I still think 'swordfish' is a better answer."

"But you are not the one asking the question."

He pulls the trigger.

I wake up to the sound of gunfire—

—and roll out of bed, hit the floor, and run toward the sound. I'm wearing pants and nothing else and for a second I'm tempted to go back for the body armor, but the gunfire just gets louder so I keep going.

As I come out of my room, I can already see that the enormous foyer in Sandoval's mansion is a fucking war zone. Windows blown out. Holes punched in the walls. Shots gouging chunks out of the marble floor. Ripping through the paintings. Vases explode, sending showers of roses and lilies into the air.

Sandoval is pinned down by the open front door. Sinclair is a few yards back. To Sandoval's credit, she's firing back at whoever's outside with a little pocket pistol.

I crawl to the edge of the room and get a look out one of the smashed windows. To my complete nonsurprise, there's an unmarked van flanked by men in balaclavas. They're even using the same kind of SIG rifles friends of theirs used when they snatched me and killed Philip.

A few seconds later, Sandoval runs out of ammo. I shout to her, hoping she can hear me over the sound of gunfire.

"Eva, get the fuck away from the door."

If she can hear me, she ignores the order. Can't say I blame her. With bullets pitting the floor around her, there isn't anywhere she can get to. It won't take long for one of the gunmen to zero right in on her head. Part of me wants her to die, but she's the boss around here and who knows what her lackeys will do or if Howard will fix me when she's gone? I need Sandoval alive.

Shouting some Hellion hoodoo, I run for her. The curse sends a pressure wave out the front door. It won't last long—a few seconds at most—but the wave deflects the bullets just long enough for me to grab Sandoval and get her away from the door. Good thing I didn't expect any thank-yous.

"Do something," she shouts right in my face.

"Fuck that. I'm not your bodyguard. I did my job already."

She looks at me hard.

"If those men get in the house, they could kill Howard."

I hadn't thought of that.

I crawl to a window and get a quick look outside. A dozen

shooters, all with rifles. I don't have my body armor or a gun, and anyway, I'm not ready to face down another murder-happy army tonight. I crawl to a heavy oak chair nearby and throw it out of the closest window. It knocks the remaining glass and curtains out of the way.

"Destroying my house is not helping!"

I ignore her as the gunmen open up on the window, knocking fistfuls of plaster down on me. I grab another chair and throw it at a window across the room. When that window shatters, the gunfire moves from me and over in that direction. It gives me just enough time to get to my window and shout hoodoo from back in my arena days.

A bright, swirling cloud forms over the gunmen's van. A second later it explodes in a blinding flash of heat and light. When I look outside again, half the gunmen are on the ground. A few of them are on fire. The top of the van and at least one of the wheels is also burning. The gunmen roll their pals on the ground until the flames go out, then drag them toward the van. I shout the curse the magician pretended to use against me in the crypt. A second later, a swarm of glittering knives appears in the air, flying down at the attackers. The blades *thunk* into the side of the armored van and the losers outside. By the time it's moving, pretty much everyone is a bloody pincushion. With flames still on the roof and a couple of tires engulfed, the van speeds away.

Before I know it, Sandoval is next to me in the window.

"What are you waiting for?" she shouts. "Go after them!"

"On foot?"

"Their wheels are on fire. They won't get far."

"They aren't stupid. Those are going to be tactical tires.

There are metal inserts inside the wheels. When a tire goes flat, they can still drive on the insert."

Sandoval looks at me like she's trying to figure out if I'm making it up. Finally, she throws up her hands and walks to Sinclair. He's still on the floor. She has to pull him to his feet.

"Don't help or anything," she says.

I go over and haul Sinclair upright, walk him to one of the few chairs not shot to shit.

"Thank you," he says.

With shaking hands, he takes a couple of pills out of his jacket pocket and dry-swallows them. If I didn't know what monsters he and Sandoval were, I'd almost feel sorry for them.

Across the foyer, Sandoval kicks enough debris out of the way that she can force the front door closed. Her face is red with anger when she looks at me.

"This is all your fault."

"How do you figure that? You didn't see this coming? I stopped their tea party. Of *course* they were going to retaliate."

She takes a long breath.

"You should have said something."

"Calm down. Those gunmen? They're good news."

"What on earth do you mean?"

"They were a tantrum. If the faction was in a position to do worse they would have. But I took out some of their key magicians."

"You mean that I should be grateful that they nearly destroyed my house and killed me and Barron?"

"That's exactly what I mean. Now, where the hell is Howard? I'm tired of waiting."

Sandoval looks me up and down, staring at my scars and bruises.

"Put a shirt on for god's sake. You're hideous."

"I'd rather see Howard."

She pulls Sinclair from his chair and walks away with him.

"Dress and meet us in my office."

"Howard better be there."

Sandoval doesn't say anything.

I go to my room. Get a shirt and the Glock.

THE ARTIFACTS ARE still piled on the desk when I come back to the office. Sinclair is slumped in his chair near the pill bottles. Sandoval is hunched in her desk chair like a cranky gargoyle.

I say, "Where's Howard?"

"He's not coming," she says. "We have other things to talk about."

"Like what?"

"The assassination attempt on me tonight. I'm not going to sit by and let them kill me like the others."

"Great. Good luck with that. What does it have to do with me?"

She points a perfectly manicured finger at me.

"You're going to get the people that did this tonight."

I walk to the desk.

"That's not my job. I did my job. I'm not expecting flowers for it, but I do expect you to honor our deal."

She picks up a necklace made of finger bones. The chain holding them together is broken, so they all fall off. She pushes the bones into a pile with the other artifacts.

"I'm going to honor it, but circumstances have changed."

"Changed how? Did something happen to Howard?"

"He's fine. What's changed is that, while you might have saved the city from obliteration, you've made me the faction's target."

"Lady, you've been their target since day one. Tonight would have happened with or without me."

"Not like this," she says. "You have to pay for what happened."

"Pay how? And bear in mind that you're talking to a man who killed fifteen people earlier and a few more just now. Let's call it an even twenty."

"Calm down, Stark," says Sinclair. "There's no need for threats. Just listen to her."

I pull the Glock and shoot the water bottle on the table with his pills.

"Keep quiet. This is between Eva and me."

Sandoval looks at Sinclair, then up at me.

"Our original understanding was that you were to stop the destruction of Los Angeles before Sunday. You've done that. And bully for you. However, it's still Friday night, which gives you plenty of time to find the faction's leaders and—since you're so fond of doing it—kill them all."

"That wasn't our deal."

"This is a new deal."

I go around the desk and pull Sandoval to her feet.

"Even if I was interested, how do I know you'll stick to this new deal?"

She says, "Because I want you gone as much as you want to be gone."

I put the Glock to her head.

"Hurry, Eva. Convince me."

Her heartbeat just jumped about 200 percent.

"I'll give you one million dollars."

"Why don't you make it a gajillion and throw in a pony?"

"Two million."

"Still not interested."

She puts a hand on my gun arm and gets closer.

"I mean it. You can have the money right now. I'll transfer it to any account you want."

I press the gun harder into her head and force her back into her desk chair.

"Look at me. Do I look like I have bank accounts?"

"I'll open one for you."

"Forget it."

She puts her hands on the desk, lacing her fingers together.

"You don't seem to understand what I'm getting at. I'm offering you two million dollars, *plus* Howard's services. These two things are a package deal. You're either going to be a rich live man or a penniless dead one. What's your choice?"

I look back at Sinclair. He's paler than ever. "Did you come up with this together?"

Before he answers Sandoval says, "No one tried to kill Barron tonight. This new proposition is mine."

"Tell me why I shouldn't kill you both right now."

She moves her laced fingers from the desk to her lap.

"Because then you'll end up unmourned in a pauper's grave. And just think of it. You were *this close* to being with your lady love, but you were too stubborn to go all the way."

One trick I don't know how to do is to stop time. I know

people who can do it. Not for long, but it's still a pretty impressive trick. I wish I could do it right now just to have a little time to think over the situation. I trust Sandoval and Sinclair even less now. But I can't see any way around this if I'm getting back to Candy. I need Howard more than any of these pricks need me. And I wouldn't mind having two million dollars to start a new life with.

I look down at her.

"I guess I don't have a choice."

"Of course you have a choice," she says. "They're just not very good choices."

I let my gun hand drop to my side.

"Okay. I'll do it. But no tricks, no renegotiations or technicalities. Fuck with me one more time and we all die together. And you'll go a lot messier than I will."

"It's agreed then."

"Not yet. Get Howard in here. I want to see that he's all right."

Sandoval takes her phone from a pocket and punches in a number.

"Howard, will you come in here, please?"

"Excuse me," says Sinclair.

I look at the wheezing creep.

"My heart," he says. "May I take my pills?"

"Go ahead."

Eva goes to the bar and pours some tonic water into a glass. Gives it to Sinclair. He gulps it down with the pills.

"Thank you," he says.

Sandoval pats him on the shoulder and goes back to the bar. She pours herself a whiskey.

"Would you like one?"

"I want Howard."

"Patience."

"Never say that to an angry man with a gun. They could go off."

She laughs a little. I don't like it, but I let it go for now.

A minute later, a door opens and Howard comes in. He stops abruptly when he sees Sandoval grave, Sinclair next to a bullet hole, and me clearly wanting to shoot everyone in the room.

"You wanted to see me, Eva?"

"No," she says. "He did."

She points at me with her glass.

Howard gives me a timid look. Through the big wire-frame glasses he looks like a myopic mouse.

"How can I help you?" he says.

I go over to him.

"When we start the process, how long will it take to finish?"

"An hour on the outside."

"Side effects?"

"Nothing serious," he says. "A little dizziness. Some nausea. Fatigue. But they'll pass quickly."

"What I mean is, will I be able to leave immediately after we're done?"

He bobs his head.

"I don't see why not. Of course, you'll want to take some meclizine before you go."

"What's that?"

"A seasickness drug," says Sandoval. "So you can say bon voyage to the captain without puking all over his yacht."

"Yeah. I want some of that."

Howard looks at Sandoval.

"I take it we're not proceeding tonight?"

She stares into her whiskey.

"Change of plans, Howard. We'll do it tomorrow evening."

"That's fine," he says. "I'm all set up and ready to go."

I say, "Keep it that way. I don't want any waiting around tomorrow."

"I understand entirely."

"No you don't. Playing with dead things and being one are different."

"Of course," he says. "I didn't mean to offend."

Sandoval waves him off.

"Thank you, Howard. You can go now. We're just about done with Mr. Stark."

"Thank you. Good evening, everyone."

Sandoval and Sinclair wish him a good night. I'm a bit more conflicted. Tomorrow, I'm going to either buy him all the drinks in L.A. or squeeze his head until it pops. I hope it's the first thing. Sandoval was right. I'd rather be a rich live man than a broke pile of bones.

I say, "Now the sixty-four-thousand-dollar question. Do either of you know where to start looking for the heads of the faction?"

"Not a one," says Sandoval.

I look at Sinclair.

"I can give you names," he says. "But I don't know where they are."

I sit on the edge of Sandoval's desk.

"Great. I guess we can rule out the courier trick. Odds are they've figured that one out."

"I would say so," she says.

"You want this done by tomorrow night, but you have zero information that can help me?"

"Well, there's Barron's list."

"Yes," he says. "There's Jonas Cornetto . . ."

I toss him a pad and pen from the desk.

"Write it down. I can barely remember my own name right now."

"Poor dear," says Sandoval.

"Don't be smug. This is your ass on the line, too."

"What I mean is that you already have what you need to find the faction."

"You mean Marcella."

"Whatever her name is. Ask her. You're very convincing with a gun in your hand."

Sinclair hands me a list with six names.

"You're sure of all of these?"

"Absolutely," he says.

He reaches for his pills again. His skin has gone from larval white to dead-frog green.

I look at Sandoval.

"Keep Kermit alive until tomorrow. I want to be able to kill both of you if things go wrong."

"Naturally."

"And get started on the bank account thing and the money. I want it set up when I get back."

"It will be ready for you."

I head downstairs with my list while Sandoval pours pills down Sinclair's gullet.

I knock on the bowling alley door before going in.

I open it a few inches and say, "It's me. Don't stab me or anything."

"Are you alone?" says Marcella.

"No. I'm with Eleanor Roosevelt. She wants to talk about war bonds."

"Come in."

I go in and close the door. Marcella sits at one of the scoring tables. Her face looks better than yesterday. Still bruised, but some of the swelling has gone down. With her shirt gone, she's just wearing a bra and pants.

On the way down I stopped by my room and took a shirt from the closet. I hold it out to her.

"Trade you. A shirt for a knife."

She sets the knife on the table and I bring her the shirt. She snatches it out of my hand. Turns around and buttons it. I grab the knife before she changes her mind.

"You could have brought me this yesterday," she says. "Or were you hoping for a look at my tits?"

"I was a little distracted hoping I wasn't going to get shot to kitty litter by a bunch of your people."

She turns to me, still tucking the shirt in.

"You look like you came through it all right. You want to know about my night?"

"Not really. I mean, you did torture me."

She blows a little air between her lips.

"That wasn't torture. That was a motivated discussion. What they did to me with cigarettes? That was torture."

I'm not going to argue about the relative merits of cigarettes versus cattle prods. I look at her.

"Did anyone bother you again?"

"No. But I didn't get much sleep, if you know what I mean."

I hold the list out to her.

"With luck, neither of us will be here much longer. Just answer some questions."

She looks at the paper but doesn't move to take it.

"What happens to me when I tell you everything you want to know? Who's going to kill me? You or them?"

"No one is going to kill you."

She puts her hands in her pockets.

"You're going to send me back to Hell then."

"Nope. Worse. I'm going to let you go."

Marcella frowns and half turns away.

She whispers, "I don't think they'd like that upstairs."

"Fuck upstairs. Once I get my treatment, you Wormwood people can kill each other off however you want."

She nods at the paper.

"That's my ticket out of here?"

"First class and all the cocktails you can drink."

She puts her hand out. Looks at the list, wads it up, and throws it away.

"You've got to be kidding," she says.

"I just want to know where they are."

"Forget it. Kill me now. It's better than what they'll do to me."

"Listen—"

"Besides, that list is a joke. Those idiots were big-time in Wormwood one point oh. They're not the ones who run the new Wormwood."

I sit down at the scoring table, hoping that will relax her. She sits down across from me.

"Fine—who does run it? One name. And a location."

"No," she says. "You don't know what they're like. They might kill me just for losing you. At least right now they'll do it fast."

I look at her eyes and listen to her heart. Check the microtremors around her mouth. She isn't playing. She's genuinely scared.

"One name," I say. "One name and not only will I let you go, I'll do it anywhere in the world. The way I pulled you through a shadow yesterday? I can take you anywhere you want to go."

"Unless you can get me to Mars, forget it."

I sit back and look at her. Without torturing her for real, she's not going to give me anything. She's Wormwood scum, but torture is something those creeps upstairs would do and I'm not going to become them. Instead, I reach into my back pocket and take out the scroll. Set it on the scoring table.

I say, "What's that?"

"Fuck!" she says, and jumps up from the table.

I hold up the scroll.

"What's on here? Your credit rating? It can't be any worse than mine."

"Have you touched it? Do you know what it's written on?"

"Yeah. Vellum."

"*Human* vellum, you moron. And guess what? It's not that old."

I unroll the scroll on the table.

"Is that what you're afraid of? If you talk you might end up someone's grocery list?"

"Don't joke about it," she says. "They peel that off you while you're alive."

"You've seen it?"

Marcella wraps her arms around herself and shakes her head.

"No, but I've heard it being done."

I point to the symbols.

"What do they say?"

She glances at it, then moves away again.

"That mystical shit isn't my department. I just gather information."

"You kidnap and torture people. Is that where the vellum comes from? Is it part of the torture?"

She takes a breath and sits down on one of the benches.

"I don't want to talk about it."

"You think they'll do this to you if you talk."

She looks at the floor but doesn't say anything.

"My offer still stands. I'll take you out of here."

"They'll find me. You can't run from them."

"Then help me wipe them out. That way, we're both free."

"No," she says, and I can tell she means it.

I roll up the scroll and get up.

"That's it?" she says.

"That's it."

"You really are a Boy Scout. I'd have a cattle prod on your balls and be waterboarding you in hot tar by now."

"In Hell they do the same thing, only with boiling shit. I can still taste it in my dreams."

I head for the door.

Just as I'm about to leave she says, "Atticus Rose."

I look back at her.

"The Tick-Tock Man?"

"You've heard of him?"

"Hell yes."

Atticus Rose is the king of Tick-Tock Men in L.A. He makes mechanical familiars for the richest Sub Rosa in the city. I tried to shut him down more than once.

"Where can I find him?"

"He runs an antique store in West Hollywood," she says.

"Familiars and mystical objects for Wormwood?"

"Something like that. I don't remember the name of the place," Marcella says.

"I'll find it." Before I get up I say, "Why the change of heart? Why give me the information now?"

"Because you didn't try to hurt me."

"That's not enough. Why?"

"If you find Rose or kill him it won't make any difference, you know. What's happening won't be over. It's never going to be over until our side wins. If it takes forever, the people at the top will never let up. They're not looking for power but salvation."

"You still didn't answer my question. Why?"

"Maybe when this is over you can be the one to kill me. I know you'll do it fast so it doesn't hurt, Boy Scout."

"We'll see. Thanks for the name."

"Thanks for the shirt," she says. "And tell those bastards upstairs to bring me a damn sandwich. I'm starving."

"I'll see what I can do."

ANGELIC BAZAAR IS on Sunset Boulevard near La Cienega in West Hollywood. From the outside, there's nothing special about it. Look through the window and you'll see the usual big-ticket trash that litters most antique and decorator shops in this pricey part of town. Old dressers and armoires. Stand mirrors. Beds and adorable little side tables, perfect for a Waterford crystal vase full of dead flowers. It lives up to its name though. There are more angel sculptures, figurines, and paintings here than at a Vatican garage sale. Enough that it feels like the place is trying to overcompensate for something. Like maybe a connection to the Wormwood faction. A BE BACK SOON sign hangs on the front door, so there's not much for me to do but wait for Rose to get back.

Across from the Bazaar are a café and a bar. It's just after noon and I wouldn't mind a drink, but I'd rather get it at Bamboo House. So, I head to the café. It's not bad inside. The decorations are what I think they call midcentury. Kidney-shaped tables and bright fake-leather swivel chairs. Lighting fixtures that look like stars and UFOs. The Jetsons would feel right at home here. The place is so ridiculous that even I don't hate it. I'm dressed in the young-executive Beverly Hills clothes Sandoval's people gave me, and I've disguised my low-rent face with a glamour, meaning there's a reasonable chance that the café will let me stay.

I still have some of Sinclair's money in my pocket so when a waitress comes over and doesn't throw me out I order coffee. That seems to confuse her and she starts naming alternatives.

"Maybe you mean an Americano? Maybe a flat white or a macchiato?"

"Those all sound like wrestling holds. I just want coffee."

"Maybe an espresso?"

"Wait. I know what that is. It's the one in little cups, right?"

She laughs. I think she thinks I'm flirting. I guess that's better than thinking I'm crazy and giving me the bum's rush.

"Yes," she says, still smiling at me. "It's the one in the little cups."

"Great. I'll take four of those."

She raises one eyebrow at me.

"Let me guess. You're a late riser or you tied one on last night."

"Yes and yes. I had a little accident and my hosts didn't have Vicodin, so I had to make do with bourbon."

"Sounds a lot like my house. Only we *always* have Vicodin around."

"If I'd known that I would have come in earlier."

She puts a chipped red fingernail on the table for a second, then holds out her hand.

"I'm Alyx," she says.

I shake her hand.

"Hi. I'm Stark."

Shit. I should have made something up. I really *do* need coffee. Or was I just caught off guard by talking to someone I don't want to strangle?

"Nice to meet you," she says.

"You too."

"Do you work around here?"

"I'm just back in town and sort of freelancing for now."

She screws up her face in a parody of deep concentration.

"Let me guess. You're either a graphic designer or you do something in tech."

"Are guns tech?"

Her mouth comes open.

"Oh my god. Are you a bodyguard?"

"Something like that."

"That's so hot."

"Thanks, I guess."

Alyx looks around the café.

"This is just my day job, you know. I'm really an artist."

"Really. What kind of stuff?"

"Hot-rod and old-school pinup stuff mostly. Sometimes I do band posters and flyers."

She's wearing a sleeveless T-shirt and her arms are heavily tattooed with old flash designs. She points to a mermaid and a medusa lounging in a martini glass.

"These are both my designs," she says.

"They're great. Do you have a site where I could see more?"

"Sure. I'll get you the info," Alyx says, then points at me. "That's four espressos, right?"

"Exactly."

"Be back in a second."

She goes to the barista and says something to him that I don't think is my order. He looks in my direction and whispers something to her. They both laugh. I'm not sure what that means. Did I just get made as an impostor in my nice clothes and fake face? I'm tempted to leave, but the BE BACK SOON sign is still hanging on the door to Angelic Bazaar. If I leave, my only choices are to loiter on the street like a high school weed dealer or steal a car and hope I can find parking close enough to keep an eye on the store. I decide to stay in the café for now and hope that whatever it was they were laughing about doesn't involve anyone spitting in my coffee.

Alyx comes back a couple of minutes later with two cups of thick coffee.

"Two double espressos," she says.

"Perfect."

I take a twenty from my pocket and hold it out to her. She puts up her hands.

"They're on the house."

"Do you treat all your customers like this?"

"It wasn't me," she says with a grin. "It was Jason."

She points back to the barista. He waves, so I wave back.

"He's got a thing for bad boys."

"What makes you think I'm bad?"

She nods down at me.

"You've got a glove on one hand, so either it's hurt or you're hiding an identifying mark."

"Maybe I'm just into Michael Jackson."

"And your wrist. Are those handcuff marks?"

I look down and, yes, my damn wrist is still bruised.

"It is, but it was all a misunderstanding."

"So, it wasn't recreational handcuff play . . . ?"

"Recreational for someone, but not for me."

"Too bad," Alyx says. "Handcuffs go great with Vicodin."

I sip my espresso. It's thick as molasses and the caffeine would revive a dozy rhino. I just wish I could taste the damn thing.

"An artist and a doctor. Is there anything you don't do?"

"Not much," she says, pulling a card from her pocket. She puts it on the table. "That's my card. It has my site on it."

Above the URL is a color drawing of a topless girl in leathers on a motorcycle. The banner underneath reads "Kiss and Kill."

"Very nice," I say.

Alyx cocks her head.

"It's a self-portrait."

I can't help smiling at that.

"You like bikes?" I say. "Too bad I didn't ride mine."

"What kind is it?"

Interesting question. I can't really tell the truth—that it was made by Hellion craftsmen when I was the Devil and I drove it all the way back from Hell. But it would be fun to say.

"It's custom. Modeled it on a '65 Electra Glide."

"The moment you started talking I knew you were a Harley guy."

"Is that a good thing?"

"As long as you're not like those rich guys down on Melrose who only drive on the weekends in the city."

"I hate those guys."

"Me too."

She waits a beat before saying, "So, when can I see it?"

"The bike?"

That's a really good question. Where *is* the Hellion hog? I left it at Max Overdrive, but that was a year ago. It could be anywhere by now.

I say, "It needs work before I can take it out again."

I look out the window at Angelic Bazaar, but the damn sign hasn't moved.

"What do you ride, Alyx?"

"A Ducati Monster 797. Is that the wrong answer, Mr. Harley?"

"Like I said, it isn't a real Harley. And Ducatis are nice bikes."

"Then you should let me take you out for a ride sometime. Just until you get your Harley back."

"Alyx," calls Jason, the barista.

She turns and he points to other customers who've come in since we started talking.

"Shit," Alyx says. "I've got to go. Check out my site."

"Thanks. I will."

As she moves to another table, she says, "And whatever you do, don't look at the back of the card."

I take a sip of coffee and flip the card. There's a phone number there. I put it in my shirt pocket.

What is it about this face and these clothes? Alyx was nice to me, and so was the barista. Carlos was nice. So was the girl at Donut Universe. Although, come to think of it, I wasn't using a glamour that night, so she was nice to my real face, which is just as puzzling. But really, it's moments like this one with Alyx that make me question my place back in this world. Who am I supposed to be? When I look like myself I tend to scare small dogs and cops. Even Sandoval couldn't stand the sight of me and she's with Wormwood. Who knows what kind of sick shit she's seen over the years. Candy thinks I look all right, which is the only thing that really matters. I don't know what Alessa thinks or what Candy has told her about me. How could she explain all my scars? "His mom swaddled him in burlap and razor wire when he was a baby . . ."

What am I supposed to be now that I'm back? What if Candy doesn't want me anymore? Am I going to spend the rest of my life wearing this fake Steve McQueen face, going through the world like somebody I'm not? What I am isn't much, but at least it's real. Did I come back to live a lie for the rest of my life?

I sip my espresso and watch the traffic on Sunset. No one goes near Angelic Bazaar. I check the boomerang-shaped clock over where they prepare the coffee. I've been here a half hour. Atticus Rose is really stretching the definition of "Be Back Soon."

I finish the second double espresso and regret it immediately. It leaves me wanting to run around and throw furniture—but in a good way. Not good stakeout behavior.

Alyx notices that I'm done with my coffee and comes over.

"You went through those fast. You want another double?"

"Yes, but I already want to bench-press that bus out there, so I probably shouldn't. What do you have with less caffeine?"

"Everything," she says. "Literally everything here has less caffeine than what you just drank."

"Can you narrow it down from everything?"

"Sit tight. I'll get you something."

As she moves off, I check the Glock in my suit jacket. I don't know why I do it. Nervous energy. The same energy that makes me check the black blade in a pocket I've torn in the other side of the jacket. If Rose doesn't get here soon, I'm going to be even harder on him than I'd planned. It's Saturday and I technically have until midnight to find and kill the faction's board of directors. I know if I can find them, I can do it no matter how many guards they have or what hoodoo they're using. But right now I'm sitting with the coffee jitters and they're winning because every twitch I feel is another second off my life.

What if I fuck this up? What will it be like to rot? Will it hurt? Rotten meat smells bad, but if you're the rotten meat can you smell yourself? How long will it take for me to fall apart? Will I decompose from the edges in? My fingers and toes coming off, and then my hands and feet? I bet I'll be conscious for the whole thing. That's how this stuff always works. The moment you want to be out of it, that's the moment when you're most alert. The worst part is that Sandoval and the others will get to watch it happen. I bet they'll even chopper Roger in for a ringside seat. Rose better be here soon or I'm going to force-feed him every goddamn angel in his shop.

A few minutes later, Alyx comes back. She sets down a plate and a tall glass.

She says, "Here's some orange juice and a grilled cheese sandwich. Citrus is good for the caffeine shakes. So is food. I see you keep looking out the window. Who are you waiting for?"

I take a sip of the juice. There's no taste, but the pulp feels good going down.

"You see that store over there? Angelic Bazaar? I'm waiting for the guy who runs it."

Alyx crosses her arms and frowns.

"Oh. Him. He comes in here sometimes. Kind of weird. Always orders a latte and three chocolate chip cookies. Then he puts about nine packets of sugar in his latte. And he never tips. Not once."

I glance out the window.

"Some rich people are like that."

"Are you going to bodyguard him?"

"Can you keep a secret?"

She leans in closer. "Not boring ones, so make yours good."

"I'm going to do the opposite of bodyguarding."

She straightens up again.

"I said it before, and don't think I'm hitting on you—although I am—but that's hot."

"And it's our secret, right?"

"Totally."

"Even from Jason."

"Aww."

I look over at him slaving away at the steamed milk machine.

"You can tell him when I'm gone. By then, it won't matter who knows."

"It's a deal."

I push a twenty at her.

"And this time you have to take it. I'm not paying you. I'm bribing you to keep my secret."

She picks it up and presses it to her chest.

"I feel so dirty."

"Not as dirty as he's going to feel."

She gestures to my pocket.

"You looked at the back of my card?"

"I did."

"Good. Call me or I'll hunt you down like a dog."

Flirting has been fun, but now I'm starting to not like it so much.

"I should be straight with you. I don't normally look like this. At all. These aren't my clothes. Hell, this isn't even my face. I know that sounds weird, but it's the truth."

Alyx folds the twenty the long way and holds it to her upper lip like a mustache.

"So, you're in disguise. We're all in disguise."

"But I'm *really* in disguise."

"Okay, Danger Man," she says, folding the twenty into a paper airplane. "Just remember one thing."

"What?"

"I'll hunt you like a dog."

I hold up my orange juice.

"Thanks for the caffeine cure."

I take my time with the juice and sandwich. When I'm done, I'm feeling better. But Rose still hasn't shown up and I'm getting sick of looking at his damn BE BACK SOON sign. I look at the café's boomerang clock. I've been here almost two hours. If I stay I'm going to feel obligated to keep eating and drinking just to pay for my seat, and it's hard to be scary during an interrogation when you have to piss.

I wipe my mouth on a paper napkin and get up. Stare at the store for one more minute hoping for some kind of activity.

Nothing.

Fuck this.

Alyx intercepts me on my way to the door.

"Going to do some unbodyguarding?" she says.

"That's the plan."

She looks away, then back at me.

"Look, I hope I wasn't too weird or anything earlier. It's just that, believe it or not, we don't get that many interesting people in here. I mean, yes, we get lots of artists and musicians and stuff, but they can be such a pain in the ass. And anyway, it was nice meeting you."

I look at her with my fake face and want to tell her that she didn't meet anything like the real me.

"Thanks. It was great meeting you too. And, no, you weren't too weird. You're about as charming as it gets, which, now that I say it out loud, sounds like something an idiot would write in your high school yearbook. That means I should get going."

"As far as idiots go, you did all right."

"Thanks. See you around, Alyx."

"You know you will. Hunt you like a dog, Stark. Like a dog."

The sun is high in the sky as I jaywalk across Sunset to Angelic Bazaar. There's a Japanese restaurant next door with a small parking lot. At one end of the lot is a billboard. Behind the base of the billboard, there's a nice shadow. I step through and come out in the back of Angelic Bazaar. Atticus Rose's office is nearby.

It's like the shop. All old furniture and plush sofas, maybe a little more worn than the stuff out front for sale. There's a too-large statue of the archangel Michael on a corner of his desk. I never liked Michael, and since he tried to kill me, I like him even less. I climb on Rose's desk and turn Michael around so that he's facing the wall. I don't like staring at his rear end much either, but it's better than that smug face. Seriously, what the hell is wrong with archangels? They're all crazy in one way or another, and I'm saying that as the son of an archangel—Uriel. At least he never tried to kill me. Hell, in his own fucked-up way, he even tried to help me understand who I am. But like the mortal father who raised me, he didn't stick around long. Although he had a better excuse. He was murdered. The whole archangel thing depresses me. This whole store depresses me. But Atticus Rose is a Tick-Tock Man. He's not just selling end tables to the Martha Stewart crowd. Where's his workshop? I know that whatever he's making for the faction will be awful. Maybe awful enough that it's an excuse to kill him. But not until he tells me where to find his bosses. My time is running out. Howard better be as good as Sandoval says he is. If I end up back in Hell for good, I'll wait for them until they die and, like Alyx said, hunt them down like dogs.

On a table, there's a crystal dish full of dried rose petals. I dump them on the floor and light up a Sherman, flicking the ashes into the dish. Candy taught me that kind of civilized behavior. I might still be a monster, but I can be a tidy one.

I'VE KILLED THE whole pack of Shermans by the time I hear the front door open and close. There are a few tentative footsteps into the store.

"Hello?" says Rose.

It's after nine o'clock and I swear I can feel my body starting to curdle. It puts me in a bad mood. I have the light on in his office, so that he'll know exactly where I am.

"All that cigarette smoke. I can smell you back there," he says. "I'm calling the police."

"I wouldn't do that if I were you, Atticus."

He doesn't say anything. I know he's dialing. I go to the door of his office and bark some hoodoo. The phone is up next to his face when it bursts into a mass of shattered plastic and electric sparks. Rose staggers back. Half turns away from me. When he turns back, he has a little pistol in his hand. I step out of the way while barking more hoodoo. He flies back a few feet and the gun goes spinning into some dark corner of the store. When I approach him, Rose doesn't move, but lies there trying to catch his breath. I pull him to his feet and shove him toward his office.

I have hold of the back of his jacket and say, "I want to see your workshop."

"What workshop?" he says. "I send all of my merchandise out for repairs."

"Not *that* workshop. I mean your Tick-Tock Man lair."

He grabs on to a heavy armoire so I have to stop to keep from running him over.

"How do you know about that?"

"I know all about you, Atticus. I chased you underground once. Make me chase you again and the only underground you'll see is me shoveling dirt on you in your grave."

He whirls around and looks at me. Stares at me hard.

"I don't know you. What kind of shakedown is this? Do you know who I work for?"

"Sorry. That was rude of me," I say as I let the glamour fade.

"Stark?" he gasps. "You're dead."

"People keep saying that, but here I am. And yes, I know who your bosses are. That's why I'm here. I want to know where to find them."

He gets a funny look on his face. Half snarl and half smile.

"You're out of your mind."

I slap him and shove him against the armoire. Go through his pockets to make sure he doesn't have any more surprises. There's nothing interesting. Keys. Wallet. A pocket watch. Some cash. I throw it all on the floor.

"Show me your workshop."

"No."

"Do it or I'm going to start breaking your fingers so they never heal right. Then try staying in the Tick-Tock business."

"Go ahead," he says. "It will hurt, yes. I might even break down and cry. But Wormwood works with some of the most important Sub Rosa in town. They'll perform a healing spell and I'll be working again tomorrow."

"Not if I break them with Hellion hoodoo. Trust me, Atticus. Those posh Bel-Air magicians have never seen the kind of Baleful magic I know."

He nervously rubs his hands together.

"I . . . I can't."

"I'm on kind of a tight schedule here, Atticus. So let's start with something easy: take me to your workshop *now*."

He croaks, "I can't."

"Okay. Let's do it my way."

I bark some Hellion and one of the walls collapses, crushing the furniture and statues underneath.

"Not through there I guess."

I pull down another wall. This one shatters some very old-looking stained glass windows hanging from the ceiling.

"Stop it," he says. "How do I know you won't kill me?"

"Play nice and I'll let you go. It's your bosses I want. And like I said, I'm in a bit of a rush."

He points back to his office.

"The floor in front. Step on the three floorboards nearest the office twice. Then the two next to them three times."

"I'm not in a dancing mood. You do it." I put the black blade into his back and say, "Just don't do anything dumb."

He nods abruptly. Steps on some boards I would have never found. The first twice. The second set, three times. A trapdoor in his office floor opens.

"Lead the way," I say.

There's a short staircase down to a large workshop below the store. It's a chaotic zoo of half-constructed mechanical animals. Some are as small as hummingbirds and some as large as tigers. There are snakes and lizards on one table. Cats, dogs, and candy-colored parakeets on another, some limbless, some with no head. A tank nearby is filled with skinless mechanical fish, all graceful silver muscles and tiny, intricate gears.

Really, it's beautiful. A crazed Santa's workshop full of sinister puppets that will one day be familiars to a horde of upper-crust bastards. If I let Rose live that long.

I push him against one of the tables and pick up what looks like a finished red squirrel. I hold it out to him.

"How do you turn it on?"

He gives me a look like I'm an idiot.

"It's not a fucking Furby. You don't turn it on. Its energy sublimes from a small crystal where the animal's heart would normally be."

"How do I sublime it?"

"Talk to it," he says. "Gently. Like waking a friend."

"Are you fucking with me?"

He reaches for it.

"Give it to me."

He cradles the squirrel in his arm and rubs its small chest with his index finger, all the while cooing at it like it's a baby.

A minute or so later, the squirrel's eyes flutter open. Its paws begin to move. It sits up and looks around. Climbs Rose's arm and perches on his shoulder.

"That's amazing," I say.

"Thank you. The small ones are my favorites. They're the most work but are endlessly charming."

"Does it bite?"

"Never."

"Let me hold it."

I take it off his shoulder and it runs down my arm. I let it hop onto the table where I found it. In the funny herky-jerky way that squirrels move, it sniffs and touches some of the other half-finished familiars. While it's sniffing a nightingale, I pick up a hammer and smash the squirrel to pieces. Gears, fur, and claws fly across the table and onto the floor.

I hold the hammer out to Rose.

"That's you in about thirty seconds. Give me a name and a location."

He stares down at the remains of his adorable red rat.

"Look at me. A name."

"I can't. No matter what you do to me, they'll do worse."

I smash the hammer on the table.

"I'm so tired of hearing that from you faction people. Don't tell me they'll do worse because you don't know what I'll do unless I get a name quick."

He looks at me.

"You are on a schedule, aren't you? How interesting."

I smash a raven and a rattlesnake.

He puts his hands on the table behind him and leans back.

"The answer is still no."

Rose doesn't just manufacture animals. The last time I ran

into him, he'd even created a few pretend humans. They hurt people. They killed them. I don't like him for it.

I bring the hammer down hard on his left hand.

He screams and cradles his crushed mitt to his chest.

"You bastard," he says. "You fucking animal."

I point to him with the hammer.

"That hand they can fix in the hospital. The next one I'll smash with hoodoo and you'll never use it again."

He half-walks, half-stumbles down the rows of tables. I follow him, resting the hammer on my shoulder.

He stops at a table set off by itself against the far wall.

"Do any of these look familiar?" he says.

The creatures on this table aren't like the others. None of them are from this world; they come from other dimensional planes of existence. Most I've only seen in drawings.

When he sees me staring, Rose says, "These are my most prized creations. Not even captains of industry or the governor could afford one. These go to heads of state."

I tap the hammer in my hand.

"Or heads of Wormwood."

"Exactly," he says.

There's a scaly, white boa constrictor with a face like a boiled baby's. A beautiful bare-breasted sphinx. With her eyes closed, it looks like she's asleep. At the far end of the table is a small manticore. You see them all over Hell, although they're usually bigger. It has a craggy humanlike head, the body of a lion, and a thick scorpion tail.

I rest the hammer on the table near the sphinx.

"What if I smash every one of these? It won't just be money you're out, will it? Important people are waiting for these."

"Very important," he says. "Very dangerous."

I hold the head of the hammer and use the wooden butt to push the sphinx slowly to the edge of the table.

Rose smiles nervously at me.

"Please don't."

One more push. The sphinx falls and explodes. It's a terrible sight. It really was lovely.

Rose puts his good hand to his mouth. I think he's on the verge of tears. His legs are shaking. He leans his back against the wall.

"What time is it?" he says. "You took my watch."

"I don't have one either."

He leans his head against the wall. Stares at the ceiling, thinking.

"Well, I came in around nine and you've been manhandling me for, what, half an hour?"

"Something like that."

"In that case, I will give you a name," he says.

"What is it?"

"Bruno Morrell. Do you know him?"

"Should I?"

He lowers his head and looks at me. If he was tearing up before, he's calm now.

"If you work for the false Wormwood you must know Eva Sandoval."

"Know her and hate her. Why?"

"Because by now, there's nothing you can do to keep Bruno from killing the bitch."

There's a ball-peen hammer that I missed down at his end of the table. Before I know what he's doing, he uses it to smash the manticore's human head. The creature jerks once, and the scorpion tail snaps out—burying itself in Rose's heart. He's dead before he hits the floor.

There isn't a single decent shadow on this side of the room. I sprint past the birds and cats and dive into a good one near the stairs.

I COME OUT in Sandoval's office, but it's empty. I run out into the shot-up foyer, but it's empty too. Voices drift from a room on my right. I pull the Glock and hold it by my side. Listen for another second, then head in.

All of them are there—Sandoval and Sinclair, Howard, and the roaches. They're drinking coffee and eating croissants in a kitchen as large as the whole main floor of Max Overdrive. Everyone looks up when I burst in. Everyone is chatting, except for Sandoval, who's looking at papers spread out over a comically large cutting board. Sinclair is on one side of her and on the other side is a younger man. He's clean-cut and drably handsome, like a TV game show host. He must be one of the roaches, but I'm not sure. Aside from Sandra, I never paid enough attention to them to tell them apart. I stand there by the door looking stupid.

Sandoval looks up at me.

"Why can't you ever enter a room like a normal person? Did you do what I asked?"

I ignore her. Grab a croissant from the table and throw it at the crowd on the other side.

"Catch, Bruno."

People are creatures of habit, slaves to their impulses and reflexes. Tell someone it's raining on a sunny day and ninety-nine times out of a hundred they'll look at the sky. Tell someone wearing loafers that their shoe's untied and they still can't help but look down. No one likes getting hit in the face. Toss something at someone and they'll try to get out of the way or grab it. Always.

Bruno tries to grab the croissant. He's the game show host, and too far away for me to grab. I snap the Glock up and fire, but he's already figured out his mistake and dived behind Sandoval. He gets a choke hold on her and drags her back, grabbing a butcher knife from the counter. He tries to stab her in the side, but Sandoval puts her arm out and the blade goes all the way through. She screams and spins away, exposing just enough of Bruno's side that I get two good shots off. Both into his stomach. I don't want him dead yet. I want him alive, awake, and in pain. Panicked and bleeding out, he's going to tell me what Atticus Rose wouldn't.

When I get around the table, he's on the floor oozing blood. Sandoval is next to him. I'm waiting for someone to help her or for her to faint and get out of my way, but she's no different than Bruno. Sandoval is as much a creature of reflex as him and when a good part of your professional life has been about control, murder, and revenge, you act accordingly. Screaming like an air-raid siren, she yanks the butcher knife from her arm and slams it down into Bruno's chest.

I yell, "No!" but she doesn't hear me or doesn't care. She puts her weight on the blade, driving it in farther. I grab Bruno and shove her away. Howard is on her immediately, wrapping a hand towel around her arm to stanch the bleeding.

I drag Bruno to safety, but it's already too late. With the

bullets in his stomach, a knife was just too much for his system to handle. He's dead.

It takes me a couple of seconds to clock that Sandoval is shrieking at me.

"What the hell was that?" she says.

Howard holds on to the towel, which is already soaking through with her blood. Everyone else has their phone out, calling whatever passes for 911 in Wormwood world.

I shout back at her.

"Why did you kill him? He had information. Shit you wanted."

She looks at me hard.

"You haven't killed them yet, have you? Do you even know where the faction is? What the hell have you been doing all day?"

I drop Bruno on the floor. Once again, I'm covered in another idiot's blood.

"I've been working, not standing around the kitchen having snacks with the enemy. Goddammit. He was my last link to the faction."

She looks at the wound in her arm and then at Bruno.

"He's dead?" she says. "Howard, is there anything you can do to revive him?"

He looks at me and Bruno's blood, spread out like wings around him.

"I'm sorry, Eva. My work takes time and he's lost so much blood. By the time I could bring him back, his brain would be too damaged to be of use."

Sandoval looks at me.

"What about you, Stark? You know Hellion tricks. Bring him back."

I take some paper towels and wipe as much blood off my hands as I can.

The truth is there *is* something I could do. The Metatron's Cube ritual. Powerful blood magic. But to do it, I have to come very close to death. This time though there's a catch: I'm half-dead already. If I slit my wrists and drift even deeper into death, I don't know if I'll be able to come back again.

I look at Sandoval.

"No. There's nothing I can do. There was one chance to find the faction and you fucked it up."

Even wounded, if Sandoval was a wolverine I can tell that she'd already have one of my legs off and would be working overtime on the second. She's used to getting what she wants and seeing that she's not going to this time, she radiates a primal hate so pure that you could bottle it and sell it as napalm.

Sandoval's towel has soaked through. Sandra hands Howard a fresh one and as he cinches it around Sandoval's arm, she grits her teeth and winces but refuses to make a sound. When it's over, she picks up the bloody towel in her good hand and throws it at me.

"You let that bastard do this," she says. "You wanted him to kill me."

I drop the paper towels on the floor.

"Don't be stupid. I just *saved* your life. And I'm still trying to get to the faction and complete our deal."

"There is no deal!" she screams.

I look at the kitchen clock.

"It's barely after ten. I have two hours until midnight."

She looks at me and screams again. "There is no *fucking* deal. No bank account. No money. No Howard. There's *nothing.* You wanted Bruno to kill me, so now I'm going to watch you die."

I go to Sandoval and stand over her. "That's a really bad idea, Eva. No one likes a fibber."

She smiles at Howard, then at me.

"Go on then. Beg me. Beg me for a little more time or another chance. Beg me and I'll let Howard make your decay easier. From what he tells me, without the right potions the process is pure agony. Hours of it. Beg me, Stark."

"I have two hours left. You're not going to cheat me out of them."

"They're gone. You forfeited them the moment you let Bruno touch me. For all I know, you were working together."

"That's insane. Why would I do that?"

"Because you're deranged," she says. "You said it to me in the bowling alley: 'I thought deranged was why you wanted me.' I suppose I did at the time. I should have known there was no way to be reasonable with someone like you."

"Listen—"

"It's over, Stark. You failed me and yourself, so you're dead. And when you're gone and the doctors have stabilized me, I'm going to come home and personally slit the throat of that faction whore downstairs."

In the distance, there's the sound of sirens coming up the hill.

I might have played the madman a bit too well. Sandoval is in shock and scared—as scared of me as she is of the faction. There's not going to be any talking her out of her decision. Not now anyway, and I don't have time to wait for her to come around.

Still, I have the Glock and the black blade in my jacket. I could kill every one of these pricks and make a run for it. But what will that get me? How long will I last? Between the arena and L.A., I've been stabbed, shot, burned, poisoned, blown up, and run down by cars and Hell beasts as big as cars. I was once almost snapped clean in half by the claws of a giant crablike thing. A couple of times, I've held my stomach together to keep my intestines from spilling out. But I've never decayed to death. If Sandoval is even half right it will be the worst thing I've ever been through, and I've been to Fresno.

A second later, and the sirens are right outside. Bright red lights strobe against the kitchen windows as medics bang on the front door. The roaches scuttle out to let them in. When the others turn to watch, I make my move.

I shove Sandoval out of the way, grab Howard, and haul him into a shadow.

WE COME OUT on Las Palmas, across the street from Max Overdrive.

Howard's head swivels back and forth like a hyperactive pigeon's.

"What happened? Where are we?" he says.

"Somewhere it's just you and me and you can fix me up like you were going to tonight."

"I don't have my equipment," he says. "My potions or books."

"You mean you don't have Sandoval's permission. You don't need it anymore."

"Yes, I do. I can't do anything without her say-so."

He tenses and takes a step into what he hopes will be a spirited dash away from me. I punch him in the solar plexus. He goes down sputtering.

"You were going to say 'You don't know what Wormwood is like. Crossing them is worse than horseradish on ice cream.' I've been hearing that from you assholes for days. Worry about Wormwood later. Right now, I'm the only monster you should be concerned about."

I try to pull him to his feet, but he's dry-heaving and can't get his legs under him. Crouching, I toss him over my shoulder and carry him across the street to the store. The lights are off and I don't see anyone, so I shadow-walk him inside.

When we're there, I dump him on the floor between the Hammer horror movies and Giallo sections. He lies there like a pile of British beans. I need time to think. The one thing he said that concerns me is that he doesn't have the equipment he needs to put me back together. In theory I could take him to Sandoval's and have him get the gear, then take him somewhere safe to do the procedure. But how can I trust him to get the right tools? He could grab something that would kill me instantly. It's what I'd do. I'm reasonably sure that if I could get the things together, I could make him put me right, but I don't know what he needs. I need to find someone who has that kind of knowledge. Vidocq is the only person I can think of who might. But if I go to him, not only will he have to deal with my being back and ready to check out again, it will get him on Wormwood's bad side. I'm not sure I can do that. That's problem one.

Problem two is that until I can figure out problem one, I need somewhere to stash Howard. I suppose I could leave him in the Room, but that makes me nervous. Even if I sealed all the functioning doors, he's a necromancer and that means he has a good knowledge of all sorts of hoodoo. Plus, he's smart. He might just figure a way out. I could tie him up or knock him unconcious, but I still don't trust him in the Room. What if he knows a way to keep me out? Then I'll be truly fucked. No, I need somewhere on Earth to put him. Somewhere he doesn't know and where no one is going to bother him.

There's a footfall on the stairs from the upstairs apartment. I start to grab Howard when I hear a *clank*. I know the sounds of that walk.

A few seconds later Kasabian comes down. He isn't scared when he sees me this time. He just looks exhausted.

"What are you doing here, man?" he says. "And who the fuck is that on the floor?"

Howard has raised himself up on one elbow and is looking around the store. I give him a little kick and he doubles up again.

"This is Howard. He's a necromancer and he's going to fix me. Make me fully alive again."

"Oh yeah? Well, good for you. Why is he here?"

"I kind of kidnapped him from Wormwood."

"And you brought him to us? What the hell for?"

I go over to him.

"I need someplace to stash him while I figure some things out."

"No." Kasabian shoves me and sticks a finger in my face. "Just *no*. You and the corpse fucker can get your asses right the fuck out."

"Listen to me—"

"No," he says again. "I knew the moment I saw you the other night that you were going to make our lives miserable again."

"It would just be for a day."

Kasabian puts his head down on the counter. Finally he says, "If you care about Candy or Max Overdrive or even me, please, take your friend out of here and don't come back."

"I'm coming back. I'm going to be alive again soon."

"Fine," he shouts, getting back up from the counter. "Then come back when you're alive and not dragging in trouble with you."

"You're overreacting."

"I'm not. I'm scared. You want to bring Wormwood around here? You stupid prick."

"They're never going to know."

"Yes, they are," says Howard. "I'm going to tell them."

We both look at him.

He says, "I'm going to tell them everything about this place. Max Overdrive, is it? That shouldn't be hard for them to find."

I walk back and crouch down next to him.

"What makes you think you'll live that long?"

"Death threats?" he says. "Now I'm definitely going to help you. You've made it so enticing."

"There are worse things than death."

He smiles at me.

"Damnation? Nice try. That's the very first provision in my contract with Wormwood. Exemption from damnation. You can't scare me with Hell."

"I could just make you wish you were dead. I mean, look at Kasabian."

He says, "Thanks, man. Bring me in as your worst-case scenario. Fuck you too."

"I have the black blade. I can cut off your head and keep you alive forever."

"And how am I supposed to perform your resurrection without a body? No. You don't scare me, Mr. Stark. You might as well send me back."

"I'll kill you before I send you back. If I'm going to die, so are you."

"And we're back to death threats, which give me no incentive at all to help you," he says. "You're exactly the type of bastard who'd let me do my work and then kill me out of spite."

"What if I took some kind of blood oath? One of those ones that will kill me if I welch on the deal?"

"That's a good try, and in different circumstances, I might accept the offer. But not with you."

"Why?"

"Because you're deranged. You said it yourself."

"He's got you there," says Kasabian. "You really are a fruit bat."

I look from him back to Howard.

"Offer me another deal," he says. "See how far that gets you."

He's right. There's no way I'm going to convince him. Not now, at least.

I whisper some Hellion hoodoo and Howard falls over with a thud.

Kasabian says, "Oh shit. Did you kill him? We don't need dead people around here."

"Calm down. He's just unconscious. I'm going to keep him like that until I figure things out."

"No. Get him out of here."

I look at the back of the store.

"Does Candy still use the storage room for band practice?"

"No. It's just full of junk."

"Perfect."

Kasabian follows me as I carry Howard to the storage room.

"Please don't do this. I'm asking you to be a person for one minute and get him out of here."

I dump Howard behind a box of old skin flicks. The store doesn't even carry those anymore, so no one is likely to look there.

I turn around to Kasabian.

"Listen. I have maybe twenty-four hours before I melt like a Morlock in *The Time Machine*."

"I love that movie," he says. "You mean the original, right? Not the stupid remake."

"Of course I mean the original. I always mean the original."

"Yeah. At least you're smart there. Now get him out of my store!"

"I'm not lying to you. I'm not here to trick you or fuck with you. This is me as fucked up and scared as I've ever been. I only have one chance at staying in the world. You don't want me around and maybe Candy doesn't want me around either, but I have to be human enough again to have that conversation. I mean it, Kas. Help me with this. And after, if Candy tells me to take off, you'll never see me or hear from me again."

He thinks that over for a minute.

"That's something I've wanted for a long time."

"Then you'll do it?"

"Twenty-four hours."

I waggle my hand in the air.

"Maybe a little longer. I'm only going to get one shot at this."

"And if it doesn't work out, what happens to Sleeping Beauty back there?"

"Go to Vidocq. Get a sprig of Dragon's Tooth root, mix it with some whiskey, and pour it down his throat. It'll erase the last month of his memories. Everything. Then just put him on a bus and let him ride around until his brain works enough to get home."

Kasabian looks at me hard.

"If Candy gives you the boot, you're gone this time?"

"Forever."

"And even if she doesn't, you're not moving back in here."

"I promise."

"It is nice watching you beg," he says.

"Then I can leave him?"

He takes a deep breath.

"Yeah. Okay. Just one more thing . . ."

There's a scrape as the front door opens. I don't wait to see who it is but walk into a shadow. All I hear as I disappear is Candy saying, "Hi, Kas. Who are you talking to?"

I'm long gone before he can answer.

SANDOVAL'S MANSION IS dead quiet when I get back. I come out in my room and change into my regular clothes. Put the

Glock, the Colt, the black blade, and the vellum scroll in my coat. On my way to the bowling alley, I hear a couple of voices from Sandoval's office. One man and one woman. But there's nothing urgent in their voices, and I have a feeling they're a couple of roaches left behind to watch the place while Sandoval and her entourage take a gold-plated ambulance ride to a Wormwood clinic. Maybe Sandoval and Roger can share a room. Do puzzles and go to physical therapy together. Maybe discover that they both secretly love Jell-O. Have a real TV-movie bonding experience.

Rest up, you two. You're both going to be dead soon.

I knock on the door to the bowling alley and go in without waiting for a response. Marcella sits at the scoring table, relaxed and bored.

"I knew it was you," she says. "The others don't knock."

"Mom believed in manners."

"Like dragging people to Hell when you're mad?"

"No. The polite part is when I bring them back after they get the message."

She stands up. Stretches.

"I'm still not sure Mom would approve, Boy Scout."

"I always was a disappointment. How about you?"

"I was on the disappointing side too. Until I found Wormwood."

"This Wormwood or the faction?"

She comes over, rolling up the sleeves on the shirt I gave her.

"There's only one true Wormwood and it's not the one upstairs."

"Right. It's the one looking for, what did you say?"

Marcella raises her chin slightly and says, "Salvation."

"I don't know what salvation means to them, but I bet there's a lot of tentacles and screaming involved."

"You couldn't be more wrong. It's a holy thing we're doing."

"I swear to everything that shits and crawls through Hell, if you say it's a crusade, I'm going to leave you here."

She looks me in the eye.

"Sensitive about righteous people doing righteous work?"

"No. I just spent a year on a crusade. I'm sick of lunatics telling me there's absolution and ice cream over the next hill."

"You just had the wrong leader," she says.

"And you're one holy-roller inch from me leaving you here with the fuckers upstairs."

She glances at the door, then at me.

"Where are we going?" she says.

"Disneyland, to ride the teacups. Now come on."

I take her arm and haul her toward a shadow. She tries to pull away, but I'm heavier, stronger, and a lot more pissed off right now.

"Fuck you," she yells, and tries to claw my face. I push her out of the shadow on the other side.

Marcella lands on her ass at the corner of Hollywood and Vine.

She looks around, a little stunned. I put out my hand to help her up and she knocks it away. Grabs a light pole and pulls herself to her feet.

"What kind of trick is this?" she says. "Is this another part of Hell?"

"Yes, but not in the way you mean."

She gives me a funny look, halfway between fury and

blind panic. I get a twenty from my pocket and slap it into her hand. She still doesn't get it.

I say, "I'm letting you go. That twenty won't take you far in a cab, but it will get you out of the neighborhood. There's a couple of old pay phones on Sunset just past Fairfax. I don't know if they still work, but they're worth a shot. Call your people. Go home or wherever the fuck you assholes hold your tent revivals."

She stands there like a stunned deer.

"If this is a trick it's going to make your mom cry, Boy Scout."

I turn around.

"No tricks. See you around, Marcella."

"Why?" she says.

"Because you're Wormwood, which makes you garbage. But if I left you back there, everything they want to do to me they'd do to you. I can't stop them right now, but I can take that away from them, at least."

I leave her there. I don't know if she gets in a cab or goes for pizza. I just walk away.

Ivar Avenue is a block west. I head up to Bamboo House of Dolls. I need time to think. Along the way, I put on a glamour. Everybody likes this face. Who am I to argue with that?

The bar is buzzing when I get inside. It's nice to see that the place can still pull a crowd, at least on the weekends. There are more Lurkers tonight, too. Some blue-skinned Ludere and a table of always-loud, always-drunk Nahual beast men. Being in a crowded bar alone can be depressing, especially if it's one you're used to spending time in with friends. There's only one good reason to ever come to a bar on the weekend by yourself, and that's because no matter how crowded it gets, there's always one lone, sad seat at the bar that no one will take. It's an unconscious thing. No normal person will touch the seat because on some animal level, they know that it's reserved for loners and losers too broke or pathetic to even pay for companionship. A perfect place for me tonight.

Carlos gives me a nod and a pitying half smile when he sees me.

"Good to see you back. Jack Daniel's, right?"

I say, "Right on the money," and put my last twenty on the bar.

Carlos disappears for a couple of minutes. I'm sitting quietly, trying to listen to the music, but it's too loud, and anyway, my brain is running on overdrive trying to process the last few hours.

I'm going to die soon unless I can convince the one asshole in the world who knows how to fix me that I'm not going to kill him when he's through. It doesn't help that I had a somewhat colorful reputation before I died. And it helps even less that all Howard has seen me do since I've been back is kick the shit out of Roger and blow holes in Bruno. If I was him, I wouldn't trust me either. So how do I get him to work some magic on me? What I need is a heavyweight psychic. Someone who can get in Howard's mind and convince him that fixing me is the best idea he's ever had. And then I need Howard's equipment. Fuck. Even if I took him back to Sandoval's house, could we get everything we need before a herd of Wormwood bulls came charging inside, shooting and ruining everything?

I can't do it. I can't figure a way out of this. I'm fucked.

I'm going to die again. And this time my body will be reduced to bloody chum, so there's no putting me back inside it. I might already be starting to rot.

My right index finger taps nervously on the twenty on the bar. I stop it and look at my hand. Did I get all of Bruno's blood off? I swear my fingertips look darker. I remember the marks on my sides and back I saw in the bathroom mirror. Were those bruises or lividity? I swear, my skin feels looser, like if I gave it a yank, it would come apart like cotton candy. I touch my stomach. The bullet wound *feels* closed, but I'm not sure anymore. If I stood up too quickly, would it rip open again? If it did, I'm sure I could make it through the crowd and outside, but why? Just so I can bleed out in the gutter?

No. This isn't getting me anywhere. I need to slow down and think this through again. Or do I? It might be time to admit that I fucked up in a way there's no getting around. I've died before. I've gone to Hell before. What's the big deal? At least this time I know that Candy and Max Overdrive are doing fine. Even Kasabian is doing all right. Maybe I just need to stop, catch my breath, and appreciate the moment. I still have twenty dollars. If I nurse a couple of whiskies like a rookie, I can make them last an hour. This is probably my last time in Bamboo House of Dolls. I might as well enjoy the moment.

Carlos comes back with my drink and I slide the twenty to him. He picks it up, looks it over, and sets it back down again.

Great. Sinclair slipped me a counterfeit bill. I can't even get a decent drink before I turn into cold beef stew.

I start to get up when Carlos says, "This is the second time you're in here and you still haven't said hello properly."

He slides the bill back to me. I don't touch it.

I say, "What's the right way to say hello?"

He shakes his head, like he's disappointed he can't teach a mollusk to play fetch.

"Asshole, the right way is, 'Hello, Carlos. Pour me an Aqua Regia.'"

I stare at him.

"How the hell did you know?"

He pinches my cheek.

"The pretty-boy face. Whenever you want to look like regular people, you always use that same stupid face. Get rid of it, man. It's giving me the willies."

"I can't. I don't want people to know I'm back. I fucked up and might not be around too much longer."

Someone down the bar signals for a refill. Carlos shoves two beers in front of him and says, "Don't bother me again."

When he comes back over he says, "Were you really dead all this time?"

"Yeah."

He leans in closer, whispering.

"Look, if someone is after you, you can always hide in back."

I take a sip of my drink.

"It's not like that. I'm back but, you see, I'm only fifty percent alive. If I don't fix things, I'm going to be a hundred percent dead again."

Carlos stands back and glances around the room.

"You're nothing but trouble, aren't you?"

"Mom says I'm her special little angel."

"Drink your drink," he says. "I'm closing early."

I grab his arm. "Don't do that, man. You've got a nice crowd in here. This is your living."

"That's right: it's *my* living. And that means I'll run it any way I like."

He throws a switch behind the bar and the jukebox goes quiet. The crowd moans. Carlos stands on a crate behind the bar and whistles, loud and piercing.

He says, "Ladies and gentlemen, thank you for coming, but I need you to finish your drinks and clear your asses out of here. Family emergency."

There are a few "aww"s and more moaning, but everyone does what they're told. The last thing the kind of people who come to a place like Bamboo House want is to get banned. It takes another ten minutes or so for the crowd to pay up and shuffle out the door looking for other, less interesting places to get wasted. A few of them look at me, the one guy not moving. They're wondering if I'm privileged or in trouble. I'm wondering the same thing, but I'm also enjoying the excuse Carlos used to shut the place down. Even if he didn't mean anything by the word "family," it was still nice to hear.

After he hustles the last stragglers out and locks the front door, he looks at me.

"You ready to go?" he says.

"Where?"

"To meet my brother-in-law. The *brujo*."

"You really have a *brujo*? I always thought that was a joke."

"It's not. Get your ass outside and let's see if he can do anything about your ridiculous situation."

I get up slowly, afraid my skin might slide off at any moment.

"Carlos, I don't know what to say. Thank you."

"Shut up. You're going to pay me back plenty when he fixes you. Sandman Slim got the crowds in here before and you're going to do it again when you're better. You're going to sit at the bar, sneer and ignore people, and tell anyone who wants an autograph to go fuck themselves."

"Like old times."

"Damn straight."

I follow him out the back and around the corner to a brilliantly polished red and black 1970 Ford Torino.

Dying or not, I can't help looking it over.

"Carlos, I had no idea."

"That's why I don't park it near the bar. I don't want any drunks puking on it. And if you think for one second about stealing it, I will shoot you in the head myself."

He unlocks the doors and we slide inside on the black vinyl seats.

"I'd never steal this one," I tell him. "But if I live, I'm definitely going to have to steal something like it."

"You're going to live," he says. "You're the only thing that's going to let me throw the damned karaoke machine in the trash. I'll drag your ass out of Hell myself for that." He looks at me. "Now, do what I told you. Get rid of that stupid face."

I drop the glamour.

He says, "That's better. I'm not bringing home Beaver Cleaver."

IT'S ONLY A fifteen-minute ride to Carlos's place. He lives just north and east of the bar, in the Los Feliz area, just off

Franklin Avenue. It's an okay little neighborhood, a mix of old apartment buildings and one- and two-story single-family homes.

He pulls us into a two-car driveway. The other car is a gray Honda Civic. Boring as dirt, but just as polished as the Torino. The house is two floors, done in mission style. It looks like it's from the forties. It could use a little work, but there are desert plants outside that give it a nice, lived-in look. He locks the Torino and sets the alarm before taking us inside.

Like the outside, the living room looks comfortable and lived-in. It's a crazy combination of overstuffed easy chairs surrounded by modern and antique everything else. There's a Victorian desk in the corner, but the coffee table is delta shaped, like the ones at the café. There are stuffed mariachi frogs and a jackalope head on the mantelpiece over a fireplace. Around the room are old gas-station signs and thrift-shop paintings that someone has modified. Robots in old barnyard scenes. UFOs and dancing girls in landscapes.

Carlos smiles, looking at me trying to take it all in.

"Like it?" he says. "Most of it's Ray's. He's a collector, only he can't decide what he collects, so he collects everything."

"I love it," I say.

"Good. Be sure to tell him that when you meet him."

"Is Ray your brother-in-law?"

"The one and only."

Carlos goes to an open door that leads to another room.

"Ray, you home?"

"I'm in the kitchen," comes another voice.

"Well, come on out here. We've got a guest."

"Coming."

Ray comes out a few seconds later, wiping his hands on a small towel. He's in a white shirt and tan pants. In good shape. He's sandy haired and wearing Buddy Holly glasses. Ray could be a computer programmer or an ad writer. Whatever he does for a living, he doesn't look like any *brujo* I've ever seen. He puts out his hand as he comes in.

"Hi. I'm Ray," he says.

We shake.

"I'm Stark."

He walks back to stand by Carlos.

"I know exactly who you are," he says, smiling. "I've seen you at the bar a few times. You're the one who brings in all the trouble *and* all the business."

"See? He knows all about you," says Carlos.

Ray is a little taller than Carlos. He says, "Hi, babe," then leans down and gives him a peck on the lips.

Turning back to me, Ray says, "Let me guess. He told you I'm his brother-in-law."

I nod.

"That's what he tells everyone."

Ray looks at Carlos affectionately.

"For as long as I've known him. He thinks it's hilarious."

"It *is* hilarious," says Carlos. "It's just I'm the only one with a sense of humor."

"Would you like some coffee?" says Ray.

I hold up a hand. "Only if you're having some."

"Three cups it is," he says, and goes back to the kitchen.

Carlos leads me into the living room and we sit down.

I don't say anything for a minute and Carlos says, "So, now you know my dirty little secret. I live with a pack rat."

I say, "Ray seems really nice."

"He is."

Carlos leans his arms on his knees, looking a bit more serious.

"There's certain stuff I don't talk about at the bar," he says. "Stuff like my home life."

"Or your car."

"Especially not my car."

I pause for a minute, trying to phrase the question right.

"Do you think anyone is going to judge you? I mean, especially the crowd at Bamboo House?"

He leans back in the easy chair and nods thoughtfully. Then smiles faintly.

"Easy for you to say, Mr. Can Beat Up Five Guys at Once and Not Break a Sweat. When someone bashes me—and they have—I go to the hospital and have to close the bar for days." He shakes his head. "It's not worth it."

I lean in a little closer.

"You know I'll fucking destroy anyone who tries that, right?"

He nods as Ray comes in with the coffee.

"I appreciate the thought," says Carlos. "But you're not always around. Especially lately. Which brings us to why you're here, so let's just focus on that, okay?"

He looks at Ray and slaps him on the leg.

"I had a feeling this was more than a random social visit," Ray says.

"That it is," says Carlos.

I reach for the coffee.

"You need cream or sugar?" says Ray, but Carlos waves a dismissive hand at me.

"He drinks it black, like some kind of animal. You could probably serve him tar and he wouldn't notice."

"Carlos is right," I say. "Not about the tar. The other part."

Ray takes a sip of his coffee and sets down the cup on the delta table. I drink mine too. I can't taste anything, but I want to be polite.

"Why don't you tell me about why you're here?" says Ray.

Before I can answer, Carlos says. "Despite appearances, Stark here is dead."

Ray cocks his head and looks at me.

"I wouldn't have guessed," says Ray. "You wear death well."

I pick up my coffee but don't drink it.

"It's not quite as bad as Carlos says. I'm only half-dead."

Carlos says, "He didn't exactly say it, but I'm guessing he pissed off a necromancer who was supposed to make him all the way alive."

"That's pretty much it," I say.

"You got to be careful around those people. Necromancers are weird little fucks. I still think you should come by trivia night. Maybe we can find one of those guys to fix you up."

I set down my cup, realizing that it wasn't coffee I wanted, but a cigarette.

"I'd love to, but, what did you say, that's Tuesday or Wednesday? I'm not going to last that long. According to the people who brought me back, I'm only going to have a few more hours."

Ray says, "Maybe I can talk to the necromancer. See what's going on. Maybe convince him to help out. Where is he?"

"Unconscious behind a stack of porn in a closet. I kidnapped him."

Carlos laughs. Ray gives him a look, and I must also be giving him the cockeye, because he says, "I'm sorry, man, but you are such an asshole. You never make anything easy."

I lean back and laugh too. It feels good.

"I thought kidnapping him *was* the easy way," I say. "But all it did was scare him. And we don't have access to his equipment."

Ray is more serious.

"Do you know what kind of spell he used?"

"No. But it's supposed to be something obscure. The people who brought me back were real clear that he was the only one who knew how to do it."

"Let's hope they were exaggerating."

"Can I ask you something?"

"Shoot," says Ray.

"You're not quite like other *brujos* I've met. Though, I suppose that's not a question. I guess I'm curious what kind of *brujo* you are."

Ray hangs his head down for a second, then brings it back up.

"That's another one of Carlos's dumb jokes. I'm not a *brujo*."

"You're *my brujo*," says Carlos.

"Thank you, but that doesn't really help Stark, does it?"

I say, "If you're not a *brujo,* what do you do? Are you Sub Rosa?"

"No," says Ray. "My grandfather was, but he rejected the community and never did any magic. I'm strictly home-schooled by my grandmother. She had a lot of old books, including some of my grandfather's. She taught me things."

Carlos says, "His *abuela.* She was a real *bruja.*"

"That she was."

Ray takes another sip of his coffee.

"Okay, Stark, let's get you upstairs and check you out."

FROM THE OUTSIDE, it's an ordinary room in any suburban house. There are no runes, wards, or charms on the door to indicate that it's anything other than a guest room or where someone ties flies for fun. But it's very different when Ray ushers us inside.

The room immediately reminds me of Vidocq's apartment. Lots of old, stained tables covered in potion ingredients and glass lab equipment for mixing magical brews. There are books everywhere and an old apothecary cabinet the size of a steamer trunk.

I say, "Nice setup," and Ray beams.

"I put some of it together, but most of it comes from my grandparents. My folks got me the alembic and the Erlenmeyer flask for Christmas when I turned eighteen, though. They wanted me to quit all this silly magic business when I was younger, but when they realized I was serious, they were very supportive."

"They sound like good people."

"They are. Are you ready?"

165

"Sure. What do you want me to do?"

"I don't have a real medical examining table, so the conference table in the corner will have to do. Carlos, will you help me with it?"

"Sure."

As they hustle the table to the middle of the cramped room Ray says, "Stark, if we're going to do this right—and I hope you aren't the shy type—I'm going to need you to strip."

Carlos laughs.

"Do you know how many times he's come into the bar covered in blood? Shy he isn't."

"That's a relief."

While they set up the table, I take off my clothes and toss them into a relatively uncluttered area below something that looks like a whiskey still with TV rabbit ears on top.

As Ray drapes a clean sheet across the table I say, "Can I help with anything?"

"Nope. We're just about ready for you to hop on."

Carlos glances over at me while Ray makes final adjustments to the table. The look on Carlos's face isn't reassuring.

"What the fuck have you been doing, man?" he says.

My first thought is that he's never had a really good look at my Kissi arm. Or seen how scarred I really am. There isn't much more than an inch or two of my body that doesn't have some kind of mark on it. Then I look down at myself and see it's so much worse. The bruises I'd hoped would be fading by now are dark and livid. Some are stiff, like hematomas. Others are pulpy soft.

"Shit."

"Shit is right," says Carlos.

Ray looks over to see what Carlos is talking about. He has good control of his face. He's done this before. Ray never looks shocked, but the momentary spike in his heartbeat and his pupils dilating tell me all I need to know.

"Let's get you on the table now," he says. "Lie down faceup."

I climb onto the table and do what he says. Carlos keeps staring.

"Ray has a better bedside manner than you," I tell him.

"I'm sorry," Carlos says. "All those times I made fun of you. I didn't know how fucked up you really were."

"Don't worry about it. The bruises are mostly from the last couple of days."

"I'm not talking about the bruises."

"The scars are old. They help keep me alive. And they remind me of where I came from."

"Remind me to never go there."

"I wouldn't recommend it. Except for the Aqua Regia and Maledictions."

"What are Maledictions?" says Ray.

"The kind of cigarettes we smoked in Hell."

He looks at me.

"You're serious, aren't you?"

"I'm afraid so. Look, if you don't want to do this . . ."

I start to get up, but Ray pushes me back down.

"No. We're doing this, and we're doing it right now."

He goes to the apothecary cabinet and pulls a few things from what, to me, looks like nothing more than a wall of little doors.

I point to it.

"How do you know what goes where?"

"I've been working with this cabinet since I was five. I know every drawer, every door, every inch of it."

Ray comes over to the table with a collection of herbs and some small bottles about the size of shot glasses. He looks at me again and takes a breath.

"You understand that we're still in the diagnosis stage, right?"

"Got it."

"I'm going to put some of these items on your chakra points," he says. "Some of the plants might sting and the glass vessels might be a little cold."

"I've been through worse."

"Goddamn right," says Carlos.

I look at him.

"You're not making me at all self-conscious."

"Sorry. He's the doctor. Also, I guess I thought you were exaggerating when you said you were part dead."

"I wish I was."

Ray begins laying out his magic tchotchkes. He starts at the top of my head, then moves to my forehead, my throat, and works his way all the way down to my groin.

I try to look at him without turning my head.

"What happens now?"

"We wait," he says.

"For?"

"The diagnosis. Try to lie still. Breathe gently in through your nose and out through your mouth."

I do it, feeling slightly silly lying naked in my bartender's home, covered in flowers, nettles, and weird chemical brews. If this was college, I'd swear the whole thing was a hazing ritual. Only it's not, I remind myself. You're dying, so lie still and suck it up.

I'm there for about five minutes. Every minute or so, Ray takes one of the items off a chakra and replaces it with something else. He was right. A few of the items sting. A couple burn slightly. All of the glass is cold and the annoying thing is that it stays cold.

A few more minutes and Ray moves all his diagnosis gear off the table.

"Okay," he says. "You can get dressed."

I roll off the table and while I'm pulling my pants on I say, "Did you figure it out? How to put me back together?"

Ray doesn't say anything. Carlos is with him over at the apothecary table. Both of their backs are to me. I get my boots on and go over.

"What's the verdict, doc?"

Ray shakes his head and says, "I don't know."

Black and wilted flowers shed petals next to bundles of herbs so dry they crumble as we look at them. I pick up one of the shot glasses. Whatever he put inside is laced with tiny pink and purple veins, and has the consistency of curdled milk. I point to the mess.

"It's not supposed to look like that, is it?"

"I'm afraid your necromancer friend was telling the truth," says Ray. "You're dead—half-dead—in the most peculiar way I've ever seen."

"You've done necromancy before?"

"I'm not even talking about necromancy at this point. I've never seen *anything* like this before."

He holds up what looks like a crumbling rosebud.

"It's like your body isn't just dying, it's dying in such a way that it's sucking the life and vitality out of anything around it."

I take a step back from them.

"Is it all right for me to be here? The last thing I want to do is hurt either of you."

"Don't worry about it," Ray says. "We're more alive and a lot bigger than these flowers and nettles. It's just that I've never seen anything dying so aggressively before."

Ray sets down the rosebud and I watch it crumble to dust.

I say, "Is there anything you can do to stop it?"

He uses his hand to sweep all the dead plants into a little heap.

"No. There isn't. Not right now. But I can research your condition. The one bit of good news is that if your necromancer used an obscure spell it means someone else has used it before and that it's going to be in one of my books. The bad news is that it might take me a while to find it."

"Right now, time is as big a problem for me as dying. I just don't have much of it left."

Ray takes a small vial of purple liquid from one of the apothecary drawers.

"But I think I can give you a little more time," he says. "Drink this."

"What is it?"

He looks at me.

"I'll make you a deal. You drink it and I'll tell you why while you're doing it."

"Deals like that make me very nervous."

"Me too," says Carlos. "Can't you just tell him?"

"I can and will. While he's drinking it."

I look at the vial.

"I don't suppose I have much to lose."

"You really don't," says Ray.

I pull out the stopper and start drinking. It's the sourest-tasting thing I've ever had in my mouth. And it's slow going down. The vial isn't big, but the neck is narrow.

Ray says, "It's a Spanish corpse preservative."

I almost choke, but when I start to take the bottle away, he puts my hand back to my mouth.

"Keep drinking and I'll tell you the rest."

I do it.

"Grandma got the recipe in Barcelona. It's a preservative for corpses people think might be vampires or shape shifters. It was customary to dismember a body and rearrange the limbs before burial so that the corpse couldn't reanimate and dig its way out of the grave."

I finish the potion and hand Ray the vial. Wipe my mouth on the back of my hand.

I say, "But I'm not a corpse."

"Yes, but you're close enough that I'm hoping the preservative will still work on you."

"I suppose that makes sense."

I go back to my clothes and pull on my shirt. I'm as sick of looking at my rotten skin as they must be.

"How long do you think it will give me?"

Ray crosses his arms and thinks for a minute.

"Ordinarily, you could keep a fresh corpse intact for a week with this potion."

I put on my coat.

"But I'm not exactly fresh, am I?"

"No, I'm afraid not."

"So, how long have I got?"

"A day," he says. "Maybe two."

I think about it.

"That's a hell of a lot longer than I had before. Thank you, Ray."

He shrugs.

"I wish I could have given you better news."

"You didn't have to help me at all, but you did. I won't forget that. For a day, at least."

I turn to Carlos. He shakes his head, tense and frustrated.

"Relax," I tell him. "These people were never going to let me off easy."

He says, "You need to hang around with a better set of monsters."

"Now you tell me."

Ray puts a hand on my shoulder.

"What are you going to do with these remaining hours?"

"I'm not giving up. I'm going back to Howard, the necromancer, and see if I can talk him into fixing me."

"Good move," says Carlos.

"And if I can't, I'm going to kill him and as many other Wormwood members as I can before I fall apart."

They both look at me.

"Sorry. Wormwood are very bad people. Like evil-Terminator bad."

"Okay," says Ray. Then, "You know, if you wanted, you could stay here while I research your condition. That way, if I find anything, we can get started immediately."

"Thanks. How about I go talk to Howard and text you when I'm done?"

"That sounds fine."

Ray gives me his number. I look at them awkwardly.

"I don't have anything to pay you back with. No money for sure. I don't even have time to help you clean up the mess I made."

"Don't be an asshole," says Carlos.

"He's right," says Ray. "I'm happy that I could help at all."

I stand there feeling stupid. Like an anxious kid. I'm out of practice with gratitude these days. I put my hands in my pockets and feel the scroll. Take it out and look at it.

"Let me ask you one last thing. How are you with old languages?"

Ray thinks about it.

"Some of the spells in the old books are in pretty obscure languages. I guess I'm passable at them. Why?"

"I'm going to ask you to do one last thing and then I'm going to get out of your hair. Can you read this?"

I hand him the scroll. Ray unrolls it and a small smile comes to his lips.

"Wow. I haven't seen this since I was a kid. It's Tammixlin, a pretty obscure dialect of Enochian script."

"Then you can read it?"

"Sure," he says. "It's pretty simple, really. It's just a list of names."

"Can you write them down for me?"

He unrolls the scroll all the way.

"All of them? That's going to take some time."

"That fucking word again." I think for a minute. "Is my name on there anywhere?"

Ray scans the scroll.

"No."

"Damn."

I think for another minute.

"How about Pieter Holden or Megan Bradbury?"

Ray runs his finger down the scroll.

"Yes," he says. "They're both here."

"In that order?"

"Yes."

"How about Franz Landschoff and Jared Glanton?"

He scans.

"Yes."

"Still in that order?"

"Yes. What does it mean?"

I look at the scroll over Ray's shoulder.

"It's a kill list. People a faction of Wormwood wants dead."

"Damn," says Carlos. "Are you sure?"

"Is there anyone before Pieter Holden?"

Ray nods.

"Barron Sinclair."

"That's it. It makes sense. Sinclair was taking fifty pills a day when I was with him. They poisoned him or cursed him, but they fucked up."

"Is this something that can help you?"

"I don't know."

There's a periodic table on one wall. Taped to the corner is a snapshot of Ray and Carlos in tuxes at some kind of party. They look very happy.

"Tetsuya Shin. Is she there?"

"Yes. Is she another Wormwood person?"

"Yeah. Everyone I just named, except for Barron, is dead."

"Does that help you?"

"I don't know. Maybe? Give me the next few names."

"The next name is Thomas Abbot."

Goddammit.

Ray thinks for a minute.

"Isn't he Sub Rosa?"

"He's the fucking CEO of all the Sub Rosa in California."

"Do you know him?"

"Yeah. He gave me a job once."

"Do you want any more names?" says Ray.

"I don't know. Sure."

"Alessa Graves."

That stops me cold.

"Are you sure you're reading it right?"

Ray looks over the scroll again.

"Yes. Alessa Graves. Do you know her?"

"Do you think there might be a lot of Alessa Graveses in L.A.?"

"That doesn't sound like a real common name," says Carlos.

"It doesn't, does it? But it doesn't make sense. I know an Alessa Graves. She's pretty ordinary as far as I know.

All those other names, they're big important people. Why Alessa?"

"Maybe 'cause of her dad," says Carlos. He has his phone. "I Googled her. It looks like her dad is head of a big anticorruption bureau in the DA's office. Could that be it?"

"That sounds like someone Wormwood would like to take down. Maybe through his kid."

"What are you going to do?" says Ray.

"Try and stop them."

He glances back at the scroll.

"You said the necromancer's name was Howard?"

"Yeah. Jonathan Howard."

"Jonathan *Lee* Howard?"

"I don't know."

"You might want to check on him."

Goddammit. This is exactly what I need right now.

Carlos says, "Can't you just call the cops about all this shit?"

"Definitely not." I check my pockets and coat for my weapons. Everything feels right. "Cops don't scare Wormwood. They probably own most of them, anyway."

Ray keeps staring at the scroll.

"Do you want to know about the other names?"

"No. These two are enough to deal with."

"I mean the nonhuman ones."

I go back and look over his shoulder again. Ray points to a few indecipherable scribbles.

"I was just reading you the human names. There are other sorts of names scattered throughout the list. Protective spirits, Orishas, primitive protodeities. All sorts of mystical creatures."

What was Marcella telling me all the time? The faction is a God-fearing bunch on some kind of holy mission. If she was telling the truth, the mystical names make perfect sense. The faction doesn't just want to control this world. They want to control or destroy the hoodoo one too.

"I have to go," I tell Ray. "But do me a favor and write down the next couple of inhuman names. Maybe there's something I can learn from them."

"Now you're saving elves and fairies?" says Carlos. "Go and kick that necromancer's ass into gear."

"I will, but think about this. We're talking about mystical beings. Some of them are going to know heavy magic. Maybe one of them can help me."

"That's bullshit. You're doing your hero thing when you should be looking out for number one."

"Trust me, I am."

Ray gives me a piece of paper with a couple of long, complicated names on it in black pen. He holds out the scroll and I put it in my pocket.

"Where are you headed?" he says.

"First to Thomas Abbot's place."

Carlos says, "You need a ride?"

"No thanks. I've got my own way."

Before I go I say, "This is probably going to look weird."

"What?" says Ray.

I step into a shadow.

AND COME OUT by the ocean in Marina del Rey.

But I'm too late.

Abbot's boat is already on fire. The idiot lives on a yacht in the harbor. It's surrounded by locked fences and bodyguards, but I'm sure it's a tempting target because instead of being a normal home where normal people might be able to run away, you can fucking sink this one and kill everybody without even hitting them.

The yacht is only a few yards out from the dock. The fact Abbot didn't just sail off means the engines must be down. But someone must be alive inside. As the faction killers shoot and throw curses at the boat, people on board are doing the same right back at them.

I step into a shadow at the edge of the dock . . .

. . . and come out on the burning deck. I'd intended to slip out in the main cabin, but I don't know this boat that well, and anyway, the damned thing keeps moving, rocked by the currents and blasts from the curses.

I dive into a kind of fancy sitting area away from the fire and the shooting. The interior is mostly kindling, but there's carpet inside. When I start to get up, I'm face-to-face with one of Abbot's bodyguards, and he has a very nice, new Kimber pistol pointed at my forehead. I don't have any choice. Before he can fire, I punch the dummy on the side of the head and kick him off when he goes limp. I didn't knock him out or anything, but he'll be seeing stars and chirping birds for a while. As I go farther into the boat, I drag the guard behind me out of range of the fire.

There are bodies on the floor of the main cabin. Some shot and others fried by curses. Six, maybe eight bodyguards fire back at shore through shattered windows. I leave the punch-drunk guard in a corner and look around for Abbot. He's at the far end of the place, throwing big balls of white-hot plasma back at the dock. He looks scared and I'm not sure he's thinking things through. Burning plasma will back off most sensible people, but one, the people outside are Wormwood, so we can rule out sensible, and two, if he keeps throwing hoodoo at the dock, he's going to set it on fire, and it's the main escape route for him and his people. Wanting very much not to get shot by the faction or a guard, I hunch over like a damn fiddler crab and run as fast as I can down the length of the room. I don't get shot, but splinters and shrapnel tear through my coat into my left shoulder and side. When I'm near enough to Abbot, I throw myself onto the floor and crawl up beside him.

"Hell of a night, huh?"

He spins in my direction and raises a hand to start a curse. Then he recognizes me. Freezes for a second. Starts to lower the hand. Changes his mind and raises it up again. I slap it out of the way and grab him.

"Asshole, if I was with them I could have killed all of you and raided the fridge by now."

"How are you here?" he yells over the sounds of gunfire and hoodoo.

"You mean, how come I'm not dead?"

"Yes. Where have you been?"

"Dead."

"What?"

I can see that he's reconsidering feeding me a plasma blast so I say, "It's a long story and I'll tell you later. Aren't you more concerned about not dying?"

"Very much."

"Then come with me."

"What about my people?"

"Bring them. Getting crowds through the Room isn't easy, though, so you're going to have to hold hands and I'll pull you out."

Abbot shouts orders to the few guards left alive and they form a scared-shitless conga line as I grab Abbot's hand and yank all of them through the nearest shadow.

The smoke in the cabin makes my lungs ache, not because it's noxious but because I haven't had a cigarette all day and now it's all I can think about.

I bring them out in the parking lot, well back from the faction shooters.

The moment we're clear, a couple of the non–Sub Rosa guards raise their rifles. I reach over and pull the barrels down.

"Leave them alone. Let the boat sink." I look at Abbot. "Let them think they killed you."

"He's right," Abbot says. "Everyone with a weapon, put it down."

Reluctantly, the guards follow their orders. I don't know any of them, but I get the feeling some of them know who I am. The ones frowning want to run. The ones who don't want to run want to shoot me, despite anything Abbot might say.

I look at him.

"Do you have a car? I can take you to the city through the Room, but you're going to need to get around once you're back."

He points across the lot.

"We have a van over there. Let's go."

We duck-walk as fast as we can across the lot to an SUV the size of a freight train. The doors are thick with armor and the windows are two-inch-thick ballistic glass. Of course Abbot has one of these. He's the Sub Rosa Augur, king high fuck-all, and this is L.A. Cars are sacred objects here. It wouldn't do for a big shot like him to be seen in anything less than a four-wheeled Stealth fighter.

We slip out of the lot while his burning yacht slumps onto its side, leaking oil and diesel fuel. The water ignites and the damned boat goes up in one big *boom*. The fireball lights up the whole marina. But swaddled in all this bulletproof glass, all anyone hears is Abbot talking to himself.

"Damn it. I forgot my phone charger."

WE DRIVE TO a Sub Rosa safe house near LAX. It's a rusted and half-collapsed metal-frame warehouse just north of the airport. A typical Sub Rosa dump. They pride themselves on selecting places with the shittiest exteriors possible, while the insides are something else entirely.

It looks like the warehouse used to store bathroom supplies. Pipes and U-joints spill from rotting crates. Local kids have used the pipes to smash mirrors and piles of porcelain toilets. The sound of rustling wings echoes down from where birds have built nests along the roof beams.

The desolation always ends if you know the proper path, though, and Abbot leads us to an office at the back of the warehouse. Invoices and shipping orders are still tacked to a corkboard, and a lone wooden desk chair rots in the corner. Abbot ignores all of that and heads for an old-fashioned girlie calendar on the back wall. It's like something from the fifties. A model in worker's coveralls, the front zipper open to reveal a lot of skin, lounges seductively on a stack of shiny pipes. Every plumber's dream girl, abandoned here how long ago? Abbot flips past January to February. It's a leap year. He presses his thumb against the 29 at the bottom of the page, and the back wall swings open like a vault door. He goes inside and the rest of us follow.

Lights flicker on in a spacious living room decorated like a high-class hunting lodge. Big rooms. Dark wood along the walls and the ceiling beams. The furniture looks like it was stolen from the lobby of a fancy hotel trying to pass itself off as folksy. I've seen worse Sub Rosa layouts, dripping with gold and animal heads on the walls like a narco boss's palace.

Abbot heads to a living room area with sofas facing each other and quaint tables with Tiffany lamps.

"Why don't you all go into the kitchen?" he says. "There's plenty of food and drinks. Relax. Decompress. You've all had a hard night and I appreciate everything you did. I'll come and talk to you individually later. Right now, though, I need to talk to this one."

Abbot points at me. Everyone looks in my direction.

I shrug and take out a battered pack of Shermans.

"Can I smoke in here?"

"Under no circumstances," Abbot says.

I point to a sideboard in the corner of the room.

"Can I at least have a drink?"

"Of course."

I get a bottle of bourbon and two glasses and sit on one of the sofas.

Abbot's bodyguards reluctantly file into the kitchen. It must be hard on them. On the one hand, I just saved them.

On the other hand, I'm a known menace. It's why I like free-lancing. Less wear and tear on your psyche.

Abbot sits down on the sofa across from me. I pour two sizable glasses of bourbon and push one to his side of the coffee table. He doesn't move to pick it up. I pick up mine, raise it in a toast, and drink half. The perfect thing to clear the smoke out of your throat.

Abbot says, "So, tell me seriously. Where have you been for the past year?"

My injured shoulder is beginning to itch. I take off my coat and pick pieces of yacht wood out of my skin. When I start to set a bloody splinter on the table, Abbott shoves a year-old copy of *Vogue* from the end of the table under it.

"I told you. I was dead."

"Be serious."

"I am. I was dead and in Hell. Then somebody brought me back."

"Who?"

"You're not going to like it."

"Who?" he says a bit more insistently.

"Wormwood."

He leans against the back of the sofa, then forward again.

"Which version of Wormwood was it?"

Should have known he'd know the dirt.

"The original."

"Why did they bring you back?"

"To stop the faction from blowing up L.A., which I did. You're welcome."

Abbot frowns.

"They knew about that? I thought we were the only ones."

"Pardon me for asking, but I've been gone and don't know who the players are anymore. Who is 'we'?"

"The Sub Rosa, of course."

I look at Abbot hard. His pupils and heartbeat are funny.

I say, "I get the feeling there's more to that sentence. Like it should be the Sub Rosa . . . and somebody else."

Abbot looks in the direction of the kitchen, like he's regretting sending his goons away. Finally, he looks back at me and says, "I mean the Sub Rosa and the group you call the faction. They've been trying to take over the city, both the Sub Rosa and civilian worlds. We stepped in to stop them. I thought we had a deal."

"You made a *deal* with the faction?"

He sits up straight. "Are you judging me? It sounds like we both made deals with the Devil."

"No. I know the Devil. He wouldn't pull shit like this."

Abbot thinks for a minute.

"You said you stopped the destruction of the city. That might explain the attack tonight. I thought we'd reached a deal where they would cease all mystical activity in L.A. They probably think that we're the ones who stopped them."

I pull the last pieces of wood out of my shoulder. I'm not bleeding right. My blood flows slowly and is the wrong color. Almost black. Abbot notices.

"Are you a Drifter?" he says. "A zombie?"

"No. But I'm not fully alive yet. That was my deal with Wormwood. I stop the event and they make me whole again."

"What happened?"

"There was a disagreement over who fulfilled their part of the bargain. I'm not sure who won the argument, but I'm still half-dead."

"I guess neither of us got what we wanted from Wormwood."

"They're good at that."

Abbot says, "I wonder if I should call them and try to set up another meeting."

"That's a bad idea. You think they attacked you because I kicked over their sand castle? I think they were going to kill you all along."

"What makes you say that?"

I take out the piece of paper Ray gave me. There are a few holes where splinters and shrapnel shot through. I hand it to Abbot.

"Do you recognize any of these names?"

He takes the paper and looks it over.

"Nothing except for my own," he says.

I pour myself another drink.

"It's a kill list. A friend translated it for me from a scroll made out of human skin. All the names I recognized are dead or dying."

"And my name is there."

"Right after a long list of Wormwood big shots."

Abbot says, "I take it this list wasn't created in the last twenty-four hours?"

I shake my head.

"The faction mystics trying to blow up the city had it at their ritual. I got it from one of them."

"I'd like to talk to them. Do you know where they are?"

"Under about a hundred tons of rubble where the Chapel of St. Alexis used to be."

"Of course," he says. "Los Angeles is lucky you're not an exterminator. You'd burn half the city to get one fly."

"It would have to be a very bad fly."

The kitchen door opens a few inches and I can see the face of the guard I punched on the boat.

"Is everything all right, sir?" he says.

"We're fine. Thank you," says Abbot.

The guard glares at me and lets the door fall shut.

I look at Abbot.

"You're going to tell him about me saving you tonight, right? I don't need more enemies right now."

Abbot glances back in the direction of the door.

"Don't worry about them. They're loyal and they understand orders. They'll leave you alone if I say so."

"And you're going to say so, right?"

"Of course," he says a little lightly for my taste. But I have to trust him for now. Like I said, I don't need more enemies.

He pushes the list back to me.

"I still don't understand why Wormwood would make a deal. Why not just come after us?"

"I spent some time with a faction member. Sometimes she talked like she was at a tent revival meeting. I didn't believe all of it, but I do believe one thing. The faction is on a crusade. A goddamn holy war."

"Against the Sub Rosa?"

"Against anyone who isn't a true believer."

"In what?"

"I have no idea. What do you know about them?"

Abbot takes his first sip of bourbon. He holds on to the glass, rolling it between his hands.

"Honestly, not a lot," he says. "We know they're well funded and equipped, and that they're very good at what they do."

"You haven't been able to get anyone on the inside?"

"Not a single person." Abbot leans back against the sofa. He says, "So, you've been dead for a year."

"That's right."

"Some of us thought that you might have faked the whole thing. That you'd grown tired of L.A. and the endless fighting and had decided to retire."

I look at him.

"You know that Audsley Ishii is dead, right?"

"Of course. Your friend Candy killed him because he allegedly killed you."

"He didn't allegedly anything. He put a fucking knife in my back. Do you think I got her to murder an innocent guy just so I could have a weekend in Cabo?"

He sets his glass on the table.

"No. That's the part that didn't make sense. I knew you were capable of disappearing, but I had Candy thoroughly checked out. There's nothing in her background indicating that she's capable of cold-blooded murder."

"Did you blow her cover when you checked her out? The Feds are still looking for her. That's why she's been wearing a glamour and going by Chihiro all this time."

"That's not true," Abbot says. "Those investigations have all been dropped. After Marshal Larson Wells was arrested, the Golden Vigil operation was shut down and all its cases closed. There's no warrant for Candy. Or you, for that matter."

"Lucky me. I'll get a dog and a Prius."

Abbot smiles.

"You couldn't afford them."

"That must have been nice for you. Me being dead, you didn't have to pay my salary all this time."

"But I have been paying it. To Candy."

"What are you talking about?"

"You really never read the paperwork when I put you on retainer, did you?"

"Not a word."

He sets down the glass.

"Aside from health insurance, which it looks like you could use right now, there was a wrongful-death provision. Audsley Ishii had been an employee of the Augur's office. Even though he'd been dismissed, he killed you over a disagreement that stemmed from that job. When he killed you, it initiated the wrongful-death payout. Candy, being the closest thing you have to a next of kin, has been getting your salary the whole time you've been gone."

I study his face, and this time I'm sure. Abbot is telling the truth.

I say, "Thanks. You could have been a bastard about it, but you weren't. I appreciate that."

Abbot picks up his glass.

"We had a deal and I honor my deals. Now that you're back, I'll start the paperwork to reroute the money to the account we set up for you."

Maybe this is part of what Kasabian meant when he said they'd been doing great without me. Having my Sub Rosa money without me around to break things or bring trouble down on the store could be one of the things that helped turn the store around.

I have a little more bourbon and think.

"Don't do it," I tell him. "Keep sending her the money. I only have a day or so before I might die again. She can use the money more than me."

"If you don't die, do you have any of your own money?"

"Not a cent."

"Do you have a place to live?"

"The bus station is a place."

Abbot leans forward again.

"We have an apartment near Universal City that we keep for out-of-town dignitaries. You can use it until we figure out what to do with you."

"What do I need an apartment for? I just told you I'm probably going to be dead soon."

Abbot puts his hands on the table.

"Don't talk like that. We'll figure something out. I have the best magicians, the best necromancers, the best of everything at my disposal. What kind of spell did they use to bring you back?"

"I don't know. No one will tell me. But it's supposed to be pretty obscure."

"That's not much to work with. But I'll get people looking into it. If you find out anything, get in touch as soon as possible. You still have my phone number?"

"Yeah. But why are you doing this? You don't owe me anything."

He looks at me hard.

"Is it so inconceivable that someone might do something

for you *not* because they owe you something but because they simply want to?"

"Yeah. It's a little weird."

"Then that's one reason why I'm the Augur and you're not. I like you, Stark, whether you believe it or not. I enjoy doing things for people I like, and I have the resources to do it."

"That sounds like the kind of thing that could get a person in trouble."

"Not true. Even if you're not getting paid, we still have a contract. I can use any resources I want to help an employee."

I look at him.

"An employee?"

"Sorry. Contractor."

"That's better."

"It's settled then. I'll get people started on the problem, and you'll get in touch if you learn anything. And here, take this."

Abbot gets out his wallet and hands me what looks like a small gold coin. When I look closer I see that it's a lot more like a milagro in the shape of an eye.

"What's this for?"

"Your shadow-walking trick is impressive, but if you get sicker, you might not be able to do it. If you get stuck somewhere and need help, just break the coin in half. We'll find you."

I turn the coin over in my hand a few times.

"Thanks."

"My pleasure," Abbot says. "Do you want to go and see the apartment?"

"Can you just give me a key and let me find it on my own? I can move faster than your van through LAX traffic."

"Of course."

He takes out an ordinary house key and hands it to me.

"The entrance is through a strip mall on Cahuenga near the In-N-Out Burger by the Hollywood Freeway. There's an out-of-business nail salon. The key opens the front door and the apartment entrance is through a supply closet at the back. It's one of the bottles of skin lotion on a shelf by themselves. I forget which one, but there are only three. Just pick up each one until the door opens."

I can't help but laugh at the setup.

"Nail salon. Skin lotion. Got it."

Abbot points to the kitchen.

"Do you want anything to eat before you go? The cook makes amazing garlic lamb."

"Some other time. I appreciate all this."

"Thanks for saving us tonight."

"I'll see you."

"Stay in touch."

"Right."

I go out before any of the guards come back. I'm tired of the way they're looking at me.

MAX OVERDRIVE IS closed when I get there, late enough that even Kasabian isn't screwing around inside. I go in near the storage room, terrified that someone found Howard or that he woke up and wandered away.

There's no reason to worry about Alessa and Candy tonight. The faction will be doing cleanup and recon in Marina del Rey. Looking for bodies. Picking up shell casings. Maybe sending divers down to the boat to search for bodies. They'll find a few, but not the one they want. With luck they'll either keep looking or assume Abbot burned in the fire. Me? All I want right now is a little clear head space. No Wormwood. No faction. Just me and Howard, a couple of regular guys doing regular-guy stuff. No pressure. Maybe some beer and pizza. Then he does his hoodoo and I send the fucker on his way. That's all I want, which is exactly why I'm sure I'm not going to get it.

My left shoulder is wet. The places where I pulled out splinters aren't even trying to heal. More good news.

I open the storage door as quietly as I can and move stacks of porn out of the way. At least things aren't completely screwed. Howard is still curled up like a sleeping kitten in the corner. I grab his arm and pull him into a fireman's carry, then push the storage door closed with my boot.

When I turn around, Kasabian is staring at me from the door of his little apartment in the corner of the store. He doesn't say anything. Just sighs and slowly closes the door again, watching me until the door is completely shut. I almost feel like apologizing, but I don't have time. Plus, he hasn't exactly been sympathetic about my current situation. And he has a home. I have a Sub Rosa squat in a nail salon. Fuck it. Let him sweat a little.

I leave through a shadow and come out on Cahuenga near the In-N-Out Burger. There's a minimall next door, so I hustle Howard over there as quickly as possible. I can do without being mistaken for a body snatcher by some solid citizen itching to dial 911.

The mall is pretty much as Abbot described it. A dull slab of commercial concrete with a liquor store, a sandwich shop, and an auto parts place. The nail salon is in the center of the mall. I don't bother with the key when I get there. Just shadow-walk through the windows. The glass is covered with white paper and a FOR RENT sign with a dummy phone number at the bottom. I haul Howard to the supply closet in the back of the salon. When I get there, I have to set him down and catch my breath. I'm getting weaker. I should be able to throw Howard's limey ass like a shot put halfway down a football field. Now I'm sweating after only fifty feet. Maybe I should have eaten something at the safe house. Can I even digest food anymore? The bourbon went down all right, but that's God's own medicine. If there are any chili dogs in here, I'm going to have to fire one up.

When my legs stop shaking, I find the shelf with three bottles of skin lotion. Pick up the first one. Nothing. This porridge is too hot. I try the one in the middle. This porridge is too cold. One more try. If I'm wrong, then Abbot set me up and a Sub Rosa SWAT team is going to burst in here with flash-bangs and grenades laced with hoodoo poison.

Only one way to find out.

What do you know?

This porridge is just right.

A seam in the cheap wood paneling splits open and a narrow section of wall swings back out of the way. I don't bother picking up Howard this time. With a fistful of collar, I drag him through the door.

It's dark inside. I feel on the wall for a light switch but come up with nothing. It occurs to me that I've been living in cars and civilian homes too much lately. This apartment is a pure Sub Rosa product. Switches are beneath them.

I say, "Lights," and the place is suddenly like premiere night at the Egyptian Theatre.

How can I describe the place? The walls and ceiling are rounded, like we're living in a goddamn UFO. The tables and cabinets have rounded backs to fit against the walls. There's an orange shag carpet and an avocado-green sofa covered with enough plush pillows that you could break a leg if they ever avalanched. The place is ringed by oval windows, and I can see lights beyond them. Aside from the sofa, the rest of the furniture is all smooth molded white plastic with the same warm seventies hipster colors on the chair seats and backs. The apartment is basically a Hugh Hefner bachelor pad in a *Star Trek* swingers' resort.

When I go to one of the egg-shaped windows, I'm looking out at around forty years ago. Sub Rosa homes can be pretty much anywhere in time and space. This one is high on a hillside looking down over L.A., only it's not current L.A. It's the city when disco ruled the legit clubs and early punk shows were blasting away in warehouses and little spaces that were only clubs in the sense that you could pack in too many people and sell them shitty beer. It's almost tempting to climb out one of these windows and go down into the city. Breathe in that prime seventies L.A. smog. Maybe steal a Mustang and head down Sunset to see who's playing at the Whisky A Go Go and the Roxy. Hell, the Masque club might even be open. I always wanted to see that place, but it was long dead before I was in diapers. On the other hand, when you're leaking black blood all over yourself with a passed-out necromancer on the floor, it isn't the best time to plan a road trip. But if I don't die, I swear I'm going to see what's down that hill. I prop Howard up on the sofa and go looking for the bathroom.

Everything in there is round too, even the mirrors. The bathroom counter is wave shaped and trimmed in wood like I'm in a goddamn Hobbit house. I drop my coat on the floor and check the bathroom cabinets. There are bandages and peroxide in the back of one. In theory I ought to be able to stop the bleeding with a healing spell, but I've never been good at those, and in my current state, I might get the thing backward and turn myself inside out.

I clean my shoulder as well as I can but find that I have a few splinters and some shrapnel in my side. I pull the pieces out and I start bleeding there too. I use up all the bandages wrapping my shoulder and midsection.

I rinse out my bloody T-shirt and leave it hanging in the bathtub. I don't want to give Howard anything to gloat about, so I need to cover my rotting body. Luckily, there are some clothes in the master bedroom closet. The only shirt that fits is a blood-red button-down number. On the same hanger is a blue seventies kerchief. That I throw in the trash.

Howard is still upright when I go back into the living room. I mumble some Hellion hoodoo, and in a few seconds, he starts to come around. As his eyes try to focus, I get hit with another wave of fatigue. I pull over one of the plush plastic chairs and sit down while he tries to remember what words are.

Finally, he's conscious enough to see me and the crazy room.

"Where am I?" he says.

"In Bilbo Baggins's spaceship."

He rubs the back of his neck.

"What did you do to me? My neck and back hurt."

"You were in cold storage for a little while, but you're fine now. It's time for us to have a talk."

He looks at the pile of colorful pillows on the other end of the couch.

"No. I'm not performing the spell," he says.

"Why not?"

"I told you earlier, I don't trust you. Even if you took an oath not to hurt me, you're tricky enough to find a loophole where you could get someone or something else to do it."

"You mean, find a loophole just like Sandoval did to me?"

"I don't know anything about that. I just know that she's always upheld any contract I've had with her. You, on the other hand, are a lying murderer, so my position stands."

This is one of those moments when being Sandman Slim, having a reputation like that, is not a goddamn asset. With a track record like mine, it's hard to fall back on a "Let's be reasonable" argument.

"Is there something I can give you? I'm a big fan of bribes. Tell me something you want and I'll get it. Money? Bonds? A Rolls-Royce? A whole fleet of them?"

He lowers his head, almost in disappointment, it seems.

"You can't buy me or convince me of your good intentions. I have nothing for you. If you're going to kill me, get on with it. If you're going to let me go, then let me go."

I pull my chair in closer, until I can practically smell his mouthwash.

"First off, *I'm* the madman here. Don't explain my options to me. Second, you're not going anywhere until I'm alive again. I'm going to seal this place tight, so that I'm the only one who can get in or out. If I'm going to die, I'm going to spend those last few precious moments with you, liquefying all over your nice suit. After that, you can stay in here until you're bones and gristle too. And after that, I'll be waiting for you in Hell with a lava tuxedo just your size."

Howard pats his hands on his knees.

"Empty threats. I'm exempt from damnation. You can't touch me in the afterlife."

"First off, Heaven is out for you. For everyone really, but especially for you, so don't even worry about that. Second, I'd try to explain all the ways I can hurt you in Hell, but I don't have time. Let me simply impress upon you that I can find you anywhere in the afterlife and make your eternity a fucking misery."

I grab him and use the last of my strength to throw him a few feet across the room.

"I'm going to find a way to fix myself without you. And when I do, you and me are going to have words."

Howard sits up and adjusts his suit.

"You have no idea how absurd you are. When I say that the spell is obscure I mean that it only appears in one book and I had the only copy left in the world. Do you know what I did with it?"

"What?"

"I burned it. You see, I have a photographic memory. I didn't need it anymore and I didn't want anyone else to have those secrets."

"What was the name of the book?"

He purses his lips for a moment.

"Goodness. I can't remember."

I step on his hand. As he winces I say, "This isn't the time to fuck with me."

I step off his hand and he cradles it against his body. But he still doesn't look scared. In fact, he's the opposite.

"Why don't you try hypnotizing me?" he says. "Maybe I'd spill my secrets then. But wait. How many languages do you speak? Ludovico's Ellicit is written in six, and none of them are currently spoken on Earth."

Ludovico's Ellicit. That's not much, but it's the most I've had to go on since Wormwood brought me back. Before Howard realizes that he gave something away, I whisper the hoodoo I used earlier and he falls over unconscious again. I drag him into a small guest bedroom and roll him onto the mattress. I seal the room with a little more hoodoo and leave him there, safe and sound for now.

I can't find a bar in this dump, but I do find the kitchen. The refrigerator is fully stocked. I pile some chicken and potatoes on a plate and heat them up in the microwave. The chicken tastes like cardboard and the potatoes like wallpaper paste. But I finish everything. The food is going to either kill me or give me back a little strength. With food in my empty belly, I'm more tired than ever. I have to get some sleep, but before I do I text Ray.

Ludovico's Ellicit. That's the spell.

I sit there groggy and wondering if I have any options left.

There's one I can think of. I hate to use it, but I don't have time to be subtle anymore.

If you need help, call Vidocq. A friend.

I give Ray his number and collapse on the couch. I set the

alarm on my phone for one hour. That's as long as I can spare doing nothing.

I sleep right through it.

If I dream anything, I can't remember it. All I have is a sense of drifting in absolute darkness and feeling like a complete idiot. Hell I can take, but I hope that isn't my eternity.

SUPPLIES. I NEED supplies, but I don't have a dime. I go through every drawer in the living room, hoping the Sub Rosa left some petty cash. There's nothing, but I do finally find the liquor cabinet. With the bourbon now on the living room table, I head into the guest bedroom and go through Howard's pockets. I come up with two hundred in cash and an American Express black card. The cash I keep. The card I don't trust.

If I start stinking, I'm not sure I'll be able to tell, so I go into the bathroom and brush my teeth twice. There's shaving cream and a razor in a cabinet but before I lather up I realize that I don't need them. My beard has stopped growing. Also, my face looks funny. I think. It's hard to tell at this point. I see rot everywhere. What complicates things is that eleven, now twelve years in Hell left me pretty pale. But have I lost what little color I had left? And are my lips turning blue? I start to put on the glamour but get nervous. How much energy will it take to maintain it? Do I have enough to spare right now? In the end, I decide against it. The outside world will just have to deal with my regular face.

I shadow-walk out of the UFO house onto Hollywood Boulevard. The sun is like an anvil and the heat is like a hammer pounding on my skull.

Stumbling into the first tourist shop I see, I grab a pair of cheap Ray-Ban knockoff sunglasses and slip them on. The world is suddenly a little less horrifying. I also pick up a couple of black I LUV LA shirts, with hearts and palm trees on the front. They're so hideous that if I thought I was going to last long enough, I'd want to be buried in them.

I give the nice lady some twenties and she snips the plastic price tag off my shades. Under my coat, I can feel the towels I taped to my body starting to soak through. My next stop is a corner market where I pick up some Tabasco sauce, sriracha, plums in hot red pepper, and four boxes of cling wrap. There goes another twenty and something.

Back at the UFO mansion, I strip off the red shirt and rinse it in the sink. The left side is never going to be red again, but I hang it up to dry next to my other shirt. It's riddled with holes and still a little stiff with blood. I leave it where it is and pull off the towels I wrapped around me.

Immediately, dark blood falls in big drops onto the floor. I pour more peroxide over my cuts and open one of the boxes of cling wrap. My side is bleeding the most, so I wrap my torso first. I go around eight times, from my waist to my armpits. My whole body feels stiff and awkward, but I'm not raining as much muck onto the floor.

Wrapping my shoulder is a little trickier, since I have to do it one-handed. After a few awkward attempts, I get the job done. I'm officially one big blood sausage, ready for frying.

Before I leave the bathroom, I wipe my blood off the floor with one of Abbot's nice towels. It's so vile with my toxic blood that I don't even bother putting it in the hamper. I just stuff it into the kitchen trash.

While I'm in there, I take a couple of slices of chicken, coat one with sriracha and the other with Tabasco. I get a little tingle from the sriracha, but I can't really taste it. Next I try the dried plums in red peppers. I might as well be eating Styrofoam. I spit out the plums and throw everything else in the trash with the towel. I swear, if I don't taste food again soon I'm going to eat Howard just to show him what happens to a man too sad to chance a bad burger.

When I go out later, I'm wearing a glamour. Even if it takes some extra energy, I need to do some things without people staring at me.

The first thing I do is steal a brown Subaru. I don't even know what model it is. It's simply the most boring wheels I can find. Cops are generally color-blind when it comes to brown cars, and this Subaru is too boring for even a soccer mom. It looks like it was made for people into competitive tire filling.

On my way to Max Overdrive, I stop at a little grocery and buy an insulated chest. Fill it with beer, cold cuts, and ice cream. Anything that will keep me cool so I don't rot in the heat.

If it was night, I might just watch the store from across the street, but it's the middle of the afternoon. There's no way I wouldn't be noticed hanging around. Besides, sitting in a broiling-hot car all day isn't stalking. It's a stakeout.

STAKEOUTS ARE BORING. I've been on them before and they never get any better. I have a beer and some ice cream to cool down, then some sliced ham to keep my strength up. I forgot to buy bread or mustard, so I shove the naked slices in my mouth one by one. I think of every old joke about how divorced guys are supposed to live. All I need are some week-old pizza boxes around to complete the look.

Even with the cold food and beer in my belly, I still feel hot. I shrug off my coat and it's better for about a minute, but half of me is still mummified in cling wrap. I turn on the car and run the air conditioner for a while. It helps, but after half an hour, the engine starts to overheat, so I have to turn the damn thing off. The air outside is dead, so opening the windows doesn't help. Eventually, there's nothing left to do but take one of the bags of ice from the cooler and hold it in my lap like I'm trying to nurse it.

This might be the most pathetic day of my life.

I wonder if this is one of those things they call a "teachable moment." What it's supposed to teach me, I have no idea. Maybe that I should have stolen an ice-cream truck? Anyway, there's nothing at all humiliating about clutching ten pounds of ice like your firstborn while the damn bag leaks all over your crotch so it looks like you pissed yourself with joy. I crack open another beer to celebrate fatherhood and keep reminding myself that I'm doing this for Candy.

What the hell am I going to do about Howard? I can't kill him and he knows it. I can't trust him, but I can't let him go either because then the faction will get him. Should I tell him he's on the kill list? Would that make things better or worse? I don't need him making dumb decisions and he's plenty scared now. If he was even more frightened, he might go off the rails completely. I need to think about it.

I check my phone. Nothing from Ray yet.

Tick-tock. Tick-tock.

The street cools down a little after dark. I put my coat back on. I'm parked halfway down the block from Max Overdrive, so when a car ahead of me pulls away, I move up the Subaru. Now I'm only one house down from the store.

I'm smoking one of my last Shermans—I forgot to buy cigarettes too—when Candy sticks her head in the driver-side window and yells at me. I'm not used to Candy screaming right in my face and it's even weirder when she's wearing her Chihiro glamour.

"*Who the fuck are you and why have you been watching us all day?*" she shouts. Then, "And why do you have a bag of ice in your lap?"

She must have spotted me and gone out the back of the store and around the block to sneak up on me. Good for her. I deserve to be yelled at for not watching my rear.

Now I'm more glad than ever that I put on the glamour. I've been going over it all day, whether I should reveal myself since it might be the last time we ever see each other. But that's junior high romance-novel stuff. She doesn't need to see me die again. And if I do live, I don't know if my body is ever going to be right again. I mean, even if I figure out what Ludovico's Ellicit is and get cured, I might look like Freddy Krueger's foreskin forever.

She's getting angrier by the second. I have to tell her something.

I say, "Thomas Abbot sent me. He's worried about you."

Candy takes a step back and looks at me for a minute. She's not entirely convinced, but she's not going to eat my face right away.

She says, "What's Abbot worried about? Everything is fine here."

I decide that I can tell her some of the truth, enough so she knows I'm not the enemy.

"It's not you he's worried about. It's Alessa."

That gets her interest. She leans back down to the window.

"What's wrong with Alessa?"

"Nothing. He's just worried that there might be people who want to hurt her."

"What? Why? We run a video store. Who cares about us?"

I'm about to say something when someone shouts at me through the passenger window. It's Alessa.

"Hey, fucker, what's your problem with us?"

She sounds as mad and dangerous as Candy. I suddenly like her a little more.

Candy says, "He said Thomas Abbot sent him."

Alessa reaches in and flips open my cooler.

"He's a bum with a cooler full of beer. And it looks like he pissed all over himself. Abbot wouldn't send this loser."

I look from Alessa back to Candy.

"I know this setup looks a little strange but trust me, I'm here to help."

"Help yourself and get out of here," says Alessa. "I already dialed 911."

She holds up her phone to show me.

Two LAPD cruisers swing around the corner and stop by the car. All four cops get out and head for us.

I look at her.

"I wish you hadn't done that."

"I bet you do," Alessa says.

"You don't understand. They might not be cops."

"Wishful thinking."

The first cop to reach us is an older guy right out of central casting. He has a gray crew cut with a five o'clock shadow and the weary gaze of a guy who's seen it all. Imagine a more malevolent Joe Friday. He stands by Candy.

"Did one of you call the police?"

"I did," says Alessa. "This creep has been sitting outside our store all day drinking and god knows what else."

Friday shines a light in my face, then swings it over to the cooler, where he spots all the beer.

"Have you been drinking, sir?"

"Yes, but I also have ice cream and cold cuts. I can show you."

The light swings back to my face.

"License and registration, please."

I don't want to get shot, so I keep my hands on the wheel while I think. I'm in a stolen car and I've been legally dead in California for years, so a driver's license isn't in the cards. In better times, I could hoodoo up the paperwork. But I don't know if I can do that and maintain the glamour.

"Sir?" says the cop.

Before I begin a whole new string of lies, two more LAPD cars pull up alongside the first two.

Shit.

I look at Alessa.

"This is why I wish you hadn't called the cops. Now they know you're home and vulnerable."

"What are you talking about?"

I never get to answer because by the time I turn back to the cops, the four new ones—all faction members—are executing them.

Two to the chest and one to the head each. Twelve shots. Four dead cops.

I kick open the driver's-side door and shove Candy out of the way as one of the faction cops opens up on us. I pull her around to the back of the car and grab my na'at. But Candy doesn't stay put. She leaps and knocks Alessa to the ground. When Candy stands up again she's turned full Jade. Her eyes are red slits in black ice. Her nails grow into curved claws, and her mouth is full of white shark teeth.

She jumps across the car like a beautiful animal and rips out the closest faction member's throat. He's dead before he drops. I throw out the na'at like a whip, taking out one cop's gun hand, then whip again, and the tip of the na'at goes into his heart. Candy has another cop pushed up against a squad car, her teeth in his neck. Faction cop number four moves around the Subaru looking for Alessa.

He's too far away for the na'at, so I throw the black blade. Let me tell you, being in a severe state of decay doesn't help your aim. Instead of his heart, the knife lodges in his shoulder. The cop staggers back and fires at me. Gets me once in the side and again in the leg. I stumble toward Alessa, shouting Hellion hoodoo. The street shudders in a mini-earthquake, knocking the cop off his feet. I get in front of Alessa and when the cop hits the ground I put a bullet through his head.

Keeping Alessa behind me, I drop my hands across the hood of the Subaru, aiming for the last cop. But he's already sliding down the side of his squad car, his head at a funny angle and Candy wiping blood from her mouth.

She comes around the side of the car and hugs Alessa. When I try to stand my leg barely holds me upright. I grab the black blade from the dead faction cop's shoulder and put it in my coat before Candy has a chance to recognize it.

"Thanks," she says. "I'm sorry I didn't believe you earlier."

I start to say something, but I have to lean against the Subaru.

Alessa grabs my shoulder.

"He's hurt. Should we call an ambulance?"

"No!" I shout. "No more calls. We can't stay here. There might be more of them."

"Where do you want to go?" says Alessa.

That's when I fall over. I'm bleeding again. Hitting my leg was bad enough, but that dead fuck ripped my cling wrap with his other shot. I'm going to be a mess.

Candy says, "Help me get him inside."

"No. We have to go," I say, but they've already pulled me to my feet.

With Candy on one side of me and Alessa on the other, they walk me into Max Overdrive. Where, once again, I fall on my damn face.

I point at the door.

"Lock it and kill the lights."

Alessa runs over and does it.

I crawl into a sitting position and lean against the front counter.

"Who were those guys?" says Candy.

"It's complicated. Now, we have to get out of here."

"How? You can't walk, we don't have a car, and those cop cars are blocking yours."

I hobble to the window and look out. She's right.

There's only one way I can get them out of here.

I say, "Where's Kasabian?"

"Probably hiding in his room," says Alessa. "I'll get him."

I hobble back to the counter. I have to lean on it, but I can stay upright this time.

Candy comes over and sets her hand on my back.

"We have to get you to a doctor."

"No doctors. I don't have time. I can fix this. We just need to get somewhere safe first."

"Where?"

I look at her through the darkness in the store. She's so beautiful it's like a punch in the heart. I can just make out her true face through the Chihiro glamour. She looks great and I want to tell her that, but I look away, trying to think of an exit out of here that doesn't involve shadows.

Alessa comes back with Kasabian. He takes one look at me and says, "This is exactly what I was talking about. Everywhere you go, it's a disaster."

"Wait. You know this guy?" says Candy.

Kasabian looks at me, then back to her.

"No. I've never seen him before."

Candy pulls me over to the window, where light from a street lamp shines in.

First she frowns. Then she stares. Then her mouth opens a fraction of an inch.

From the moment I got shot, I've been worried that the glamour wouldn't hold. I just hoped that being in the dark for a while, I'd figure out how to get everyone clear without them seeing my face.

"Stark?" she whispers.

"Hi, Candy. Sorry about all the blood."

She grabs me in the kind of hug that under other circumstances I'd cherish. But with a bullet in my side all I can say is, "This hurts kind of a lot."

She eases up but won't let go of me.

"Where have you been all this time?"

"Dead. But I'm better now. Sort of."

Alessa comes over too.

"I saw you die. I saw them take your body away," she says.

I can hear sirens in the distance. A lot of them.

"I promise to explain everything, but we really have to get out of here."

Candy looks at Kasabian.

"You knew he was here, didn't you? Why the fuck didn't you say anything?"

"Because the last time he came back from Hell he cut my head off," he says. "I didn't know what he'd cut off this time if I said anything."

"Can we talk about all this later?" I say. "We need to move."

"Where?" says Alessa.

"To a Sub Rosa hideout. We can't get out on the street, but I can take us though the Room."

"I thought you didn't have control of the Room anymore," says Candy.

"That's complicated too. Help me to that shadow and let's get out of here."

"What's the Room?" says Alessa. "Why a shadow?"

"Just watch," says Candy. "You're going to love this."

"WHOA," SAYS ALESSA when we come out. And, "Whoa," again when she gets a look at the UFO bungalow.

"You live here?" she says.

I hobble into the bathroom, trying not to get blood everywhere.

"Temporarily. Thomas Abbot loaned it to me. It's a Sub Rosa house. Wormwood—the psycho cops—aren't going to find you here."

Candy follows me inside. I sit on the edge of the tub and wrap a towel around my leaking leg.

She says, "That was Wormwood outside the store?"

"Yeah."

"What did they want?"

I point to Alessa in the living room. She sees me and comes in.

"Those guys were there for *me*?"

"I'm afraid so."

Kasabian sticks his face in the door.

"What did you do to get them mad at Alessa?"

I throw the towel at him.

"I didn't do anything. Her name is on a Wormwood kill list."

"Why?" she says.

"Your father works in the prosecutor's office, right?"

"Yeah."

"It's probably something he did. Or he's going to do. Anyway, it's the only connection I can figure between you and Wormwood."

Alessa holds up her hands. "Okay. Everybody stop a minute. Who is Wormwood?"

Candy helps me stand up.

"You explain it to her," I say. "I'm going to take a shower."

"You're shot. You can't be on your own so soon."

There's real concern in her voice. It's good to hear after all this time.

"I'll be fine. But I'm not healing right. I'm going to need your help bandaging me up."

"Okay. I can do that."

"One thing. My body. I'm a lot more fucked up than you remember."

She smiles. "I've seen you plenty fucked up. I think I can handle it."

"We'll see. Just remember I warned you."

She helps me up and gets my coat off. The three of them take a good look at my blue-black right arm. Alessa stares at my prosthetic left one.

"What the fuck did you do?"

"All of you clear out," I say. "I don't need anyone gawking while I get these wounds clean."

Candy hustles the others out of the room. Stops at the door.

"You sure you're going to be okay?"

I say, "I'm fine. Thanks."

"Call me when you get out."

"I look a lot worse naked, but I'll need your help and I don't think those two are up for it."

"I'll be right outside. Knock when you're done."

"Got it."

She closes the door and I strip off the rest of my clothes and the cling wrap. I took a shot on the right just below the ribs. There's no exit wound, so the bullet is still inside. The second shot hit the meaty part of my leg where it meets my hip. That one went all the way through. The only good thing about being this close to dead is that my sense of touch is pretty dull. Normally, either of those shots would hurt like hell. Now they're bee stings and my biggest problem is the blood.

I get in the shower and turn it on hot. At least I think so. Anyway, I stand under the water long enough that I start to feel a little better.

When I've scrubbed the blood off and the wounds clean, I towel off and knock on the bathroom door. Candy comes in immediately. Still bleeding, I get back in the tub.

"See that cling wrap over there?"

"Yeah," she says.

"That's what's holding me together. I need you to wrap my shoulder, body, and leg tight."

She says, "Okay," and gets right to it. No hesitation. I've missed her so much.

It takes a few minutes to get me mummified enough to stop the bleeding. When it's done, we sit on the side of the tub in the steamy bathroom and look at each other.

"Hell of a way to let someone know you're back," she says. At first, it sounds like she might be mad, but she smiles when she says it.

"It's not exactly the grand reunion I'd hoped for."

"How long have you been back?"

"About four days."

Now she does look a little mad. "And you didn't come to see me? Didn't call or anything? What the fuck is wrong with you?"

"I wanted to, but I couldn't."

"Why not?"

"I was fucked up in a hundred ways. I still am."

I tell her about Wormwood, how they brought me back, and how Sandoval and Howard wouldn't finish their end of the deal.

"That's why you're like this? You're not completely alive?"

"Worse. I'm dying again. That's why I didn't call. It didn't seem fair to show up just to die in front of you again."

She looks at me hard. "I'm a big girl. You could have let me choose for myself."

"I know. I'm sorry."

We sit there quietly for a minute.

I say, "You and Alessa look happy."

"We are," she says. "I was in a pretty dark place after you died. She helped me through it. We've got a nice life now."

"I'm glad. Kasabian tells me that the store is doing well too."

"Better than ever. This last year, we've really pulled things together."

She looks at me. Turns a little white.

"That sounded weird. I didn't mean it's been good because you weren't there. It's just, Alessa has a lot of ideas and is good with business."

"It's okay," I tell her. "I'm happy it's all going so well."

"Thanks," she says, barely above a whisper.

"I should get dressed."

"Do you need help?"

"No. I'll be fine."

I get up and hobble to the sink.

"You're such an asshole," says Candy. "Come here."

I lean on her while she helps me into my pants and boots.

I feel a weird mix of happiness and sadness that I'm with her again because the first thing we're doing together—cleaning me up after I've gotten shot—is exactly what Kasabian told me they'd grown past. She goes into the living room and comes back with the other I LUV LA shirt. Helps me put it on. She even slips on my glove and gives my hand a tiny kiss. Dressed and clean, I don't feel that bad.

"What now?" she says.

"I need food."

"I could eat too."

"I'll see you in the kitchen in a minute."

When she's gone, I check myself in the mirror. My face and lips are blue, like I've been holding my breath since New Year's. I brush my teeth again and go to the kitchen.

Candy has laid out what looks like every piece of food in the house on the kitchen island. Alessa is next to her chewing a baby carrot.

"What will you have, sir?" says Candy.

"It doesn't matter. I can't taste anything."

"Oh."

"Sorry. Meat. I need protein."

She piles a plate high with chicken legs and slices of roast beef. When she's done she says, "You want it warm?"

"Sure. Thanks."

As she carries it to the microwave, I look at Alessa.

"Chihiro . . ."

"It's okay to call her Candy. She explained everything to me after you . . . you know."

"Right. Anyway, she tells me that you've really turned Max Overdrive around."

She nods. "I didn't think I could work at the same place day after day, but it's kind of our world that we made together. It's cool."

"And Kasabian?"

She smiles. "He takes a little getting used to, but he's fun to have around."

"'Fun' isn't the word most people use about Kasabian. It's nice that you get along."

"He's a hoot. And he knows a lot about movies. More than I'll ever know."

"Probably more than all of us put together."

She picks up another carrot and says, "Can I ask you a question?"

"Of course."

"What's the story with your arm? My uncle had a prosthetic leg, but I've never seen anything like yours before."

I tear off a piece of sliced chicken and eat it.

"I lost my arm in a fight. Someone thought it would be funny to give me this ugly one."

"Why don't you just get a regular one?"

"It doesn't come off."

She looks at me.

"It's attached? Like it's magic?"

"Exactly."

Alessa sighs.

"I didn't believe in magic until I met Candy. I don't mean the 'Oh, baby, you're so magic' kind of thing. I mean real magic."

"What convinced you?"

"All the weird movies the witch brings us. Movies that never got made in this world."

"Do you have a favorite?"

She thinks for a minute.

"La Femme Nikita 2."

"There's a second one? I'd like to see that."

"Come on by. You know where we live."

I can't tell if Alessa is being casual or giving me a hard time with "You know where *we* live" and "our world that *we* made together." But she might be thinking the same thing about me with Candy dressing and undressing me. Really, neither of us knows the other at all. This is the first time we've said more than a few words to each other. However, she's not shy.

She says, "So. I guess we're both in love with Candy."

I eat another piece of chicken.

"I guess we are."

"What are we going to do about that?"

"I have no idea."

"Me neither."

I flex my left hand, feeling more than a little self-conscious.

"Tell me something," Alessa says. "Why did you jump in front of me back there?"

"You mean, why didn't I let you get shot?"

"Yeah. I mean, I get why you were watching the store. Those guys could have hurt Candy. But why help me?"

"I don't let friends die."

She sets down her carrot.

"We're friends?"

I really want a cigarette. I wonder if Abbot would mind if I smoked in here.

"Friends of friends," I say. "I wouldn't let anyone Candy cared about get hurt."

She grunts quietly, not entirely convinced.

I take the Shermans from my pocket. Alessa perks up when she sees them.

"Can I have one of those?"

I open the pack and look at her.

"There's only one left. Want to split it?"

She really wants to say no.

"Fuck it. Sure."

As we head for one of the porthole windows Candy says, "Where are you two off to?"

"Smoke break," says Alessa.

Candy frowns.

"You said you were quitting."

"I am. But I almost got shot tonight."

"Plus, there's me," I say.

"Plus, there's him."

Candy looks at us a little nervously.

"Play nice. Both of you. We'll figure things out."

"I know," says Alessa.

We go into the living room and I pop one of the windows open. Forty-year-old L.A. air drifts in. I wish I could smell it. Johnny Thunders, Nico, and Sergio Leone are breathing that air.

I light the Sherman, take a puff, and hand it to Alessa.

Neither of us talks for a while. We just pass the cigarette back and forth.

I tap some ashes out the window and say, "I'm dying. By this time tomorrow I might be dead for good."

Alessa says, "Does Candy know?"

"I told her. She's going to be upset if it happens."

"Don't worry. I'll take care of her."

"Good."

I give her the last puff of the cigarette. She stubs it out against the sole of her shoe and tosses it out the window. I close it and we head back to the kitchen.

"In the meantime," I say, "you and me don't have to be enemies."

Alessa stops.

"And if you live?"

"Not then either as far as I'm concerned."

"This is going to get complicated."

"Not if I die."

She gives me a look. "Stop saying that. You think I want someone Candy cares about dead?"

"It would uncomplicate things."

"No it wouldn't. They'd just be complicated in a different way."

"You're probably right."

"Fuck," she says quietly.

"Yeah."

We start back to the kitchen.

Alessa says, "Let's just see how things go."

"That makes sense to me."

"Thanks for the cigarette."

"Anytime."

Candy looks relieved when we get back.

"Eat," she says. "Both of you."

I start on the meat she microwaved.

Kasabian comes in.

"I see you're still dragging the necromancer around," he says.

"What necromancer?" says Candy.

"Jonathan Howard," I say between bites.

"Can he keep you from dying?"

"Yes. But he won't. That's why I kidnapped him."

Kasabian sits at the kitchen island and glares at me.

"A shootout, dead cops, party to a kidnapping, and now we're running from the Wild Bunch. Great to see you again, buddy."

"Shut up and eat."

When we finish, Candy says, "What happens next?"

We leave the leftovers on the island and go into the living room. I take Ray's piece of paper from my pocket.

"Ray, a sort of *brujo* Carlos introduced me to, is researching ways to fix me. I gave him Vidocq's number, but even with his help, I don't know if they'll come up with anything."

"Okay. But that doesn't answer my question."

I hand her the paper.

"I'm going to see the next name on the kill list."

"Hijruun," she says. "What kind of name is that?"

"I met a Hijruun in Hell once. A cackler. He was selling some curses to Azazel."

"What's a cackler?" says Alessa from the couch.

"They're weird, ugly fuckers," says Kasabian. "Big bags of bones. And when they talk, they always sound like they're laughing."

"You think Hijruun might know something that could help you?" says Candy.

She hands me the list.

"Cacklers know a lot of arcane hoodoo. And I can't just sit

around here. Maybe if I warn Hijruun about the faction, he'll trade me some information."

"Sounds like a plan," she says. "Do you know where Hijruun lives?"

"Technically in an alternate reality, but it's a close one, so I can get there through the Room."

"Great. I'm going with you."

Alessa stands up.

"Wait. You told me he did this kind of stuff all the time."

"He did," says Candy. "When he was well. Look at him now."

She goes to Candy.

"You told me, months ago, you were glad to not be doing this kind of crazy stuff anymore. The running around. The guns and magic and killing. You said you were happy."

Candy looks at me a little guiltily, then back at Alessa.

"I am happy. But, well, *look* at him."

Alessa shifts her weight, getting angrier.

"I am. Are you? He looks horrible. But according to you and Kasabian, he was always like this."

"Not always," says Candy.

"Always," says Kasabian.

"Now he shows up after all this time, almost gets us shot, and you go running back to him," says Alessa.

"It's not like that," Candy says.

"Then how is it?"

Candy takes Alessa's hand.

"I love our life. I'm not running back to him. But Stark and me have a lot of history together. That means something."

Alessa looks at me. It's all in her eyes. She's not angry.

She's scared. Not that I'm going to steal Candy from her, but that I'm going to do something dumb and get her killed.

"Alessa's right," I say. "I created this problem the moment I agreed to work for Wormwood. It was a selfish and stupid bargain and it makes me pretty much as bad as them. But it was my choice. I'm not dragging anyone else down with me."

I start away and Candy says, "Don't leave yet."

She hustles Alessa into one of the side rooms. I head into the bathroom. Kasabian follows me in.

He says, "Spreading hope and sunshine wherever you go."

I open the medicine cabinet and go through it, looking for anything that might help heal me. I look at Kasabian.

"Once upon a time, I thought we were friends, Kas."

"That was then. This is now. Friendship only goes so far when one of the friends spends all his time trying to get the other killed."

"You know that's not true."

"I'm not saying you mean it. You just can't help it. You said it yourself. You're a shit magnet. And you're going to fuck up me and the girls."

I toss bottles of pills and ointments into the sink. But I set aside a tube of antibiotic cream.

"The three of you are going to stay here. I only have a few hours left. It will be morning soon. If you don't hear back from me before dark, go home. You'll be safe and I'll be gone for good."

"And if you do come back?"

"Odds are I won't."

"What about Sleeping Beauty in the boudoir?"

I'd almost forgotten about Howard.

"If I don't come back, let him go. But punch him in the balls for me. Just once."

Kasabian nods. "I can do that." He leans against the wall. "This is a little weird," he says.

"What is?"

"Saying good-bye like this. The first time you were gone, it was pretty abrupt. Now it's sort of like putting down the family dog."

I look at him.

"I'm going to take that as a compliment."

He shrugs, then asks, "You'll be okay if you go back to Hell, right?"

"I always am."

"It's just . . . there's no malice in this, okay? I want you to be all right. I just want you to do it far away."

I stop pawing through the cabinet and look at him.

"Whatever happens, that's the plan."

"Okay," he says. "I hope shit works out for you."

"Thanks."

"You just scare me a lot of the time."

"I understand."

"When you go—if you live—you should take some movies with you. Anything you want."

I stop again. For Kasabian that's as close to flowers and Valentines as anyone is ever going to get.

"Thanks. I'll probably take you up on that."

"Yeah."

Candy comes into the bathroom.

"Kas, would you wait outside for a minute?"

"Sure," he says. Then, "Later."

"See you."

When he's gone, she closes the door.

She says, "It's set. I'm going with you."

I grab a bottle off the shelf. Finally, something I can use.

"Are you sure? I won't have the last thing I do in the world be fucking things up between you and Alessa."

"It's okay," she says. "But I made her understand. If you die and I could have helped but didn't because she might be mad, that's guaranteed to fuck things up for us."

"Spreading hope and sunshine wherever I go."

"What?"

"It's just something Kasabian said."

"Don't listen to him," she says. "He's a scaredy-cat who doesn't like the furniture getting moved around."

"That's the thing. I don't want to move your furniture around."

"And you're not. This is something I want to do. We'll get through this and when you're well again, we'll figure out the other stuff."

I gesture to the door with the bottle.

"Kasabian said I could take some movies with me."

Candy smiles.

"It sounds like true love."

"He's always been a romantic."

"What's that you've got?" she says, looking at the bottle.

I hold it up so she can see it.

"Tincture of asphodel," I say. "Hoodoo Adderall. It's like an energy drink made with rocket fuel."

"Cool. I could use that at the store on weekends."

"If I live, I'll steal you a crate."

She laughs.

"Stealing Sub Rosa speed. Just like old times."

"You know it."

"Are you ready to go?"

"Almost. Would you see if there's any duct tape around? If I start falling apart, I might need something stronger than cling wrap."

"I'll check the kitchen cabinets."

We go back into the living room. Alessa and Kasabian are sitting together on the couch. Alessa's eyes are red. Candy squeezes her shoulder as she goes past.

I go into the bedroom and wake Howard.

He looks at me and tries to hide his smile. He fails.

"You're looking well," he says.

I sit on the end of the bed, trying to look as nonlethal as an extra from *Night of the Living Dead* can.

"I'm here to make a deal. Tell me what you want to do Ludovico's Ellicit."

"You know what I want. I want to be free of you. I want to go back to Eva's house."

"You're safer here right now. There's a lot of gunplay around town. But if you fix me, I guarantee I'll leave you alone."

"What kind of guarantee?"

"There are people in the next room. One person in particular. I've promised them I'll leave them alone too. I care more about them than anything, including me. If you help me out, I'll make the same deal with you."

Howard's raises his eyebrows a little.

"Is Sandman Slim offering me true love like his lady friend outside?"

"I'll throw in something else too."

"What?"

"Protection. You know what I can do. You help me out, I'll keep Wormwood off your back."

"How?"

"By killing them."

He frowns.

"You see, it's that kind of behavior that makes me hesitate. You kill the things that upset you. But I upset you. You'd kill me if you could, but you can't. Not right now at least."

"What if I swear in front of them? I'm not going to lie about that in front of Candy. Not for my life. She'd hate me for it."

"Very dramatic," says Howard. "Believe me, if I thought that helping you would keep me safe, I would do it."

"Let me ask you something. What's your middle name?"

"Lee. Why?"

I cannot catch a fucking break in this life. Or maybe I can.

"Exactly how good a necromancer are you? I mean, could you bring yourself back to life?"

"Another empty threat?" says Howard.

"It's a real question. I only bring it up because your name is next on the faction's kill list."

Howard sits up a little straighter.

"'Kill list'?" he says. "What do you mean?"

I get up off the bed. I have to touch the wall to keep from swaying on my bad leg.

"I took it off a dead faction magician. You're good with languages. Read it yourself."

I toss the scroll on the bed. Howard grabs it and stares at the names.

"This is bad," he says.

"Is that your professional opinion?"

I grab the scroll back and roll it up slowly, giving him time to think things over.

"In the end, I don't have to do a damn thing to you. The faction will do it for me."

"Why didn't you mention this before?"

"Are you freaked out?"

"Yes."

"There you go. I didn't need you any more freaked out than you already were. You need to make some rational fucking decisions and you need to make them now."

Howard gets it. He leans against the headboard and crosses his arms.

"I'm going to have to think about this," he says. After a minute he says, "What about money?"

"All I have is the money I stole from you while you were out. Want it back?"

He gives me a look.

"I mean real money. If I help you, Eva will never forgive me. I'll need to get away and be able to take care of myself for a long time when I do."

I lean against the wall, tired again.

"Are you asking me to rob a bank?"

"Of course not. I want you to rob *Eva*," he says. "There's a safe in the floor under her desk. The cash is clean and there are bearer bonds. Jewelry and gold too, from what I understand. I might be persuaded to help you for that."

"Done," I say, and hold out my hand to shake. Howard looks at my overripe mitt and just nods.

"I'll take your word for it."

"Then we have a deal?"

"I'm going to have to think about it."

"I won't be gone long. Have an answer for me when I get back."

"Of course."

I go out, reseal the wards so he can't escape, and meet Candy in the kitchen. She holds up a big roll of gray duct tape.

"Ta-da."

"Great."

I put it in my pocket and check myself for weapons. I have everything, but I wish I had more damn bullets.

"You ready?" I say.

Candy says, "Give me one minute."

She goes back into the living room and talks to Alessa. They hug. I think Alessa is crying again. I turn away and swallow the tincture of asphodel. A warmth moves quickly from my heart out to my limbs. I feel strong again. I don't look any better—the asphodel doesn't change the color of my hand—but I feel good enough to do a little healing hoodoo on my leg. The wound knits together almost instantly. I know this stuff is temporary, but for however long it lasts, it'll be great not feeling like a moldy sponge.

I go into the living room. Alessa is back on the couch holding Candy's hand. After a few seconds she lets go.

She says, "Are we just supposed to sit around here while you two are gone?"

"No," I say. "Call your father. Tell him what happened and that people might be after him. Don't tell him where you are. His phone might be bugged. Just tell him that you're safe."

"Anything else?"

"Do you think our other friends are safe?" says Candy.

"I don't know. Call them too, Alessa. Tell them to get over here. Allegra. Brigitte. Vidocq. Carlos and Ray too."

I write Ray's number and instructions for getting into the salon on a pad, pass it and the key to her.

"What do you want me to do?" says Kasabian.

"I don't think Howard can get out of the bedroom, but if he does . . ."

"I know. Punch him in the balls."

"You got it."

I look at Candy.

"You ready?"

She leans down and kisses Alessa.

"Soon, baby," she says.

"Soon," says Alessa.

I take Candy through a shadow, pretty sure that no matter how much Howard hates me, it's not half of what Alessa is feeling right now.

EACH OF THE thirteen doors in the Room leads somewhere I want, but the place didn't come with a user manual. I've learned to move through it by trial and error. Truth is, I haven't used most of the doors, and I never use the thirteenth—the Door to Nothing. It's sealed shut. Where it leads, I never want to see again. Going from what I remember about Hijruun, I take Candy through the Door of Mist. I'm not worried about what's on the other side. I'm worried that I might not remember the cackler right and we could waste time running around the wrong reality.

"Compared to some places you've taken me, this isn't so bad," says Candy.

We're in a dense forest. Golden light filters down through the trees in bright shafts. The air is clean.

Fucking nature.

"I just hope we're in the right place."

"How will you know?" she says.

We start up a hill on a white trail that's like walking on a soft carpet. Please don't let me die here in Tinkerbell country.

"Hijruun is an important magician in his world. Plus, I think he has connections to the royal family. He lives in a tower in a deep valley."

"This hill?" says Candy.

"I hope so. I've never been through this door before, but the Room knows what I'm looking for."

Red and white flowers line the path on both sides. Moss hangs from the lower tree branches.

I say, "I think we're at least in the right reality."

"How do you know?"

"You like the flowers?"

"Sure. They're pretty."

"Look closer."

Candy steps to the side of the path and picks one of the buds.

"Shit!" she yells, and throws it away. "That flower was a fucking eyeball," she says.

I point to the trees.

"Look at the moss."

She squints into the gloom.

"It looks weird. Is it moving?"

"Yeah. They're bundles of nerves. They're on all the paths. Like surveillance cameras."

We continue up the hill and over a rise. With the potion in my system, I feel like I could climb goddamn Kilimanjaro.

"This carpet is nice," says Candy. "Are all the trails like this?"

"I think so. Anyway, it's not carpet."

She kicks at the path with the toe of her boot.

"Ewww. Are those bones?"

"Very old bones. Cartilage. Remains of anything that dies in the forest."

"Jesus. You take me to the nicest places."

She looks at the bones again.

"You think there are people in the road?"

"No. Anything that talks gets buried. These are just birds and mice and things."

Candy bumps into me, trying to keep away from the eyes on the edge of the trail.

"You might have told me about some of this before."

"I didn't know if we were in the right place."

"Still. Whenever you take someone somewhere that's made of eyeballs and bones, it's just good manners to warn them."

"I'll remember that."

I almost say, *I'll remember that for next time,* but catch myself.

"Okay. We're in the right world. Where is Hijruun?"

"If we're lucky, right down there."

I point to a tower standing at the intersection of four trails.

Candy starts walking faster but falls back when my bad leg won't let me keep up. Still, when we make it there a half hour later, I'm feeling good.

"Okay. That's impressive," says Candy.

"This is the right place. I remember Hijruun describing it to Azazel."

The tower is around fifty feet high and capped with a vaulted roof that gently rises and falls, like the building is breathing. The main structure is made entirely from gravestones that have been cut to fit together like a massive jigsaw puzzle. The courtyard area is surrounded by high curtains of animal bones.

"You could have told me about that too," says Candy.

"If you don't like that you're not going to like the doorbell."

Candy looks and shakes her head. "I'm definitely not touching it."

"Always leaving me with the dirty work."

"You *are* the dirty work."

A large pair of pink, healthy-looking lungs hangs on a hook near the door. I squeeze them and a horn blares somewhere inside the tower.

Candy rubs her nose.

"That's gross. You're gross."

"That's half the reason you like me."

"True. You really do take me to the most glamorous places."

"You better hope he doesn't ask us in for tea and crumpets. You don't want to know what those are like."

"Still gross."

I give the lungs another squeeze, but no one comes down. When I try the knob on the gravestone door it swings open.

There's a long spiral staircase. Every few feet, candles burn within holders made from ribs and vertebrae. Books and papers are scattered on the stairs. A small table by the door is on its side.

I look at Candy.

"Do you have your knife?"

"Always."

"Keep it ready."

She takes it out of her jacket.

"No one's home?"

"I don't think so. But they left in a hurry."

"Do you think the killers got here ahead of us?"

"I doubt it. Those faction pricks would have burned the tower as a warning to everyone else."

"What are we going to do now?" says Candy.

I think for a minute.

"Fuck. I'm going to have to do some tracking hoodoo."

"Are you strong enough for that?"

"I don't have any choice. I'm not going to sit around and rot."

"How can I help?"

We go outside. I take out the black blade and kneel on the ground.

"Keep your eyes open. If anything weird comes at us, let me know."

"Weird?" she says. "What's your standard for weird here? Someone riding a bicycle made of tits and assholes?"

"Definitely let me know about that. I wouldn't want to miss it."

With the blade, I cut a magic circle into the ground. I don't have a map of the place to use as a reference, so I'm going to have to use some extra-elaborate hoodoo, which is going to tire me out and take a lot longer to set up.

A gentle wind blows through the forest, passing through the bone curtains and making them rattle like bamboo wind chimes.

I'm on my knees trying to carve intricate mystical scripts and sigils into the ground and it's not working. Everywhere around here is covered in the bone carpet we walked to get here. Cutting it is easy, but it's too soft to hold the hoodoo forms I need. I'm going to have to dig down until I hit dirt and start over. This is going to take forever.

I've gouged out a couple of clumps of bones when the wind stirs and the curtain rattles again.

"Stark!" yells Candy.

Something bursts through the hanging bones, something we didn't see earlier because it too is bones. It's ten feet tall, with a head like an elongated fish skull. Its entire body is made out of smaller animal skulls, some with jutting horns and antlers. It moves quickly and quietly, knocking Candy flying with the back of its arm. Over its head, the bone mountain holds a cleaver that's as long as I am tall. When it swings the blade down at me, I know I'm fucked. My bad leg is too far gone for me to move quickly. All I can do is roll away and hope for the best. The little skulls on its back giggle and guffaw at me.

I get lucky with the first blow and it misses. The cleaver goes in so hard that the ground shakes. It takes it a couple of tries for it to pull the thing free.

"Hijruun!" I shout.

If he hears me, he doesn't care.

The moment the cleaver comes free, Hijruun swings at me again. I can't move out of the way this time and my injured arm isn't going to stop a blade that weighs as much as a narwhal. Without thinking, I reach out with my prosthetic hand—and catch the cleaver. The impact just about knocks me over. While on one knee, I grab the top of the cleaver with my other hand and spin my whole body. There's a loud *snap* as Hijruun's hand breaks off at the wrist. He falls to his knees, howling and cackling with laughter.

Candy jumps on him from behind, holding her knife to his throat. She's gone full Jade, so I wave with both hands to get her attention.

"Hold on. It's Hijruun. The one we're looking for."

I look down at him. He nods and the little skulls titter.

"Kill me quickly, Hell beast," he simultaneously laughs and howls. "That's the only favor I ask of you."

"Calm down, you bony fuck. I didn't come all this way to kill you."

"Liar!" he chuckles. "I remember you from Azazel's stable. You're the slim one. The monster who kills monsters."

"I haven't worked for him for a long time. In fact, I'm the one who killed him."

"Then damn you for that," Hijruun chortles. "I have been without decent access to the Hellion court since he died."

I put away my knife and tell Candy to do the same. She does and transforms back into her human form.

I say, "There is no Hellion court anymore. The place is a shambles."

"So I understand," says Hijruun. "The war that shredded the place, was it your doing?"

"Not entirely. But I helped."

Hijruun rises to his full height. His one bony hand holds on to his broken wrist.

"If you're not here to kill me, might I retrieve my hand?"

"Just the hand. Leave the cleaver where it is."

"If you insist," he laughs.

Talking to him is unnerving. When everything I say is a joke, I can't gauge his tone. And he doesn't have a heart or eyes, so I'm screwed there too.

He pulls his hand free of the cleaver and holds it to the end of his wrist. The bones knit back together in a few seconds.

"Now, monster who no longer kills monsters," he giggles. "Why have you come all this way?"

I get closer.

"Don't get me wrong. I still kill monsters. But not today. Today, I'm here to warn you that someone is coming to kill you."

"If not you then who?"

"Have you ever heard of Wormwood?"

That gets some big yuks. He howls, sniggers, and guffaws for a long time. I can't tell if he's scared or thought the question was genuinely funny.

"And here I was running from you," he chuckles. "I ruined some books escaping my tower."

"Sorry, but I didn't have your number. It sounds like you know who Wormwood is."

"That I do," he laughs. "But why would Wormwood care about me?"

"I don't know, but your name was on a list of people to be murdered."

That really cracks him up. He laughs and laughs, but I get the feeling that might be how a cackler sounds when it's in pain.

"I'm not surprised," Hijruun says with the smallest chuckle. "So many friends in so many realities have been taken. And you say it's been Wormwood's work?"

"Yes."

"But which one? Each is more awful than the other. I can scarcely believe such malevolence," he screeches.

"I know what you mean. I'd like to kill them all."

Hijruun looks at us with his hollow eyes.

"Neither of you is human, am I right?"

"I'm half-human," I say.

"Then forgive me cursing you and all of your kind. Of all the evils I have seen in the centuries of my existence, I've never seen a species so dedicated to its own ruin and corruption."

"What do you mean?" says Candy.

Hijruun looks at her, then back to me.

"You know of Wormwood and the newer so-called Wormwood? Tell me which one is worse."

"That's easy. The faction. They're religious nuts killing everything in their way, in any reality, to get control of the world. Never trust a crusader."

He looks at Candy.

"And you agree?" he giggles.

"Absolutely."

"Then what do you say to the ultimate goal of the original Wormwood? Do you judge their betrayal of the human race less harshly?"

I say, "I don't know what you're talking about."

Now he laughs for real.

"You're in a war and you don't even know your enemy's motives and goals. Perhaps you should go back to your old ways, slim one. You were a better assassin than a soldier."

"What does 'betrayal of the human race' mean?" says Candy. I can hear her worry for Alessa in every syllable.

Hijruun and his skulls whoop.

"The faction, as you call them, longs to serve a God who has no use for them. But the earlier, older Wormwood still lives only to serve itself. They've made a compact with God's rebel angels to steal every mortal soul that is or has ever been to prevent them from entering Heaven. This will end the great war and things in the afterlife will regain their balance. As a half-human, you must be so proud."

He's laughing harder than ever now. It's distracting. I can't think things through.

"That doesn't make sense. Even Wormwood members die. What's going to happen to their souls when they go?"

That cracks him up even more.

"Nothing, because they won't die. Part of their bargain with the rebels is a Heavenly elixir. It will render them as immortal as the angels themselves. This will make them kings of their world and lords of every human soul unto the end of time. It's enough to make one laugh."

And he does just that.

I look at Candy. We both know it, but she's polite enough not to say it. This is who I've been working for. People who are going to own every human in existence. Wormwood can already buy and sell damnation. What will happen when they can sell immortality too? The kind of people who can afford that are exactly the kind who shouldn't get near it. And I've been their stooge from the second I got back, paving the way for them to wipe out the faction and buy eternity for themselves and their friends. Now I am going to kill all of them. And I deserve to die along with them.

"Stark warned you," says Candy. "Isn't that worth something?"

"Of course," laughs Hijruun. "My kind pays our debts. Ask what you will."

"He's dying. Can you do anything to stop it?"

The big bag of bones looks me over. After a while he says, "You wish to live forever?" Hijruun giggles.

"No. Just my normal time."

The cackler thinks, the skulls along his body whispering and laughing at something we can't hear and probably wouldn't understand if we could.

"There might be a way. A potion. Something very old. I have the makings in the tower. Come," he snickers, then stops and looks at me.

"Will you encounter either Wormwood again, do you think?" laughs Hijruun.

"I'm sure of it."

Hijruun touches one of the skulls on his side and it pops open, revealing something gleaming inside.

"Please give this to them," he snickers.

It's a small clear crystal, about the size of my thumb.

"What is it?"

"A surprise," Hijruun howls. "Now come. Let us see about your potion."

We barely get twenty feet.

They come out of the trees, down the bone trail, and through the eyeball thicket. All in balaclavas and heavily armed. When they're rushing us like that, I can't tell how many of them there are, or if they're Wormwood or the faction.

As if that matters anymore.

Hijruun grabs his enormous cleaver and slices the closest gunman in two, then swings it back, using the blunt side to crush the skull of another.

Candy goes Jade and drops back behind the bone curtain, before bursting out again and bringing down two more gunmen.

I can't move as fast as Candy or Hijruun, so I empty the Glock and the Colt at the shooters. Each bullet hits, but the bastards are wearing body armor so all the shots do is make them dance a little. I retreat around the side of Hijruun's tower and disappear into a shadow. When they come around for me, I jam the black blade into the base of the second shooter's skull. By the time the first one has turned around, I've disappeared again. Come out by the side of a tree, swinging the na'at like a sword, slashing through his armor. As he falls, he fires wildly. I dive for cover, but not before a shot ricochets off my Kissi arm and slices my cheek. Perfect. I'm going to die even uglier now. By the time the idiot hits the ground, he's blown through his clip, so I pigstick the bastard through the heart.

Just as I turn to check on Candy, something hits me in the side of the neck.

I rip it out.

It's a tiny dart.

I fall.

There's a gunman standing right over me.

I get one last look at Hijruun lying facedown on the bone trail and Candy being chased into the forest by a couple more shooters.

And I pass out.

I DON'T KNOW how long I was unconscious. My head hurts like someone ran over it with a tank, but that could be the drugs or the fact I got shot in the fucking face. Blood is steadily oozing, down my cheek. I touch the wound and my hand comes back slick with something the color of old motor oil.

"Anyone got a Band-Aid?"

We're in a big room. A huge damn room. Four of the masked shooters stand over me with their rifles ready to put many more holes in my body. That's the last thing I want right now, so I stay down with my hands in plain sight.

One of the shooters squats next to me and yanks off their balaclava.

It's Marcella.

"Did you find that pay phone I told you about?"

She shakes her head.

"I gave a cabbie the twenty to borrow his phone."

"That is simpler. But doesn't he have your pricks' phone number now?"

Marcella sighs dramatically. "We had to take him into custody. If he's good, we'll make some modifications to his memory and send him home with a new phone."

"You keep telling yourself that, but Wormwood doesn't have a good track record with catch and release."

She cocks her head at me.

"You keep saying 'Wormwood' like the organizations are interchangeable. *They're* the ones who want nothing more than to murder humanity. *We* want to improve it."

"From what I've seen, you're both pretty okay with the idea of mass murder. What about your ritual at the chapel? There are four million people in L.A. How many were you looking to kill? One million as an object lesson to the others or all of them so you could repopulate the city with your Stepford Assholes?"

Marcella looks up at the other shooters. They haven't moved an inch. She stands up.

"What if I explained our position to you from the beginning? Would you even listen?"

"Not by the hair of my chinny chin chin. Wormwood explained and justified itself to me before. It was all lies. Your bunch? You're the same shit just in a shiny new package."

"There's nothing I can say to change your mind? Just to get you to be quiet for a while and listen?"

"Nothing."

She looks past me to somewhere in the distance.

"You look a lot worse than the last time I saw you. If you just cooperated a little, we might be able to help you."

The blood running down my neck is making my shirt and coat sticky.

"I don't want your help, but can I at least stop this damn bleeding?"

"How?"

"I have a bandage in my pocket."

Marcella says, "You're aware there are three associates here who'll shoot you if you try anything smart."

"Don't worry. I haven't done anything smart in years."

Very slowly, I take the duct tape from my pocket and show it to everyone. Cool. No one shoots me. I pull out a couple of inches and tear it off with my teeth. I'm still not shot. Things are going great. With my coat sleeve, I clean my cheek, then smack the tape into place. I put the roll back in my pocket and show everyone my hands.

I say, "How do I look?"

"Like a pail of manure dragged down a bumpy road and dumped into a river of puke," says a familiar voice from behind me.

He comes around the side and stands with Marcella.

"It took a while," says Marshal Larson Wells. "But you finally have the face you deserve."

I look around the room. I'm surrounded by men and women in sharp business suits. A lot of flag lapel pins and BLUE LIVES MATTER buttons. All of them have little cross tie tacks and the power of the Lord in their hearts. Beyond them are military vehicles and long racks of impressive weapons.

Oh Hell.

The faction really isn't Wormwood.

It's the Golden Vigil.

Wells leans down a few inches for a better look at me and says, "How's my favorite pixie today?"

He says "pixie" the way he always does. The way a redneck says "faggot."

The Golden Vigil is the first bunch of bastards I worked for. Soon after I crawled out of Hell the first time, Wells and his people picked me up and offered me a job. Didn't offer it so much as said they'd kill me if I didn't take it. The Golden Vigil was a secret paramilitary group that, in theory, policed Lurkers, magicians, and all kinds of questionable mystical activity for the government. I don't know if it was by design or just the kind of volunteers the Vigil got, but they were also psycho religious fruit bats. And I thought they'd been disbanded after Marshal Wells put a bullet through Mason Faim's head.

I smile at him with my gray teeth and black gums.

"Hi, Larson. I thought you were in jail for murder."

"Don't throw my name around like that, son, or you will be sorry," he says. "And as to your other point, I'm not in jail because you can't murder someone who isn't human. It's in the Constitution."

"Where?"

"Well, it will be soon enough."

"Mason was a human—a backstabbing bastard, but human enough. You shot him in front of a hundred witnesses."

"Wrong," he says, "and watch your language. The person you refer to as Mason Faim was an unclean spirit possessing the body of a dead man. He had committed a number of gruesome murders and deserved to be shuffled off this mortal coil forever. Amen."

"But it was still a scandal, Wells. How do you live with yourself over that?"

"Just fine, thank you. Time with like-minded brothers and sisters and solitary prayer brought me back to my senses. A good union kept me in government service. And a keen awareness of Wormwood's growing power brought me and these good people right to where we are today. Hallelujah."

"Hallelujah," say a few of his lackeys.

My head is finally clear enough that I can sit up straight. I swivel around to everyone, giving them a good look at my rotten face.

I say, "The Elmer Gantry act is very convincing, but why pretend you're Wormwood? That doesn't make any sense."

"It makes perfect sense if you think about it, but you're not a thinking creature, so let me explain. Wormwood is an old organization with invisible tentacles—literally in some cases—in virtually every part of government, business, and the lives of ordinary citizens. Wormwood is a brand as much as an organization. And when we replace it with our new and righteous order . . ."

"You'll get royalties on Wormwood sneakers and hand out political endorsement deals to your favorite cross burners and good, down-home lynch mobs."

"You should be quiet and listen," says Marcella.

"I was listening to Wells's line before you ever held a cattle prod. I know him better than you ever will."

Wells turns to his people. Points down at me.

"Delusions of grandeur," he says. "The sin of pride and so many others. I'd say all of them, but Stark here cannot be accused of sloth. And I suppose the Lord is grateful for that one small thing."

The Vigil laughs in that dead way that everyone laughs at their boss's bad jokes.

I say, "From what I hear, God isn't taking your calls these days. Wormwood, any version of it, isn't getting through the pearly gates."

Wells turns back to me.

"What makes you think we've tried to get in touch with the old coot?" he says. "Do you remember Aelita? The angel the Lord sent to guide the Vigil in its early days?"

"I remember you mooning after her. I remember a psycho who ran the Vigil by day and plotted God's murder by night. Is that the same righteous Aelita you're talking about? The wannabe god killer?"

Wells points at me like P. T. Barnum showing off the dog-faced boy to the masses.

"That's her in a nutshell. And I doubted her. Then when she was gone it broke my heart because I thought she'd died in sin. But now I know she was right."

That I didn't see coming.

"When I speak to you of the Lord," Wells says, "I do it in the broadest sense of a wise and righteous ruler of Heaven and Earth. The creature who sits on Heaven's throne now is a monstrosity who will be brought low. He will be vanquished and he will pay for the crime of sitting on a throne to which he was not entitled."

"I heard he steals cable too," I say, struggling to my feet.

Wells says, "That kind of humor only makes clear the debauched ethic of your life. You have nothing to say. Nothing to contribute. And you do it all day long, profane and blaspheming all the while. And so proud of yourself and your transgressions."

I look past Wells at his Brooks Brothers flock.

"He's just jealous because I'm more of an angel than he'll ever be."

"It's true," he says. "This thing before you isn't just a debased human; he is half angel. Let that be a lesson to you. You might think that you were born into righteousness, but if a celestial being like this can fall so low, so can any of you without eternal vigilance."

The room goes silent as the idiots let Wells's warning sink in. I can't stand it.

"Does anyone have a cigarette? I promise not to kill anyone with a goddamn cigarette. I'm not picky. I'll even take a menthol."

Wells punches me. I can tell it's hard because my head moves. But I can't feel a thing. I test the duct tape. It's still in place.

"Where are my artifacts?" he says. "I know you stole them."

"Which artifacts are those? There are so many of them these days. I blame the Internet."

"The holy objects you took from our brethren at the Chapel of St. Alexis."

"Oh, those artifacts. What does everybody want with them? What I saw looked like flea market junk."

"What they're for doesn't concern you. But you don't really think you stopped anything with your stunt at the chapel, do you?"

"I kind of hoped."

"Where are they?"

"I forget."

Wells fiddles with his tie.

"That pixie you travel with. What's her name this week? Candy? Chihiro? Whore of Babylon? She's still alive, back where you abandoned her. But that can change at a moment's notice. It's nothing at all to send some men to hunt her down like the monster she is."

One bit of good news, then. Candy is alive. Wells wouldn't lie about something like that. It would be a sin.

"Your artifacts were shot to pieces by your idiots at the chapel."

"The scroll too?"

"That I burned."

He blinks once.

"Is that true?"

"Once I figured out it was a kill list I burned it to keep anyone else from using it."

"Oh, James," he says. "What have you done?"

I look at the concern on his face.

"It's not just a list, is it? There's something else on the scroll."

Wells shakes it off.

"A few sacred rituals. Sigils. Invocations. Don't concern yourself. The scroll is nothing that can't be replaced," he says.

I can't see his eyes, but the microtremors around his mouth tell me that he's lying when he says not to be concerned. I fucked up something big. He'll never outright let on what it was, though, so I'm going to have to keep my eyes open.

"What you did at the chapel was a setback and so is this. But delayed is not destroyed. We will prevail. I'd say that with luck you'll live to see it, but I don't believe that's in the cards for you."

I want to say something, but he's got me there. And I don't have time for these games. Without knowing how much longer the energy drink will last, I need every second to find Candy and keep looking for a cure.

Wells starts away from me.

He says, "It's been delightful catching up, Stark. Maybe we'll have time to do it again before your demise. Take him to his special accommodations."

The three masked gunmen perp-walk me to a room across the big facility the Vigil uses for its headquarters. I glance back at Marcella, who trails behind Wells.

My accommodations are a room with a row of three cells. A sleeping man occupies the one closest to the door. The cabbie is my guess. There's a curtained cell at the end of the block. It's weirdly bright down there.

I understand why the moment I see the cell. The Vigil pricks take my weapons, put them in a plastic evidence bag, and shove me in the cell.

"Can I have my tape, please? I'm bleeding other places too."

One of the goons takes the tape from the bag and throws it into the cell.

"Bless you, my son."

The cell is completely surrounded by lights. There isn't a single shadow anywhere. If I was as strong as I should be, I might be able to break the cell lock and smash some lights. Create enough shadows to get out before they could stop me. But right now, I'd lose at arm wrestling to a butterfly. I'm not breaking out of anything.

When they're satisfied I understand how fucked I am, the guards file out with my gear.

There isn't even a chair or a cot. Furniture might cast enough of a shadow for me to escape. All I can do is sit on the floor.

My first thought is that I might be able to stretch enough tape over the bars to create a shadow on the floor. I hold up my hand, trying to figure out some angles.

Nothing. I could use up the whole roll, but with the way

the lights are set up, all I'd get is a dim spot on the floor. Nothing good enough for me to shadow-walk.

I take off my coat and drop it on the floor. I'm bleeding under the cling wrap, so I wrap tape around my arm, body, and leg. The skin on my right hand looks like it's about to slough off, so I wrap that too. I'm more tape than man at this point. You'd think there would be a tipping point where, if you're wrapped in enough of this stuff, it would give you super tape powers or something. I could cling to the wall like Spider-Man or seal leaking pipes with a single bound. But nothing happens. I put the tape back in my coat and sit there bleeding.

MAYBE THE TRANQUILIZER wasn't completely out of my system after all because the next thing I'm aware of is someone whispering my name.

I open my eyes and Marcella is right outside my cell.

I get up and go to her.

"If you're here to gloat, I can't stop you. But if you're here to read me the gospels, fuck off."

"Neither, you idiot," she says. "And keep your voice down."

"Why?"

She holds out the evidence bag and pushes it through the bars of my cell.

I look at the bag but don't touch it.

"Is this Wells's trick so he has a reason to shoot me?"

"No. You're as stupid as the marshal said. Listen: You helped me when you didn't have to. And I don't think you're quite as bad as the marshal does. So, decide what you want to do right now. They'll realize the cameras are off in a minute and we'll both be finished."

I take the bag and start filling my coat with gear.

"What about the lights? I still can't move."

"Leave that to me."

She takes a metal strip from her pocket and goes to a lamp by the side of my cell. Slips it into the back of the lamp. There's a spark and it goes out. She does it to one more lamp.

"Is that enough shadow?" she says.

"Yes. But what's going to happen to you?"

"Don't worry about me. Just go."

"Come with me."

She shakes her head.

"I can't do that. For good or ill, this is where I belong."

I start for the shadow at the back of the cell.

"If they catch you, say it was my fault. Say I used hoodoo on you."

"Go," she says.

I take out Abbot's gold coin, drop it on the floor, and crush it under my boot. Then I'm gone.

I COME OUT by Hijruun's tower. He's still facedown on the trail, his bones broken and splintered by gunfire.

I yell into the forest a couple of times.

"Candy!"

When I don't hear anything, I open the tower door.

There's a trail of blood leading up the spiral stairs. I get out the na'at and start up.

Candy is just a couple of turns above me. She's pale and shaking. Barely conscious.

Blood runs down the right side of her face. There's a gash across her forehead full of dirt and clotted blood. I brush her hair out of the way to see how seriously hurt she is. As I do, she opens her eyes.

"Yay. You're not dead," she says weakly.

"They just took me to the principal's office and gave me detention."

"I'm sitting here bleeding. You can at least tell me what really happened."

"I am. I met the head of the Wormwood faction and he locked me up."

Candy says, "How did you get out?"

"A friend—or, well, I don't know what the hell she is—let me out."

"Are the faction people as crazy as you thought?"

"Marshall Wells runs the faction. You do the math."

Her eyes widen.

"Shit."

Then she laughs a little. Points to her bloody face and my duct tape.

"We match," she says. "Like those old couples wearing 'I'm with Stupid' T-shirts."

"That's us. Just a couple of bleeding morons. You ready to go home?"

"Yes, please."

I help her to her feet and take us through the wall, back to the UFO mansion.

WHEN WE GET there we both collapse.

Alessa screams Candy's name and runs over.

I have a hard time getting to my feet, but hands pull me upright. I look around and see Brigitte and Carlos.

"Hi," he says. "Want a sandwich? There's turkey in the fridge."

Brigitte grabs me in a big hug. I want to hug her back, but in my current state it feels wrong.

She takes my face in her hands.

"Jimmy, what have you done to yourself?"

"Don't get too close. You might catch something."

"Don't be stupid," she says. "You're always beautiful to me."

She kisses me on the lips. Even though I can't feel it, it's nice. I look at Carlos and he puts his hands up.

"Don't look at me, man. I'm not kissing your ugly ass."

"Where's Ray?"

"He's with Vidocq, looking at old books. Neither of them would come."

"Tell them not to be stupid and get over here."

Carlos makes a face.

"No one tells Ray to do anything when his mind is made up. Anyway, he says Vidocq's apartment is pretty safe."

"Yeah, I guess so. There's hoodoo on it. No one can see it unless he wants them to."

Candy is propped up on the couch. Alessa is next to her, holding her hand. Allegra is there with her medical bag. She's cleaned most of the blood off Candy's face and is smearing a clear ointment on her wound. I go over in time to hear, ". . . after they took Stark, one of the assholes hit me with his rifle butt."

I look over Allegra's shoulder.

"Is she going to be all right?"

"She'll be fine. There's red mercury in the salve. The wound will be closed in another minute or so. It's a concussion I'm worried about," she says. Then adds, "Hi, by the way."

"Hi to you."

"When I'm done with Candy I'm going to want to look at you."

"Forget it. I'm a corpse. You're not going to have anything in your bag for that."

"You just might be surprised. Sit down and take off your shirt."

The look Alessa gives me lets me know not to sit on the couch. I go across the room and drop down into one of the plastic spaceship chairs.

When I get my coat off, Kasabian is in front of me.

"What?" I say.

"Nothing, man. Nothing at all."

"Did Howard give you any trouble while we were gone?"

He just stares at me.

"You could have gotten Candy killed, you fuck."

"You think I don't know that?"

"You better stay away from her from here on out."

I look at him. He's as mad as I've ever seen him and I've seen him shooting at me.

"Are you threatening me, Kas?"

"Considering your current state, yeah. I am. Leave Candy out of any of your stupid future plans."

I say, "Thanks."

"For what?"

"For sticking up for her. You're not quite the asshole I remember."

"Well, you are, so watch yourself."

He heads back to the couch, where Allegra works on Candy.

I go into the bathroom, take off my shirt, and look myself over. I'm bleeding under the cling wrap, but the duct tape is holding me together pretty well. But my skin feels loose, like it might all fall off in one big sheet. My joints ache and feel stiff. The first signs of rigor mortis? I flex my arms and fingers to loosen them up.

"Is there anything I can do to help?" says Brigitte from the doorway.

"No. It's funny, don't you think? The two of us used to kill things like me."

She leans against the door frame.

"You're not a Drifter, Jimmy. I was the one who was almost a zombie, remember? I know what it feels like. You're nothing like that."

It's true. Brigitte was bitten when we were out Drifter hunting. We found a fix for her, but it was a close call.

"Thanks. But I think Kasabian is right about one thing. I spend a lot of time getting my friends almost killed."

"When did you force any of us to do anything? Everything we did we did because we wanted to."

"Still. I get the distinct feeling that coming back was a bad idea. People were safer when I was gone."

"Safer and better off aren't the same thing," says Brigitte. "Has it been quieter? Yes. Has it been as interesting? No."

"Look at Candy. Look at Alessa. Look at Kasabian clanking around on that metal body. That might be too interesting for my taste anymore."

Brigitte comes in and sits on the edge of the sink.

"What does that mean? Suicide? Exile?"

I flex my stiff knees.

"Is it too late to run away with the circus?"

She looks at the ceiling.

"You're impossible when you're like this. A maudlin child."

"I'm joking. I'm not going anywhere but six feet in the ground. This body won't last much longer and the hoodoo speed I took, I can feel wearing off."

She brushes some dirt off my face.

"If you've already written your epitaph, why do anything?"

"Because I have to make sure all of you are safe. That means securing this place and me killing some people before I go."

Brigitte looks at me.

"At least when you talk that way you sound alive. Now, how can I help?"

I point at the stuff from the medicine cabinet that I dumped in the sink.

"You can look through those bottles and see if I missed anything marked 'energy' or 'restorative' or 'invigoration.' Something like that."

She begins picking through the bottles.

Allegra comes in a couple of minutes later.

"Well, aren't you a sight?" she says.

"The good news is that I feel worse than I look."

"That's hard to imagine."

She puts down her bag and looks at my shoulder and side.

"I can't see anything through all that plastic. Take it off."

"I'm just going to start bleeding again."

"Then get in the tub first."

I slice everything off with the black blade. My blood has gone from burned motor oil to the color of squid ink. There is no way for it to get darker, which, in its own weird way, is a relief.

Allegra frowns as she looks at my wounds.

"Does that hurt?" she says over and over.

"I told you. I can't feel much of anything."

"Your skin feels like soft cheese."

"That's very reassuring, doctor."

She gives me a look.

"Normally, I'd try to keep things simple, sew you up or cauterize the wound, but I'm not sure your skin can handle either of those."

"Is there anything you can do?"

"I have a potion that might stop the bleeding."

"Try it. I'm sick of leaking like an inflatable sex sheep."

Allegra looks up at me. "Do they really have those?"

"Right down the aisle from the pancake-shaped Fleshlights."

"Now I know you're making stuff up."

"Everybody likes a good breakfast. Some people want to make sweet, sweet love to it."

"I'm not going to ask how you know that."

From the sink, Brigitte says, "I'm sorry, Jimmy. I can't find anything."

"That's okay. It was a long shot."

"What are you looking for?" Allegra asks her.

"A restorative of some kind."

Allegra looks at me.

"Are we doing speed now, too?"

"I need something to help me keep moving. If I stop, I'm afraid I'll fall apart."

She goes to the sink and dampens a washcloth.

"I might have something for that too. Let me clean you up and we can try it."

She wipes the blood off my wounds and uses a small spray bottle to apply a potion. The bleeding doesn't stop, but it slows to a trickle.

Allegra says, "I've never seen this not work."

"Like you said. I'm made of cheese. It just happens to be the kind with holes in it. Anyway, it's better than it was before."

"You might still want to use the plastic to make sure the wounds stay closed."

"That's what I was thinking too."

She paws through her bag and hands me a couple of triangular pink pills.

"This might give you a little more energy."

I dry-swallow them. They taste like licorice.

"How do you feel?" she says.

"The same as before."

"I'll let you have one more, but that's it."

I swallow the third pill and wait.

"Anything?"

"Nothing."

She looks back in her bag.

"Those are some very powerful stimulants. If they're not working, I'm not sure what else I can give you."

"Don't worry about it. I just need to keep going for another two or three hours."

"What happens then?"

"Don't worry about it."

"Oh," she says softly. "I wish you'd come to me earlier."

"I wish I didn't have to. Anyway, you don't work on dead things. Thanks for trying."

She gets up and gives me a little hug.

"I'm going to go back and check on Candy."

"Good. I'm sorry about you and Vidocq."

"Me too," Allegra says, and goes back to the living room.

Brigitte helps wrap me back up in cling wrap. After Allegra's cheese comment, I put extra plastic around my legs and duct tape everything in place.

"How do I look?"

"Awful. Simply awful."

"Come on. I need food if I'm going to keep going."

Brigitte helps me get dressed. On the way to the kitchen, I go over to Candy.

"How are you feeling?"

"A lot better," she says.

Alessa leans into my line of sight.

"Don't even talk to her. You've caused enough trouble."

"It's all right," Candy says. "I've been through lots worse than this."

"And that makes it okay?"

"That's not what I meant."

"You come up with all kinds of excuses for this guy, but listen to me. This is not a healthy relationship."

"Don't talk about Stark like that. He stuck with me through some really tough times. He's the one who came up with Chihiro when the Feds were looking for me."

"And why did you need to invent Chihiro? Because he dragged you into one of his messes."

"No. It was because I almost killed somebody."

Alessa looks at her.

"I never told you because I was embarrassed. A while ago, something happened with the potion I drink to suppress my Jade feeding urges. I almost killed someone. The Golden Vigil arrested me and were going to send me to an internment camp. Stark saved me."

Alessa keeps staring. Then she says, quietly, "I never said he was a monster. But helping you then doesn't make up for what happened today."

Brigitte takes my arm and pulls me into the kitchen.

"They need to work this out between themselves," she says. "We shouldn't eavesdrop."

I look back at the two of them.

"It's like being at your own funeral and finding out what people really think of you."

Brigitte opens the refrigerator.

"What do you want to eat?"

I follow her over.

"Meat. I think protein helps me keep going."

Carlos and Kasabian come in while we pile food on the kitchen island.

"That's all there is?" Carlos says.

I pick up a piece of chicken.

"We've pretty much cleaned out the fridge."

He checks the cupboards for spices. Slams the doors shut.

"This is the whitest kitchen I've ever been in," he says. "I was going to make some food at the bar, but I can't work with this *Brady Bunch* shit."

"If I live, I'll pass that on to Abbot. In the meantime, have some bologna and mayonnaise."

He does an exaggerated shudder.

"You're going to turn me into a vegetarian."

Everybody eats and tries not to listen to the argument in the living room.

Soon, Allegra comes in and stands next to me.

She says, "Candy doesn't have a concussion."

"That's great news."

"Mind if I join you?"

"Of course not," says Brigitte.

She passes me a plate and I hand it to Allegra.

While she piles on food, I try to eat another piece of sliced turkey. It gets halfway to my mouth before I drop it. My stomach cramps. I run into the bathroom and vomit. All I can hope is that what came up is just food and no important organs.

Allegra comes in as I'm rinsing out my mouth.

"What happened?" she says.

"I don't think my body likes food anymore."

"That might be why the pills didn't work. Your digestive system has shut down."

"Meaning the drugs aren't going to work on me anymore?"

"It's doubtful," she says.

"That's good to know."

I go to Kasabian.

"Do you have any cigarettes?"

He pulls a pack from his pocket and slaps them into my hand.

"Thanks," I say as he walks away.

I open one of the egg-shaped windows and light up.

Candy and Alessa continue their tense conversation. Everybody else retreats to the kitchen.

About halfway through my first cigarette, I notice movement on the hillside. I keep smoking but watch the rocks and scrub below. Something metallic flashes for an instant and is gone. A gun? Another piece of equipment? Someone is definitely coming up the hill.

I crush the cigarette and toss it out the window.

"Everybody listen up," I yell. "I think there's somebody outside, which means we can't stay. Grab whatever shit you need and get ready to move."

Kasabian comes out of the kitchen.

"What are you talking about? I thought we were safe here."

"We were. And now we're not. We're leaving in one minute, so get ready."

Everybody runs around grabbing things. I go into Howard's room.

"Get up. We're leaving."

He says, "I heard you yelling. What's wrong?"

"Armed people are coming up the hill."

"They found me then. I knew Eva and Barron would send someone for me."

"What makes you think it's Wormwood?"

He looks at me suspiciously.

"Who else could it be?"

"The faction. I just escaped from one of their cells."

"You're lying."

"What if I'm not? What do you think those faction freaks are going to do to you if they find you?"

He thinks for a minute. Then, "Where are we going?"

"I'm not telling you."

He frowns but follows me into the living room.

I go back to the window. Whoever is down there is a lot closer than they were a minute ago. I wish I hadn't used the locator coin at the Golden Vigil's headquarters. I liked the idea of Abbot finding them then, but I like the idea of his finding us now a lot more.

I check my guns. Both are empty. The knife and na'at won't work from this distance and anyway, there are too many of them. I pat my pockets. The only thing I come up with is the little crystal Hijruun gave me.

I still have no fucking idea what it is, but I open the window and throw it out as hard as I can.

Someone shoots and the window explodes. More gunshots come through the wall.

I duck and head for the others as they run for the other side of the room.

Before I shadow-walk them out, the gunfire stops and screaming tears through the open window. I run back over and look out.

The side of the hill is swarming with skinless snakes. They're nothing but slithering lengths of squirming bones, but they have fangs and they're using them to rip apart whoever was coming up the hill.

I run back to the others.

"Are we safe?" says Kasabian.

"Not even a little."

I grab his arm and pull everyone into a shadow.

We come out at the corner of Sunset Boulevard and Las Palmas.

"Let's go to the store," yells Kasabian.

We don't.

Before we can even move, three blacked-out vans pull U-turns and head in our direction.

I yank everyone into another shadow.

We come out on Venice Beach. More vans pull into the parking lot behind us.

This time I take us out to LAX. We're there about thirty seconds before airport security heads our way. A few seconds after that, more vans pull up.

"How are they doing this?" yells Kasabian.

"Is it a locator spell?" says Candy.

I drag us into another shadow.

"I don't think so. I think it's something simpler."

This time we don't come out anywhere. We stop in the Room.

I pull everything out of my coat and pockets and drop it on the floor.

"What are you doing?" says Carlos.

"Looking for something."

"A tracker?" says Candy.

"Exactly. They had my gear for a while. It has to be there."

She gets down on the floor with me and starts checking my weapons.

"What will it look like?" she says.

"I don't know. It's Golden Vigil equipment. It could be anything."

"Are we safe here?" says Alessa.

"Completely. Even God can't get in here."

"Then why don't we just stay here?" says Howard.

"Because Stark might die," says Allegra.

I check the Colt. Look down the barrel. Examine the cylinder.

"She's right. There are things I have to do. If I left you here and died, you'd never get out. If I stay here and die, you'll still be trapped."

"What's this?" says Candy. "I don't have one of these on my knife."

She hands me the black blade and points to the pommel.

She's right. There's a small bump in the center. It's absolutely smooth. Nothing you'd ever find if you weren't looking for it.

"Do you think that's it?" says Carlos.

I flip over the blade and smash the pommel into the floor of the Room. When I check the knife again, whatever was on it is gone.

I show Candy.

"Good eye," I tell her.

"Thanks."

Alessa helps her to her feet.

"What do we do now?" says Brigitte.

I load my weapons back into my coat and look at Carlos.

"Let's go see a couple of bookworms."

"Now you're talking," he says.

VIDOCQ'S APARTMENT IS actually my old apartment, the one I shared with Alice when she was alive. After Mason Faim sent me to Hell, Vidocq took over the place and used some clever hoodoo to make it invisible. You can't see it unless he wants you to. And if the wrong person ever does get a look at it, they'll forget it instantly. It's a good deal all around. L.A. is an expensive burg and Vidocq has been living rent-free for twelve years now.

I bring everyone out in the lobby of the building and we ride the freight elevator up. It wasn't technically necessary to come this way. I could have just taken us out in the hall by Vidocq's door, but I wanted one last elevator ride upstairs. I rode this way with Alice a million times and, later, with Candy. If I'm going out, I'm taking a few good memories with me.

As the elevator whines and jostles us on the way up I look at her.

I say, "How are you feeling?"

"Better. Whatever Allegra gave me really helped. How about you?" she says.

"Good. I've got another couple of hours in me."

"That's not what I mean. I mean being back here."

"It's fine. Some nice memories."

"And the bad ones?"

"Those too. I don't want to forget anything."

She reaches out and holds my hand for a second, then lets go. Smart. If there was ever a time for letting go, this is it.

When we get upstairs, I lead everyone down what looks like an empty hall that dead-ends at a window.

"How's your head doing?" says Carlos. "I think you took us the wrong way."

I look at Alessa. She and Howard are the only other ones

who've never been here, and she's looking at me like I've finally lost it.

I don't say anything. When I knock, all they see is me
banging on a blank wall. It's even stranger for them when the
wall opens up and Vidocq is there.

"James," he says, pulling me inside. He's French and two
hundred years old, so he can't help greeting everyone like he's
Louis the Sun King. "Let me look at you," he says. "You look
like shit."

"Good to see you too, old man."

"At least your absence wasn't eleven years like your last
trip. How was your time in Le Merdier?"

"Dusty. There was a judge down there. He spoke more
languages and was crazier than you. If I live, I'll tell you all
about it."

Ray comes over and frowns.

"I was hoping the potion would last a little bit longer."

"I'm still on my feet. That's enough for now."

Carlos goes over to Ray.

"I didn't expect to see you over here," Ray says.

"It was the kitchen. All white bread and American cheese.
These fuckers can do magic, but they're afraid of spices," says
Carlos.

Since Vidocq took over the apartment, it's always been
full of moldering books and pamphlets, weird alchemical
lab equipment, and cases full of potions and elixirs. Now
that Allegra is gone, his tools have completely taken over the
place. There's hardly a table or countertop that isn't stacked
with books or stained by his noxious brews. The life of a
bachelor alchemist, I guess.

Howard immediately heads for Vidocq's books.

"Keep an eye on that guy," I tell him. "He's a necromancer, a liar, and a book burner."

"Thank you. I will."

On his way to intercept Howard, Vidocq runs right into Allegra. They back away, a little shy and awkward. I get the feeling that this is the first time she's been to the apartment since she moved out.

"*Pardonne,*" he says.

"It's okay," she says. "It's nice to see you. You're looking well."

"You too."

Fuck me. In a minute they're going to start talking about how nice the weather is. Almost every relationship in this room is broken or bruised in some way. Carlos and Ray are the only happy people, and they're only here because I roped them into something I shouldn't have.

When I look back at Allegra and Vidocq, she's going over to check on Candy and he's heading for Howard. Teen angst crisis averted.

Ray calls me to a side table. He's leaning over an old book the size of a goddamn washing machine. On the page the book is open to is an enormous gruesomely detailed image of a flayed man. Someone has scribbled notes in Latin all over the page. I can't read a word of it.

"You're going to need a new coloring book. Someone finished this one."

Ray flips the page and runs his fingers down a crowded panel of what looks like Cyrillic text.

"People call this the Flayed Man Codex. Sometimes the

Flayed Bible," he says. "It's an amazing repository of ancient dark magic."

"You think there's something in there that can help me?"

"I don't know. It's a mix of languages. Between Vidocq and me we can read the French, Latin, and most of the German, but this section on death magic seems to be in Russian. We're stuck."

I look around the room and spot her.

"Brigitte, can you read Russian?"

"A bit," she says. "Why?"

"We can't tell if this borscht recipe says sour cream or marshmallows."

She comes over and pushes me out of the way.

"You're such a nuisance."

Ray moves aside and Brigitte stares at the page for a minute, then looks at us.

"You're both idiots," she says. "It's Ukrainian."

"Can you read it?" says Ray.

"My mother is from Kiev. But this is an old dialect. I'm not sure I can make out all of it."

"Why don't we go over it together and see if anything sounds useful?"

"Is it to help Jimmy?"

"Yes."

She looks at me with a sly smile.

"I have my own TV show now, you know."

"So I heard."

"I should be drinking champagne at the Chateau Marmont."

"But instead you're on the run with a bunch of crazy people and a dead man."

She flips pages of the book.

"Do you remember what I told you long ago?"

"No. What?"

Brigitte touches my duct-taped cheek.

"If you were just ten percent less scary . . ."

We both smile.

"Not much chance after this I guess."

"First you must live. And then we shall see."

She takes her hand away and points to some bolded letters.

"This says something about the resurrection of the dead."

"Really?" says Ray. "What else?"

She reads a bit more and frowns.

"No. It's about the resurrection of farm animals. Sheep and cows."

"Keep reading. Maybe there's something about people later."

I lean into her ear and say, "Moo." Give her a peck on the cheek.

She smiles and shrugs me away.

"Move, you silly oaf. Some of us are working."

Everything I do or say at this point feels like some version of good-bye. At least I'm getting the chance this time. When Mason sent me to Hell and when Audsley Ishii killed me, it happened too fast to say anything to anyone. It's good to have a little more time before I might make a last exit.

Kasabian is eyeing Vidocq's liquor cabinet.

"Be careful," I tell him. "Not all this stuff is for drinking."

He points to a brown bottle near the top.

"My first clue was the frogs in this one."

I pull out a bottle of Angel's Envy rye from the bottom shelf.

"Try this. They make a bourbon, too, but the rye is better."

He looks at me suspiciously for a few seconds, then holds up the bottle to inspect it for pickled vermin.

"I'll think about it," he says.

"That's sipping whiskey, not the plastic-bottle generic stuff you buy."

"Yeah, yeah. Don't tell me how to drink."

I give him back his cigarettes.

"What are these?" he says.

"Your cigarettes."

"You never give back cigarettes."

"Don't take it personally. My brain probably isn't getting enough oxygen."

He puts the cigarettes in his pocket.

I look at Brigitte studying the book with Ray.

"You never told me if Brigitte's show is any good."

"It's real good," says Kasabian. "Stylish, you know? All neon and hot guns and shiny skirts."

"And she's good in it?"

"They're talking about making it into a movie, so you tell me."

"That's good to hear."

I put out my hand to him.

"See you around."

After a second's hesitation, he shakes the hand.

"You leaving?" he says.

"I've got a couple of things to do."

He looks away and nods.

"You know all that stuff I said about things being better without you?"

"Yeah?"

"Well, they're true. But that doesn't mean I want you to croak or anything."

"Good to know."

"Okay," he says. "Later."

"Later."

I check the room for a good shadow. There's one in a corner where the wall separates the living room from the kitchen.

"Hey, Stark."

I look around. Candy is sitting on Vidocq's battered sofa with Alessa on one side and Allegra on the other. She beckons me over.

"Where do you think you're going?" she says.

"Who said I was going anywhere?"

"I know that look when you're scoping out ways to leave."

"I was just going to take a walk."

"Where?"

"No place special."

She frowns. "This is a very bad time to be lying."

"I have some business I have to finish up."

"You're going to save the world in your condition?"

"No. I'm just going to break some things and scare some people."

"Wormwood?" Candy says.

"Yeah."

"You said Wormwood was everywhere. How can you hurt them?"

"I can't destroy the organization, but I can take down some of its leaders. Knowing those rat fucks, there'll be a power struggle to see who's in charge. That ought to slow them down for a while."

Allegra says, "And you're going to do that all by yourself?"

"If I pray real hard, I'm sure I can get the baby Jesus to watch over me."

"You just blew up a church," says Candy.

"Okay. The Devil then."

"That's more like it."

I take a couple of steps away.

"See you soon."

"Wait," Candy says. "You need to stay here. What if they find a spell or something to fix you?"

"I have my phone. And let's be serious. I appreciate what they're doing, but what are the chances of them finding anything in the next couple of hours? The only person who can help is Howard and he's not going to budge."

"I could *make* him," says Candy.

"I know you could, baby, and I appreciate it. But don't. You're already hurt because of me. I want to go knowing you're safe."

She gets up. "I want the same thing. If you're going to go, I want to know it's not lying in some alley somewhere or in a Wormwood jail."

"That's not going to happen this time. I'm doing one small thing and coming right back. I promise."

Candy starts to say something, but Alessa cuts her off.

"Let him go," she says. "He knows what he's doing. This is his thing, right?"

"Right," I say.

Candy's face gets red.

"I'm afraid if you go you'll never come back."

I go over to her.

"I'll be back. I promise. No matter what shape I'm in. I'll be back."

She looks away.

"I'm not going to forgive you if you don't. Not this time."

"I'll be back."

Alessa tugs her hand and Candy slowly sits down again.

"Take care of her," I say.

"Go do whatever it is you're going to do," says Alessa.

Vidocq and Howard are arguing about whether getting high on ayahuasca is the door to universal consciousness or just a good way to meet girls at parties.

I put a hand on Howard's shoulder and turn him toward me.

"Eva Sandoval. She's not the type to stay in the hospital long. With all the shit that's going on, where would she hide? And bear in mind that if you lie, I'll hurt you more than being dumped on prom night."

"At home," Howard says. "The mansion is the only place she feels safe. It's protected by powerful curses."

"The faction got through them pretty easily when they shot up the place."

"She'll have added more layers of protection. By now, the mansion will be impregnable."

"We'll see. Is there any chance you'll help Vidocq and Ray keep me from turning into Frosty the Snowman?"

"Not while I'm held against my will."

"Trust me. No one wants you here. But you're not going anywhere until I say."

"I'll keep an eye on him," says Vidocq.

"Between you and Candy I don't think he's going anywhere. By the way, I used to have bullets here. Are there any left?"

"One box. I'll get them."

He brings them to me and I load the Colt. I feel a little bit better. I put it in my waistband at the back.

"I'll see you soon."

"Where are you going?" Vidocq says.

"Bowling."

This time I don't look around. I don't want any teary eyes, plaintive looks, or what-the-fuck-are-you-doing stare-downs. I shadow-walk out of the apartment, giving myself 90 percent odds that I'll never be back.

I COME OUT in Sandoval's bowling alley. It's dark and when I turn on the lights, it looks like no one's been there since I let Marcella go.

Out of nowhere, my leg and arm joints stiffen. I flex them hard, trying to break up whatever is happening inside. It feels like there are wads of broken glass under my skin. Eventually, though, everything gets loose again. I don't know how regular corpses deal with this shit.

While I catch my breath from the bout of rigor mortis my phone rings. I answer it quick before anyone in the mansion hears it.

"Hello?" I say, barely above a whisper.

"Stark. Where are you? And why are you whispering?"

It's Abbot.

"I'm in enemy territory, that's why I'm fucking whispering. Whatever you want, make it quick."

"We found the headquarters of the Wormwood faction. You won't believe who they really are."

"The Golden Vigil."

There's a pause.

"How did you know that?"

"Because I escaped from there like a half hour ago."

"That was *your* coin that called us? I gave you that for your personal protection."

"I didn't have a chance of taking them down and I figured you did. You did, didn't you?"

"We have control of the facility and most of the personnel. A few of them got away and I know there are others in the field. We're in the process of rounding them up."

"Do you know where Eva Sandoval lives?"

"Of course."

"I'm pretty sure there are Vigil people outside right now. But leave them alone. I'm going to need them."

"For what?" Abbot says with an edge in his voice. "What are you planning?"

"You can arrest anyone you want in twenty minutes. Is there anything else?"

I already know the answer to the question, but I want to hear it from him.

"We haven't found a fix for your situation, I'm afraid."

"If it's any help, the ritual is called Ludovico's Ellicit. I probably should have told you before."

"I really wish you'd said something earlier. We could have been looking this whole time."

"Sorry. I was busy getting shot and trying to navigate a tricky relationship situation. Love sucks sometimes, doesn't it?"

"Stark?" he says in a funny tone. "Are you all right? You sound a little strange."

"What? I can't have relationships? I once ruled Hell for a hundred days. Did you know that? There are plenty of people in L.A. who'd appreciate seeing that on a dating profile."

"You're not making sense. Wherever you are, I want you to come back to the Golden Vigil facility. It's safe here now and we have medics who can help you."

"I don't need a Band-Aid. I need to finish up some work before I fall apart."

"Come in now," says Abbot. "We can protect you while we look for a way out of this."

"Thanks. You're okay for a guy who owns a yacht. I'll talk to you later. Remember: Ludovico's Ellicit."

I hang up and listen at the door to make sure there's no one outside. When I'm sure, I go upstairs quietly.

There are six armed guards in the mansion foyer. I go through a shadow and come out by the kitchen. Four more guards in there. That means there are going to be guards scattered all over the mansion. The grounds too, probably. I mumble some Hellion hoodoo. The guards in the kitchen and foyer drop to the floor and start babbling like babies. The sounds of falling bodies come from upstairs too. It wasn't my best hoodoo or the strongest. It's a confusion curse that won't last long, but I'm hoping it'll hold just long enough for me to get my work done.

BECAUSE SHE HATES it, I shadow-walk into Eva's office. She and Barron are having a nightcap and watching the news on her million-inch TV. On the screen is a helicopter shot of vans and cop cars around a warehouse in East L.A. The news is reporting it as a raid on a terrorist compound. That's a smart way for Abbot to have played it. There are enough Sub Rosa in the police department and local FBI office that he could call in some favors and make it look like the Golden Vigil takedown was good, clean law enforcement. Your tax dollars at work. Let Marshal Wells count rosaries, meditate, chant, or whatever the Vigil does in jail for a couple of days. Then, if Abbot can play it right, the badass part of the Sub Rosa—the part no one likes to talk about—will swoop in and haul the Vigil's true believers off to a hoodoo black site. I have no idea what happens then and I'm not asking. Life is too short. Way too short for some of us.

I say, "You two must be breathing easier, huh?"

Barron chokes on the pill he was trying to swallow. I walk over and slap him on the back a couple of times. He drains a glass of water and just sits there, too exhausted by the choking fit to care that I'm close enough to snap his neck.

Sandoval, on the other hand, cares a lot. She's on her feet, clutching the TV remote like it's a gun.

I put my hands up.

"Don't shoot. Think of the children."

She turns off the TV and tosses the remote on her desk.

"I was praying you'd be dead by now."

"I couldn't leave without one last good-bye."

She stands there coolly, like she's staring down a poodle that just shit on her chinchilla long johns.

"Have you killed Howard yet or just tortured him, hoping he'll save your precious life?"

"How do you know he hasn't already told me how to fix my complexion problem?"

"You wouldn't be here if he had. From the looks of you you don't have much time left. You'd be spending it doing the ritual."

I walk slowly around the room. Sandoval stands her ground but doesn't want me behind her, so she has to follow me, turning around in place. We're like an ugly little carousel covered in bones and bad meat instead of bouncing horses. Barron sits in his easy chair gobbling pills like they're sweet potato fries and he hasn't eaten in a year.

"What if I told you that I don't care about the ritual anymore? That I'm not afraid of Hell, I'm not going to get fixed in time, and I want to have one last little blowout before I go?"

Sandoval looks at me.

"If you were a normal person I'd say you were lying, but it being you, I don't know. I can't imagine the life you came back to is what you'd hoped for. Your lover in the arms of someone smarter and much less ugly than you. Your business thriving without you. Finding that many of your friends are doing better without you and that the ones who aren't are still happy that the chaos you drag with you like Jacob Marley's chains is no longer infecting their lives. Now that I think about it, even someone as crude and dull witted as you must find it almost unbearable."

I say, "You left out the part where I haven't had a proper drink or smoke since I got back. You think I want to live without Aqua Regia and Maledictions forever? I'll have all I want in Hell. And I won't share any of it with you."

"This is where we're supposed to cower in fear, isn't it?

The threat of eternal damnation hanging over our sinful heads. I'm positively quivering. Are you quivering, Barron?"

With drugs in his belly, he's looking a lot better now.

"Like a violin string, Eva," he says. "I don't know when I've been more terrified."

They both laugh.

I wave a finger at them.

"I know the punch line here. You have a secret. You're immortal. While everybody else slinks around the Hellion shit pits, you'll live forever on caviar and ambrosia."

"Something like that," says Sandoval. "In fact, exactly like that."

"How are you feeling over there, Barron? Are you looking forward to eternity choking down those horse pills?"

"Not at all," he says. "I'm getting a little better every day. Even if it takes a year or ten years to get back to normal, what do I care? What's a decade when placed against eternity?"

"You know the faction did this to you, right?"

"Who cares? They're being dealt with right now."

"You mean what's on the news? The faction's pretty big. I wouldn't count on them catching everyone, at least not tonight. But there's something more important you ought to be thinking about."

"What's that?" Barron says.

"How did the faction get to you? I mean, you're part of the team working with the rebel angels. You're a Mafia made man. And yet, somehow they got to you. How do you think that happened?"

"What makes you think the faction did this to me? You have no proof."

"Sure I do. It's a kill list. A friend translated it for me. All of your dead Wormwood friends are there, and in order. Pieter Holden, Megan Bradbury, Franz Landschoff, Jared Glanton. I guess they didn't rate the immortality serum, did they? Just you and Eva and who else? That's the funny thing about immortality, though. Being alive doesn't necessarily mean walking around eating tamales. How does spending eternity in a coma sound? It's still immortality, but probably not the kind you were hoping for."

Barron looks at me.

"Do you have the list?"

"In English? Just the interesting parts."

I hand him the piece of paper. He looks it over.

He says, "Do you know anything about this, Eva?"

Sandoval looks at me like she wishes her eyes were jackhammers and I was a chocolate Easter bunny.

"Let me see it," she says.

She reads it over. Wads up the paper and throws it on the floor.

"It's a list of names. He probably made it up himself. Nothing that comes out of this animal's mouth is the truth."

"That girl's name," says Barron. "Alessa Graves. How would he possibly know about her? We were looking at her father ourselves. And there was an incident outside of the store where she works."

"He could have added her name because he knew about her father. He could have staged the incident himself."

I go and stand next to Barron.

I tell him, "She's never going to give anything up. Any questions you have, she'll have a quick answer. Eva worked this all out ahead of time. When she decided to feed some of you to the faction and run Wormwood herself."

Barron gives me a dirty look, but when he turns to Sandoval his hands flex nervously.

It should be noted that everything I'm saying is absolute bullshit. I'm completely winging it. I don't know who poisoned Barron or why. But I know these Wormwood pricks are paranoid, which makes them easy to fuck with.

"Hey, Barron. When's the last time you checked your pills? I hate to think that someone might be keeping you sick on purpose."

"Eva . . . ," he starts.

"Stop listening to this idiot," shouts Sandoval. "You're ill and he's manipulating you."

"But how did the faction get to so many of our people?"

"You know as well as I do that they got some of their spies among us."

"And who let that happen?" I say.

Sandoval looks at me.

"I was stabbed, for Heaven's sake," Eva says.

"Not very badly."

"It's true," says Barron. "You weren't in the clinic long."

She shoots him a look.

"Of course not. They used healing magic. It took no time at all."

I lean down to Barron.

"Ask her why she killed Bruno, the one guy who could have told you how the faction was infiltrating your operation."

"Eva?" he says.

"He attacked me!" she shouts. "There was blood everywhere. I don't remember much after that."

"But at least you have your arrangement with the angels, right, Barron? I'm sure she's above making any side deals."

He rubs his chest and gulps down a couple more pills. When his hands are steady, he pulls a small pistol from under his jacket and points it at Sandoval. His voice is rough when he speaks.

"Do you have some kind of deal with Stark? You let him take Howard."

"Shut up, Barron," says Sandoval.

We're finally where I wanted.

"Howard is the key to the angels, isn't he? All that spooky secret hoodoo he knows. I knew you weren't keeping him around just for my benefit."

"Do you see what you did?" Sandoval shouts at Barron. "You've told him everything."

Barron looks at me, a puzzled expression on his face. When he looks back at Sandoval she has her own pistol out. Without missing a beat, she shoots him in the head. Barron slams into the back of his chair, knocking his pills off the table. They scatter in a hundred directions on the floor.

"I'll make you another deal," she says. "Bring back Howard and we'll see about having him fix you."

I cut a sigil in my right arm with the black blade.

Sandoval takes a step back, disgusted by my black blood soaking into her Persian rug.

"What the hell are you doing?" she says.

"I'm weak, Eva. But blood magic, it supercharges every spell and curse you can cast."

She levels her pistol at me.

I have to time this just right.

"I just turned off the mansion's hoodoo defenses. Those faction assholes waiting outside should be breaking in here any minute."

Sandoval smiles.

"What are they going to do? Shoot me?"

"You shot Barron."

"He'll heal, and when he does, I'll shoot him again. The idiot."

"Maybe they can't kill you, but they can put you in a cage at the bottom of a mine shaft for the next million years. How does immortality sound now?"

There's a crash in another room. Footsteps. Shouted orders.

"Bye, Eva."

"Good-bye, Stark," she says.

Remember when I said I had to time this just right? I should have factored in that my body is moving slower than normal.

Before I can step into a shadow, Eva fires her pistol twice. One of the shots hits me in the stomach. I don't step out of the room so much as fall on my face.

I DON'T FEEL a thing. If it wasn't for all this blood I'd think an old lady bumped me with her purse on the bus. Not that I ever ride the bus.

I lie on the floor of the Room wrapping duct tape around myself until the roll runs out. It seems to take a while, but I'm not sure. Time has gone a little sideways. Space too. When I get to my feet, I try to lean on the wall but I can't find it. I can see it, but it seems infinitely far away. I keep heading for it and, lucky for me, trip over my own feet. I find the wall with my forehead when I fall against it. That doesn't hurt either, which just makes me laugh.

Usually I love the Room for its silence and solitude. But I don't want to die here alone. I get to the closest door and step through it.

And come out on Hollywood Boulevard. I'm not sure if it's still night out, but it sure seems dark. The street is pretty much deserted. The closest street sign is hard to read. It wobbles and the letters are smeared like we're having an earthquake.

Are we having an earthquake? I know I am.

It takes a couple of minutes, but I'm pretty sure the sign says Ivar Avenue, which puts me near Bamboo House of Dolls. That means Max Overdrive is west. But, for the life of me, I can't remember how far. Nothing to do but start walking. Go west, young man. Someone said that, right? Power through the desert. Try not to eat all your cattle or each other along the way. Brave pioneers. Manifest Destiny. Make America great again.

Fuck that noise.

Where was I going?

Got it.

Max Overdrive. Man, my brain isn't working right. And I think I'm bleeding. Must have cut myself shaving.

Goddamn, I'm hilarious.

Where was I going? West. Right.

Let's get this wagon train moving.

I start walking. I'm pretty sure that's what I'm doing because I keep bumping into buildings and parked cars. It's hard to tell. I'm looking at the pavement a lot more than I am the street. From a distance I probably look more drunk than gutshot. Good. At least people will leave me alone. Unless I run into some cops.

Oh man. Whoever is in charge of the universe right now, please don't let me run into cops. I don't need the hassle and they don't need me punching them because there's no way I'm spending whatever time I have left in a drunk tank.

I miss Candy. I mean, I was just talking to her, but I still miss her.

I already miss the world too. Considering what a shitpile it is in daylight, L.A. is sure pretty at night. All light and the outlines of buildings floating against dead black sky and stars. I wouldn't want to die anywhere else.

Shit. There must be an earthquake. All the buildings are on their sides.

Scratch that. It's me. Must have missed a step. I have a hard time getting up until someone helps me to my feet.

Please don't be a cop. Please don't be a cop.

And it's not.

He's a scruffy little guy. Or maybe he's tall. Everything seems to be both at once.

"You doing all right tonight, pardner?" he says.

Because I'm hilarious I say, "It's my birthday."

"Congratulations. Looks like you've been having a good time."

"The best. I love birthdays. Do you love birthdays?"

"I love *your* birthday," he says. "Did anyone slip you a little cash at your party? Maybe an envelope or a little something from Grandma?"

He keeps pushing me. I look down and see that he has a knife against my side.

It's so fucking funny. I can't help laughing.

He laughs along with me.

"I mean it," he says. "Give me your cash. All of it."

He doesn't sound fun and friendly anymore. I think it makes me sad, but I can't be sure because I'm still laughing.

He pushes the knife a little harder, so I push him back. Pretty hard, I guess, because he goes flying into a parked car and drops his knife. I stumble over with the Colt in my hand and stick it in his face.

I say, "L.A. sure is pretty at night."

He's frozen there on his knees.

"Don't you think?"

"It sure is," he says.

"What's your favorite part?"

He shifts his shoulders nervously.

"The people?"

"The lights," I say.

"The lights. Yeah. You're right."

I pull the last of Howard's money from my pocket and hold it out to him.

"Take it."

He hesitates.

"I said take it. You have to. It's my birthday."

I keep the gun on him while he reaches for the bills.

When he has them I say, "Get up."

He does, very slowly. Everything is slow now. It's like one of those science shows where it takes a droplet a minute to splash into a pool of water.

When he's on his feet, I put the Colt away and he runs off.

"Go west, young man."

I'm not sure he heard me or if I even said it out loud. But I'm sure he got the message.

Happy birthday to me. Happy birthday to me.

Wait. It's not my birthday. That was a joke.

It occurs to me that I might not get to Max Overdrive.

I make it to a bus shelter and drop down onto one of the incredibly uncomfortable seats to wait for something. Not a bus. I'd rather be dragged behind a burning pickup truck into a barbed wire lake than ride the bus.

Wait. I remember now. I'm dying. I'm waiting to die.

I lean back against the plastic wall of the bus shelter.

There's an old man sitting a few seats away.

"L.A. sure is pretty at night," he says.

It takes me a while to process the words, but I get there.

"Yes it is."

He says, "Don't you think it's time to let go? To come home?"

I stare at him but can't see anything until passing headlights illuminate his face.

Oh.

"Hello, Mr. Muninn."

"Hello, James."

"It's been a while."

"It's been busy in Heaven."

"That's what people tell me."

Who's Mr. Muninn? That's a complicated question and I'm not good with complicated at this precise moment. You'll just have to trust me when I say that Mr. Muninn is the grand marshal of the big parade. To be a little clearer, he's God. Yes, that God. The one in all the books. Not a bad guy either. We're friends. More or less. Less a lot of the time. I never pictured him waiting for a bus.

"You don't have to do this," he says.

"What's that?"

"What you're doing. Dragging your battered body all over creation. Just sit back and relax for a while. I'll take care of the rest."

I look at a bright red neon sign across the street.

CHECKS CASHED.

I point at the sign.

"Isn't that nice of them?"

Mr. Muninn swivels his eyes toward the sign, then back at me.

"You're babbling," he says.

"It's my birthday. I get to babble."

"It's not your birthday."

"I know why you're here."

"Why?"

"You want me to go to Heaven with you."

"Does that sound so bad?"

I sit up straighter.

"The war in Heaven is still a mess then?"

"In some ways, worse than ever. The rebels' plans . . . they'll do anything to win. They make me feel ashamed of myself for what I've created."

"I know about their deal with Wormwood. Steal all the souls. Stick them on the wall like bowling trophies."

"For the record, it was Wormwood that developed the proposal. Not the angels themselves."

"Your point being that even though you're at war with the rebels, mortals are still worse."

"Not quite as simple as that," he says. "But yes, essentially."

"I had a weird year, too. Want to hear about it?"

"I know all about it. You killed the archangel Michael on my doorstep."

"I forgot that part. Mostly I remember driving forever and never getting anywhere. But I guess that's Hell for you, huh?"

"You don't have to go back there again."

"Right. You're going to whoosh me off to Heaven. That's the thing, though. If you can take me to Heaven, you can make it my birthday. Come on. Do it."

He shakes his head.

"You know, most people would jump at the chance I'm giving you."

"I've been to Heaven. It wasn't so great."

"You saw the gates. It's not the same thing. It's like saying you looked at a picture of an ugly doll and it's the same as seeing *Bride of Chucky*."

I lean back against the shelter wall.

"You've seen *Bride of Chucky*?"

"Of course not," he says. "I was just trying to speak your language so you'd understand."

I reach over and slap him on the knee.

"I appreciate it. I know I don't look it, but complicated emotional responses are a little beyond me right now."

Mr. Muninn is holding a cane. He leans forward on it.

"What exactly is it you're trying to accomplish here?"

"I have to break the contract between Wormwood and the rebel angels."

"How are you going to do that?"

"I'm going to kill Jonathan Howard."

"And how are you going to do that? Poison him? Shoot him? He's immortal."

I take out the black blade.

"I'm going to use this. Remember this knife? An assassin's blade. And it will kill anything. Including angels. If it will kill an angel, it will kill Howard."

He applauds lightly.

"It seems you have some faculties left. All right. Let's say you kill him. What about your personal situation? With Howard gone, you'll be killing the one person who knows the ritual to bring you back."

"Fuck Ludovico and the Ellicit he rode in on. Howard was never going to do it. It was just a stalling tactic."

"It seems to have worked."

I laugh again.

"I guess you're right. Still, what you want is for me to lean back, close my eyes, and sleep the big sleep. I can't do that. If I'm going to die, I'm going to go out messy."

He taps his cane on the ground.

"Alice sends her regards," he says.

"Tell her hi for me. How's Samael?"

"He's fine. Busy as always."

"Is he still the Angel of Death?"

"No," says Mr. Muninn. "He lost that job when he loaned you the knife that severs souls from their bodies."

"Oh yeah. It was nice of him. That knife sure came in handy Downtown."

"I'm sure it did."

I want to look at the stars, but the roof of the shelter is in the way.

"What's it like these days, being God and Lucifer at the same time?"

He picks a thread off the knee of his pants.

"I'm feeling spread thin. Endless war in one place. Endless suffering and confusion in the other. That's another reason I thought you might come with me. Perhaps you'd consider taking over Hell for a while. Nothing permanent. Just while I sort out some things in Heaven."

I give up on the stars and look at him.

"I was a terrible Lucifer, remember? What about Samael? He's too smart to take the job, isn't he?"

Mr. Muninn adjusts his ass on the uncomfortable seat.

"I thought about asking him but decided against it. He's a good boy. But a bit rash sometimes."

"Yeah. He'd get bored and start a whole new war with someone."

"You could rule Hell with Alice," he says. "I'm sure she'd agree to accompany you."

"Now you're just making me mad. I'm not dragging Alice to Hell and you're a bastard for dangling her in front of me."

"It was just a passing thought."

"I bet spiders were a passing thought too and look how that turned out."

Mr. Muninn doesn't say anything. He knows there's no excuse for spiders.

I turn and look at him hard.

"Are you even here or am I talking to myself?"

He taps his cane again.

"I suppose that's for you to decide," he says. "But if you're going to kill Mr. Howard, you ought to get to it."

"I thought you'd be more on my side. If I take him out, it's one more fuck-you to the rebel angels."

"I am grateful," he says. "But I think you're making things harder on yourself deliberately."

"No, I'm not."

"You had a moment's weakness and agreed to work for Wormwood. Now you're punishing yourself for it."

"Shouldn't someone?"

He stands and the neon light from across the street flashes in his eyes.

"Deciding punishment and mercy is, traditionally, my job."

I wave a hand at him.

"You're not even here. I'm just talking to myself."

"If that's what you wish. Good night, James."

"Good night, bus shelter. Good night, moon."

Another car goes by, but there's nothing to light up this time. I'm in the shelter alone.

I knew it.

There's something on my leg.

It's his cane. Anyway, it's *a* cane. I probably found it or traded someone magic beans for it. However I got it, it's good to have. I can't stand up straight, so it helps me get to my feet.

I'm heading for a shadow on the corner when, I swear, a meteor crashes into me. I drop the cane and go down hard on my back.

I might have blacked out for a second because the next thing I'm aware of is an alien looking down at me. A pretty one too.

"Are you all right?" she says. "That skateboard asshole almost knocked you into the street."

Her antennae bounce around amusingly as the alien helps me to my feet.

She squints at me.

"Oh shit. It's you."

"Who's me?"

"You're going to buy all the donuts in Donut Universe if you live through the weekend, remember?"

I smile up at her.

"I remember you. You're not an alien at all."

She helps me to my feet. Gets a good look at my purple and blue face.

"Oh my god. You look horrible. Did somebody beat you up? You need to go to the hospital."

I pull away from her.

"No hospitals. I don't have time."

"You look like you're ready to die," she says sternly.

"I'm fine."

I look at her, wanting to remember her face.

"What's your name?"

"Janet."

"Thanks, Janet, for the donuts and the help."

"You should really see a doctor."

I give her a wave.

"Thanks for the help."

"You helped me once," she says.

Under normal circumstances I'd ask what the fuck she's talking about, but this is now and the cane is the only thing keeping me on my feet. I stumble away from her into a shadow.

EVERYONE LOOKS UP when I get back to Vidocq's. I hold my coat closed so they don't see the new blood.

"How did it go?" says Candy.

"Great. By now, one of them is under arrest, the other is in a coma, and, with luck, Thomas Abbot is taking everyone else in."

"That's it then, you're finished. You can relax while Vidocq, Ray, and Brigitte find a cure."

I look at Kasabian.

"Could I have some of that whiskey I gave you earlier?"

He gets the bottle and pours me a tall glass. I drain it in one gulp.

He says, "I thought you said that was sipping whiskey."

"Sipping is for people with time to kill."

"Nice cane," says Allegra.

"Yeah. It was a birthday present."

"It's not your birthday," says Candy.

"I fibbed."

Allegra says, "Why don't you come over here?"

I lean against the wall.

"I'm fine where I am."

"You can't walk over here, can you? Not without the cane."

"I'm fine. I'm just really fond of this wall."

Vidocq crosses to me with a bottle of blue amber. He gives me the once-over. Opens my coat and closes it again.

"Listen to me. You can't keep going like this."

"I'm almost done. Just one thing left."

"Leave it. Let me put you in the Winter Garden."

The garden is a kind of hoodoo coma. It slows everything in your body, even death.

I shake my head.

"You haven't found anything yet, have you?"

"I believe we are very close."

"You thought you were close before. You put me in the garden and I could be there for years. I've already been on ice lately. I'm not doing it again."

"At least let Allegra help you."

"In a minute. I have something to do first."

I get out the black blade and cup it in my hand so it's out of sight, then push past Vidocq and hobble over to Howard.

He's sitting in a chair by himself near the window and looks up when I get there.

"How are Eva and Barron?" he says.

"They're not riding to the rescue. I can guarantee you that."

He sits back.

"I know you didn't kill them because that's impossible. What did you do?"

"Not all that much really. When it came down to it, Eva shot Barron. He's not dead, but he's got a bullet in his brain. His eternity is going to be fun. After that, I left Eva for the faction to find. The rest of the faction is running wild in the streets, so if you think there's someplace you can escape to, there isn't."

He looks out the window.

"You're here to kill me, aren't you?"

"You're the last connection to the rebel angels."

He takes a deep breath. His nostrils open wide, like he's taking one last sniff of the world.

"You know about that," he says.

"Eva and Barron gave you up. It was a nice deal. But it's over."

"And you really think you can kill me?"

"I've killed plenty of angels. You can't be any harder than that."

I get the knife ready. Howard sees it. He tries not to show fear, but his pupils expand to the size of basketballs.

"I'll do it," he says.

"Do what?"

He cups his hands in his lap.

"I'll do Ludovico's Ellicit. But there are certain conditions."

"What?"

"We can't perform the ritual here. It has to be somewhere special, a location only I know."

"That's not the condition."

"I don't trust your friends," Howard says. "Especially the alchemist. He could hurt me. Therefore, the ritual will take place with just the two of us. If you'll agree to that and let me go afterward, I'll do the Ellicit."

"Don't listen to him," says Candy. She's right behind me. "It's a trick."

I tap the black blade against my leg.

"Why would you do it now when you wouldn't before?"

"Look at you," Howard says. "Before, I could have performed the ritual and you could have killed me immediately afterward. But now? Even after I perform the Ellicit, it will be hours before you pose a threat."

"You're so sure of that?"

"Quite."

"Why's that?"

He glances at the floor.

"You've dropped your knife."

I look down. The bastard is right. Sometime while we were talking, the blade slipped from my hand. It's sticking straight up in the floor. Candy pulls it out and hands it to me.

She's beside me now.

"Thanks," I say.

"Stay here," she says. "Go into the garden like Vidocq said."

"No. There's no guarantee I'd ever come out again. With Howard, I stand a chance."

Ray and Brigitte are over by the big book.

"Thanks for trying. I won't forget it."

"What are you doing, Jimmy?"

"Going with a sure thing."

I look at Vidocq.

"Is it all right if he takes some samples?"

He throws up his hands in disgust.

"Take it all," he says. "It's nothing but junk. With all of it, I can't figure out how to save my friend."

Howard is already pulling bottles and herbs out of Vidocq's stores. He stuffs it all in his jacket pockets.

"That's everything I need," he says.

Candy is holding on to my arm.

"Don't go. Don't leave me again."

"That's the whole point. I'm doing this so I don't have to leave. I'll see you soon."

I lean over and kiss her on the cheek and whisper, "No matter what happens, I'm killing this guy. But I have to take this chance first."

She loosens her grip for just a second.

I grab Howard and we're gone.

WE'RE ON THE street by the converted industrial building where Vidocq lives.

"What now?" I say.

Howard looks up and down the street.

"We're going to need a car. I hear you have a knack for stealing them."

I walk past a few until I find an older-model Mercedes convertible. Jam the black blade into the door handle. It opens without setting off the alarm. I slip the blade into the ignition and it starts without a hiccup.

I sit in the driver's seat for a minute as the street tilts one way and then the other.

"Maybe I should drive," says Howard.

"Maybe you should."

I have to use the cane to get out and walk around to the passenger side.

When we're both in I say, "Put the top down. I want to feel the wind."

"I didn't think you'd be feeling much of anything at this point," he says.

"I'm just being optimistic."

He looks at me.

"I suppose if I'm driving, you can't slit my throat or kick me out. All right."

He plays around with the dashboard buttons until he finds one that retracts the roof.

"Seat belt, please," says Howard, slipping into his. I do the same. Actually, it feels better this way. Strapped in like this, I'm less likely to slide onto the floor. I'm feeling weak right now. Even with the cane, I'm not sure I could stand.

I say, "Where are we going?"

"You'll see. It's not far. Depending on traffic, we should be there in thirty minutes."

Even belted in, I slide down some in the seat. I did a piss-poor job with the duct tape. My stomach is still bleeding. I hope whoever details this car knows how to get blood out of leather.

Howard steers us to the 405. It's all I can do to keep my eyes open.

My vision is going funny again. The city is one big blur.

This isn't the first time I've come this close to death. A little over a year ago, when High Plains Drifters were all over the city, one of the bastards bit me. I started dying then too, on my way to being a full-blown flesh-eating zombie piece of shit. The funny thing that happened was that as my mortal half died, my angel half started taking over. And it was a real bastard. Half cold-blooded killer and half Dudley Do-Right. Running around doing good deeds. Ruining my reputation. But he's not here now. I was hoping he'd show up. He was strong and might be able to keep us going or, at least, think things through in ways I can't. I should have known he wasn't going to this time. As my body dies, so does he. I wish I could feel him now. It's kind of lonely here. No angel. No Candy. No friends. No smokes or whiskey or donuts. Just me and a clown I'm only counting on to keep his word to prove he's stronger and smarter than me. It's okay. I'll take whatever I can at this point.

I'm glad I made Howard put the top down. I can feel a little bit of the breeze and smell the freeway exhaust fumes. It's very soothing. L.A. aromatherapy.

I wonder where Eva and Barron are right now. Does the Golden Vigil have them, or Abbot and his people? It's nice to know they're fucked no matter what.

I look over at Howard. His face smears like the city lights and I'm afraid for a second that I'm going to black out. But I pull it together and push myself back into a better sitting position where I can feel the wind.

I say, "Howard."

"What?"

"What are you going to do with immortality? I always wanted to know how you plan out something like that. What are you going to do with yourself? Learn to play the piano? Then what? Learn to paint? Then what? Learn to sail? Go skydiving? Wrestle gators in Florida for tourists? How do you spend forever?"

He smiles, delighted by the question.

"All of those things and more," he says. "You see, you and your friends are bound by time. You're linear thinkers. Tomorrow, and tomorrow, and tomorrow. I'm not bound by time. I can let my imagination roam freely. The first thing I'll do is put Wormwood back together again, bigger and better than before. I'll pursue my study of magic. Can you imagine what that will be like? A magician with all the time in the world and all the resources of Wormwood at his disposal. In a hundred years, I'll be running this whole bloody planet. After that? Who knows?"

I watch the stars streak by.

"At least you've kept your modesty," I say. "It's your best quality."

"That's just the thing. I don't need to think in ordinary ways anymore. Modesty. Ego. Benevolence. Malevolence. All the old definitions and mores fall away when your future is infinite. I'll have to invent a whole new way of being."

"It's going to get lonely, don't you think?"

He considers that for a minute.

"I'll allow for a few more of my type. Just a few carefully selected individuals who can grasp the enormity of this gift."

My eyes are getting better. I can focus again. The wind is really helping me feel alive again. I look around at the buildings and the nearby cars.

"Hey, Superman," I say. "Have you checked the traffic lately?"

"It's not too heavy. We're making good time."

"That's not what I mean, shithead. I mean have you looked at what's around us?"

He checks the mirrors and looks side to side.

"Cars. Trucks. Vans. What are you getting at?"

I look around again. Twist around so I can see the rearview.

"There are two unmarked vans on either side of us and at least one behind us."

He glances at me.

"What does that mean?"

"It means the faction found us."

He looks around again.

"How?"

"How the fuck do I know? Spy satellites? Facial recognition pigeons on the freeway signs? Ballerinas with Uzis? What does it matter? Just hit the fucking accelerator."

"But I don't drive. Not often. I have a chauffeur."

"Of course you do," I sigh. "If you can't drive, then get off the freeway. Maybe we can lose them in the streets."

"Will they let me?" he says. There's real fear in his voice.

"They're not going to kill a bunch of civilians with witnesses around. They'll let us off. How much farther to where we're going?"

"Just a few minutes."

"Okay. Take this next exit and let me think."

Howard jerks the wheel and we scream across three lanes of traffic, almost flipping as he turns onto the exit.

"Good plan. Kill us before they can," I tell him. "You're doing great."

There's a red light at the bottom of the exit.

"What now?" he says.

"Keep driving."

"Don't stop?"

"Keep going!"

He does it and we almost get T-boned by a semi.

"I said go through the light. I didn't say 'Don't look where you're going.'"

"Sorry."

There's a puddle of something at the bottom of the off ramp. As the Vigil van hits it, I bark some Hellion hoodoo.

The puddle expands and deepens. The van hits it easily going sixty. It spins out, does a complete three-sixty, and clips the side of the van coming down right behind it.

The first van is stuck, but the second one stays on us.

Best of all, doing that hoodoo didn't just weaken me, it goddamn well hurt. That can't be a good sign.

I push up my sleeve and cut myself again. Luckily, Howard's eyes are plastered to the road and he doesn't see me. This time when I do some hoodoo, I just whisper it.

A car from each side of the street flips into the air and explodes. When they come down, they block both lanes of the two-lane road.

"What was that noise?" says Howard.

He glances in the rearview mirror.

"What did you do?"

"Nothing. Keep going. And slow down."

"All right."

Behind us, the second van slams into the burning cars. It skids and flips onto its side.

He looks in the rearview.

"Was that you?" he asks. "Are we all right now?"

"No. There's at least one more van. Get back on the freeway. Head south, toward LAX."

"LAX? Where are we going?" he says suspiciously.

"Richard Branson is taking us to Narnia in his laser blimp. Just get on the fucking freeway."

He steers us onto the 405 and heads south. I can't see the third van, but I know it's behind us.

My head swims. I hope Howard gets us there soon. I don't want to let him know how bad I am, but I can't help groaning.

"What's wrong?" he says.

I bend my arms up and down.

"Rigor mortis. Each time it hits, it's harder to break through."

"Interesting," he says in a tone that should be reserved for viewing dissected frogs and roadkill.

Just north of the airport I say, "Take this exit. Head for those warehouses over there."

He takes us down a side road to a cluster of metal buildings.

"See that collapsed one over there? That's where we're going."

"Are you sure?" he says uncertainly.

"Yes. And speed it up. The van is back."

Howard hits the gas and fishtails the car, almost spinning us into the metal fencing along the road. But he gets control again and we head for the warehouse. I undo my seat belt and pull out the Colt. Twisting around in my seat, I fire at the van's front tires. It takes all six shots, but I manage to hit one.

In the rearview, Howard sees the van lurch. He smiles, but it disappears quickly.

"It's still coming," he says.

"They're running on the rim. It'll slow them down. Keep driving."

He pulls the Mercedes to a stop by the collapsed warehouse.

"Kill the lights," I tell him.

When it's dark, I pry myself out of the car with the help of the cane and Howard follows me inside the building. I use my phone to light the way.

We pass the same scattered pipes and shattered toilets I went by the last time I was here. Birds shriek at us from the ceiling. Howard stays close to me.

"Are you sure this is the right place?"

"Shut up."

Lights slide over the interior of the warehouse as we reach the office in the back.

Howard says, "The van is outside."

"We're almost there."

I cut myself again and bark some hoodoo. Rotting wooden crates all over the warehouse burst into flame. The birds go wild. The ones that can't find a way out through the roof swoop down and fly out the front, right through the Vigil crew.

When we reach the office, I stay by the door and point to the fifties girlie calendar.

"Find February twenty-ninth."

A few seconds later Howard says, "I found it."

"Now push the number."

Something clicks and the wall swings open. I grab Howard and shove him through. Push the wall back into place.

We're back in the hunting lodge safe house. I collapse on the sofa.

"What is this place?" says Howard.

"A Sub Rosa meeting house."

"Like the other place you kept me?"

"Bingo."

He looks back over his shoulder.

"Are we safe?"

"For a little while."

I get out my phone and text Abbot.

We're at the LAX house. Golden Vigil outside. You might want to hurry.

A few seconds later I get, *We're on our way. Stay there.*

Can't. Have to get somewhere. Carlos says you need more spices in the kitchen.

Who's Carlos?

I put the phone away.

"You ready to go?"

"Where?" says Howard.

"Wherever we're doing the ritual."

He nods. "We need to get to where the San Bernardino Freeway intersects with the 5."

I try to visualize the place. My mind keeps wandering, but I get it.

"A crossroad. You need a crossroad for it to work."

He pulls a sprig of something from one of his pockets.

"Are you surprised?"

I try to shake my head, but it hurts. Damn rigor mortis.

I say, "'Go to the crossroads and call him three times.'"

It's a line from F. W. Murnau's *Faust*. I already made one bad bargain recently. Am I making another one? What if Howard gets away? What if he's lying? What if, no matter what I tell myself, I'm so desperate to live and be with Candy that I'll agree to anything? My mind is too fuzzy. I'm weak and I hurt too much to be sure.

"Invoking the Devil? I never took you for such a traditionalist," says Howard. "Ludovico's technique was much more modern and efficient."

I look at my hands. A couple of my fingernails have fallen off. I'm leaving bloodstains on the sofa.

"Do I need to do anything?"

"Can you stand?"

"Do I have to?"

"Technically, no. But it gives the ritual a bit of elegance," says Howard.

"Fuck your elegance. Let's go."

"Lead on."

I stagger us through a shadow onto a freeway overpass.

We come out in the breakdown lane at the exact spot where the roads meet.

The San Bernardino Freeway and the 5 are busy any time of day or night. Cars and semis speed past us and under us. This is a wind I can feel. The pressure of each truck as it passes almost knocks me over. I lean against the metal guardrail. Even with the cane, it's hard to stay upright.

"Are you ready?" says Howard.

"No. I want to wait for Labor Day, when the leaves start to change."

"Is that a yes?"

He's enjoying himself a little too much.

"Yes."

"Good."

With his foot, Howard brushes away some broken glass and twisted metal from the ground—signs of a recent crash—and gets down on his hands and knees. He takes something from one of his pockets and carefully draws a large circle, then a smaller circle inside it. He squares the interior and adds a pentagram. In the blank space between the two circles, he begins writing. Some of it looks like abbreviated Greek, some of it like angelic script. The letters themselves begin to melt together into snakelike squiggles chasing each other round and round the interior of the circle. It's a neat trick if Howard is doing it, but it's entirely possible that my vision is going funny again.

I say, "How much longer?"

"Not much," he says. "You want it done properly, don't you?"

I don't answer.

He pours one of Vidocq's potions into the center of the pentagram, then drops in what looks like a handful of dried moly flowers. The potion begins to glow. First a pale pink, then a deep blue, and finally a swirling mist of black and rose.

"How are you doing up there?" he says.

"Hungry. I'm looking forward to being able to eat again."

"I'm sure you are. Just a couple of minutes more."

"I'll be over here thinking deep thoughts."

As the light grows brighter, Howard gets to his feet and begins a low chant that I can't quite make out. Whoever this Ludovico guy was, he took his sweet fucking time designing this ritual. On a good day, I could have conjured a herd of zebras, a large sausage pizza, and Ernest Borgnine's ghost, and reunited the Misfits, by now. But Howard just keeps yammering away. Every now and then, he sprinkles a glittering powder that makes the mist seethe momentarily.

Our little snake oil act isn't exactly stopping traffic, but the freeway is clogged as people slow to rubberneck at us. What do we look like to them? One of us is praying over the tiniest disco light show in history, and the other is a wobbly

Crypt Keeper ready to topple over the guardrail onto the road below.

"I need a few drops of your blood," shouts Howard.

"You didn't tell me Ludovico's Ellicit was blood magic."

"Is that a problem? You're already bleeding."

I look into the swirling lights at our feet.

"That's not the Ludovico, is it?"

"Of course it is, you idiot."

My legs and arms cramp as a wave of rigor hits me. A semi roars by and blasts its air horn at us. Startled, I drop the cane. But I can't even fall over. My body is rigid against the rail.

Howard comes over, smiling.

"Not feeling so good, are we? Relax. It will all be over soon. But I still need some of your blood."

Howard grabs my arm.

As quickly as it came, the rigor eases and I can move again. I pull my arm free of Howard's grip. That doesn't go over so well with him. He grabs the cane and swings it like a baseball bat into the side of my head. It hits and I drop onto the road like a dead flounder. He beats me with the cane a few more times while I'm down, just having fun. Cars honk and people video us. It's L.A. Blood lust runs deep.

When beating me isn't fun anymore, Howard throws the cane away and drags me to the swirling mist. He squeezes my arm where I cut myself earlier. Black blood flows into the magic circle. The dancing light seethes for a few seconds, then goes out. I'm able to roll away a few feet, but that's all.

The center of the pentagram begins to sizzle. Pieces of it fall away. The burning continues to expand and pieces of the circle continue dropping into a dark abyss. The incandescence stops at the edges of the larger circle. There's a void the size of a manhole in front of me. Howard gives me a kick on the side of the head with his nice shoes and drags me toward it.

"You were right. This isn't Ludovico's Ellicit. Although, to be precise, it *was* the Ellicit until the point where I added your blood," he says. "What to do with you was a problem, you see. I could send you to Hell, but you're perfectly comfortable there. I could kill you, but, again, you would go right back to Hell, which solves nothing. Altering the Ellicit was the only solution."

The piece of shit has been dragging me this whole time, and now my bruised and woozy head dangles over the freeway chasm.

He says, "Most people think that the opposite of life is death, but that's not true. The opposite of life is nothingness. That's what reversing the Ellicit has conjured—perfect, perpetual nothingness. You can spend eternity there thinking about your wasted life. Or going mad. Whichever suits you."

He drops my head and tries to shove me into the hole. My dead nerves don't feel a thing, but I can smell my flesh burning. Before I slide in, I manage to get my arms around one of his legs and hang on like an angry tick.

I suppose if I'm really leaving for good, the freeway is the best place to do it. If nothing else, L.A. is the city of roads and I'm an L.A. boy. Plus, I'm not going out entirely dead. Just Hollywood dead. I hate not making it into the movie, but maybe they'll include a couple of my scenes in the director's cut.

Something thumps repeatedly against my back and I realize that Howard is beating me with the cane again. I can't look up at him, but every few seconds, a car passes by and throws his shadow on the road. He's working Casey Jones hard to get me loose. And he's doing it. My arms are loose. I slide a few inches down his leg.

Goddammit, I don't want to go, especially not at the hands of a ten-dollar corpse fucker. But only the lucky ones get to choose how they go out and that's not me.

Candy was right. I should have stayed at Vidocq's. Candy was right about a lot of things. I miss her already.

There's a skid and a thump. The undercarriage of a car flashes overhead. All of a sudden Howard's gone and there's nothing for me to hold on to.

I fall into the dark.

WHAT'S TERMINAL VELOCITY in nothingness? Is there air drag? Updrafts? I wish I'd brought a book. I suppose I could Google it, but I don't think they have Wi-Fi in nothingness.

How long do I fall? How far? Am I going to float in nothingness or fall forever?

Do those questions even matter in a total void situation? If there's no up or down, how do you measure time or distance? I don't think you can and everything is the same forever, which I'm guessing is part of Howard's "going mad" plan for my future.

I wonder when that starts.

Has it started already?

My head feels funny.

Is today my birthday? I can't remember.

But I met a cute alien. That was cool.

How long have I been here?

I'm going to miss touching things and smelling things the most, I think.

I hope Candy isn't too mad when I don't come back. I hope Alessa takes good care of her.

How do you tell time here? Has it been a million years yet?

Something happens to my hands. My wrists get tight. I brace for another bout of rigor, but it's not like that. My arms stretch and my head falls back.

Soon, I see something, which is strange for a void. And what I see is even stranger than that.

It's a palm tree.

I didn't expect to see one of those in nothingness. I mean, if there are trees, it kind of defeats the whole concept of nothingness.

Someone slaps me. I'm sure of it.

"Stop yammering," a woman says.

There are palm trees *and* women here? Things are looking up for nothingness.

Someone slaps me again.

I say, "Where are you?"

"I'm right in front of you, you nitwit," she says. "Your eyes closed again."

I open them and she was telling the truth. She's right there.

Mustang Sally, the highway sylph. The queen of the roads. Wherever there's a path, a track, or a rut around here, Sally is there watching over it.

"Sally. What are you doing here?"

With one hand, she pulls me the rest of the way out of the hole.

"Saving your ridiculous life," she says. Then she gets a

good look at me. "Oh dear. I'd heard that Hell had aged you, but I didn't expect this."

"Who said Hell aged me?"

"People. Spirits. Agents of the road. I hear it all."

Sally always looks like she's on her way to the best parties. She's dressed in an all-black iridescent floor-length gown. Even on the filthy road, not a speck of dust sticks to her.

I look into the hole.

"How long are your arms? I was falling for like an hour."

She sees I'm wobbly, so she gives me the cane and pushes me against the guardrail. Even with that, I can't stand up anymore. I slide down to a sitting position on the ground.

"You were falling for a second or two," she says. "And you were only down about an inch."

"Still, you're really strong."

Sally makes a face, watching the cars go by. Some honk at her. She waves to them.

I look around. There's a silver Bugatti Chiron parked a few yards away. The right front fender is crumpled.

I point.

"You broke your car."

"That's life on the road. Do you like it? It's tribute from someone who owes me more than a car could pay. I'll return it to him tomorrow so he can get me another."

"Sorry if this sounds uncivilized, but why did you save me just now?"

She looks at her nails.

"I just happened to be passing by."

"That was convenient."

She gives me a little kick with her pointy designer shoe.

"Besides," she says, "I couldn't let you disappear. You still owe me a car, remember?"

"A little. My head is kind of fuzzy. What kind of car was it?"

Sally leans against the guardrail.

"The exact model doesn't matter. But something big and powerful. Red. And not recent."

I have to think about it for a minute.

"Wasn't it a Catalina fastback? Late sixties?"

She stands up again.

"That will do."

"Where's Howard?"

She makes a face.

"By the Bugatti. He's a bit of a mess. So are you, but you're in one piece."

"What are you going to do with him?"

"I thought I'd leave that to you. We could chuck him into that little hole I pulled you from or we could do it my way. Leave him where he is. Let his spirit wander the roads and freeways of the city with all the other lost souls forever."

"But he's immortal. I mean, I think so. Yeah, his body's a mess, but won't he wake up alive again at some point?"

Sally looks at me, annoyed.

"Immortality? On my road? Darling, there's only room for one immortal here and it's not a moth-eaten necromancer. He's as dead as anyone else. Just another highway ghost."

I try to pull myself up but fail miserably. "Let's do it your way. Let him thumb rides forever and no one will ever stop, right?"

"No one. He won't even know he's dead at first. Some

of his kind spend years frightened and confused before they admit what's become of them."

"I like that. But what about the hole?"

"What hole?" she says.

I look back and Howard's shaft to the void is closed.

"As for you, get off your rear and get in the car."

I try to stand up. I can't do it. With both hands on the guardrail, I try to pull myself up, but that doesn't work either.

I sigh, embarrassed.

"Sorry. I might have to spend eternity right here with Howard."

She comes to me and puts out her hands.

"Men are such babies."

I reach for her and with no effort whatsoever, she pulls me to my feet. I can't walk, so she tosses one of my arms around her shoulders and puts one of hers around my waist. We walk like that, very slowly and clumsily, to the Bugatti.

She opens the door, but when she starts to help me in I stop her.

"I'm going to bleed all over your nice seats."

She pushes me inside and belts me in.

"I told you I was getting a new one. Bleed to your heart's content."

Sally revs the engine and, being the freeway sylph, a spot opens for her in the traffic. She blasts onto the road, cutting across six lanes, a pure spirit in her element.

She says, "Where am I taking you?"

"Back to Vidocq's I suppose."

"You don't sound happy. Isn't that where your friends are?"

"That's why. I'm just going there to die in front of everyone."

She looks at me longer than makes me comfortable at this speed. But these are her roads. Traffic moves apart for her.

"If I understand things correctly, they're trying to find a fix for your current situation."

"Yeah. They're nice people. And Vidocq and Ray are smart. Maybe they'll figure something out."

"Then why are you hesitating?"

I close my eyes.

"Can't we just drive awhile? It's really nice here with you."

"Of course," says Sally. "It's always nice on the road."

She hits the accelerator and the road turns into a blur streaked with the glare of chrome and glass that looks like Christmas tree lights.

A moment later she says, "It's the girl, isn't it? You're afraid of losing her."

"Already lost her," I say. "Everything that's happened since I've been back makes it crystal clear how much better off she is without me."

"Is that what she says?"

I don't answer.

"It's the guilt too," says Sally. "About your naughty arrangement with Wormwood. Mr. Muninn told me."

I've slid down in my seat. It takes some effort to turn my head to her.

"You know Mr. Muninn?"

"We're acquainted, celestial to celestial. He doesn't think you're in your right mind."

"I sold out. Gave in to my worst enemy. Came back and

made everybody I care about miserable. And almost got some of them killed."

"Which ones?" Sally says.

"Candy and Alessa."

"Why would Wormwood want to hurt them?"

"It wasn't actually Wormwood that time. And it was only Alessa. She was on a kill list. Candy would have just been collateral damage."

Sally thinks about it.

"But if Alessa was already on a list to die, how is that your fault? It sounds like your being there saved her life."

"Maybe. But that was the only good thing."

"And you deserve to be punished," she says in a mocking tone.

"You don't understand. I don't work for monsters. I kill monsters."

"And now you're the worst monster of all."

"I don't know. Maybe."

We tear down the roads for a few more minutes. I have no idea where we are.

"Your friends must hate you for what you did," she says.

"Stop it. Please. Let's just drive."

"So you can die in my car?"

"You said you were getting a new one."

We go for a few more minutes, then my phone rings.

"That's your phone," says Sally.

"I know."

"Are you not answering it or *can't* you answer it?"

"A little of both."

Sally lets go of the wheel and starts going through my pockets.

I close my eyes, getting ready for the crash. But it doesn't happen. Of course it doesn't. No car would dare crash Mustang Sally. The steering wheel moves by itself, keeping the Bugatti going straight and smooth.

She comes up with the phone and thumbs it on.

"Hello? Yes, he's here. But he's pouting or something. Says he wants to die. Anyway, he's being the most annoying baby. Me? I'm Sally. Can I give him a message?" Sally listens for a few seconds more and says, "Thank you very much. I'll tell him."

She hangs up and puts the phone back in my pocket.

When she doesn't say anything I ask, "Who was that?"

"He didn't say."

"What did he want?"

"Something about how everybody hates you and you're a terrible person."

"Is that really what he said?"

"No. I forget. I wasn't listening. Let's just drive."

"It's your car."

"All cars are mine. You should know that by now."

Sally yanks the steering wheel hard to the right and we scream across the freeway as she pulls a perfect one-eighty through an open space in the concrete road divider no wider than a couple of shopping carts. If my heart was still beating, it would be going really fast right now.

"Where are we going?"

"Want to see a movie?" says Sally.

"What movie?"

"I don't know. Let's see what's playing at the drive-in."

WE COME OFF the freeway and blow through the streets of
Hollywood like a cruise missile. Red lights turn green. Lanes
open before us. When the cars slow, Sally takes us down side
streets I've never seen before and swings us back onto the
boulevard well past the traffic snarls.

I say, "Howard had a deal with a lot of badass angels and
you ruined it. They're going to be pissed."

She screws up her face like she smelled curdled milk.

"How boring, worrying about what angels think of you."

When she spots the Devil's Door, Sally twists the steering
wheel, sending the Bugatti onto the sidewalk. The drive-in
lights are off, but the gate is open. Sally doesn't slow but blows
through them and squeals to a stop by the concession stand.

She gets out and comes around to my side. When I open
my door my legs don't work. Sally stands there for a minute
looking at me.

"Really?" she says. "You're going to make me do this?"

Sally likes road food. The kind of junk you find at gas station food marts. Cupcakes. Stale cookies. Potato chips. She
pulls me out of the car like I weigh about as much as a bag of
Twinkies and carries me in her arms to where some startled
people I know are waiting for us. Sets me on the ground like
I'm light as a feather.

"Thanks, Sally."

"You're going to owe me a much nicer car before this is
over with."

I raise myself a few inches on my elbows.

Ray, Brigitte, and Vidocq come over.

"It's going to be okay," says Ray.

Vidocq says, "It's not quite Ludovico's Ellicit."

"But we think it's from the same region," adds Ray. "It's a kind of necromancy, but different."

"Now you're just confusing him," says Brigitte. She kneels down and puts a hand on my arm. "The spell is a little creative, but we think it will work."

Sally stands next to Candy.

They're a little behind me. It hurts to turn my head, so I mostly listen to them.

"Are you Sally?" Candy says. "Thanks for bringing him."

"I take it you're the one he's running away from."

"Running away?"

"According to him, he's done something unforgivable. I think he's exaggerating, but I'm not the one he's in love with, so what does it matter what I think?"

"I don't understand."

"Of course you do. Do you think you can save him?"

"We're going to try," says Candy.

"You might want to shake a leg."

Sally winks at me as she goes by and sits on the Bugatti. A wink is as close to a get-well card as she'll ever give you, but it's plenty for me.

Candy comes over and props me up against her. In the distance, Flicker and some of the others are rearranging the parking spaces into a hexagram. In the center of the hexagram, Kasabian and Carlos seem to be trying to light a pile of wood on fire.

Allegra is by me. She takes a stone from her bag and places it on my forehead. It turns black and crumbles. She rubs a purple salve on my cheek. It too turns to ash and falls off. She puts a leaf into each of my palms and closes my hands. When she opens them again, you can probably guess what they're like.

She closes her bag and curses quietly.

"I don't know what to say, Stark. I'm sorry."

"It's okay. I know embalming isn't your specialty."

That wasn't the right thing to say. When she moves away, I think she's crying a little.

I look up at Candy and nod at the screen.

"What's playing tonight?"

She says, "Saving Private Asshole."

"Porn? Kasabian will be happy."

Candy looks at Sally, then back at me.

"Was Sally right? Do you want to die?"

"How's your head?"

Candy frowns.

"Is that what this is about? I got a bump on the head?"

I try to push myself upright. I make it a few inches, then lean back against her.

"It's your head and everyone else's," I say. "I was ready to fuck over the world to come back. I'm afraid if I stay, I'll bring more trouble down on everyone."

"Leaving isn't entirely your decision."

"Yeah, it is."

"Then get up and walk away."

"I can't."

Candy gestures with her hand to the others working.

"All the people you were fucking over are here to help you."

"That was the old me. Not the Wormwood me. Buy them a popcorn and send them home."

Carlos and Kasabian finally have their fire going. Are they having a cookout? Is this my going-away party?

Candy says, "That's a shitty thing to say after everything they've done for you. If you want to send them home, tell them yourself."

I try to say something, but my mouth doesn't work anymore.

Candy takes my hand, but I pull it away and drag the Colt from my waistband. It's so heavy I can barely lift the thing.

"Stop it," says Candy.

I drag it up my body so I can get it as close to my head as possible.

"Stark?"

It takes a lot of effort, but I pull back the hammer.

"I'll never forgive you."

Someone grabs my arm and snatches away the Colt.

Alessa squats on her heels with my gun in her hand.

"I already cleaned up your mess once," she says. "If Candy wants you to live, you're going to live."

Carlos and Kasabian come and stand behind her.

Carlos says, "What the fuck was that? Was he going to shoot himself?"

"He's not thinking straight. Is it ready?" says Candy.

"We're still working on the bonfire," says Kasabian.

"We're not the outdoorsy type," says Carlos.

"Please hurry," says Candy.

"You two are ridiculous," says Sally, looking at Carlos and Kasabian. She says, "This is how you start a fire."

With a plastic gasoline can in her hand, she gets a few yards closer to the pitiful flames lapping up from the wood and tosses the can overhead. It makes a perfect arc through the air and lands on the pile. A second later, it explodes in a beautiful, rolling orange ball that lights up the entire theater. The wood is now a roaring pile of burning timbers.

The others run back to us.

"Is everyone all right?" says Brigitte.

Flicker leans down in front of me. She's wearing a set of dirty workman's overalls.

"Who is that?"

"Sally," says Candy.

Flicker looks again.

"Mustang Sally? Damn, Stark. You do have interesting friends."

Candy looks at Vidocq and Ray. "This all sounded like such a good idea a little while ago. Now I'm not so sure."

"There isn't any choice, I'm afraid," says Vidocq. "Look at him. How close to death he is."

Ray says, "Vidocq is right. I can't give you any guarantees tonight except one: he's going to die if we don't do something. And by the look of him, we need to do it now."

Candy brushes my hair back. Some of it comes off in her hand.

As the rigor tightens me I want to say, *I don't care anymore. Do whatever it is you're going to do.* But Kasabian does it for me.

"Are we ever going to do this?" he says.

"Okay," Candy says. "Let's go."

Ray nods, then says, "Stark needs to wear this."

He takes a length of rawhide with a pouch hanging from it and places it around my neck.

"Don't worry," he says. "It's just salt and gold dust."

Brigitte takes a brush, dips it into a small bowl, and flicks something over me that smells like a dead whale's backwash.

"I know it smells awful, but it's necessary."

When she's done, she nods and says, "Good luck, Jimmy."

I have a very bad feeling I know where this is heading and there's nothing I can do about it. Rigor mortis has hit again, and I don't have the energy to shake it off. All my limbs cramp and I can't move.

"I guess we're ready," says Candy. "I don't think he can walk there himself. Can someone help me?"

Everyone grabs a piece of me and carries me to the edge of the bonfire, close enough that I can vaguely feel the cling wrap harden and the adhesive on the duct tape begins to loosen and melt.

They set me down in a salt circle, pry open my mouth, and pour brine down my throat. I choke and sputter but keep most of it down.

As everyone stands back, Flicker pats me on the shoulder.

"Don't worry, Stark. We made a good hexagram for you. Number thirty. Very powerful. Radiance. The phoenix."

Fuck me.

Carlos squeezes my arms.

"Buena suerte."

Candy gives me a kiss on the cheek.

"See you soon," she says.

And pushes me into the fire.

I've used fire a lot in my fights, both in the arena and since returning to the world. I've been burned badly both places, but I've never been thrown into the equivalent of a furnace before, and a magic one at that. Let me describe how it feels.

It fucking hurts, which is so unfair. How long has it been since I've felt anything at all? And now my nerves are working again just in time for me to baste in my own filthy juices.

The cling wrap melts into my skin and the duct tape bursts into flame. My hair goes next. Then my clothes. I don't want to tell you what happens to my eyes.

I feel my skin crisp, then bubble and swell. That part doesn't last long. My fat begins to melt, which is extra fun because it's flammable and I burn even hotter. I keep waiting to go unconscious. Hoping for it. I try to think of hoodoo that will knock me out. I've been knocking out assholes left and right for days, but when I need to remember the curse it's gone. Maybe because my brain is boiling in its own juices. Maybe because these are magic flames and I'm supposed to be awake to enjoy every moment of the ride. Maybe it's part of my punishment for Wormwood.

I don't know how long it takes for the meat parts of me to cook away, but I'm happy when they do. Burning bones don't hurt as much as skin. Not that it's fun turning to ash. How hot does a fire have to be to destroy bones? Fourteen hundred, maybe fifteen hundred degrees? This is definitely a hoodoo fire. Nothing Kasabian was involved in could ever work this well.

And then there's none of me left to burn. I'm gone. A bodiless consciousness floating into the air as black vapor and airborne ash. Finally, I have my wish.

I float into the sky and come down all over L.A. as wildfire debris, making people's eyes water and throwing them into coughing fits.

That's it, fuckers. I saved your dumb asses more than once. Let me choke you a little as I vanish into the sky.

I spread across the city, growing thinner as I go. I swirl around buildings, trapped by convection currents. I'm sucked into air-conditioning systems and blown out through giant vents on skyscraper rooftops. I mix with car exhaust and grill flames in food trucks. I drift into bars and churches, mixing with incense and the smell of candle wax. I envelop the hills like a fog, wrapping like Marilyn Monroe's mink stole around the letters in the Hollywood sign.

Then the currents change and I'm drawn into a whirling tunnel of flame—a fire devil—that drags me back to the scalding center of the hexagram.

And then, weirdly enough, something in the fire begins to twitch. I stumble forward to the edge of the flames.

I seem to have feet again. And hands. And they're not burning. They're bright like the fire. I lurch forward a few steps and trip over something.

It's the wood around the bonfire.

A second later, I'm out of the flames and glowing red like a goddamn piece of charcoal.

Everything is too bright. I can't see anything but my own luminous body, incandescent with heat. I don't know what else to do, so I walk a few more steps.

I begin to shiver. It's a frigid world outside of the fire and I can feel my skin cooling rapidly.

Eventually, I can see again. Nine people stare at me like I'm Jesus returned to Earth or the beast from twenty thousand fathoms.

One more step and I fall to my knees. But it's okay. I can

get up again. And I felt the ground. It was hard and now my new damn knees hurt.

Candy runs over and puts out a hand.

"Stark?" she says.

She reaches for my arm and then snatches her hand away like she touched a hot skillet.

Ray and Vidocq throw freezing buckets of water over me. I stand there naked and steaming, white vapor curling off me as I cool.

Soon, the steam disappears.

Candy touches me again. Smiles. Throws her arms around me.

That's something I didn't think I'd ever feel again.

I look at my right hand. It looks like a real hand again and not a mummified tarantula. Pale scars still crisscross my body. My breath comes easily and when I touch my chest, I can feel my heart beating.

"Will somebody give this fucker a robe or something so he doesn't stand there feeling himself up all night?" says Kasabian.

Candy gives me a beaten-up robe we stole from the Chateau Marmont when we squatted there last year. I can feel the soft fabric against my skin, the grit of the parking lot under my feet.

"Stark?" says Allegra. "Can you talk?"

It takes me a couple of tries, but I manage to get out, "I think I'm okay."

People crowd around me. Hugs. Pats on the back. Kasabian and Alessa stand apart from the congratulations, which is probably best for all of us.

Behind me, the bonfire is just about out, like all of its heat went into my body and when I walked away from it, all its power came with me. In a few more seconds, it dies completely. Carlos and Vidocq dump buckets of water on the embers.

Ray and Brigitte show me a couple of pages scrawled with tight handwriting. My eyes don't focus well enough yet to read it.

"What does it say?"

"It's the spell we used to bring you back," says Ray.

"What kind is it? Resurrection? Spirit binding?"

Brigitte covers her mouth when she laughs. Ray looks a little embarrassed.

"It's not either of those," he says. "It was used by farmers in Eastern Europe in times of famine."

Brigitte says, "It restores spoiled meat to an edible condition."

I look at Candy and back to them.

"You're saying I'm a ham sandwich?"

"Exactly," says Brigitte.

"I can live with that."

Vidocq comes over and Carlos follows with something in a rag. He holds it out to me.

"I guess we got a little distracted. We forgot your stuff in your coat."

"The scroll too?"

"Yeah. Sorry, man. This is all we could salvage from the fire," he says, handing me the rag.

It's the black blade, and it's perfect. No fire on Earth, even a hoodoo one, was ever going to hurt it. I wrap it back in the rag.

"Thanks a lot for everything. Really. Everyone."

People nod and murmur.

Flicker taps me on the shoulder.

"So, Stark, that really is Mustang Sally over there?"

"Yeah. I'll introduce you."

Sally drops her cigarette and stubs it out as we go over.

She looks me up and down in my bare feet and my stolen robe.

"You look like a rakish hobo," she says. "It suits you."

I put a hand on Flicker's shoulder.

"Sally, this is Flicker. This is her place."

Sally smiles at her.

"Nice theater you've got here. There aren't enough drive-ins left in the world."

"I totally agree," Flicker says. "You're welcome here anytime, Sally."

Flicker pulls some theater passes out of a pocket in her overalls.

"These are for you. Please come back. Whatever you want to eat or drink, it's on me."

Sally looks the passes over.

"I might just do that. What's playing here next?"

I say, "It's seventies week, right?"

"That's right," Flicker says. "Starting with *Foxy Brown* and *The Getaway*."

Sally thinks about it.

"I might just come back for that."

"Anytime. Really. It would be an honor to have you."

"That's sweet of you."

Sally turns to me.

"I changed my mind about the car you owe me."

"You don't want a Catalina?"

"I want a 1958 Chrysler Dual Ghia L6.4."

"That's a very specific car. Why that one?"

"Frank Sinatra gave me one once. It was a lovely ride," she says.

"You knew Sinatra?"

She gets into the wrecked Bugatti. Starts the engine.

"*Everybody* who drives here long enough owes me," says Sally. "Have a good night, lovelies."

Sally backs out of the theater and does a one-eighty without stopping. Hits the gas and is gone.

"Thanks for letting us make a mess of your place," I tell Flicker.

She claps her hands together.

"Thank you for introducing me to Mustang Sally. As far as I'm concerned, we're even."

We go back over to the others.

Candy looks me in the eyes and says, "You look tired."

"I kind of am."

"Where were you planning on sleeping?"

I think for a minute.

"Abbot said I could use the UFO place. I'll head back there."

"It's all shot up and the food is lousy."

"I gave all my money away so I can't stay in a hotel. Besides, I don't think they'd let me check in wearing just a robe."

"Come on with us. You can crash on our couch at Max Overdrive tonight."

I look at Alessa.

"That's okay with you?"

She nods.

"We talked it over."

"Okay then."

There's not much left to say, so with one last look around, Candy, Alessa, and I pile into Ray's Honda and he gives us a ride back to the store. It's right around dawn.

When we get out he says, "Come by Bamboo House tonight. I'm making tamales."

"We'll do that," says Candy.

I guess they go that night. When I finally wake up, Candy tells me that I've been out for twenty-four hours.

It's the best sleep I ever had.

NEW CLOTHES ARE waiting for me on the kitchen table when I wake up. Boots. Leather bike pants. A new coat. And a clean Max Overdrive T-shirt. There's a note too.

There's coffee in the pot. Just heat it up.

I get dressed and turn on the coffeemaker. Candy comes in just as I'm pouring myself a cup. I start to pour her one too, but she shakes her head. I take a sip of mine.

"Holy shit."

"You can taste again?" she says.

"Yeah. It's strange. I was just a couple of days without taste or touch, and now that all my senses are back it's like they're all new again."

"That sounds exciting. It almost makes me wish I could do it."

I drink some more.

"Figure out another way than the one I used. It wasn't worth it."

Candy takes my hand and pulls me over to the couch. We sit down. There are coasters with cute anime creatures on the table. I set my cup down on one of those.

"It's good to have you back," Candy says.

"It's amazing to be back. But listen, I've got to know. What ever happened with Audsley Ishii? The last thing I remember is you jumping him."

"Yeah, that. It was a big mess," Candy says. "Alessa was freaking out and someone called the cops. I managed to get clean clothes on before they got here. You gave me Thomas Abbot's number, so I called him and—I don't know how he did it—but he fixed everything with the police. No one got arrested. Then they took your body away in an ambulance."

"And that was that?"

"And that was that. We never heard another word. I suppose Wormwood must have known about things right away. When I called the morgue about your body they said they couldn't find it."

I pick up the coffee and drink a little more. The heat goes through my whole body.

"Wormwood kept me on ice until they wanted me back."

"What happened to Howard?"

I don't want to look at her, so I look at the floor.

"It was stupid to leave with him. He tried to fuck me over, just like you said he would, but Sally saved me. No one is going to see him again."

Candy moves the coasters around for a few seconds, then says, "Were you really going to kill yourself back at the drive-in?"

"I don't know. I was a little crazy right then."

"You didn't look crazy to me. You looked like you knew exactly what you were doing."

"You don't get it. I went against everything I ever believed in when I threw in with Wormwood."

She leans back against the sofa pillows.

"I would have done the same thing."

"Really?"

"If I was in Hell and away from you and Alessa and everybody else? I would have done anything to come back."

I pick up the hot mug and hold it until I can't stand it anymore.

"I'm having a real hard time with this."

"I can tell," Candy says. "But you've had this bigger-than-life idea of yourself ever since I've known you. You were super-special Sandman Slim for so long you think you have to be that all the time forever."

"You really think that's what I'm like?"

Ignoring the question, she goes on. "And then there's what happened to Alice. You're still guilty about that."

"I always will be."

"I bet she's forgiven you by now."

"Maybe. I saw her when I was Downtown this last time."

"Alice is in Hell?" says Candy.

"No. She came there with some other angels. She *is* an angel, I should say. She and her friends helped keep the rebel angels off our backs. I don't think we would have survived without them."

Candy puts her hands together.

"That sounds like forgiveness to me."

"Still. Her death is my fault. So are all the things I've

done to you and Kasabian and everyone else. I don't know anymore if I go looking for monsters or I just bring them with me."

Candy puts her hand on my back.

"You need to go to Allegra and spend some time with her. She said before you went away this last time that you'd agreed to try medication for your PTSD."

"I did. Now I'm not so sure about it. What do you think?"

"I think you should take a chance on anything that might make you happy."

"I know that makes sense, but I don't know. I've been me for so long, what am I going to be if that's gone?"

"Wouldn't it at least be interesting to find out?"

She takes her hand away. I miss it already. We sit for a minute, and I soak that in—taking what I can get—until Candy says, "What was Hell like this last time? It must have been horrible being back."

"It was strange. Stranger than anything I went through down there."

I tell her about the Magistrate and his mad crusade. And about the weapon that was supposed to save Heaven but turned out to be nothing but a carny gaff. Last, I tell her about almost going to Heaven.

"See?" she says. "After all that, of course you jumped at the chance to come home."

I drink more coffee and use the mug to point downstairs.

"I like what you've done to the store."

"Oooh. Nice deflection," she says. "I take it we're not talking about you anymore?"

"I can't right now. I just can't."

"It's okay. I get it."

She looks at the door.

"The store is doing really well now. Did Kasabian tell you that we have bands in sometimes?"

"He did. Do you and Alessa still have a band?"

"Yeah. We're really good now. You should come and hear us."

"I'd like that."

Candy screws up her lips a little bit.

"Alessa thinks we need a logo, but I have no idea how you get something like that."

I pat my pockets and then remember that my other coat burned up in the bonfire, along with just about everything else.

"Across Sunset from an antiques store called Angelic Bazaar is a café. There's a cute waitress inside named Alyx. She showed me some of her designs. She's really good. And I think you'd like her. Tell her the bodyguard sent you."

Candy raises her eyebrows at me.

"My. You do work fast, Mr. Stark."

I wave a hand at her.

"It's not like that. I was wearing a glamour. She thinks I'm some pretty boy from central casting."

"Still. You charmed her."

"The face charmed her. Everybody likes that damn face. I have to get another one."

"Or maybe figure out something to do so you don't have to wear glamours anymore."

I finish the coffee and put down the mug. I want more, but it doesn't feel right asking.

"How are you with still being Chihiro?"

Candy shrugs.

"I'm pretty used to it. I don't think of her as quite me, so when Alessa and I go clothes shopping it's like we're buying stuff for our crazy friend."

"I almost forgot to tell you, Abbot said that when the Golden Vigil disbanded last year, all of their cases were closed. There's no warrant out for Candy anymore. You can go back to being you."

She frowns.

"But the Golden Vigil is back. Doesn't that mean their old cases are back too?"

"I don't know. Can they do that?"

"I think they can do anything they want. I'm going to stay Chihiro for now. It's what everyone is used to at the store and in the band. Having her just disappear would take more explaining than I want to do right now."

"I can understand that."

I touch my coat and feel the black blade inside. Even though I don't want it to, it feels comforting.

I say, "It might sound weird to say, but I'm glad that you and Alessa got together before I disappeared."

"Before you were *murdered*," says Candy.

"I'm glad there was someone to take care of you."

Talking about Alessa, I can see her relax.

"She really saved me. Kasabian tried his best to help, but he's just not the nurturing type. But he bought us a lot of beer."

"He bought himself a lot of beer and let you have some."

Candy wags a finger at me.

"You really need to ease up on him. He's changed a lot since you've been gone."

"I'll try."

Candy takes my empty, pours more from the pot, and brings it back to me.

"So. The other thing," she says.

"The other thing?"

"You, me, and Alessa."

"Right. That."

I move around a couple of the coasters.

"I don't want to get in the way. I'm not going to get in the way. I'll walk out of here right now if you want."

Candy looks at me.

"You would, wouldn't you?"

"If that's what you want."

"See?" she says, a tone of exasperation in her voice. "You're playing the hero again. Stop it."

I pick up my hands and drop them in my lap.

"I'm not sure what I'm supposed to do right now."

"Listen," she says. "The three of us were figuring things out when you were killed. I want to go back to that. I want to figure out how we can make this work."

"Alessa has had you to herself for a year. How's she going to feel when some dead guy suddenly appears and you go off with him?"

"First of all, I'm not going off with you. And I'm not going off with her. You and me were together for a year or so when I started seeing Alessa. If you were okay with me seeing her I'm sure she'll be okay with me seeing you."

I swirl the coffee around in the mug.

"That sounds complicated."

"You and me were always complicated. Now it's the three

of us. That's only one more. Between us, we can figure out the complication."

I set down the mug.

I don't have to go away. My gut unknots itself.

"Okay. I'm in if you are."

"I'm in."

She smiles and bumps her shoulder into mine.

I say, "Kasabian won't be happy. He wants me long gone."

"No he doesn't. He missed you. Just not the guns and monsters."

"I'll try to keep them to myself."

"Try to not keep them at all."

"Even better."

Candy turns on the sofa and sits on one foot.

"What are you going to do now?"

"I'll see if Abbot will let me stay at the UFO place. I know it was kind of a wreck, but maybe I can do something about that in my copious free time."

"That's good, but I meant do you know what you're going to do with your life?"

"Not a clue. Kasabian said I could have some movies."

"I think we can let you have movies whenever you want them."

"Good. I have a year to catch up on."

The door from the store below opens and Alessa comes in. She smiles at us.

"You're finally awake," she says.

I take a last sip of coffee and get up.

"Yeah. I should get going. Thanks for letting me crash here. I'm sorry I stayed so long."

"It was no problem," Alessa says. "After all the craziness at the drive-in it seemed smart to make sure you were all right."

"I really am. See you later."

Candy jumps up and gives me a kiss on the cheek.

"I'll call you."

"Sure."

For once, I leave the store by the front door like a normal person. Kasabian nods to me as I go out. I nod back. When I'm outside, I go around the short alley at the side of the store and walk through a shadow by the Dumpster.

Come out in Eva Sandoval's office.

The place is a wreck. Bullet holes in the walls. Chairs and tables knocked over. Blood has soaked into the green felt on her pool table. Her desk lies on its side. I push it out of the way and pick up the rug underneath.

Howard might have been a murdering necro-prick, but he wasn't lying about Eva's safe. There's a square door and key-pad just a half inch below the level of the floor. I listen for footsteps or any other sounds in the house. When it stays quiet I whisper some Hellion hoodoo to check for any magical traps, but whatever curses Sandoval had around the place were used up last night.

I bark a bit more hoodoo and the safe door slams open. I don't really know what I'm looking for, so I grab everything and stuff it into my coat pockets.

When the safe is empty, I close it, replace the rug, and push the desk back where it was. I'm tempted to steal some other stuff, but what? There are paintings, sculptures, and expensive carpets everywhere, but none of it is anything I'd want.

But I can't leave the place entirely unlooted. I go back to the desk one more time and paw through the drawers.

Lucky me. I find a few more packs of Shermans. I squeeze those into my pockets with Eva's other loot. On my way out, I take the only other thing worth having: a bottle of her very good bourbon.

A Sub Rosa cleanup crew must have been to the UFO mansion while I was asleep. The place is put back together again just like the first time I saw it. No bullet holes. All the windows intact. I go into the kitchen and open the refrigerator. Yep. Same boring food as before. But right now, all food is exciting, and soon I'll go to Bamboo House of Dolls and have Carlos's tamales.

I unload my pockets on the kitchen island.

There's fifty thousand dollars in cash in five ten-thousand-dollar bundles. There are stocks and a pile of bearer bonds, which, according to *Die Hard,* are very valuable. Abbot will know about them. There are boxes of diamond earrings, pearls, and other shiny stuff. I'll have to have people over and let them figure out who wants what. The bottom of one pocket is already ripped because I stuffed four small gold bars in there. I figure that those should go to Vidocq and Ray. They can use them in their hoodoo spells. Or just cash them in and buy a new TV. That's all right too.

I leave everything on the kitchen island, grab a glass, and go into the living room with Eva's bourbon. I pour a shot and toast her.

You brought me back and then tried to kill me, so I guess we're even there. But if I ever see you or Barron again, I'm taking your heads down to the bowling alley and not stopping until I roll a three hundred with each of you.

I turn on the TV and flip through the channels, but what I'm really thinking about is the windows. I wonder how far it is down from them to the hillside below. If I bought one of those collapsible home fire-escape ladders and hung it outside, I wonder if I could reach the ground. It's L.A. sometime in the seventies outside. How can I not check that out?

Abbot doesn't have to know.

No one has to know.

I mean, what's the worst that could happen?

I FALL ASLEEP with the TV on. Babies sleep a lot, right? I guess new bodies need sleep too. And I didn't piss myself, so I'm still one up on babies.

It's about three in the morning, everything on TV is garbage, and I don't have any movies yet. I grab my coat and shadow-walk to Donut Universe.

The woman working the counter is my alien friend from last night. She looks startled when she sees me.

"Wow, you look a lot better."

"Thanks for helping me out. I think I'd still be lying there without you."

She gives me a sly smile.

"The last time you were in you said you'd buy out the store if you were still alive. Are you a man of your word?"

I spread a thousand dollars of Sandoval's money on the counter.

"Is that enough?"

She holds up a hundred to the light to see if it's counterfeit.

"It's a start," she says. "But I have a better idea."

She brings me a black coffee and an apple fritter.

"Voilà."

"You remembered."

"On the house," she says.

"Won't you get in trouble?"

She leans across the counter and speaks in a low voice.

"Look around. It's just us and a couple of drunk convention guys who don't want to go home to their wives."

"Thank you . . ."

She points to her name tag and says, "Janet."

"Janet. Right. I'm Stark."

She shifts her weight a little nervously.

"Actually, that stuff isn't really free."

"How much is it?"

She pushes the thousand back to me.

"Sit down over there. I get off in fifteen minutes."

"Anything for free donuts."

"If you finish your coffee, come back for more."

"Great. I'll be over there."

I drink the good coffee and eat my fritter. Janet is a little odd, but the last week has been pretty fucking odd—with dying, not dying, burning up, not burning up, going back Downtown for a few minutes, and being a cling-wrap mummy—so why not end it that way?

What the hell am I going to do with my life? I think going part-time at Max Overdrive is probably out of the question, so what else is there? I could go back to work for Abbot, but that's eventually going to lead to more monsters and I'm going to try to avoid them for now.

I should call Allegra and talk to her about PTSD stuff. But no yoga or soy burgers.

Maybe Carlos needs a barback at Bamboo House. But not on necromancer night. Never on necromancer night.

The UFO mansion is kind of big and empty to be there all the time alone. Candy and Alessa have music night at Max Overdrive. Maybe I could have movie nights at my place. Or is that too pathetic and obvious? I'm not twenty anymore. Of course, when I was twenty I was Downtown fighting bug-eyed fuckwits in the arena. Maybe I get to do some twenty-year-old things? I'll think about it.

"Mind if I join you?"

Marshal Wells slips into the booth across from me. He smiles and clasps his hands together.

"You're looking good, James. What *is* your secret?"

"Lots of greens. Prayer. Faith in the baby Jesus."

Wells unclasps his hands.

"You see? I try to approach you in a calm and respectful manner and you resort to cheap blasphemy."

"I didn't think it was cheap. It felt just about right to me."

He doesn't talk for a minute. Just looks me over.

Eventually he says, "Who did you sell your soul to this time?"

"You're talking about my miraculous resurrection?"

"You look better than even before you were a moldering piece of human garbage."

I eat a piece of my fritter.

"There weren't any demon deals or satanic payoffs. Just good old American know-how."

"You're what that circus at the drive-in was about," says Wells.

I rap my knuckles on the table once.

"It was great. You ought to try it. Treat yourself to a spa day."

"No thank you. I have more important fish to fry. Which reminds me. Don't worry about your friend Marcella's future in the Vigil. I executed her."

I want to jump across the table and throttle him, but I stay where I am, trying to show him as little as possible. It's a pointless thing to do. Wells knows me well enough to know what I'm feeling and what I'm thinking about.

"Nothing to say?" he says. "No clever quips or animal violence?"

I look at him hard.

"How many people do you have outside?"

"Enough to put you down like the dog you are."

"And the innocent people in here?"

"They're your responsibility. Do something dumb or just sit there and listen."

I reach for my coffee, and almost imperceptibly, he flinches. Unfortunately, I think that's all the satisfaction I'll get out of him tonight.

I say, "I have a friend coming over soon, so make it fast."

"Then listen hard, Mr. Stark," he says. "The first thing I want from you is my scroll."

"I told you. I burned it."

"I don't believe you."

"Would you believe me if I told you it was a mistake?"

He turns his head slightly and says, "What does that mean?"

"The scene at the drive-in? My coat ended up in the fire. And the scroll was in my pocket."

He stares at me.

"Why should I believe you?"

"It's the truth."

"You told me you'd burned it before the drive-in."

"I did. That was a lie."

"But now you're telling the truth."

"Yes."

"Why?"

"Because the truth is so stupid," I say. "You see everything in gigantic, CinemaScope Old Testament terms. Plagues. Seas parting. People turned into pillars of salt. But the truth is smaller than that. I fucked up."

Wells hangs his head for a few seconds. When he looks up, he's as hard and mean looking as I've ever seen him.

"Listen to me. Things are coming. They're bigger than you or me or any of the pissant sinners around us. I know that you think I'm going to tell you to stay out of the way. But I'm not. Feel free to jump into the fray anytime you want, James. I welcome it. I *long* for it. You think you're protected from on high by Thomas Abbot and his pixie friends? Let me tell you, he won't be able to help you. There is no one you can turn to, nowhere you can run where I can't find you. And when I do, I'll burn you down and everyone and everything you've ever loved."

I look at him with my heart racing.

"You know what I'm thinking?"

"I don't, James. What are you thinking?"

"I think you're a cheese Danish guy. Cherry would be too sweet and decadent. No, you're definitely cheese. Admit it. I'm right. Why don't you get some coffee and I'll buy a whole box for you and your lackeys outside? What do you say?"

He looks at his watch.

"Fortunately, I have an appointment on planet Earth," he says. "Enjoy your pastry. You look almost like a human being with that thing. That's how I want to remember you. Almost human, but not quite, and more dangerous because of your proximity to normalcy."

Wells slides out of the booth.

I look at my fritter.

"'Proximity to normalcy' is a nice turn of phrase. You ought to do a needlepoint, frame it, and shove it straight up your ass. Keep it there with the rest of your wisdom."

"Good night, James."

"Good night, Larson."

As he's walking out, Janet comes over with coffee and a pile of donuts.

"Who was your friend?" she says, sitting down. "He didn't look happy."

"He isn't a friend. You know those people you never want to see again, but you seem to run into them everywhere? That's him."

"Oh good. He looks like a cop. I was afraid for a minute you might be one too."

"I'm about as far as you can get from a cop and still be a biped."

Satisfied, Janet takes a bite of an eclair.

"How's the coffee?" she says, covering her half-full mouth with her hand.

"Good. How's your donut?"

She swallows.

"Good. Now it's time for you to pay for your dinner."

"That doesn't make me at all nervous."

"It's just a question. Questions, actually. Several of them."

"Shoot."

She says, "Last night you looked like someone worked you over with a tire iron and you walk in here tonight like nothing happened."

"I don't think that's technically a question."

"It will be later, but I have another one first."

"Let me have it."

"When I helped you up, you disappeared. You didn't run away or hide in a crowd. You *disappeared*. How did you do that?"

Shit.

"You saw that?"

"I sure did."

I take a bite of fritter, stalling for time.

"It's not a big deal. It's just a trick I can do."

"*I* thought it was a big deal," says Janet. "I could use it around here sometimes with the creeps that come in. Can you show me how to do it?"

"I'm afraid it's not that kind of trick."

She leans over the pile of donuts and speaks in a quiet, conspiratorial voice.

"Are you one of those magic people? I've seen them, you know. When it's late like this and nothing's happening I watch people. It's not spying really. Just people watching, you know?"

"What have you seen that makes you believe in magic?"

"Sometimes they goof around. Make napkins move or the coffee refill itself."

I brush off the comment.

"Those just sound like tricks you could learn off You-Tube."

She points at me. "Which is exactly what a magic person would say. You're going to have to try harder than that to convince me that you didn't disappear in a puff of smoke."

"There was smoke?"

"There should be. It would be a much better trick."

"I'll remember that."

She looks down at the table.

"You don't remember me, do you?"

"Sure. You helped me last night."

"That's not what I mean. It was during the whole craziness with the zombies last year. You came in and said you were an angel and that I should go home and lock the doors."

Right. "I remember that. Only the way I recall it, I didn't say I was an angel. You did."

She looks at me hard.

"You saved my life. I never forgot you, but I guess you forgot me."

"Of course not. You gave me free donuts then, too."

She smiles again.

"Another question: How did you get all those scars?"

It always comes down to my stupid face.

"All of them? I got them at different times."

Janet reaches across the table and touches my nose.

"How about that one?"

"You want the truth?"

"Absolutely."

"It was from a *xiangliu*. It's a really big snake. With nine heads."

She drops her weight against the back of the booth.

"You'll notice I'm not laughing or mad. Guess why."

"Why?"

"I believe you."

I look out the window. A day ago I thought I'd never see Hollywood Boulevard again and here I am now eating donuts with a nice alien.

I say, "It's okay talking like this."

"I think so too."

"But you should know that I'm involved with someone."

That gets her attention. "Boy or girl?"

"Girl."

"Where is she?"

"With a friend."

"It's three in the morning. Kind of late to be out with a friend."

"They're really good friends."

She pushes some powdered sugar around on the table with her fingertip.

"I'm friendly. Can't we be friends?"

This is nice and I come up with four thousand reasons why I should leave right now. But I don't. Instead of saying "Good night," my mouth says, "Sure. Why not?"

Janet is friendly, and at least for the moment, I'm pretty alone. We drink coffee and talk about nothing. She's older than I thought.

"I've got one of those faces," she says. "I get carded all the time."

We talk until the place starts to fill up with people on their way to work. After everything that's happened, it's nice to sit and talk to someone who doesn't know about the awfulness of it. And someone who isn't scared of my real face.

I look at the clock.

"It's getting busy. I should give you your booth back."

"Yeah. I should get going too."

Before I get up I say, "Let me ask you a question this time."

"Go for it."

"If someone moved into a new place, are movie nights something grown-ups do?"

"What kind of movies?"

"That's the big question. I mean you could have a bad-movie night or a good-movie night."

"What's your idea of a bad-movie night?"

"How about *Face/Off* and *Battlefield Earth*?"

"A bad Travolta festival. That is pretty bad."

"Too bad?"

"Not with the right people."

"That's what I thought."

I get up and so does Janet.

She says, "Can I come to your movie night?"

"I didn't say I was doing it. It's just something I'm thinking about."

"Do you like drive-ins?"

"In fact, I've had some very intense times at drive-ins."

She fans herself like she's scandalized.

"Really?"

"Not like that."

"The Devil's Door is having a seventies festival."

"I heard about that."

"I'll remind you the next time you come in."

"Next time."

"Aha," she says. "Then there is a next time."

"I mean, I come in all the time."

Janet puts her donuts in a bag.

"Sure, sure. That's what you meant."

I nod at the door.

"I should go."

Janet points over my shoulder.

"Look at those guys," she says.

When I turn, I feel her put something in my hand. The two guys, however, just sit there.

When I look back for Janet, she's gone. And she slipped me a piece of paper with her phone number. Nicely done. She has some disappearing tricks too. I start to throw her number away, but after a moment's hesitation I put it in my pocket instead.

Maybe I'll have a movie night after all.

Or maybe steal a car and go to Flicker's. Not with anyone necessarily. But maybe. Who knows?

I walk down Hollywood Boulevard in the morning sun for a couple of blocks.

Really, whether I have a movie night or not, go to the drive-in or not, it's good to be alive.

And not a monster in sight.

ABOUT THE AUTHOR

Richard Kadrey is the *New York Times* bestselling author of the Sandman Slim supernatural noir books. *Sandman Slim* was included in Amazon's "100 Science Fiction & Fantasy Books to Read in a Lifetime" and is in development as a feature film. Some of his other books include *The Wrong Dead Guy, The Everything Box, Metrophage,* and *Butcher Bird.* He also writes comics.

RICHARDKADREY.COM

MORE FROM RICHARD KADREY

The Grand Dark
"*The Grand Dark* is a miracle of the old and the new: a tale of Weimar decadence that is also a parable for our New Gilded Age .... It's a fun and terrifying ride, gritty and relentless, burning with true love and revolutionary fervor." —Cory Doctorow

Hollywood Dead
Life and death takes on an entirely new meaning for half-angel, half-human hero James Stark, aka Sandman Slim, in this insanely inventive, high-intensity tenth supernatural noir thriller.

The Kill Society
Fury Road becomes a battle between Heaven and Hell in the ninth book in Richard Kadrey's bestselling Sandman Slim series.

The Perdition Score
Sandman Slim returns in a stunning, high-octane thriller filled with the intense kick-ass action and inventive fantasy.

Killing Pretty
Sandman Slim investigates Death's death in this hip, propulsive urban fantasy through a phantasmagoric L.A. rife with murder, mayhem, and magic.

The Getaway God
Sandman Slim must save himself—and the entire world—from the wrath of some enraged and vengeful ancient gods in his sixth high-octane adventure.

Kill City Blues
Kadrey returns to his bestselling Sandman Slim series with a high-octane fifth adventure.

Devil Said Bang
Combining outrageously edgy humor with a dark and truly twisted vision, Kadrey once again delivers a masterful amalgam of action novel, urban fantasy, and in-your-face horror.

Aloha From Hell
"Richard Kadrey's Sandman Slim series is one of my favorite sets of fantasy books from the last few years..." —John Scalzi

Kill the Dead
"Sandman Slim is my kind of hero."
—Kim Harrison

Sandman Slim
"An addictively satisfying, deeply amusing, dirty-ass masterpiece." —William Gibson

The Wrong Dead Guy
In this fast-paced sequel to *The Everything Box* chaos ensues when Coop and the team at DOPS steal a not-quite-dead and very lovesick ancient Egyptian mummy wielding some terrifying magic.

The Everything Box
"A rolling bouncy-house of a caper tale . . . abounds with quick-witted characters, snarky dialogue, and surreal analogies. "
—Christopher Moore, *New York Times* bestselling author of *Lamb*, *A Dirty Job*, and *The Serpent of Venice*.

Metrophage
Los Angeles in the late 21st century—a segregated city of haves and have nots, where morality is dead and technology rules. A small group of wealthy seclude themselves in gilded cages. Beyond their high-security compounds lies a lawless wasteland where the angry masses battle hunger, rampant disease, and their own despair to survive.

Dead Set
A wonderful stand-alone dark fantasy in which a young girl is caught between the worlds of the living and the dead.